Cowboy In The City

To Perry and Beth
Enjoy the ride!
Lisa Carney

Lisa Carney

This book is a work of fiction. Names, characters, places and incidents are products of the author's imagination or are used fictitiously. Any resemblance to actual events or locales or persons, living or dead, is entirely coincidental.

Edited by Kiffin Steurer

Special thanks to Rebecca Budaj.

Front cover art by Elizabeth Dempsey EMT-P
"…still life…" by Elizabeth Dempsey EMT-P

Additional images provided by Julie Davis EMT-P

…and to Tonya…

ISBN: 0-615-33345-1
ISBN-13: 9780615333458
Library of Congress Control Number: 2009905376

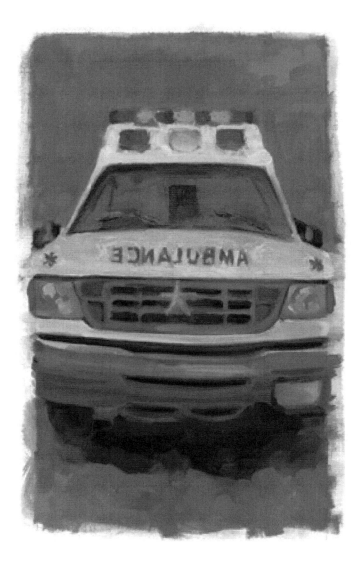

...to my heroes...

Before the beginning...

...and probably at the end too...

It was late...and it was getting later...My life was careening down narrow windy roads completely in the dark and constructed with blind corners...Careening is a subjective motion...You can feel it standing still if you're dizzy...But when you feign control careening is fun...Sitting next to the Almighty Kelly O'Brien it was intense...

*This is the story of a 24 y/o GWF who grew up wanting to be Johnnie or Roy who then grew up and met Kelly O'Brien***...who was way cooler than Johnnie or Roy could have ever hoped to be...***and suddenly it all made sense...There is no feeling more liberating than the realization that one has stumbled upon their destiny...Now I'm scared to think where else I could have turned up...There are so many fine lines in life...friend-lover...lord-devil***...blah blah blah...***And you can end up in the strangest places for a sixteenth of a degree's difference in fate's line***...I was a sixteenth of a degree away from a life as doomed whiskey tango...***Now I don't believe there is anywhere else to be***... anywhere else would not be as true...***I thought I was applying for a job...What I got was a new perspective...I began to see life for what it isn't...I saw it from the bottom up***...And I liked the view...***In fact I have grown afraid that they might try to take it away from me and if they did I don't know what I'd do...*

...ours is not a profession...it is a religion...

✫ ✫ ✫

...and I think all religions are basically the same...They all teach that the world sucks and it's because evil kicks good's ass...The only chance good has is the gods...The gods who have the right to say anything they want because whatever they want is right...

...they are gods and that's what gods do...

✫ ✫ ✫

I believe in the God of EMS...He is a he right now...but Kelly O'Brien is giving him a good run for his money...I'm able to believe in the God of EMS because I have seen him in action...This is a god who can be fair...**sometimes he just chooses to be a bastard...** *However...fair is fair and at least he doesn't care if you call him a bastard when he deserves it...*

...I don't know how Kelly will feel about being called a bitch...

✡ ✡ ✡

The God of EMS operates by certain rules...I share them as I figure them out or as they are shared with me...**only a few are allowed to the inner sanctum...***Ariel taught me my first rule*...**be careful what you wish for...***Because you will get it...Like if you wish for a code because you're bored you'll get a pedicode...And for some strange reason looking at a dead kid and knowing you wished for it kinda sucks...*

Ariel also explains that there's a special angel for drunks...kids and EMTs...Sometimes I think Ariel is my angel...I mean with her by my side I have carried a lot of drunks...cried with a lot of kids and drank with a lot of EMTs...

✡ ✡ ✡

Ours is a religion passed through stories told well...You are taught respect...Respect for yourself...Respect for your patients...Most importantly respect for learning...One reason we share the rules as we figure them out is because nobody knows all the rules yet...**maybe collectively we can come up with a complete set...**

Dark nights are the best time to learn...Sit next to the almighty Kelly O'Brien in florescent truck stops...under the neon glow of the light bar... and listen to her as the stories pour out...They tell our history...a history loaded with heroes...leaders...goats and devils...

All religions have a book that explains the rules...The book also outlines punishment for failure to comply...Some people might think regional protocols are our bible...but they're not...We have no such book...because no one can tell you how to feel holding a dead baby...

Sometimes it just gets to you and no one holds it against you if you go home and stay there...So like any good religion...guilt is all the punishment we ever need...

...bless me Hoppy for I have sinned...

✡ ✡ ✡

*So now I'm going to tell you some stories**...parables if you will...** and this is how they came to be...I listened to all their stories...I lived a good portion of them myself...I paid attention to the details...I remembered how everything felt...Everything you read is true**...It happened to somebody...**If you can feel it you know how we felt...*

...we're just people too...

✡ ✡ ✡

*It's scary when you realize that somewhere along the line you sold your soul to the Devil...We all heard the story and we all know how it ends...You enjoy the promised ride and then get pissed off because the ride doesn't last forever**...yet we fall for it every time...**Sometimes when I'm really enjoying some sick thing I get to work with I wonder "...why am I having so much fun?...how did I get lucky enough to be here?..." I always forget the part about how much it's going to cost... Some kids sell their soul to get backstage at a rock concert...I sold mine to get behind the tape at crime scenes...to approach the bench for the Commonwealth and to witness autopsies with homicide detectives...*

...oh yeah...and the chance to work with Kelly O'Brien...

CHAPTER 1-
THE BOOK OF THE PROVERBIAL DEAL

...the God of EMS said "...It is not good for the man to be alone...I will make a helper suitable for him..."

I wanted to just jump in and start sharing stories right away but it's hard to appreciate the punch line without a proper introduction...*I was talking to the pig*...See it just doesn't have the same zip. So here's the proverbial deal. I found an ad in the newspaper advertising an upcoming EMT class...*I was intrigued*...I was tired of getting expensive speeding tickets and thought I could get out of more of them if I met some cops. Seeing as I wasn't randomly going to get invited to the right BBQs I signed up and prepared to begin a respectful well-paying career that would have the side benefit of letting me drive fast legally...*there I go leading off with the punch line again*...Anyhoo...I passed the class...got certified by the state and went off to find my first job.

Now while it is true some people take this opportunity to add a little adventure to their lives and they run off to find gore and goo in the big cities of faraway lands I had no such ambitions. It was adventure enough for me just to start a new career. I didn't need to learn new streets too.

At that particular time...*in my limited geographical area*... it was all "mom and pop" companies running the show. There were two in particular that did the bulk of the hiring and gave little plebe EMTs like me their big breaks. Carter Ambulance covered suburbia and LittleCity, so they subsequently hired preppies to wear their uniforms. Valley Ambulance took care of BigCity and was known as the ranch for all the cowboys who were crazy enough to want to roam the streets of BigCity...

...I wondered...could I be a cowboy?...

I took the first job offered to me because from the outside I actually had no idea there were class distinctions...*and so I ended up a preppie...*Which was probably the best thing anyway since truth be told I didn't have a lick of cowboy in me.

So there I was in my crispy new uniform with a shiny new stethoscope around my neck and no idea what was around the next corner. I tried hard to settle in to my new digs while doing my best not to draw any attention to myself. See I was really afraid that meeting me would be all anyone would need to do to realize that I didn't belong there and then I'd be shown the door.

I could tell already that this environment held a harsh mirror up to one's own life and up until now I had just been getting by as a naïve and often scared middle-class suburban chick. I soon learned that even the preppies possessed a swagger and edge that I could not yet pull off. I immediately felt intimidated by everyone around me...*the medics...the intermediates...other basics... dispatchers...and oh yeah...most of the patients scared the hell out of me too...*This was not going to be easy...

...not even in suburbia...

✧ ✧ ✧

"...so who's the new kid?..." Jodie leaned on the passenger side window and talked over me.

"...she says her name is Casey..." My partner...*whose name escapes me...*leaned on the steering wheel and answered for me.

"...yes...my name is Casey...Liz Casey..."

"...QUIET NEW PERSON...nobody said you could talk..."

...I was definitely scared of Jodie the most...

When you're a newbie...*especially a newbie basic...*you work with a lot of different people...old...young...male...

female…straight…gay…tease…slut…prude…partier… preacher…stoner…student…mother…father…soon-to-be-medic…lifelong basic…EMS lifer***…and the always popular "…on my way to somewhere better…"***

Everybody has to check you out for themselves so you get passed around a bit***…sometimes I think they forget they're being checked out too…***When all is said and done you can spend some strange hours with some strange people and I have had partners who truly scared me. Immediately coming to mind is the guy who wore a bear tooth on a necklace that he claimed to have wrestled right out of the mouth of a grizzly. And the chick with the monkey who dated the streaker was fun at the holiday party. The guy with the full back tattoo of***…insert bow chica bow…***himself getting a blow job was I'm pretty sure everything my mother told me to stay away from.

A very strong athletic male that I met at the time clock once told me that EMS attracted many layers of multilevel dysfunctional people. Not sure why he was looking at me when he said it but it sure does make sense. Who else would be fucked up enough to wanna get involved in everybody else's crap and think they could be a productive member of society doing so?

With the buffet of partners to chose from you might think that there was some very serious thought put into matching up people. You know to take advantage of everyone's strengths and maximize the camaraderie. But as it turns out there's actually exactly no amount of thought whatsoever put in to it. By simply lasting longer than everyone else some of the old-timers ended up paired together but when you're new you have zero say in the matter and things usually come down to who fits what slots on the schedule. It almost never comes down to matching experience. My first six months were spent with people just as green as me with the only thing that set us apart from each other being how we dealt with our greenness. Most of us who fell into the mean kept it quiet and simple and hoped nobody would ask us questions we didn't know the answers to in front of anyone. We all knew who each other was too because we all had this wide-eyed scared look we shared with one another when we thought no one was looking. We also could be heard from time to time whispering *"...whoa...this shit is fucked up..."*

The scariest green from where I stood was the "Poser." You see the "Poser" possesses no more knowledge...training or ability than anyone else but the "Poser" plays it off with a *"...been there done that..."* bravado. I learned right away not to fake knowledge. At the very least people who did know what they were doing were depending on me to provide critical clues. Guessing on a blood pressure prior to the administration of a vasodilator is one mean recipe for disaster...*or so they tell me...*

The long-term effect was far more insidious. This was all about trust. Everybody has to be able to trust everybody...no hesitating...no questions asked and I sensed that if they didn't trust me they would just eat me alive and be done with it. Normally that mentality wouldn't have even fazed me. Take me... leave me...I don't care. I saw most of life's responsibilities as disposable...*apartments...jobs...relationships...*They came and they went and you always knew there was another one around the bend.

This was different though. This didn't even feel like a job. About a month into my expedition I realized I really wanted to do this and I didn't want anyone to tell me I had to go home. True some things sucked. Like twelve-hour shifts can be long and tiring at first but before you know it you're working sixteen- and twenty-four-hour shifts without hesitating. You get stuck missing a lot of meals but at least you're busy and the time passes. Truth be told this was every bit as cool as it looked from the outside. We all worked hard…saw gross things…told great stories…drove fast and partied often.

Even at the bottom of the pecking order things were fun and at the bottom was exactly where you could find me. There are three levels of certification for EMTs. Basics are basic…intermediates are in the middle and paramedics have the most training and responsibility. I was just a basic without experience…*truly the lowest of the low*…But I got hooked on the atmosphere…

…and the chance to be on the news every night…

☆ ☆ ☆

Over time I came to have a lot of respect for the medics. After all they were the ones expected to have a plan for when the crap lifts up and moves toward the fan…*a "fan plan" if you will*…Amongst themselves though the medics were a pretty competitive group and there was a lot of biting bantering that went on around them. If you were content to watch from a safe distance you could see quite the entertaining show but getting too close could be like walking right into a chopper blade.

To keep newbie basics safe from hurting themselves…*or others around them*…they are assigned to transfer shifts as opposed to being thrown into the fire of 911 work. Transfers are low-challenging…mostly boring trips between doctors' offices… clinics…dialysis centers… hospital rooms…rehab and physical therapy offices with elderly…disabled and otherwise unable-to-sit-up-in-a-car patients. In most cases the emergency happened long ago and you were nowhere near it. Some lucky medic or intermediate got to do all the cool stuff and here you are doing the shell of the call. And let's debunk one romantic notion right away: Not all old people are cute and pleasant. A lot of them are miserable secondary to being pissed off at how it's all ending. And look out Tillie if you remind them of their no-good two-timin' money-grubbin' daughter-in-law...*fun trips those are...*

Other lucky contestants include the completely gorked out which allow you to stare at the hollowed-out human for the fifteen-minute ride. You keep telling yourself that it's still a person and it's probably important to someone somewhere but at three o'clock in the morning it just looks like a cheap souvenir from the Life Gift Shop. But from how it was explained to me... that doesn't mean you should keep pushing on your patient's head to see if they'll roll with the curve of their stiff spine. You must respect life even as you learn it doesn't respect back. Every day you witness its cruel jokes playing out on all of us and you come to accept that you are either going to have to die young and tragic or take the huge risk of living past all useful humanness. It is completely possible to have your life unceremoniously drag on leaving you as nothing more than a mummy with a pulse. That's where a cool partner comes in handy. First and foremost you promise each other that if one of you ever sees the other one end up like that you'll hit them in the head with a rock and be done with it. And you mean it...*they're not just words...*

And then for those things that make you go *hmmm* you have that one other person in the world who saw exactly what you saw and therefore knows exactly how you feel. The beauty of that is you don't have to rehash it and get all maudlin and whine about sadness...*the other ducks on the pond don't want to know your ass is wet...*Instead a good partner will immediately jump in and participate in your gallows humor. And here's the thing about gallows humor: It isn't so much important that you make jokes about gross things. It's more important just to make jokes about everything. You see...that way you never forget that nothing is so important or unconquerable that it can't first just be laughed at.

Over time you can easily end up spending more time with your partner than anyone else in your life. The right one can help you stay grounded...*the wrong one can really complicate the spin...*

One day I showed up at work and the scheduling stars had aligned in my favor. It would seem that just about every new basic that was hired with me was already enrolled in medic school. That left just me and this new guy Dave Blossom with flexible schedules and the ability to fill in anywhere. So they plopped us together.

I'd seen Blossom around and he was cool. Turned out we went to the same suburban high school together without ever having met. I always wondered if we would have been friends in high school. I mean without all this crazy stuff going on all around us what would we have had to talk about? Oh well that didn't matter because here...*where it mattered...*the partnership was a good fit. Neither one of us was gung ho about telling everyone how great we were. Both of us expressed concern that someone would figure out that we shouldn't have been let in the door in the first place and neither one of us were morning people so nothing was ever so important it had to be discussed before 10 a.m.

Later on though...as shifts dragged on into their fourteenth... fifteenth...hell umpteenth hours...*and the empty coffee cups stacked up on the dashboard...*we got chatty. Who knows... maybe there's some correlation between neon lights and stress debriefing because the wee hours always made for the best conversations. Whenever we finished our shifts early instead of rushing back to the office and gathering with the rest of the herd we'd park the truck just outside the parking lot gate and sit and talk about our day. I really liked talking to Blossom. He had a real easy manner to him and for a guy he was very insightful. He also had a dry biting wit that he used to deftly dissect the sociological and psychological trends in our coworkers as a species and a herd.

Overall we knew we were getting the best post-grad education you could get and we didn't even have to take the SATs. Straight up it was honest and direct. And because of it my eyes were opening quickly to the world around me. Seems like everything I once believed in was pretty much invalid. People are not inherently nice or intelligent. And a very large percentage of the population has no desire to seek out the benefit of their fellow man. Hell…a very large percentage of the population won't even acknowledge the benefit of their fellow man if they run headfirst into it. Pretty much that task is left up to a very small minority of folks who possess nothing more than a little bit of knowledge…a good portion of heart and sturdy shield of humor.

One thing I did learn in high school that remained relevant though is that experience is life's harshest educator. See it tests you first and then it offers you the chance to get an explanation. That is if you're willing to hang around after your beating and ask insightful questions…

…everyone please put your pencils down…

☆ ☆ ☆

"…did ya ever notice…" I was deliberately baiting Blossom. "…that when we get to do a really cool call…nobody remembers we were there?…I mean…the medics hang out at the ER and talk shit and we clean the truck…"

"…yeah…fuck 'em…" Blossom smirked and squinted. "…we won't call 'em for intercepts today…we'll ride everything in ourselves…"

"…really?…"

"…yeah how else we gonna learn?…"

"…yeah…fuck 'em…" *long pause of gloating silence*
"…you know…we never really get to do good calls…"

"…maybe that's why nobody remembers we were there…"

…it's called paying your dues…

CHAPTER 2 -
THE SEARCH FOR GUIDANCE

...I know my people and my people know me...

Day in and day out Blossom and I steadily went about doing our transfers and turning in completed paperwork. Soon we found ourselves in the rotation of trucks that got to do low-priority basic emergencies. Simple stuff like fender bender accidents... slips and falls...kids with fevers...psychs. What we noticed though was that even so-called simple calls could have interesting subplots that made for good copy. Sometimes we were the closest truck to a real emergency and we got dispatched to hold down the fort until the medics showed up. Sometimes we just got to hang out and listen to other peoples' cool stories. No matter how the information was obtained I saw it all as important...

...I just wanted to be ready for anything...

✧ ✧ ✧

we gathered in a circle to hear Jim's story...

"...so the lady's gorked right..." Jim put his hands in his pockets. "...'cause she's got the rearview mirror sticking out of her forehead..."

"...Ooooooh..." *we all took a deep breath.*

"...but I look and there's this little bitty teeny foot on her shoulder..." And he took his hand out to show how weeny teeny is.

"...car seat in the back?..." *someone in the crowd asked.*

"...nope...baby in mommy..." He put his hand back in his pocket. "...at least there was...steering wheel took care of that..."

✧ ✧ ✧

coffee coffee

...why does everyone have coffee but me?...

"...Joooooooodie..." I whined through the bay door. "...you forgot my cofffeeeeee..."

She bellowed back "...yooouuuuu forgot to give me mooooneeeeyy..."

"...Damn..." I mumbled. "...I coulda used a coffee..."

✵ ✵ ✵

"...so me and Blossom get sent to SmallTown for some psych standby and we're hanging out in their police station..." I leaned on the counter eager to tell my story to someone experienced. "...and the hick dispatcher doesn't know how to give instructions over the phone to some woman whose baby isn't breathing..."

"...yeah..." Jodie put the antennae of her portable in her mouth***...not really far...***just an inch or so.

"...so Blossom volunteers me and the dispatcher throws the phone at me...I was nervous but surprisingly I kept my head well enough to talk her through the obstructed airway algorithm..."

"...cool..."

"...yeah...well it was 'cause the kid started breathin' again...then he was crying and the mother was crying and that felt awesome...I didn't want to hang up...I mean I saved this kid's life and none of us knew each other's name...you know... our destinies crossed...they'll never forget me even though they never really knew me...like the faces you recall from childhood that you never knew the names of but yet you never forget walking by them on the way to homeroom..." She adjusted herself on the edge of the dispatch counter and let me go on...*although I sensed I was losing her*"...it doesn't often work out that well... does it?..."

"...odds say that was your last good turnout...for awhile at least...plus it was probably only a seizure..."

"...so from here on out I'm pretty much useless unless I'm adversely affecting someone else's destiny?..."

"...you think too much Casey...we're just the twenty-minute ride to the hospital that delays the inevitable...state law says nobody dies in an ambulance so we're just an extra twenty minutes to accept the unreal for crying kids...scared wives and pissed off parents...don't be taking this too serious...it's not about us..."

...I didn't remember reading that in the employee manual...

☆ ☆ ☆

breaking in my first newbie...

"...Okay Slick here's another rule...the God of EMS doesn't want to think you're comfortable or having fun on the job... sneaking naps at night is acceptable if you don't take your boots off...see you'll never get comfortable with your boots on and God likes that...if you take 'em off...stretch your feet and get cozy...BANG...he gives you a sucky call..."

"...really?..." Slick nods and listens.

"...yeah and if you do fall asleep and you wake up having to pee...you got a choice to make...do you lay there...suffering in pain and chancing getting a call?...which means you couldn't pee for at least another half hour..."

"...that doesn't sound good..."

"...no it doesn't but remember...if the God of EMS sees you get up and go to the bathroom he's gonna say '...HMMPH...well I guess they don't appreciate their sleep. I'll give them a call since they're up…' trust me Slick…if your partner finds out he got a call because you got up and peed…he's gonna be pissed…"

"…yeah that makes sense…" Slick sat thinking…

…or was he staring at *The X-Files?*…

…it would appear he wasn't a believer…

There was nothing like 2 a.m. for a lot of things…hanging out in dispatch…inane conversation…dirty jokes and drooling on yourself… empty soda cans…funny little dances…vestiges of uniforms…coffee cups everywhere…and everybody was a goddamn comedian…

…we should have all just gone to bed…

lessons for the newbie…

"…I love this job man…" Sean Mahan was young and drummed the steering wheel…cruising Interstate Three-Nine-One.

"…yeah me too…" Jim was laid back and soulful…kinda the James Brown of silver-headed white men.

PPPHHOᴏᴏᴏOPPPPPLAᴀᴀᴀᴀHHHH

"**…**and that fine sir…" Mahan wistfully mused "…is a dead pigeon…" *feathers flew around us.*

"…yes it is…and there ain't nothin' you can do about that…"

…note lesson…

"…you know who's a real good medic?…" Blossom filled the bucket with soapy water.

"…I think Jesus would make a real good medic…" I grabbed the brushes and prepared to wash the truck.

"…ah no…" Blossom giggled and sprayed down the hood. "…I'm thinking more contemporary…"

"…Gandhi wouldn't have minded working through meals…"

Blossom giggled and looked up. "…what was I saying?…oh yeah…no…not Gandhi…Kelly O'Brien over at Valley…"

"…oh yeah…you've seen her work?…" I washed a wheel.

"…yeah…she intercepted me and Chad when we didn't have an ALS truck available…" Blossom sprayed a dead bug off the door.

"…she cool to basics?…"

"…she was cool to everyone…me…Chad…the patient… the family…everyone…"

"…and she knew what she was doing?…"

"…what the hell do I know about that?…" Blossom giggled and sprayed the dead bug to the drain. "…but she was cool to everyone…"

…cool…

✵ ✵ ✵

"…new girl…get over here…" I looked up from my Chinese food and Jodie was calling me. ***I am still scared of her*** "…this is my friend and long-suffering partner Fergie…she's wicked smart so don't argue with her and she's a third-degree black belt so she can kick your ass…"

I did believe Jodie but Fergie whacked her in the arm. "… don't scare the new people like that…"

"…why not?…it weeds out the weak ones…"

…I am still very scared of her…

✵ ✵ ✵

One evening me and Blossom were driving around looking for college chicks jogging in the burbs when we heard an ALS truck get sent to an address near us for a one-car MVA. Something about the way it was dispatched made it sound cool and since we were in the area we thought we'd drive by. As long as we didn't have anywhere else to be and we didn't get in the way no one would care if we poked around...*and we might get to help...*

When we pulled up we saw a Firebird with its front end disappearing into a tree and two ambulances with their back doors open. Blossom went right for the Firebird and I peeked into the back of the first ambulance. Jim was busy with an airway while Mahan simultaneously cut off clothes and put on monitor leads. I paused for a second because I couldn't see the patient's face but I thought I recognized the boots...*that was a scary feeling...* Once I caught my breath I asked if they needed a hand. Jim shook his head no and said they'd be all set so I walked down and joined Blossom at the crash and I must say...as impressive as it looked from the top of the hill...it got even more so as you got closer to it. The Firebird had to have been flying because it ended up so far off the road...down an embankment and square into a tree. That kinda cracked me up because I had always thought of Firebirds as dogs in a street race...*must have taken forever to get it up to that kind of speed...*

The more I looked at it though there was something weird about how the Firebird was sitting...*sometimes the more bizarre a detail the more subtle it presents...*Upon further inspection I found that the tree had done a pretty good job of standing its ground while two tons of metal wrapped itself around it...*literally...*The tree stood tall like a blade and sliced through the engine compartment. It split the beefy front end like a snake's tongue all the way up to the front seats. So now when someone asks me "...what's the most bizarre dashboard ornament you've ever seen?..." the answer is "...an oak tree..." Not that I get asked that question a lot. But when I do *I'm ready...*

The fire department had cut the roof off to get the passenger out and one of our medics was squatting on one of the halves of the hood of the car looking into the patient compartment. He was looking down at the dead driver who was now slumped against a tree planted in the car interior. Paul laughed...shook his head a couple of times and pulled a tarp over the driver...

...I traded my Mustang in for a Jeep...

CHAPTER 3 -
A TEST OF FAITH

...to which the angel spoke and said "...Joseph...do not be afraid to take Mary home...because what is conceived in her is from the Holy Spirit...and he will save his people from their sins..." To which Joseph answered "...are you kidding me?...that's crazier than the load of crap her father tried laying on me..."

Dark room...cement floor...silence...cement walls... sleepers...cement ceiling...**RRRING RRRING RRRING RRRING**...loud crashes...still dark..."... oof...DAMN IT...fuckin' pho...hello...yeah...okay...yeah... all right...okay..." *hung up phone* "...wake up...wake up..." *bed kicked* "...oof...sorry...we got a pedicode in SmallTown..."

"...I'm awake..."

...no I wasn't...

And so our story begins. You'll forgive me if my facts are clipped. I'm not quite used to this early morning crap...but anyway...here we go. It was 02:00 in the suburbs...nineteen hours into a twenty-four-hour shift...it was February and it was cold. Welcome to the bomb shelter under the police station where for the last twenty-four hours four cloistering walls had surrounded Blossom and me. The cold cement had conspired to keep out natural light and we had been entombed.

I didn't remember throwing the blankets off. I didn't remember finding my boots. I remembered the dark and I did remember the cold. The dark held me down and the cold bitch slapped my face as we entered the parking lot.

"...twenty-seven en route...." Hey I could see my breath.

"...RECEIVED TWO-SEVEN...EN ROUTE..." I couldn't see dispatch's breath.

"…oh no dude…a pedicode in SmallTown…" Blossom's words appeared loud but they were whispered. He slammed hard on the accelerator but the cold diesel was slow to respond. Red lights bounced back flashing off the snow banks. "…ever done a pedicode?…"

"…no way…I still haven't done any kind of code…"

"…me either…and I definitely didn't want a pedicode first…ut ALS…ming so it…okay…" I didn't reply as I barely heard. I was too busy trying to remember everything I ever heard about pedicodes***…get the baby out of the house…work stiff SIDS babies so the parents have hope…tape the head to the board…***

"…oh yeah…Sean Mahan told me SIDS doesn't happen until more like four o'clock…so we gotta keep our eyes open for signs of abuse…"

"…okay…" Something new to remember…always find something new to remember for next time***…look for things smashed with baby head…***

so we pulled on scene…

And Blossom noticed that the cops weren't going ballistic. That was a good sign***…no dead babies flying across the front lawn…***He parked the ambulance in front of the house and left the engine running to keep the patient compartment warm. The rattle of the cold diesel woke up the neighbors. Within a slipper shuffle a hundred peering eyes were on us. Every move we made was now witnessed from behind drawn curtains and cracked blinds***…move along folks…there's nothing to see here…***

"…what's up?…" Blossom asked the young cop walking toward the ambulance.

"…I don't know…my partner's upstairs with some seventeen-year-old kid…" His voice declared nonchalance and he freely gestured with his Maglite but I knew he was just as happy as we were that there wasn't a dead baby flying around. "…I don't know if she did drugs or what but her parents say she hasn't been herself all night…"

I stopped to grab the entry bag from the side door and Blossom began trudging across the snowy front yard to the house. The cop walked slowly behind him. He didn't want to be here…

…I wished I'd had a coffee…

✯ ✯ ✯

The snowy front yard glowed under the brightness of a full winter moon…New England is spooky at night…especially in suburbia where the crooked elder elms creak across the lavender sky…I think this sticks out so vividly because this was about where I woke up…

✯ ✯ ✯

Eventually we climbed one flight up to the patient's bedroom. We used the typical suburban staircase in the typical suburban house in the typical suburban neighborhood on your typical suburban frosty morning.

Entering the bedroom the first thing I saw was a pale…very pregnant teenage girl sitting on the edge of her bed. She was dressed bizarrely in a super-sized sweat suit with an orange top and purple bottoms. She looked around the room picking out each person and suspiciously eyeballing them as they filled up her bedroom. Her movements were jagged and her eyes glassy.

…so this is how Alice felt…

✯ ✯ ✯

Her mother was behind me pacing like a gerbil trapped in a shoebox. The pitter-patter of her little feet annoyed me to no end. Dad shuffled around downstairs mumbling something about insurance cards.

"...how many months pregnant is your daughter?..."

"...pregnant?...she's not pregnant..." Her mother snapped indignantly. Blossom looked at me and I looked at the mother. "...so just watch your mouth young man..."

"...okay..." Blossom replied politely under his breath. "...well then that must have been one hell of a chicken burrito she had for dinner..." The cop nervously laughed and slapped Blossom on the shoulder. My ears were sleepy and muffle the sound.

"...no...now listen...there's something else wrong with her...she went out with her friends to a school dance...when she came home she was acting strangely...and her face was pale with big black circles under her eyes...we asked her what was wrong but she wouldn't answer us and just ran up to her room... we just asked her if she felt all right and she got so angry...then about twenty minutes ago we heard her rustling around in her room so I opened the door to see what she was doing...well she starts screaming at me and thrashing around being quite disobedient..."

I couldn't move closer to the girl because the small room was crowded with people and furniture. It was odd furniture. It was pink and green...*the colors called pastel...*Her twin bed was smashed into the far corner.

The people were odd too. There were two cops in the room. They were very young and nervous...*rookies stuck on the night shift...*The mother continued pacing...*she was breathing way too fast...*Dad kept popping in to make sure everybody was doing their job getting ready for the road trip.

"...okay..." he would say. "...insurance cards in pocket... car's warmed up...let's go...and make sure you pee because we're not stopping..."

"…but Daddy…" his daughter would ask. "…can I stop to have my baby?…"

"…no my sweat darling…" he would condescendingly pat her head. "…no baby of mine is having any babies…"

"…but Daddy…"

"…no…no buts about it… now let's go…"

…you can make anything go away…

✡ ✡ ✡

The early morning hues of light made everyone look long and yellow.Yet despite the illusions my mind knew it needed to be awake and alert. I had no choice but to pay attention. Still my physical body yearned to yawn…stretch…fall down…

✡ ✡ ✡

Blossom took the girl's blood pressure and I asked questions from the foot of the bed.

"…what's her name?…"

"…Laura…" her mother answered.

"…how old is she?…."

"…seventeen…"

"…hi Laura…how are you feeling?…" Laura didn't answer. She just stared.

I asked my series of standard medical questions. The list so standard I could have done it in my sleep***…hey wait a minute…I was doing it in my sleep…***I felt with each question I was taking yet another baby step into my journey toward the ridiculous. I asked. Laura stared. I shrank with her glare and was afraid to ask any more questions. Mom chimed in but what good was she? Was I really expected to listen to a woman who either didn't recognize pregnancy or was so unable to deal with its reality that she blocked it from her mind and was truly shocked at what others felt they saw? The mother who knew every detail of her pageant daughter's body and yet continued to deny its metamorphism...

...I couldn't believe I woke up for this...

✲ ✲ ✲

Mom paused to think about the questions but all she could think of was how beautiful her baby was...How could any man resist?...How could he not help but stare?...What could she do about it anyway?...There are some things a wife can't control...it's not her place...They were a good family...anyone could see it...they had come so far... and now look at the great things they had given their daughter...Sometimes you just can't love them enough...

✲ ✲ ✲

"...c'mon Laura...come over to this chair..." I looked up at Blossom. He knew she wasn't moving but it was her mother that grew impatient.

"...Laura let's go...these people want to help you..." Her mother snapped "...we've bothered these people long enough..."

"...with all due respect ma'am...yelling at your daughter won't help..." I wondered if the cop realized yelling at the mother wouldn't help either.

"...Laura...get in the chair..."

"...Ma'am please stop yelling..."

Blossom stepped in for the cop and tried to redirect. "...Officer...could you please take Mom downstairs and get her settled in the ambulance?..."

"But...but...this is my house and my daughter and you can't tell me..."

"...yes ma'am...this way...please let us help your daughter..."

"...if you stare at the pictures on the wall they start to move..." I felt my head move with crepitus toward the girl. She was now rocking back and forth on the edge of the bed.

"...what?..." Blossom asked in muffled tones.

"...it's a movie...it's a movie...it's a...AHHHHH get out of my room...get out of my room..."

Suddenly the girl rocked into a jump and lunged on top of Blossom. He screamed ***"...what the hell?..."*** and I screamed ***"...Jesus Blossom..."*** and the parents heard. While I was busy beating up a pregnant girl trying to pry her off a pinned-down Blossom her parents were yelling up the stairs. It got real noisy. Then the cops just completely lost their minds and the next thing you know we had a true melee on our hands.

We managed to contain the girl and get her somewhat contained on the stairchair with some nine-foot straps. Two across the chest...one across her lap and one across her legs. The chair rocked back and forth as she struggled to get her arms free.

"I'll kick you...put me down...get out of my room... Mommy...Mommy..."

Blossom and I struggled to keep our balance. He took the top and I ended up down at the feet.

"...I'm gonna hurt you you son of a bitch...fuck me... don't touch me...put me Down...CUNT...CUNT..."

"Laura dear stop yelling...stop yelling right this minute... Laura..."

"...she can't hear you...now let's go...the car is warmed up..."

"...don't talk to me that way and don't touch me you son of a bitch..."

✡ ✡ ✡

The typical suburban staircase was well polished and Blossom and I might as well have been wearing wool socks. The girl's thrashing meant there was no stability as we carried the chair. Twenty-seven stairs…

Twenty-six stairs…

Twenty-five stairs…

"…Sir…do me a favor…" I hoped the young cop was up for one. "…grab my belt…walk behind me and don't let me fall…"

"…you got it…" **OOOOH TURBO WEDGIE!** "…sorry…" he sheepishly offered.

"…that's okay…" Better a lacerated butt crack than a fractured skull and flail chest from Blossom and the Virgin Mary slip slidin' down upon my body. Besides***…the stimulus fought languor…***

on to the front yard…

Dad was in the Taurus revving the engine. Mom was making snow angels on the side of the ambulance. That all changed though when Mom saw us and bolted toward the action. Naturally she brought her vocal cords.

"…Laura are you behaving yourself?…"

"…Mommy…Mommy I want to go home…they won't let me go…who the fuck are you people?…get out of my room…WHO THE FUCK ARE YOU?…get out of my room…!"

The nervous cop ran to try and restore quiet. He slid and fell butt first into the snow. Neighbors who weren't already awakened by the diesel rattle sat bolt upright from the night shrills…

…I got real dizzy…

✡ ✡ ✡

Blossom and I put the chair down as we descended the last of the front stairs. A second ambulance appeared on the front lawn.

"...cool...ALS is here..." Blossom smirked and giggled while leaning on the back of the chair. "...you know...we never did update them..."

"...that stuff's overrated..." I bent at the waist and breathed heavy clouds of cold air.

"...yeah...fuck 'em..." He giggled. "...after all we did all the heavy work..."

...they were gonna yell at us...

✵ ✵ ✵

That was the blackest coldest night I ever knew...I didn't want to be awake...the phone made me...Then again maybe I wasn't...I couldn't hear... sound was muffled...I think my toes were cold...I was scared...Blossom was giggling...

...why on earth did we stay?...

✵ ✵ ✵

Blossom and I separated. He went ahead with the nervous cop to set up the stretcher. The young cop stayed with me and for some reason became engaged with pointlessly trying to talk the girl into not hurling her and the chair she was tied to into the snow. She wasn't listening. Then again...who could listen with the mother in the background screaming about propriety and insulting morons who came into her house and disrupted natural order?*...that would have been us...*To further demonstrate her point she came flying across the yard...waving her arms...and steamrolling straight for the first object in her path*...that would have been me...*Ah...at last... a sign that I was not dreaming.

Her hurling created momentum that pitched us conveniently into a nearby snowbank...*snowbanks are not fluffy...*Sound became truly muffled as my left ear filled up with frosted flakes... Ahhhh...*ultimate brain freeze...*

Now imagine you are 25 y/o and a little naïve about the nuances of life. It's 02:40 in the morning. The noise level is overwhelming. You are lying in a snowbank. Any of the soft fluffy snow that you landed on has melted into your underwear and the hard crunchy stuff scrapes your back...a crazy woman is holding you down and spitting in your face...*nobody talked about this in EMT school...*

And then there she was. She appeared out of nowhere... *like an angel...*She pushed the mother to the side and extended her hand pulling me to my feet. Only Ariel didn't look like an angel. At least not at 02:45 in the suburban a.m. She was wearing round-rimmed wire glasses and her shoulder-length dark hair was pulled back into a ponytail and jammed under a baseball hat. Her lanky frame was covered in a wrinkled uniform that screamed *"I just woke up"* and her hands were pulled up into the sleeves of an oversized jacket in an apparent gesture to find heat. Still she descended from the moonlight and looked every bit an angel to me.

"...I'm confused..." She scrunched her forehead. "...this doesn't look like a pedicode..."

"...well..." I began brushing off snow. "...that's 'cause it really isn't..." I continued brushing. "...let me explain..." *my underwear was a lost cause.*

"...here...you got some over here..." Ariel unaffectedly assisted me.

"...thanks..."

...oooo nice to meet you...

✵ ✵ ✵

I bet you're waiting for me to finish the story…you want to know how it turned out. What was the score?…Did we win?… Did we lose?…Was it good?…Was it bad?…Did we drive real fast to the ER? It's never that easy. I can only tell you what I learned. Our patient's baby was born fifteen minutes after she got to the hospital. The girl was not only pregnant…she was very ill from lack of prenatal care and all that yelling and screaming she did was seizure activity secondary to wicked high blood pressure. This of course in no way explained Mom and Dad's behavior. Because she was continually seizing her body was low on oxygen. The baby was born blue*…he came into this world suffocating…*

I thought it was really weird that two parents could be completely blind for nine months. I know when I left the ER they were still telling the doctor that their daughter wasn't pregnant. Which technically at that point I guess they were right. I don't know how long they were able to continue ignoring reality. I can tell you what I learned. Some children are very afraid of their parents. Some parents like it that way*…my guess is everyone involved will continue to suffocate…*

CHAPTER 4 -
A DELUGE OF CALLS

*...when Lamech had lived one hundred eighty-two years
he had a son...he named him Noah saying "...this one
will bring us comfort from our labor and from the painful
toil of our hands because of the ground that the* **Lord**
*has cursed...the earth was ruined in the sight of God...
the earth was filled with violence...for all living creatures
on the earth were sinful...so God said to Noah "...I have
decided that all living creatures must die...for the earth
is filled with violence because of them...make for yourself
an ark of cypress wood...you must bring into the ark two of
every kind of living creature from all flesh...two basics...
two intermediates...two medics...two chairvan techs...two
dispatchers...and make them all work overtime... and you
must take for yourself every kind of food that is eaten and
gather it together... and make sure you have a lot of coffee...*

one day it started to snow...

"...are you and Blossom on a sixteen today?..." I don't know
why the supervisor was asking. He had the schedule in front of
him.

"...yeah...and from the looks of the weather it should be a
fun shift..." I leaned on his desk while I tied my boot.

"...well...if the snow they say is coming comes we're going to
be holding crews through the overnight..."

"...you mean like the medics?..."

"...no...I mean like everyone...so I hope you brought extra
socks..."

"...oh..." The phone rang and Travis answered it. My mind
drifted ahead to the thought of being held over on the overnight.

Strangely it sounded like fun to me...*like a sleepover at your cousins'*...Not sure where it came from but I had visions of bunk beds...pillow fights and general high jinks...*in retrospect that may have been a little weird...*

"...is there anything else Casey?..." Travis spoke and I was pulled back to reality.

"...huh?..." I focused on Travis' annoyed expression. "...uh... no...I'm good...so when are you going to let us know about the holdover?..."

"...I am now...oh...wait a minute..." Travis cleared his throat. "...so make yourselves comfortable kids 'cause no one's going home...there...is that more clear?..." *I never really got him when he talked...*

"...oh...sure...I'll let Blossom know..."

✫ ✫ ✫

So there Blossom and I were...out doing our morning transfers...*or shucks as someone had started calling them...* when the predicted Nor'easter started dumping heavy snowfall onto the morning commute. With it came diminished visibility and the morning traffic grinded to a halt. Then we heard a flurry of dispatches go out for the medics. That caught our attention because normally only the basic trucks are all out at once and the medics rotate their calls. Clear as day though...*well maybe not this day...*we heard all the medic trucks sign on the air.

"...oh...something's going on..." Blossom reached down and turned the radio up.

"...FOUR-THIRTY...FOUR-THREE-OH...I HAVE YOU EN ROUTE...91 NORTHBOUND AREA OF EXIT SIXTEEN..."

"...four-twenty-six is on and en route..."

"...RECEIVED FOUR-TWENTY-SIX...FOUR-TWO-SIX... I HAVE YOU EN ROUTE ALSO AT THIS TIME..."

"...four-nineteen...four-nineteen en route from area of LittleCity Hospital..."

"...wow...the LittleCity intermediate truck is going..." I was getting excited...*the LittleCity trucks never left the LittleCity...*

"...no shit...something's going on..."

"...drive slow...maybe we can piece this together..." Blossom nodded in agreement and we slowed our pace to the next nursing home even more. By now we were used to the medics flying around doing cool stuff without us so even if something big was going on we had no expectations of participating. But it would be cool to know what everyone would be talking about later.

"...BigCity CMED...BigCity CMED...this is Carter ALS four-twenty-six..." The radio in the back of the ambulance squawked and I recognized the voice.

"...hey...that's Jodie..."

"...GO AHEAD FOUR-TWENTY-SIX..."

"...yes ma'am...can you alert area hospitals?...multi-agency response on 91 north area of exit 16 for multi-vehicle accident... multiple patients...will advise further with updates as available..."

"...wow...multi-agency...it sounds huge..." I felt the excitement rise in me as if just hearing it all go down on the radio was enough to make me part of the event. Blossom had a grin from ear to ear so despite his calm appearance I knew he was getting a charge out of it too.

"...four-twenty-seven...we're clear from Americana Hall... what's your pleasure?..." One of our brother basic trucks cleared from a nursing home. I wondered if they knew what was going on.

"...FOUR-TWENTY-SEVEN...FOUR-TWO-SEVEN... PLEASE RESPOND PRIORITY ONE TO 91 NORTHBOUND EXIT SIXTEEN AREA...MULTIVEHICLE MVA MULTIPLE PATIENTS..."

"…hey…they're going to that accident…"

"…yeah and we're closer than they are…" Blossom was right.

"…maybe dispatch doesn't want us there…"

"…maybe dispatch forgot where we are…maybe we should tell them…"

"…yeah?…" I asked.

"….yeah…" Blossom seemed sure.

I picked up the radio mike with my shaking hand. I cleared my throat and prayed hard that my voice wouldn't crack. Pointing out a dispatch oversight on a good day can put you in dangerous crosshairs. Remember…*they have final say over who gets the puking patients…*I was pretty sure that this was just asking for some serious unwanted attention. But like a junkie peddling blow jobs I was willing to do anything to get near this scene.

"…four-eighteen…to dispatch…"

"…FOUR-ONE-EIGHT STAND BY…"*uncomfortable pause* "…FOUR-ONE-EIGHT…WHAT'S YOUR LOCATION?…"

"…four-eighteen…we're at the North End rotary…"

"…FOUR-ONE-EIGHT WHY DON'T YOU HEAD TO 91 NORTHBOUND EXIT 16 AREA…ASSIST ALS WITH MULTIPLE PATIENT TRANSPORTS…"

"…YES…WE ARE IN…" Blossom and I high-five each other. **"…WE ARE GOING TO A HUGE TRAUMA…"**

Then with one deliberate motion Blossom turned all the lights on. It was probably a silly thing to do because with the storm we weren't going anywhere fast. Still…we had to do it. The rotary put us right on 91N and it didn't take long to come up on the backed up traffic…*three lanes of it to be exact…*

"…hold on…" Blossom downshifted to low. "…I'm gonna try to drive on the median…" Surprisingly that worked pretty well and soon we were passing everybody. It's really cool to be shotgun in the vehicle passing all the locked up traffic. Everybody was looking at me and even though they were mostly pissed off at being in the jam I imagined they were impressed with my backstage pass.

As we got closer updates from the medics started coming in. From what we could piece together a car traveling in front of a pack of other cars drove 65 mph into a squall...lost all visibility... panicked and slammed on the brakes. Six other vehicles...including a sixteen-wheeler...never saw the car stop and literally ran over it. So far the patient count was in the twenties and that precipitated an *all-hands-on-deck* cry. Everyone from fifteen square miles was there...Carter...Valley...LittleCity medics...every fire department...local cops...state cops...a helicopter...every news source. It was loud...it was smelly and it was insanity.

Unfortunately for Blossom and me we never got really close to the epicenter. Basically we showed up...got assigned one patient located on the fringes of the scene with very minor injuries...and got told to get moving to the LittleCity Hospital and not stand around ogling the scenery. Not quite the adventure we thought we'd find but hey...at least we could honestly say we were there.

All was not lost in the lesson department either and this one was a good one to get out of the way. You see as a naïve suburban-raised traveler I had been going through life with the belief system that bad things only happened to people who didn't take care of the details and left life to chance. I think this philosophy single-handedly substantiated my immature arrogance which would only serve to hold me back in my quest for enlightenment. At the very least I would probably get popped in the nose a lot for pissing people off with my hollow pretentiousness.

But then I met my patient...a 60 something y/o male who had been driving his wife to a doctor's appointment when without a moment's notice he drove headlong into a vortex from hell. He was just a regular guy doing decent regular-guy stuff and his world got tipped upside down. Next thing you know he's laying on the uncomfortably cold longboard... clothes cut off so we could check for injuries...a plastic disposable blanket tossed over him and a horror show of imagery just outside the ambulance doors.

Obviously he was quite rattled. Every time Blossom or I asked him a question all he'd say...*over and over...*was "...I never saw it...I never saw it coming..."

✵ ✵ ✵

So there you have it...utter randomness with no credit given for planning ahead. It kind of eliminates the need to feel cocksure arrogance that your life is superior because you take the time to attend to the details. Injuries...some illnesses and overall crap luck can come at you out of nowhere. Next thing you know... I'm standing in your living room asking you for your insurance cards.

Basically if something crappy hasn't happened to you yet it just means you're a day closer to when it will. For creatures with such limited time we sure spend a lot of it plotting and planning and attempting to control details that are really just balls in the Bingo wheel...

...B9...B9...please head to radiation....

✵ ✵ ✵

and then it kept snowing for three days...

...and management made good on their holdover threat over and over again. All together Blossom and I worked a total of forty-five hours in three days...*that's a long time to wear your boots...*When the initial snowfall brought the "Great Crash of '93" most everyone being held captive enjoyed a huge surge of adrenaline...*at least the storm wouldn't be boring...*

For the rest of the morning every time we passed through an ER we'd see the medics from Carter and Valley hanging out laughing and talking loud. A call like that broke company lines and for a little while at least the competition took a backseat and everybody was on the same side.

When cutting the patient's goose down jacket off and learning just how many feathers they cram in those things is your only dramatic moment in the call you don't qualify for the adrenaline rush. Therefore our morning remained fairly bane. I did take away another valuable piece of experience though...*I learned you can't sweep feathers...*

After our noble if not modest contributions at the big crash we went back to being nobody newbies with a huge pile of work ahead of us. Blossom and I just resigned ourselves to the fact that we would probably spend most of the day in our truck. Just because the storm generated extra calls didn't mean the usual calls were going away. We spent the day alternating between traditional shucks and storm-generated emergencies with no breaks in between. Lunch didn't happen until 16:00 and the usually grumpy skilled care facility personnel were just downright nasty and unreasonable about our perceived lack of effort to keep their appointments on time. One nurse actually started screaming at me and Blossom "...you people are always late...and this proves it..."

I stared incoherently and Blossom just laughed. "...what are you saying?..." He looked at me "...I don't understand what she's saying..."

"...I think she's trying to say she feels bad that our feet are wet and freezing..."

"...oh..." Blossom looked back at her. "...oh...thanks..."

By now it was no surprise to us that the storm brought out the worst in people but we were committed to not letting it get to us. While the world around us talked loud and bought extra milk we strived to keep calm. Blossom brought in his Phish CDs to set a trippy tone for driving around and we figured we could always just calm our fraying nerves by staring at the gentle snowflakes falling all around us...*they were so pretty...*

We even felt soothed enough to help some poor guy dig his car out of a snowbank. I kinda thought he might offer us a tip. But he didn't. In fact he didn't even say thank you. Maybe he thought we worked for AAA...*who knows...*

For the most part the patients who needed the transport understood our situation and remained grateful. To someone who needed chemo...dialysis...radiation...trach care or any of the other life-sustaining treatments we shuttled them to...it was nice to have someone willing to keep their word and show up even if they were a half hour late. It also shouldn't take a genius to recognize that someone is busting their ass to carry you in snowy/icy conditions and a kind word from an appreciative patient can go a long way on a tough day.

Then around 17:30 the snow turned to freezing rain and all hell broke loose. All the fools who just had to stay at the office to the bitter end sprung loose on the roadways and started crashing into each other. And of course nobody believes a snowstorm should actually slow them down so while you're slippin' and slidin' on icy roads trying to carry equipment and keep your balance they still think they can zip on by you. Getting splashed by icy puddles is one thing but at one point Blossom actually had to pull me back from a freewheelin' coupe...*I never saw it...I never saw it coming...*

Two seconds to catch my breath and then back to carrying fools on longboards across the slippery roads. Oh and fools are no more pleasant to deal with than cranky old people. It may have clearly been poor judgment on their part that put them in this unpleasant situation but they are going to whine and complain and drag everyone else into it. "...it's snowing on my face...I feel like I'm drowning...oh...get me inside...I'm cold...can I have a blanket?..." Meanwhile Blossom and I are stuck carrying these morons because protocol says if someone complains of neck or back pain you have to protect their neck and spine with a collar and longboard...*your classic cervical spine precautions...*It doesn't make any allowance for it just being a ploy to cash in on an accident settlement. So many times you pull up on a fender bender and you just know that everyone in the car that got hit from behind is going to have severe neck or back pain and want to be taken to the hospital because that's step one in a lawsuit. Most days you just roll with it. An accident here an accident there... *no big deal...*Even as you see your car insurance rates doubling before your eyes you have to chalk it up to one of those things you can't control no matter how hard you yell...*so why yell at all?...*This evening however was quickly turning into nothing but accidents with plenty of Aetna pain to go around. Not to mention that by now my pant legs were so wet that the water had seeped through my doubled-up socks and down to my toes and I was cold from the inside out. I was getting tired and we really hadn't had a significant meal all day...**FOCUS GRASSHOPPER...FOCUS... STARE AT THE PRETTY SNOWFLAKES...**

Then we got sent to LittleCity to transport a respiratory distress for the LittleCity medics. Usually the chance to back up the medics pleased me and Blossom but the LittleCity medics were a group all their own. They actually worked for the LittleCity Hospital and only provided paramedic-level care out of their four-wheel-drive Tahoe so while most of the time they acted like they were above everything they couldn't even transport their own patients. They needed us for that but they didn't really spend much time chit-chatting with the basics. Unless of course the basics were hot chicks perceived to be willing to give blow jobs...*of which neither Blossom nor I were...*So we just got the usual 'tude. To complete their personalities they also enjoyed embarrassing new people which to me was about as useful as a solar-powered flashlight. You see…enlightened EMSers know that no one's seen it all so no one knows it all. True experience calms you down for the routine and mundane calls but every now and then something happens that nobody's seen and even the most seasoned vet can get thrown off their game. My ops manager …a medic of ten years… told me that he walked up to a car accident one dusky evening and found the partially ejected patient's head wedged between the door of his car and a tree. Because it was pinched off it had swelled and turned ghastly blue...*the head...not the tree...*

As the medic approached and saw the ghoulish sight he stopped in his tracks…said *"…holy shit…"* and turned around to get his paperwork book figuring he'd have to write it up for the coroner. As he turned he heard a voice say "…HEY…can you get the door?…my arm won't reach that far…" *insert creepy music…* The supervisor was last seen that night searching the backseat of his Chevette for a clean pair of underwear.

My point is that anybody can get flustered because we're all learning as we go so what's the point of intentionally showing up the new people? We all get it...*your penis is wonderful...*

To further complicate things LittleCity has narrow side streets and little money for plowing. It probably wouldn't have been so bad if the address was just off the main drag but it was actually three side streets in. The closest the plows got to it was when they were boxing it in with all the other streets' snow. Once again though we just focused on keeping things simple and getting through 'em. Blossom was driving and I was bouncing up and down trying to keep the windshield wipers free of accumulating ice and giving measurements to the nearest parked cars. Dispatch kept hounding us wanting to know how much longer we were going to be.

"…EIGHTEEN…ONE-EIGHT… ETA…"

"…EIGHTEEN…ONE-EIGHT…LITTLECITY   MEDICS ON SCENE…"

"...EIGHTEEN...ONE-EIGHT... LITTLECITY MEDICS REQUEST YOU EXPEDITE..."

It just droned on and on. Finally I had had it. I couldn't take the insanity anymore and I jumped out of the ambulance. I ran toward a woman shoveling her walk and I yelled in my best authoritative voice *"...I am commandeering this shovel in the name of emergency services..."* and I took it.

I don't think she knew what hit her but I had her shovel and I wasn't looking back. I slid down the walk and started digging out the road for Blossom. He's a smart driver and I shoveled like hell and soon we had a fair path. Then I ran back...gave the lady back her shovel and jumped back in the truck just in time to arrive on scene. Blossom giggled. "...'I am commandeering this shovel?'... what the fuck was that?..."

I reddened. "...oh...you heard that?..."

"...EIGHTEEN...ONE-EIGHT..."

"...eighteen...arrive on scene..."

"...ACTUALLY EIGHTEEN YOU CAN DISREGARD... MEDICS ON SCENE CANCEL..."

"...what the fuck?..." Blossom looked at me with frustration.

"...look...they're waving out the door at us...and laughing... it's a joyful moment..."

"...assholes..."

"...oh hey new basics...no way..." One of the pricks was walking toward us. "...how ya doin'? I'm Jeremy Davidson...what brings you out tonight?..."

I looked at Blossom and he shrugged. "...you guys needed a transport..." I answered out the window.

"...boy you're tired out already huh..." He noticed my post-shoveling redness and SOB.

"...well we made sure we expedited..." I explained.

"...for Mary?..." He laughed. "...oh not for Mary...she's a regular...snow got her a little excited...we calmed her down..." *He went on like we cared.*

"...so you're all set..." Blossom was done with the experience.

"...yeah...you guys head out..." He walked away with a swagger. "...we'll see you at the next big one..."

"...fucking pricks..." Blossom threw the truck into REVERSE. "...they knew they weren't transporting the whole time..."

"...yeah...when I grow up I wanna be an asshole too..." I rolled my window back up.

"...well you came to the right place for lessons..."

✳ ✳ ✳

Blossom and I were technically off at midnight but as expected we were told not to go home lest we not be able to find our way back the next morning. So we limped back to the garage...changed our socks...gulped down some egg rolls and crab Rangoon and I crawled upstairs to sleep in the basics' dorm. I think Blossom stayed downstairs all night playing Nintendo Hockey in dispatch.

The upstairs was more crowded than usual because of the extra crews on and the usually dark quiet room was bright and abuzz. Most nights the medics and intermediates each have their own room and the basics flop on the couches in the common area. That night there were basics...intermediates and medics flopping everywhere. I pulled a stretcher mattress out of a spare ambulance and dragged it upstairs and laid on the floor next to Jodie who had done the same thing. She was deep in an argument with Kenny Siano. He was one of the medic blowhards and at this particular moment he was going on and on about how great he was hung. He stepped into the bathroom to refresh himself and she turned to me. "...he's such a cocky bastard...watch this..."

Well ol' blowhard came struttin' out of the bathroom and stood over Jodie in an attempt to continue his perceived intimidation. Jodie didn't skip a beat and reached up over her head and pulled down his shorts. Everyone was watching to see what she'd do and on cue the whole room broke out laughing. Jodie was rolling around and pointed at his manhood. "...you brag about that?....HA HA HA HA HA HA....what's a matter?...didn't they have it in adult size?...talk about making a mountain out of a molehill....right Casey?..."

Ol' Blowhard got reeeeeeeeaaallllly embarrassed...shrunk up and crawled back to his room. We didn't see him for the rest of the night...

...that was awesome...

☆ ☆ ☆

...about six hours later...

...found Blossom and me sitting in our truck warming ourselves with the steam from our coffee. The snow was on pause but the temperatures were brutal. Dispatch had woke us up to do a dialysis transfer***...or renal run as we called them...***but we ended up getting diverted to the local military base where a C-5 crewmember had fallen on the icy tarmac and was reported to have sprained her ankle. When we pulled up on scene I commented that I didn't see any ice on the tarmac. Not to worry though...upon stepping out of the truck I immediately found some. Apparently the entire tarmac was glazed in black ice. Something that made standing back up a humorous palsy dance. I remember lying on the ground... laughing and swearing...helpless as I watched Blossom slide off into the horizon.

The rest of the morning was more of the same...driveways... roads...sidewalks...parking lots and especially outdoor stairs were all coated in ice. Patients fell...we fell and by noon our underwear and socks were soaked again. Then the snow started up and just about everyone we encountered was pissed off at the weather. We just gave up trying to be friendly.

We did have some fun later that afternoon at the Mercy. Jodie and her partner Fergie thought they were cute and ambushed us in the parking lot with snowballs but we turned the tables on them by using our stretcher as a rolling shield and through sheer wet-sock anger forced them into retreat.

We caught a quick nap around dinnertime and then headed back into the fender bender grind. By now I was so tired I started to zone out...Blossom and I had long since stopped talking

and begun a system of grunts to communicate...

Everybody else was too angry to warrant conversation so I started to fade...

...

..we did a shuck

from the Mercy to a LittleCity nursing home and I was in the back with a gork...

...

...

...maybe it was the long ride or

the heat blowing out the vent at my face...

...

...

...or the hot chocolate I had sipped in the ER

maybe I was just toast but I fell asleep...

...

...

...and I had a weird dream...

I was standing on the deck of a steamship freezing my ass off. Everything I saw or touched was cold. I think my brain may have given my motor sensory the first act off because there was no light and there was no sound...*it can do that you know...*So I stood there in the dark...shivering with my black arms tucked. As my eyes adjusted to the darkness I looked around and could see I was surrounded by black silhouetted cutouts. These were the silent passengers. The ship floated unanchored dangerously close to an even more darkly lit pier...*an odd mix of movement and stillness...*

The silence was broken... **SPLASH** ...and followed with a scream **"...MY BABY..."**

"...I should help..." I thought

. . .

. . .

. . .

So I jumped into the air...and air was all I saw for m

a

n

y

many m

a

n

y

m

a

n

y

FEET

...I don't know how many...just a lot...

SPLASH...

And as I entered the water I

       c

         o

       n

         t

           i

         n

           u

            e

             d

            t

             o

              f

            a

           l

           l

This time...not as far...

I heard water lapping on the side of the ship. I got much colder. Opening my eyes I saw the only thing that looked like color when a bright gray light cut through the water's surface. Looking up I could see the side of the ship extend into the night. It stood as high as a downtown skyscraper...*how was I ever going to get back up there again?...*

In the light twenty feet away I saw the baby drift. Its eyes and mouth were open and it made a sick gurgling sound. Bubbles surrounded its head.

*Oh little baby...*I swam to it...*I'll save you...*It just seemed that easy. If I put my arms out I was sure I could reach it. Then I'd pull it in and swim to the surface...*if I swim to the light they'll* *be able to see me...*I reached for the baby and hoped it sensed everything would be all right.

I figured it must have because its face stopped crying...the bubbles stopped and it smiled. It cooed and then the bastard became like dead weight. And it laughed while we dropped like

```
l       b     l     b     l     b     l     b
   e       a     e     a     e     a     e     a
     a     l     a     l     a     l     a     l
       d     l     d     l     d     l     d     l
             s           s           s           s
TO THE...O
         C
         E
         A
         N
```

FLOOR FLOOR FLOOR FLOOR FLOOR FLOOR

Blossom hit PARK and I woke up on the bench seat clutching my paperwork book...

Dro...
  o...
     o...
        l...
           i...
              n...
                 g...

Back to the office again where things were much quieter than the previous night. The snow was supposed to stop sometime early morning so management had cut back a few crews. The ones that were left had been pounded on just as bad as us so EVERYBODY was beat. In times like these there are unwritten rules that go into effect. Rule number one was no complaining. Remember…all the ducks have cold wet asses. Limited groaning is acceptable but that's it. Rule number two…No fucking around with people's shit. This was not the time to be putting Mahan's drenched underwear in the freezer…***there'll be plenty of time for that later…*** Finally…rule number three is if you get sent on a call just shut up and do it. And don't be calling the office from the ER to wake everybody up. Ain't nobody who wants to do anything right now but the work is still there. When your truck number is called **SUCK IT UP…**

…god I feel so angry…

The next morning found me and Blossom warming ourselves again in the steam of our coffee. If you can give me a word for the condition just past numb I'll gladly use it. I'd never felt too tired to drink coffee before but well…here it was…***this just wasn't any fun anymore…***

"…no bunk beds…no pillow fights…no zany high jinks… what the fuck?…"

"…huh…what's that?…" I may have woken Blossom up.

"…oh nothing…" ***CRAP*** that was my outside voice.

I was pretty sure if I had to do one more call I would lose it and scream and break shit. But somehow every time dispatch called…***despite the loud screaming in my head…***Blossom and I would calmly answer and go about our business. Then we caught a break late morning and got sent to the Region for a spell. Ah the Region. A land of multilayered suburbia where calls only happen about once every six hours and if it times out right you can sit a whole day and never move a wheel…My sock…w…re… sti…l… dr…y… an…we… wer… catching a breather…This was d…fini…ely goin… t..o…

. . .

. . .

. . .

. . .

"... E I G H T E E N ... O N E - E I G H T ... EIGHTEEN...ONE-EIGHT...!!!!!"

"...uhhh....eighteen answering...eighteen here..." God that radio's loud when it's waking you up. This time Blossom and I both got bagged sleeping.

"...EIGHTEEN...419 NORTH MAIN GARDEN APARTMENTS FOR THE WOMAN FELL ON ICE... ADVISE IF YOU NEED ALS...THEY'RE ALL OTHERWISE OCCUPIED..."

"...eighteen received..."

So Blossom and I headed up the street to the North Main Garden Apartments which ...*according to the brochure*...was an active seniors complex set up like condos. We had pulled down the street and were heading for the cul-de-sac when a flap-u-lator pulled us over.

"...my neighbor Shelly was getting her mail and I saw her fall down at the bottom of her driveway...she's really yellin'...I hope it's not her hip..."

"...okay ma'am...we see her...we'll go check it out...why don't you go inside...it's cold out..."

"...oh okay...thank you..."

So Blossom and I continued on to the end of the street where a little old lady was lying at the end of her driveway. We stopped pretty far away because we didn't want to chance sliding on the icy roads and running her over. There were a couple of cops on scene and they were pretty pissed off about the conditions of the streets. Or maybe they had just had a couple of crappy days like us and anything would have pissed them off. Anyhoo…it was so bad the sergeant was on his portable radio ballin' out somebody at the DPW.

"…I don't give a rat's ass…you got old people down here… we need a sander ASAP…do you understand?…"

Blossom and I looked at each other and acknowledged silent mode. We would do our best to assess our patient…cancel ALS and come up with a plan involving minimal disturbance of the atmosphere around us…*do not attract attention and nobody gets hurt…*

Shelly had indeed appeared to have broken her hip so she was worthy of scoop extrication. In my humble opinion…the scoop is probably the coolest of all basic EMS inventions. It's actually a two-piece longboard that clips at the top and bottom and can be separated to come around the patient in halves. It's great for broken hips because you barely have to move the patient to get them off the ground. After all…nobody with any significant fractures wants to be rollin' around.

Blossom stayed with Shelly while I slid back to the ambulance to get our scoop and collar bag. Just then Shelly's neighbor popped back out of her condo.

"…yoohoo Shelly…are you cold?…"

"…yes…"

"…what did she say?…"

"…we're getting her up…she's okay…"

"…no…she needs a blanket…"

"…no she's got a blanket…"

"…but no it's…whhooooaaaaaa…" And Shelly's neighbor was down.

I heard Blossom call me and when I came around the ambulance I saw him sliding over to the neighbor. He looked up and signaled that we were going to need another board. Then he started sliding his way over to the ambulance to give me a hand with stuff. He was kinda giggling and smirking and I knew it was because he couldn't believe Shelly's neighbor wiped out like that right in front of us. It was pretty funny and even I started giggling. I was worried that I'd totally lose it because I was so tired and punchy. I just got it back together when a large truck rumbled past me. I recognized the *che che che* sound but by the time I could say *"NO!!!!"* it was too late.

All the sergeants yelling had produced a sander and while Blossom and me watched helplessly our patients were sanded. Yup…sanded…right there on the ground where they lay. It was downright hysterical too because the ladies saw it coming and they were yelling in old lady words "…oh dear…no…oh my honey…we're gonna get sanded…" I will never forget the look on Blossom's face when he turned around…looked at me and burst out laughing. Despite his very laid-back nature he just lost it which in turn meant I just totally lost it. Next thing you know we're on the ground…holding our guts doubled over. All the stress…all the cold and all the wet socks and underwear of the last three days came spilling out. And we let it. In fact I was afraid I'd pull a stomach muscle if I tried holding it in.

Then the sergeant came over and told us to quit lying around on his street which inspired us to quickly get it together and finish the call. We almost lost it again when we got to the LittleCity Hospital and the ER nurse asked us if we picked our patients up at the beach but we pulled it together when she scowled at us… *LittleCity people got no sense of humor…*

After that the rest of the shift seemed pretty pedestrian and by 20:00 we were ready to have some time off. I've driven home drunk and remembered more of the ride than I did that night. When I got home there was a letter in my mailbox from BigCity College. It was in response to my application for medic school.

Oh yeah...I applied to medic school. It read: ***"Congratulations, you have been selected to begin the spring session of paramedic training...blah blah blah..."*** Yippee was all I could muster as I dragged myself off to find sweet repose...

...I'll be really excited tomorrow...

CHAPTER 5-
THE BOOK OF JAMES

*...and as the students joined the Teacher they asked
"...Teacher...is it true...what you sow is what you shall
reap?..." and the Teacher answered them so "...know this
newbies...not much of this is about us...it is as my Father
foretold...if tragic things didn't happen to tragic people
there would be no good calls..." and the students sighed...
knowing he had spoken to them the truth...*

James Zoya was snapped out of a sound sleep at 6 a.m. on
Monday. Daylight pierced the bedroom as he sprung over and
slapped the alarm clock. "...FUCK I hate that thing..." And thus
he greeted what should have been his first day off in a week.

Cathy embraced his torso from behind. "...James..." she
whispered. "...don't go in today...let Danny get his brother to
work..."

"...I can't..." He didn't say anything else and stumbled to the
shower. As the cold water gashed his face he fought for air. The
sting of the string of self-inflicted trauma set in...*cold water...
scalding coffee...bad shocks in his Jeep...*There just wasn't
any other way though. His job at the Water Department paid well
but not well enough. When they had their third kid Cathy had
to stop working...again. Three kids...one mortgage...two car
payments and life do not equal one income.

Cathy's brother-in-law gave him a second job that paid twelve
dollars an hour under the table doing landscaping. It was brutal
work. Hot baking afternoons...blisters ripped and bloodied on
the palms of his hands and posterior heels...constant dry tongue
from chronic thirst...dust baked on his shins like oven-kilned clay

secondary to the diesel-generated fumes kicked back on the deck mower. His joints throbbed from thirteen-hour days and his hips ached from tossing bags of grass.

He hated doing it. He hated being away from the kids as they grew. No choices though. In a couple of years they would've paid some bills and clawed open some breathing room. Then he would slow down...

...but they grow so fast and then they're gone...

☆ ☆ ☆

"...I love you..." he whispered as he kneeled by the bed and laid his head over her shoulder***...she was soft and warm...***He ached to climb back in bed and hold her and smell her hair. Cathy was pissed. She just laid quietly and wouldn't answer.

"...c'mon...you know I want to stay...it's just..."

"...I know..." She squeezed his hand and stopped him. "...I love you too babe..."

☆ ☆ ☆

James Zoya pulled into the Double D's parking lot. He was a junkie and he knew it. Without two plain donuts and a large black coffee with three sugars he remained useless until noonish***...shock the body keep it humble...***

Pulling into the landscaping lot he saw Tim driving the dump truck down to the pit where they dumped all their cut grass... amputated tree limbs and broken boards.

"...c'mon man...over here..." Danny was hanging on to the tailgate. "...c'mon we gotta dump this sucker..."

Ah great...***nothing quite like the smell of misty decomposing grass to start the day***...Yet he still found himself jogging to keep up with the blue Ford.

somewhere else in a diner…

"…and what's wrong with this town is the fatal tong of nepotism…" Bill was talking quite rapidly and it was hard not to stare at the corn muffin crumbs flying from his mouth…*damn Blossom for going on vacation.* "…see that's Tim Fredericks… the mayor's nephew who gets a $25,000-a-year stipend to act as police education liaison…it drives me crazy…it's why I won't live in this town…" *incoming corn muffin crumb.*

"…oh that's why…" I always thought it was because he was an EMT. Everyone knows career EMTs never own more than the car they drive and the clothes they wear…*they certainly don't live in the suburbs* "…I gotta go to the bathroom…" so I climbed up out of the booth into the parade of suburbanites…

…

…

…this much polyester in one place has got to be a fire hazard…

✧ ✧ ✧

"…today we're gonna head over to the Johnson's…" Danny was barely huffing as he pitchforked and chatted.

"…yeah okay…" James stabbed at the pile.

"…we gotta start cuttin' up that huge elm in the front…you don't mind climbin' today…do ya?…"

"…nah…it's okay…"

"…okay…you take the two stooges over with you and work on getting the thing delimbed…okay?…"

"…okay…" Just then the truck lurched forward and the two nimrods in the cab giggled.

"…hey asshole…set the fuckin' break…" Danny shook his head. "…I'm glad I got you here man…these fuckin' kids piss me off…"

...James had nothing to say...

✵ ✵ ✵

James made sure the guys got the trailer loaded and then backed the blue Ford up to the hitch. Greg spotted and Tim kicked back against the fence. It seemed like a good time to smoke a butt.

"...let's go Tim...we're wastin' sunlight..." James snapped the lock down.

"...what's the rush man?...we got all day..."

...god he pisses me off... James thought to himself. "...yeah but that doesn't mean I wanna take all day...let's go..."

"...so how's Cathy and the kids doin'?..." Greg was making an adolescent attempt at conversation.

"...they're fine..." James wouldn't cooperate. It was impossible to think about the family he'd rather be with. He'd rather you jabbed him in the abdomen with a pitchfork. Fuck anyone who thought he'd turn them into light conversation...*especially a puke kid working to earn money for a stereo system...*Greg didn't understand and figured James was a prick.

✵ ✵ ✵

The blue Ford pulled up to the house and all three of them lumbered across the front yard. James rang the bell to let the family know the morning quiet was about to end. Soon chainsaws... blowers and a mulcher would be roaring the dearth of the mighty elm...*except he would probably use different words...*Right after he rang the bell he turned around and watched Tim crush a cigarette out on the family's driveway...

...Jesus what an idiot...

✵ ✵ ✵

After escaping the polyester world of the diner doilies...Bill and I ambled back to the bomb shelter. We had eaten our carb-laden brunch and now it was time for a nap.

After all...it was 11 a.m. in the suburbs...what on earth could go wrong?...

✡ ✡ ✡

James grabbed his climbing gear. Tim and Greg were supposed to be unloading the chainsaws and fuel but when Tim saw James putting on his harness and spikes he didn't miss a beat.

"...so when do you think I could start climbing?..."

"...it's not up to me...Danny picks the crews..." James didn't bother looking at him.

"...yeah but everyone knows your word goes a long way with Danny and if you..."

"...look Tim...you're not ready to climb..." James felt himself starting to uncork and reeled himself back in. "...this isn't a game and I don't want to have to explain to your mother why you're a spot on the asphalt..." Then he walked away.

James climbed a good height and dug his heels in. He leaned back from the tree and for a moment let himself relax. It was a beautiful morning and it was going to be a beautiful day***...one last deep breath with his head back and the sun on his face...*** Then he primed the ignition and ripped on the saw.

Tim and Greg stayed on the ground and manned the rakes and mulcher and for the next half hour James methodically cut through the smaller branches clearing through to the larger ones. It was something he had done at least thirty times before. Basically you set your safety ropes...dig in your heels and keep your wits about you. It's not the world's most dangerous work but you still have to act responsibly with your safety. James leaned out and extended his arms to reach a cut. His left heel kicked out and while he was waiting for the safety rope to catch taut he realized something…

…oh my god…I'm falling…

…

…

Greg was at the truck getting new gloves. Tim was intently hacking at a stubborn branch that wouldn't run through the mulcher. James was rapidly accelerating through branches until finally he decelerated on asphalt. He hit the ground hard. The last thing he saw was the chainsaw hurling down and hitting the pavement just to the side of him. It shattered in multiple fragments. James's last thought for awhile was***…damn…that's what just happened to me…***

✲ ✲ ✲

I woke up and laid still on the bed. True it was noon-thirty and I wouldn't need another nap until four or five but Bill was up reading *Newsweek* and any movement on my part could trigger a political dissertation.

RRRING RRRING RRRING RRRING

"…we have a call in RichTown…a construction accident of some sort…"

"…okay…I'm ready…" And this time I meant it.

…I was an experienced newbie now…

✲ ✲ ✲

Bill was an old goat of a veteran tech…sort of the Bob Dole of EMS…so it was no surprise when he jumped in the driver's seat and began navigating us down the maze of suburban side streets. We heard dispatch send out an ALS truck and it sounded like they were coming from Valley Trauma Hospital. Their coming from the city meant we were

*going to be without them for fifteen minutes. PHEW...it's
not like fifteen minutes is forever...*
*   ...I've already lived through this...*

When we first got on scene I focused in on two guys and a
cop standing over a body on the driveway. There were branches
and tools scattered everywhere. It looked like a mini twister had
touched down. The patient was lying on his back with his eyes
wide open but he wasn't moving or making any noise.

"...**HEY...CAN YA HEAR ME?...**" I yelled four inches
from his ear but still no movement or noise. "...what's his
name?..." I asked one of the guys standing nearby smoking a
cigarette. "...and hey...c'mon man...put that cigarette out..."

"...oh yeah...sorry..." He crushed it out on the driveway.
"...James...James Zoya...he was cutting branches in that tree...
he must have cut his safety line..."

"...ah...good move..." I heard Bill mumble as he approached
with the longboard. "...does he have any medical problems we
need to know about?..."

"...I don't think so...uh...I mean...I really don't know him
that well...he's just a guy who works part-time with us..."

"...is there someone you can call?..."

"...uh yeah...Greg...you should call Danny...he can get
Cathy..."

"...yeah...right..." And that guy took off.

So far I knew this guy had a significant gash in his forehead...
he was acting loopy just sort of staring around and his legs were
twisted oddly in opposing directions. Just the tiniest vibration
generated from cutting through his clothes made him writhe in
pain. Everything started to make him scream. Bill fumbled with

the collar while making the cop hold c-spine. Beads of sweat gathered on his face.

"...your paramedics are here..." The cop announced while looking over my shoulder.

Bill struggled with the collar's Velcro strap. "...oh thank God..." I looked at him. His nervousness was starting to disturb me.

"...yeah...good thing..."

✡ ✡ ✡

"...what have we got kids?..." The first paramedic was Joanie. She was loud and she was large and drama was her middle name but she always talked kindly about the basics so she was all right in my book.

"...I grabbed some extra fluid..." The second paramedic was Ariel***...hey cool...I know her...***

"...approximately 30 y/o male fell from that tree while he was doing some cutting..."

"...about how far up was he?..."

"...uh...I don't know..." I fumbled with the O2 mask.

"...about twenty feet..." One of the bystanders chimed in.

"...great thanks...any history...meds or allergies?..."

"...unknown...PD's trying to get a hold of the wife...hey can I use your trauma shears?...I can't get through this belt..."

"...here ya go..." Ariel flipped me hers off her back belt and then moved in to assist with removing his climbing gear. "...he's looking shocky...does he have radial pulses?..."

I fumbled to get the right glove off***...this led to a grisly discovery...***I took the left glove off***...this led to a second grisly discovery...***

"...does he?..." Ariel asked again.

"...I don't know...he doesn't have any wrists...his hands are severed and only his gloves...a flap of skin and a couple of tendons are holding them on..."

"...splint 'em..." Joanie bellowed while tossing two hand splints and gauze at me. "...that's why we expose...okay people... let's get him on that longboard and let's get moving...jump in the truck Aire and get set up...Officer hold him here and we're gonna roll on my count...ONE...TWO...THREE..." If you want here's where you can insert loud sustained scream from the patient...*we all pretended we didn't hear it.* "...okay good... on the stretcher...head's up this end...Bill grab that strap... good...place him carefully...okay kid you drive our truck... we're going to Valley Trauma...we'll see ya there..."

...two truck doors slammed and just like that the call is over for me...

✿ ✿ ✿

Two ambulances pulled into the Valley Trauma driveway ahead of Cathy. She thought maybe James was in one of them. Despite straining to see...Cathy couldn't tell if any of the anonymous faces were her husband's. As it turns out they weren't. Around back by the emergency room entrance her painfully contorted husband was being removed from the back of an ambulance. Two basics and two medics wrestled with BP cuffs...IV solutions and splints of all kinds. Everyone hoped they looked calm on the outside but there really wasn't any way of knowing. Down the hallway and into the trauma room they pushed James Zoya's shattered self to a team of doctors...nurses and orderlies who took transfer of patient care.

Later that day I ran into Ariel who had some news about driveway guy. He underwent sixteen hours of reparative surgery. Many pins...rods and screws later Humpty Dumpty was back together...*sort of*...He was injured on an under-the-table second job so he had no coverage for his accident. The lost time caused him to lose his primary job. Six months later his family lost their house...one year later he was divorced. Now he limps and drinks too much and we pick him up from time to time passed out in various public venues.

So what have we learned people? Go ahead and try sowing hard work and love for your family but when it comes time for reaping it's all worthless if you make one mistake or have an ounce of crap luck. I don't know about you but I think that's evil. It's the great can't-do. Oh I know...where was I when God created the mountains?...

...all I know is I'm not so scared of Jodie anymore...

CHAPTER 6 -
MY ROAD TO DAMASCUS

...now as Saul journeyed on the road to Damascus...
suddenly a light from heaven flashed about him...and he
fell to the ground blind and heard a voice saying to him "...
Saul did you get your paperwork signed?..."

"...the medics see so much shit...you know..." Blossom stands in my kitchen and drags off the jay. "...and it's not the blood and guts stuff..."

"...no...that shit's cool..."

"...exactly...it's the sadness though...there's a lot out there..."

"...yeah..." I hold my hit. "...sometimes it makes me wonder why we want to be medics..."

"...'cause we figure we can handle it and it's time for some fresh minds and souls to assist the burnt-out vets..."

"...I wonder how much you gotta see before you get crispy..."

"...I don't know..." Blossom squints. "...but thank god for weed..."

...amen...

✫ ✫ ✫

...if I was my bible where would I be?...

✫ ✫ ✫

"**...HEY...**" Hoppy instructed from the center of the room. "...now listen ...there are three rules on the board...and as potential...and believe me people the thought scares the living shit out of me...but as potential paramedics you are required to know these rules..." His voice proceeded to commandingly drone on***...at least that's how I heard it.*** "...rule number one all bleeding eventually stops...rule number two...all patients eventually die and thirdly people...for god's sake...if you drop the baby...**PICK IT UP..."**

...I couldn't write fast enough...

✲ ✲ ✲

"...congratulations on getting in to medic school..." Blossom squinted and put his hands in his pockets. "...so you're going the traditional BigCity College route?..."

"...yeah...I'd like to do the accelerated program you're in but I can't travel that far..."

"...it's a haul..." Blossom pointed toward his driveway. "...had to drive three hours on my donut Friday..."

"...damn..."

"...so you gonna stay at Carter or go to Valley when you get your medic?..."

"...I don't know...is it required that every new medic go to Valley to work the streets of BigCity?..."

"...don't you want to?..." Blossom ducked from an incoming fly. "...I know I do..."

"...yeah I guess...it's just that I'm not good with change...first I get this new drug box then I get new partners and GSWs..."

"...yeah..." Blossom giggled and broke into twang. "...but you can't be a cowboy if you don't ride the pony..."

"...what the fuck are you talking about?..."

"...I don't know...it's the Portuguese wine talking..."

✲ ✲ ✲

"...so anybody I know in your paramedic class?..." Fergie never even tried to kick my ass so we became friends.

"...I don't know..." I struggled with a collapsing burrito. "...you know a lot more people than me..."

"…know any names yet?…"

"…uh…there's me…some chick from Oklahoma named Skvarla…a Sue…"

"…anyone from Valley?…" Fergie declined banana bread.

"…a couple of guys that hang out with some chick…Rickie somethin'…"

"…oh…Rickie… she hangs out with Kelly O'Brien…"

"…yeah…see you do know everyone…"

✩ ✩ ✩

"…Casey…get over here…" Jodie beckoned and I went. "…you did good on that call today…"

"…really…I wasn't sure I really helped…"

"…you didn't lose your shit and you did everything you were told…that's all we're asking out of you…when you're a paramedic you'll appreciate it…"

"…thanks…"

…and I didn't know what else to say so I shut up…

so here's what happened…

"…the Red Sox aren't going to win the World Series until they get better pitching…"

"…you're killing me Blossom…" I steered through suburban traffic. "…as long as you keep the race tight anybody can get hot at the right time…"

Blossom shook his head and dispatch interrupted. **"…FOUR-EIGHTEEN…FOUR-ONE-EIGHT…"**

"…eighteen…Converse and Stony Hill…"

"…EIGHTEEN…ASSIST ALS FOUR-TWENTY-NINE… FOUR-TWO-NINE AT ALLENCREST AND SHAKER FOR THE TWO-CAR MVA THREE PATIENTS…"

"…eighteen received…" Blossom flipped on the lights.

"…lights…wow…do you really think we need 'em?…"

"…no…but we gotta have some fun sometime…"

"…it'll almost make us look like ALS…"

"…till we trip getting out of the ambulance…" Blossom giggled and I agreed. When we pulled up on scene we noticed the medics who called for us were Jodie and somebody filling in for Fergie. Initial assessment of the accident didn't reveal anything overly dramatic or cool so maybe they just needed extra hands. Two midsize cars had met at their front left quarter panels creating crunched metal and distributing plastic pieces in concentric circles radiating outward from the crash point. There was a significant dent in the windshield of one car but there was no blood or hair sticking to it so I figured it had just crumpled. Two patients were standing next to the blue car***…they seemed fine…***Nobody was near the green car. Two cops were measuring skid marks and reciting license and registration info into their portable radios while another cop directed traffic around the lump of vehicles. The side door of 429 flew open and Jodie stuck her head out. "…Casey…Blossom…in here…"

Blossom and I looked at each other and smiled***…maybe this would be fun…***When we got inside the ambulance we saw five people. Jodie…her partner Mark…a loudmouth smelly guy… some mousy chick and an unconscious nine-month-old on the stretcher. Mark told Blossom to go check the other two patients… verify that everything was okay and do the paperwork to make it all official. Blossom turned without answering and exited the side door. I could tell he was disappointed to be going back to the basic part of the call. Meanwhile Jodie told me to hold c-spine on the baby while she got the c-collar on. It too may have been a basic assignment but at least it came with a twist. See…I had never seen an unconscious baby before***…never mind touch one…***It was kind of creepy how it laid there like a rag doll. I got all caught up… staring at it…waiting for it to move like you do at a wake and soon I lost track of what else was going on in the ambulance. Then I felt Jodie thump my forehead with her finger "…hey Newbie… you wanna pay attention?…"

Startled and embarrassed I made eye contact and nodded in the affirmative. She kept the pressure on. "…and there's no reason for me to tape your hands to this baby's head and the board… move 'em…" I realized I was distracted and I better get it together or be considered useless.

Then the action around us rumbled toward crescendo when Mark and the smelly guy got into it. In the distance I had heard them jawing back and forth but my fuzziness had kept it a wordless argument. Then as I pulled myself back into focus details emerged. Apparently the smelly guy was the baby's father and he wanted everyone to know he was in charge of his kid and nobody could do anything that he didn't want done. **"…SO YOU MOTHERFUCKERS GOT IT?…I'M MOTHERFUCKIN' IN CHARGE…"**

"…SHUT UP…" Mark looked up from the freshly inserted IV catheter and screamed back…which just made the smelly guy shout more. Jodie efficiently got the baby's spinal considerations secured and directed me to put it on oxygen. I don't think I had ever witnessed so much chaos in such a confined space…*what's the point of paying attention when nothing makes sense?*…I had never had my senses challenged and overloaded like that before…*ever*…but instead of grabbing my head and screaming **"…EVERYBODY JUST SHUT THE FUCK UP…"** I strictly focused on Jodie's commands so as to avoid the next forehead thump.

The smelly guy kept going on and on in an escalating pattern of threats though and eventually called somebody…I don't know if it was me or Jodie…a cow bitch. I was impressed by his creative string of vernacular but Mark saw it differently.

"...THAT'S IT..." Mark had had it. **"...YOU'RE GETTING OUT OF MY AMBULANCE NOW..."**

Mark opened the door and yelled for a cop. Then he turned to me. "...your partner should be done by now so get this dirtbag and his wife out of my ambulance while we try to keep their kid breathing..."

The wife only heard a partial phrase and started screeching **"...OH MY GOD...MY BABY'S NOT BREATHING...ARE YOU TELLING ME MY BABY'S NOT BREATHING?..."**

Even with her wails I wasted no time getting out and dragged her with me. On my way to putting her in our truck I flagged down Blossom. "...Mark needs you ASAP..." I made a little face so Blossom knew Mark really meant ASAP and I wasn't just being a dork. He got the idea and nodded back.

Poor Blossom though...he definitely got the short end of this call because the next time I saw him he was walking behind the smelly guy who was being helped to our ambulance by two cops. Blossom had his hands in his pockets and a smirk on his face. The smelly guy was handcuffed...upside down and very close to being dragged by his arms. Later Blossom told me he didn't know what to do because he thought he had the guy talked out of the back of the ambulance without further complications but then out of nowhere the smelly guy spit on Mark. That left the cops in no mood for fucking around so they grabbed parts and pulled. Blossom said while they were dragging the guy he was making all kinds of threats and swearing up a storm. Blossom had to walk behind them through lots of stopped suburban traffic on a warm day while everyone's got their windows rolled down and people and their children were staring at him...*hello ma'am... hey what radio station is that?...what did he do?...uh...he got into a car accident...nice horn...no we don't do this to everybody in a car accident...hey is that Beastie Boys?...*

*no really we are protecting his spine...ok have a nice day...
drive safely...we're still in town...ha ha...*

Meanwhile the mother was confiding woman to woman with me and it was kinda pissing me off...*So the baby's been sick and we were taking it to the pediatrician and he started crying... My husband started yelling at me to shut the baby up because he couldn't drive with all that obnoxious crying...so I took the baby out of the car seat and he still kept crying so my husband freaks and we drove right into that car and I can't hold on to the baby and he goes flying into the windshield...and is my baby going to be all right?...I really need to know...*

...uh...my guess would be no...

CHAPTER 7 -
MOVE CALMLY AND PREPARE TO EXODUS

*"...this is the land I promised on oath...I have let you
see it with your eyes but you will not cross over into it..."
And Moses the servant of the LORD died there in Moab...
unfortunately he did not have an active DNR and he had to
be worked for forty-five minutes...*

When I signed up for EMT class I assumed going to school
and having to pass a state board exam meant I'd earn better pay
than I did as a factory worker. Well...that would be wrong. In
fact...I have quite the vivid memory of someone asking our EMT
instructor what we should expect for starting pay. I remember
hanging on the edge of my seat while thoughts of a higher income
bracket fed my fantasy of new toys and home ownership. Then he
made a funny face and succinctly answered "...well...they have to
give you minimum wage at least..."

When I got my first job I realized it got even worse. First
they paid you a mere pittance and then they expected you to
buy your own uniforms and shoes...whatever seasonal gear you
needed like raincoats and winter jackets. There were no paid
holidays***...just all the holidays got worked...***No insurance until
you made fulltime and nobody ever seemed to work fulltime just
eighty hours a week. I asked about retirement programs and my
ops manager told me to make sure I died while I still had a job and
it wouldn't matter. Besides...no one ever retired an EMT. This
was a transient field and turnover was expected.

Every now and then a group of medics would get their
dander up and demand raises for everyone. That usually resulted
in mandatory company meetings where the owner would drive
up in his Land Rover...yell at everybody because his electric bill

went up and then explain that he bled for this company so he got the bigger piece of the pie. I never knew what that meant and the meetings never ended with raises for anyone but once he promised that he would try harder to keep up with buying toilet paper for all the bathrooms.

However…as horrified as I may have been there was no reason for me to act shocked that selfless hard work would net me anything but getting screwed. It's been going on right from the beginning of time. Take Moses for example. Living as a future pharaoh he was pretty much living as the world's first rock star. He had hot chicks everywhere…a kickin' palace on the water… he was essentially the ruler of the earth and he gave it all up to lead an oppressed nation to freedom. So were they appreciative?*…no…*Did they cut the guy some slack for all the sacrifices he made?*…no…*He went without sleep…money…food and any semblance of a healthy relationship***…not to mention not a drop of good coffee to fall back on…***and they didn't even name their nation after him. Then under the pressures of the job he snaps and his boss cuts bait with him and hangs him out to dry. Oh yes that was the earliest recorded act of risk management. Yet thousands of years later…the story having been consistently retold generation after generation…and yet we still act surprised when we discover that all that applies still applies.

We work hard and we sacrifice. One thing I learned was that while EMSers may be a little screwy in the head for wanting to be around all of life's woes they are intelligent people who easily could go to school to make more money. And some did. Some became doctors and nurses…easily the more lucrative medical careers…Some became very good lawyers and engineers who never seemed to let anything hijack their stride. But face it…if you're not standing on a four-lane highway doing your job just how daunting can it be?

But many stay and simply for the reason that they love what they do. And maybe their crusty exterior shells imply ambivalence to the world around them but the truth is they do care. They care about the work they do and they believe the world is a better place if they do their job correctly. Will that get them praise and recognition?…A simple thank you at the end of the day? How about fair wages and job protection?….*have you been paying attention at all?…*

The truth is we know the deal and so to stay and not lose our minds we lower our standards of expectation. Just let us have our kinship and group hugs and we'll work hard and long for peanuts. We're dysfunctional remember…*a little bit of love and affection goes a long way…*

✷ ✷ ✷

"…so did you hear the news?…" Blossom sprayed down the stretcher.

"…no…what's up?…" I held a clean sheet.

"…Carter and Valley got bought out by the Borg…"

"…really…is Jon Luc in town?…"

"…more like DATA…" Blossom tossed his towel. "…this new company is huge…"

"…New England huge?…" I unfolded the sheet.

"…no…NAA…North American Ambulance…they're international huge…and they're all about big business…"

"…big business?…in EMS?…that ain't going to work… everyone knows there's no money to be made…at least not big-business money…"

Blossom giggled and tucked in his end. "…not the way things are now…"

I stopped tucking and stared. "…you mean…change?…"

"…yup…"

…oh god…

✫ ✫ ✫

"…wait a minute…wait a minute…I got one…"

"…oh no…"

"…no wait…I can tell it…"

"…well you gotta stop laughing first…"

"…HEEEEEEEEeeeeeeeeee…."

"…breathe Jodie…breathe…"

"…no really…I can do it…"

"…oh my God…"

"…ohhh the pain…my stomach…"

"…Jesus…I'm outta here…"

"………………………………………………………………eee"

✫ ✫ ✫

so Blossom and I were just about to order our grinders…

"…EIGHTEEN…ONE-EIGHT…" *guess who.*

"…eighteen…"

"…EIGHTEEN…FORTY-SEVEN…FOUR-SEVEN SPRINGFIELD STREET…32 Y/O MALE…OUT OF CONTROL…PD ON SCENE…"

"…eighteen received…okay…I guess we'll be back…" I looked at Blossom. "…shall we cowboy?…"

"…giddy up…" And Blossom giggled.

the short of this story is…

There was a 32 y/o male out of control. Blossom thought it was funny because he was a 25 y/o male out of control and nobody noticed. Anyhoo…this out-of-control male was sitting on the ground in a busy convenience store gas station parking lot holding a steak knife to his neck. Surrounding him was a cop circle with their hands on their weapons and a couple of paramedics from LittleCity that came by to watch. Blossom and I set up on the outside perimeter and joked about buying the guy a gallon of gasoline. Then one of us brought up the scene in *M*A*S*H* when Klinger was going to set himself on fire...*hey who put gasoline in my gasoline?...* Blossom was dancing around poking an unlit cigarette at an imaginary Klinger and I was giggling...*probably low blood sugar...*when were rudely interrupted by one of the LittleCity medics asking us to bring our ambulance over. Seems we missed the part where the cops got sick of waiting...charged the guy and doused him with mace. Now they wanted to put the snotty spitty sweaty slimy guy in our truck...*uggggh...*

Blossom brought our ambulance over and the cops handcuffed the formerly out-of-control male's arms behind his back and laid him facedown on our stretcher. We put our stretcher straps on him and slid him into the ambulance. He was really spoogy and la-houd but he wasn't going anywhere and I figured just Blossom and I would be taking him to the LittleCity Hospital up the road. Then one of the LittleCity medics got in the ambulance and said he was coming with and I didn't see where I had a chance to say no. And it would have been one thing if the guy needed a medic. You put up with an ego if it's in the patient's best interest. But this was as basic as a basic call could get. On any other day the guy may have even gone to jail and been processed before given his humane and ethical transport to a medical facility. Now I had to give up complete control of the back of my ambulance and for no apparent good reason. And right away the two of them started yelling back and forth with each other. Normally Blossom and I try to schmooze psychs. What difference does it make if they think they're getting their way?...*if the ride is easy the night is easy...*This wasn't going to be easy. They were jawing back and forth over who had a bigger penis and then the formerly out-of-control male spit at the medic. And it was a nasty one too 'cause it was all mucousy and stringy and green and he managed to get him right in the face. It was really gross. Without hesitation the medic punched the handcuffed guy really hard in the head...*twice...*

...gotta say I didn't see that coming...

☆ ☆ ☆

"...company meeting..." I studied the notice over the time clock. "...at the Y?...since when do we need an industrial-sized conference room for a company meeting?..."

"...Valley is going to be there too..." Ariel reached over me for her timecard in the rack...*I smelled honeysuckle...*

"...why?..." I wasn't getting it.

"...because they bought both of us and we're going to merge..."

"...what?..."

"...yup and that's only the small change..."

"...you guys talking about the merger?..." Fergie threw her backpack over her shoulder and joined the conversation.

"...yeah...I'm just filling Casey in..."

"...sounds bizarre to me..."

"...oh just wait...bizarre is only the beginning..." Fergie adjusted her glasses. "...I hear a bunch of medics from both sides have already resigned..."

"...resigned...why?..."

"...because NAA is a really crappy company to work for..." Fergie pulled no punches. "...everybody's gittin' while the gittin's good..."

"...where are they going if there's only one company left?..."

"...fire departments...some are going back to school..." Ariel filled me in. "...Jim's going to Valley Trauma to work phlebotomy..."

"...so study hard Casey..." Fergie punched me in the arm.
"...you're our future..."
   ...the time clock clicked and we were gone...

☆ ☆ ☆

My next paramedic class was loud. The ten Valley students
were bragging that they were going to rule over the scrubby
Carter people. The out-of-towners were sympathizing with all of
us because of what they had heard about the new company and
the three of us from Carter sat stoically, too outnumbered to talk.
Bottom line...everybody had heard about the exodus of medics
from both companies. True a lot of them were going to better
more secure jobs with fire departments but a bunch were leaving
just to get the hell out before it hit the fan. The fact that our
graduating class would quickly rise in the seniority ranks was not
lost on anyone. The cockier students thought that was awesome
and they'd rule. The grown-up students recognized the hazards of
not getting properly mentored. I wasn't convinced I was going to
make it through medic school yet so there was no stress there.

☆ ☆ ☆

so one afternoon it was raining pretty hard...
   ...and Blossom and I were sitting in dispatch watching
Mahan work a big auto accident on the local news. We had just
started debating Chinese or Italian for dinner when a call came
in for a transfer. Dispatch relayed that we were taking a 45 y/o
male to Weston on Armory Street for a hospice admission. We
acknowledged and simultaneously cringed at the thought of our
assignment.
   Weston on Armory Street was one of the creepiest buildings
I had ever been in. Its dark and heavy architecture made you
feel like you were twenty feet underground navigating confining
twisting tunnels instead of hallways. In the seventies it was the

emergency room hot spot for the contestants of the bloodiest most violent crimes of a drug-crazed city. The worst of the worst were brought there and the air held residue from the negative energy that spilled over it night after night.

Things tragically boiled over one evening when a psychotic guy tweaking on PCP stormed in the ER. For reasons that will never be known he grabbed some random kid off a chair and hacked at him with a kitchen knife until PD and staff could finally wrestle him off. The kid died and a bunch of people including the crazy guy got beaten and sliced up. After that…most people never saw that emergency room the same and not long after that the resulting lawsuits caused the hospital to go bankrupt. The building sat vacant for years…which I believe just led to the creepiness becoming more entrenched. Most people were hoping the bankruptcy meant someone would finally take the building down. Instead an out-of-town corporation that had no sense of the local history bought the building and actually touted the virtues of retaining all the original creepy architecture in their managed care trifecta…a detox…a psych facility and a hospice. Great…just what a bunch of dying and drying-out patients need to deal with…*doom…gloom and bad juju…*

Going to Weston was bad enough but having it be a trip to the death ward in the rain was a real kick in the pants. Hospice calls by nature were always sad. To qualify for hospice care you have to be terminally ill. To qualify for a hospice admission…the end has to be imminent. Still sometimes if the person is really old or really sick you can feel better by saying "…at least it's their time…" or "…there in so much pain it's for the better…" Overall you just keep working on the notion that it's nobody you know so just keep it simple and do the call.

For those reasons Blossom and I made the trip out in quiet mode. The radio was low and we could barely hear it over the wipers smackin' the foggy windshield. We pulled up in front of the patient's house and I called us off to dispatch. We grabbed our baseball hats off the dashboard defroster where we had them drying...zipped our rain jackets and stepped out of the truck. Blossom walked quicker than me and made it to the doorbell first. The inside door was open but it was too dark to see past the screen door. A couple of minutes went by and a shadowy figure appeared at the door. He was dressed in a heavy dark overcoat with a black fedora. Under the hat you could tell he was very pale and completely hairless but other than that he didn't seem like your average cancer-ravaged hospice patient. He didn't say much...he just opened the door and we stepped inside. Normally hospice admits are so sick they're bedridden and we do all the work. It was odd not to have anything to do while he continued shuffling about gathering his personal possessions.

While we waited a woman appeared from a room in the back of the house. She asked him if he had everything and he more or less shook his head yes. He seemed to be delaying and we believed we understood. The lady kept grabbing him and spontaneously hugging him. He would hug her back but neither latched on or pushed away...*they just didn't seem to know what to do with each other*...Their awkwardness spilled over to Blossom and me and we avoided looking at each other. Blossom turned to look at family pictures on the wall and I stared, blindly focusing on the fact that this was not my moment...*I am merely a trained observer*...

So the guy had his suitcase and a plastic bag full of magazines and M&M's and we headed for the door. Blossom asked him if he wanted us to bring in the stretcher and he shook his head meekly. It was hard to tell if he didn't want to be a bother or if he was simply resolved to walking out of his house for the last time on his own terms. We let him know that it was raining pretty hard which was stupid. The guy had windows in his living room. For the lack of anything better to say we spewed out some shamelessly hollow words about him letting us know if he needed anything...*is it even appropriate to try to sound like you can help?*...I would have been happier if I could have just held up preselected cue cards...*Can I carry your bag?...Would you like a blanket or pillow?...cigar?...cigarette?...ashtray?...*

We made it to the front door and waited while he and his wife embraced one last time in the living room. Again Blossom and I avoided eye contact and instead turned our attention to our respective shoelaces. There were a few "I love you" and definite sobs and then the goodbyes were done. Blossom and I were outside now. He jumped up in the back of the ambulance and started getting the stretcher ready and I was right behind him with the patient right behind me. Selfishly I was hoping the finality of him leaving his home was past. But just as I stopped holding my breath a small voice from the house called him back. "...Dad...**WAIT**...don't go..."

I couldn't see in the house to see who was calling but the patient turned around quickly and went back up the stairs. He climbed up to the doorway where I could see a young boy come into view. Without hesitation they embraced and the little boy cried. His voice strained as he sobbed repetitively. "...I don't want you to go...please don't go..."

The patient rubbed his back and whispered "...I know son...I know..."

...it was a good day for rain...

☆ ☆ ☆

"...so it's official...Carter and Valley are one...bought by the Borg..."

"...the Borg..." Blossom laughed and shuffled at the foot of the stretcher.

"...yeah...I like that and I think that's what we should call any large company that supports vertical disintegration..."

"...you should have never taken Urban Sociology..."

"...true...but anyway...remember when we were newbies and we thought there was this big difference between Carter and Valley?..."

"...yeah...the preppies and the cowboys..." Blossom turned the hallway corner and laughed.

"...now we're going to be cowboys by default..."

"...hardly seems fair..." Blossom pretended to pull up a holster around his waist. "...I think you should have to earn the right to be a cowboy..."

"...are you kidding me Tonto?..."

"...no..." Blossom turned around and stared at me. "...I'm completely serious..." I cracked up just as we got to the nurses' station.

Blossom smiled at the nurse and she handed him the paperwork. "...thank you...but hey...seriously...there is a hidden benefit to all of this..."

"...to change?...no way...there's never a benefit to change..."

"...no...there is...there's a whole bunch of good medics over at Valley that we'll get to work with now...it'll be the best of both sides...for example...we get to work with Kelly O'Brien now..."

...cannot compute change...cannot compute change...

☆ ☆ ☆

so there we were at the Y...

...and there were a lot of us. Just about everyone from Carter was there and we numbered about fifty. I didn't know everyone at Valley but I'd say they had about one hundred. Ariel... Fergie and I sat next to each other and Jodie and Blossom were in the row behind. There were technical problems with the PowerPoint presentation so we had time to chat. Blossom was making some awesome shadow puppets in the projector light and Jodie was making awesome shadow missiles and seeking and destroying. The room was loud with joking and hearty laughter***...it's hard to keep EMSers quiet...***One of the Borg stood to speak and semi-quiet fell over the room. Blah Blah Blah was all I was hearing. This was after all just the customary ball-washing that goes on when a new company is pretending to be all about the employee and I felt no need to make any kind of emotional investment.

I started to occupy myself by looking around the room to see if anyone was falling asleep yet...when all of a sudden the two conference doors in the back of the room burst open and two on-duty crewmembers from Valley busted in. They were loud and laughing and barely noticed that they had stumbled upon the company meeting. Anyone who had been sleeping wasn't now. I recognized the one on the left as Rickie from my medic class. Pretty much everybody turned to look at them and me and Blossom giggled. When he figured I had positively identified with the strangers he whispered **"...that's Kelly O'Brien..."** while giving me the thumbs up.

I gave him the ol' hmmmph face and strained my neck to see better. My first impression of Kelly O'Brien was "...oh okay..." Eventually she sat down and the speaking Borg representative was staring at her when her attention turned toward the front of the room. She waved her hand and told him to please continue***...I thought that was pretty funny...***Then the meeting took back over and the rest of the evening was a blur.

Later found all of us at everyone's favorite Irish bar...Sully's. It was the first time many of us had ever seen each other socially and that immediately made me nervous. I'm not one to warm up quickly to new people but even so...looking around the room it seemed to me that a lot of the Valley people were pretty cool. Who knew however who'd be left after the exodus? Everyone seemed to agree that the company meeting was a total sham. Nobody was buying that any of this was good for us and it was very insulting to have it presented in such a way.

"...if you're gonna fuck me up the ass..." Mahan was heard proclaiming "...just fucking get it over with already..."

...don't you just hate it when the bar goes quiet at the wrong time?...

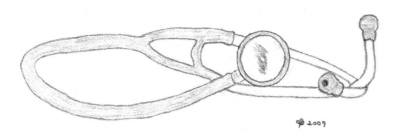

...can you hear me now?...

CHAPTER 8 -
ADIOS AND LAMENTATIONS

...how deserted lies the city...once so full of people...

Now that I look back on it paramedic school was an impulsive decision. I had barely begun feeling comfortable with my role as a basic and now I had rushed off and written a large check to an organization that would torture me for eighteen months while it decided if I was worthy to be the one that should be in the room when someone needs to come up with a "fan plan."

To prepare me and my fellow minions for such weighty responsibility Pschool hammered us with a barrage of information with the dual purpose of teaching us facts and providing us with the ability to handle stress with no sleep. It was a haze of acid-base relationships...generic drug names...lists of acronyms...miles of EKG strips...trauma kinetics...diseases...fatal errors and on and on it went...night after night...know it by Wednesday...reading for the weekend...*Ughhhhh...*

I barely had time to brush my teeth never mind work sixty hours a week.

Unfortunately to compensate for the hasty decision for which I must now pay I had to find a way to work less and make more money. I wasn't interested in working at the mall so I did the next best thing. I traded in my stethoscope for a telephone and came off the road to work in dispatch.

Cross training for school purposes was not a new idea. Many a Pstudent had walked the same trail. Some would even say it was a rite of passage that would make me a more well-rounded medic but it still took some getting used to. Blossom would come by in the morning with a coffee but it usually didn't take long before I had to send him out the door on a call. Out of habit I'd find myself walking him to the door…wanting to get in the truck with him and secretly being jealous of his new partner. In typical Blossom fashion though he was always cool about it and didn't give me any crap. Even on the days when he got stuck with a horrible new basic or cranky old guy. And it's not like he didn't have his own stresses tugging at him. Blossom was not only traveling to take the accelerated program but he had a marriage that he was juggling too. In some ways it really was better to get through school single. Even the most understanding spouse has a hard time reconciling the time commitment Pschool demands just so you can graduate and make ten whole dollars an hour.

I also missed working on the road as much as I thought I would but it was impossible to argue with the logic. Not only did I make a higher pay rate in dispatch but the downtime on overnight shifts was perfect for studying. And while the steady diet of overnights left me bleary-eyed I was able to make my classes and pay my bills. Working in dispatch also let me meet and get to know some the other kinds of species that called emergency medical services their life.

Up until that point I had only met the road warriors. People in dispatch were a voice on the other side of the radio and the occasional story about the good tech who lost their career in a truck to bulging disks or torn labrums. Now I had some faces for the voices of the people who did all of the calls but none of the calls.

The merger also marched on and slowly the lines between Carter and Valley began to blur. For a long time…while financial details were hammered out in boardrooms…each company kept their own trucks and logos but soon crews from each side were jumping back and forth to keep shifts covered and pick up overtime. There started to be more and more occasions where a two-person crew would be wearing two different uniforms on calls. It confused the hell out of the patients who noticed but we all thought it was funny...*what's the point of a uniform that's not uniform?*...The socialization also continued as we all got to know each other better. There were two Irish bars in BigCity... *Sully's and Murph's Pub*...that were public servant friendly and attracted cops...firefighters and EMSers. I had pretty much given up my social life to get through medic school but every now and then my peeps called to me and I had to answer.

One night Blossom...Jodie...Jodie's husband and I headed out to Sully's for cocktails. When we got there a group of Valley employees were already hanging out. We took a table next to them and introduced ourselves. Soon we were all joking around... buying each other drinks and hanging out like old pals. Blossom went up to the bar to get a round and Jodie pinned me to the jukebox...I don't know why...her husband was right there too... but it happened. When I freed myself and made it back to the table Blossom was standing there with his Guinness and a goofy grin on his face.

"...she's here..."

"...who's here?...your wife?..."

"...no not my wife...Kelly O'Brien...you'll get to meet her..."

"..oh...okay.."

We sat back down at the table and I watched Blossom do something I never saw him do before. My usually mellow laid-back partner got goofy and flustered. Sure he kept talking to me but the whole time he was looking around...over my shoulder... not really listening to me and I couldn't help but remind him that he could not score with this chick. Not that I thought he wanted to but that's what he was acting like.

Thankfully Kelly did eventually come in and sit down at our table. Blossom got a wider than usual smirk on his face and behaved like he was in the presence of a rock god. At first I was just really enjoying Blossom's humorous behavior but before long that thrill wore off and I actually listened to the conversation. And even though there was no "angels singing from heaven" kind of moment…it didn't take long for me to realize that she was pretty cool. She had a wicked-sharp wit and an engaging way of speaking. She spoke in rapid-fire phrases…dared you to keep up and never once looked back for approval. She laughed at her own jokes and readily admitted that she cracked herself up. But despite her thorough approval of herself, when she asked me about medic school and how I was making out I had no doubt she genuinely wanted to know. A lot of people had given me advice and words of encouragement already but no one had yet set me at ease about my decision. Fifteen minutes with Kelly O'Brien and I couldn't wait to get back in a truck and do another call...*as a medic...*

Kelly ended up hanging out a little bit with us and then she was off to entertain the next audience. Blossom knew I had drunk the Kool-Aid.

"…she's cool huh?…"

"…yeah…she is…" *why fight it?* Just then Blossom's pager went off. "…is that the Missus checking up?…"

"…yeah…" Blossom mumbled while he struggled in bar light to read the text message. "…whoa…I don't believe it…"

"…what's up?…"

"…my wife just paged me…"

"…I got that…she'd be the missus…"

"…she just got the mail…"

"…yeah?…"

"…I got the big envelope from the state…"

"…you what?…hey…you passed your medic?…"

"…yeah…I guess so…"

"…hey that's awesome…hey Jodie…guess what?…"

"…no hey wait…there's something else…"

"…yeah?…"

"…I wasn't sure how to tell you but this also means I got another job…"

"…what?…you got another job?…"

"…yeah…maybe…I don't know…I applied up north at Country EMS pending passing my state board…"

"…you what?…Country?…why Country?…when did you do this?…I thought we were going to ride with the cowboys together…" *insert awkward moment when the bar got quiet just as I said that…*Great…now everybody thinks I wanna be in a rodeo.

"…I know…I'm sorry…" Blossom was having a hard time not giggling. He took a moment and stared at his beer and then it came out. "… I just don't think I can work for NAA…I wanna do 911 but I can't do it for this company…I've heard a lot of crap about them and I want to get out while I can…"

"…yeah…I hear ya…it's just…why didn't you tell me?…"

"…I know…I thought a lot about that…they came out to recruit us during our ride time in Albany and I wasn't talking to you every day…and I didn't want to say anything until I knew for sure…you know…in case I bombed my state test and it didn't matter…and it's not that I don't want to work with you as a medic too…I just don't think I can stay…"

"…yeah…I know…I'm probably the idiot for not even trying to leave…"

"…no…you'll do well…you'll make a great cowboy…"

"…easy with that…I don't even like country music and now people are looking at me funny…" I looked around to make sure no one was staring. "… it's just not going to be the same without you though…"

"…then come with me…you'll be getting your medic soon enough…they'll hold a spot open for you…they're psyched just to get basics with our kind of call volume experience…"

I looked at Blossom and knew he was genuine with his invitation. Part of me thought it would be a really great idea to go with him and keep the team together. A bigger part of me knew however that there was no way I'd ever have the balls to do it. Change forced upon you is one thing…*proactive change is just looking for trouble…*

Anyway…I think he knew me well enough to know that I'd never do it but we left it at a maybe and I bought him a congratulatory Guinness to change the conversation. Of course this meant the rest of the night took on a different feel as more and more EMS people got off shift and showed up and more and more beverages disappeared. There was singing and laughing and a makeshift mosh pit broke out when word of Blossom's new credentials were announced…*all hail the newborn paramedic…*

I felt sad at the end of the night though because I knew something cool in my life was coming to an end. I looked around the bar and I saw a lot of potential change coming. New partners…new friends maybe…*and who knows what else…* It's just so hard to say goodbye that sometimes it makes me wish I never said hello…

Goodbye Blossom

CHAPTER 9-
BLESSED ARE THE LITTLE CHILDREN

...even as they're getting fucked up the ass...

The merger had not yet oozed through the dispatch doors so for at least now Carter and Valley dispatched their own 911 contracts. As a company we probably did about a hundred calls a day on the ambulance side and two hundred on the chairvan side. To handle the volume we had two dispatchers...one for ambulance and one for chairvan...along with a call-taker who worked both sides answering the phones. I worked a couple of shifts as a call-taker just to get my feet under me and then I alternated between ambulance dispatcher and call-taker. It really wasn't a bad gig as long as you kept track of where your crews were and remembered that losing your shit when the phone rings off the hook helps no one and irritates everyone. Seriously...sometimes it could get a little overwhelming. I had taken for granted that when I worked on the road I was only ever responsible for one call at a time. No matter how crazy that one call got no one was going to expect me to do anything else until it was completed. Telephones with ten lines didn't offer the same exclusivity.

The benefits to dispatch increased exponentially however when you factored in that no matter how often the phone rings you never have to stand in the rain or snow or deal with oppressive heat and cold...*dispatch was wonderfully homeostatic...*

One day during a lull I was feeling particularly thermo-regulated and enjoyed a brief chance to lean back in my chair and munch on a pizza slice. I also thought I'd take the opportunity to get to know my call-taker a little better. His name was Kevin although everybody called him Gumbro. I always wondered why so I thought I'd ask.

"…so why do they call you Gumbro?…"

"…it's a long story…"

"…back to your childhood kinda long?…"

"…no…around here kinda long…"

"…so…we got to 8:00 tomorrow morning…" Gumbro stared at me through his Malcolm X glasses and suddenly I felt I had made a faux pas.

"…I used to wear my hair like Bobby Brown and Dave over at Valley said I looked like Gumby…his partner said that would make me a Gumbro…get it…Gumby…homey …bro…Gumbro…" I was speechless and somewhat horrified. It really seemed kind of racist to me. "…hello…anyone there?…"

"…yeah…it's just…that's kind of…well…doesn't it bother you that everyone calls you that?…"

"…I've been called worse…"

"…yeah…me too…but just because I've been called a dyke doesn't mean I want to be called…a…a…I don't know… LesBro…"

"…you're not black…"

"…I know but…"

"…listen…don't worry about it…I'm fine…" The phone rang and Kevin seemed grateful for the escape. I spun in my chair and ate the rest of my slice while looking out the window.

✷ ✷ ✷

Being off the road for my dispatch shifts made me really antsy to start my clinical rotations. Deep down inside I was really missing the Rubik's Cube of patient assessments. What made this job challenging to smart people was all the figuring out you had to do. The constant thinking and puzzle-solving that goes into every patient encounter. It starts with figuring out where the address is and how to get there from here in the quickest manner and then figuring out what's wrong with your patient and figuring out how to get them out of the tight spaces they always seem to be found in. For example there is a very long standing tradition that if a person falls and breaks their hip in the bathroom they will end up twisted around the toilet like a baggie tie. Your mission...should you accept it...is to safely and as painlessly as possible extricate the baggie tie and get it to the hospital in a timely manner. Bear in mind that there's barely enough room in most bathrooms for the patient, never mind throwing in two other adults and their equipment and narrowing the work area down to the back of the toilet. I loved it and I loved the fact that no matter how difficult the task we don't get to give up or say "...no...I'm not doing that..."

It reminds me of the old Irish story. Brian and Ryan are walking home down a narrow windy wooded road when they come upon a tremendously high stone wall that extends for miles on either side. Brian looks at Ryan and says "...what are we going to do?...we have to get home and there's no way over or around the wall..." Ryan takes off Brian's hat and throws it high and it flies over the wall. Brian shrieks "...what the hell did you do that for?..." To which Ryan then answers "...well now there's no two ways about it...we have to get over the wall...'cause we can't go home without yer hat..." See...it doesn't matter what you have to do or why you have to do it...just do it...*failure is not an option...*

My initial EMT-Basic training was more about mechanical and technical tasks but my paramedic training was an amazing body of facts and figures to absorb and process along with new hands-on skills. After I completed my eighteen months in the classroom I got to spend sixty hours in the Valley Trauma Emergency Room being taught by RNs how to start IVs quick and clean and draw up all kinds of meds while working around angry pissed-off people. They taught me how to assess patients who couldn't speak or speak a language I understood. I moved on to an OB rotation where I saw three babies being born up close and personal. I saw firsthand the damages lingering in trauma patients in the ICU and witnessed people having multiple heart attacks while on CCU monitors. The OR would have been the coolest since I got to wear scrubs and intubate surgery patients but every time I turned around some surgeon was yelling about misfit paramedic students blocking their board.

Two hundred hours and a lot of cafeteria meals later I was cleared to get rolling on my two hundred hours of ride time with an experienced medic who would hopefully help me transition from "head full of knowledge" to "hands-on practitioner." To prove I had made the journey I collected signatures on skill signoff sheets and I needed about a bazillion of them before I could take my state board. There were a lot of hoops I was going to have to jump through to get my medic. Skill signoff sheets were probably the biggest hoop. Because of that skills become like cards in a poker run with dozens of paramedic students hawking patients hoping to pick up an IV...endotracheal intubation... cardiac defibrillation or any other of the skills necessary to qualify to pass go and collect the next two hundred hours. Some students got caught up in the actual skill acquisitions focusing more on the technical performance. I wasn't so worried about how to do things. I worried more about recognizing when to do them...*I wanted to be a master puzzle-solver...*

Ride time or riding third was definitely another step in paying your dues. You don't even have the dignity of a seat in the ambulance. You get shoved in the back and have to strain your head through the opening up front to hear what anybody's saying. Sometimes I didn't bother and I'd just lie on the stretcher while we drove from call to call. Rest of any kind was also as coveted as any skill.

Ride time was measured two ways. First you had to ride a minimum number of hours along with completing a minimum number of skills. If you finish your time but not your skills you just keep on a ridin'. For some poor fools the agony has dragged out so long that they have to wonder if it's even in the cards for them.

Something inside me told me I would get all my skills so I didn't worry too much to start. I plugged along with nothing really exciting to show for it but I picked up IVs...assessments and some med administrations along the way. Mostly I tagged along on chest pains...difficulty breathings and not feeling wells...*the staples of medic calls...*Occasionally someone would be in a lot of distress and the medics would shove me out of the way and tell me to watch. I didn't mind because it was just as important to me to watch someone do it right a few times before I pretended I knew what I was doing.

One Friday night I finished my dispatch shift around 21:00 and was hanging out drinking coffee...hoping something cool might come in. Sure enough a call came in for an intercept in MiddleCity for a woman down. Now a woman down can mean a lot of things. For one thing there have been times when a woman down is actually a man. And people go down for a lot of reasons. They fall...they faint...they drink too much...shoot too pure heroin...lay down because they're tired and sometimes they're not even down when you get there. However...there is always the chance they stopped breathing or having a pulse and that's why they're down. Then they're a code...the ol' Ace of Spades...a cardiac arrest and a cardiac arrest means a plethora of skills. You can get your tube. A tube of course being an endotracheal in**tub**ation or ***I'm going to put this tube down your throat to help you breathe...***They can net you defibs and a bunch of med pushes and a fun assessment to write up. Unfortunately though there are only so many people who are going to code in a given period of time and with paramedic students flooding the ride time schedule in droves...codes become a coveted...rare occurrence. Therefore, if you get a shot at a code you take it. In fact my *Ode to* *the Code Gods* had become **"...I don't wish for anything bad to happen...I just want to be there when it does..."**

So when the call for a woman down came in I didn't wait for the medics to ask me if I wanted to tag along. I grabbed my skills book and jumped on the stretcher for the ride. The two medics were Paul and Tracy. I hadn't ridden with either one of them before but they had each intercepted Blossom and me on separate occasions. Paul was a tall skinny guy who had been a medic about five years even though he was a couple of years younger than me. Tracy was older and knitted a lot. In fact she had kids not much younger than me. And speaking of Tracy's kids...

I remember one night...

...we had a small going-away party for a guy who was leaving for a job in North Carolina. It's hard to get too crazy while you're on duty but right after dinner there was a lull in the action so we broke out the snacks and got sugared up. Tracy brought in an awesome chocolate cake and Fergie...Blossom and I all dove in. A couple of cups of coffee later and we were feeling all right. Not long after though something weird started to happen. I felt kinda speedy and couldn't stay in the building anymore. Next thing I know Fergie and I are in the parking lot laughing at Blossom like he was in his underwear or something. Then Fergie ran up to the side of a parked chairvan and started rubbing it.

"...you know what I've always wanted to do?..."

"...pet a chairvan?...'cause that's what you're doing..." I started laughing so hard I could barely stand.

"...no...I want to drive a chairvan..."

For some reason that sounded like the best idea ever to me. "...yeah ...let's boost a chairvan...come on let's go..."

Next thing I know Fergie and I are whippin' around in a chairvan. I'm driving ninety miles an hour out of the parking lot while Fergie's opening and closing the door yelling "...you wanna get on?…you wanna get off?…Ah-hah aha ha…you wanna get off!!!…" When we stopped whippin' around we came back to find Blossom standing on top of our ambulance yelling at a C-5 flying by. What was really weird was that as zany as we were behaving nobody else seemed to notice or care. In fact…other than Tracy knitting in the garage I don't even remember anyone else being there for all this. It was like everyone disappeared. Then in an undetermined amount of time I got really tired and left Fergie and Blossom to go up to the dorms for a nap. In fact I was so tired that when one of the new basics came upstairs really excited about a bomb scare at the LittleCity Mall I could barely muster a yahoo...*I just assume we didn't have any more calls that night...*

A few shifts went by and one day when Blossom and I were driving around he said "…you know…you can put acid in cake frosting…"

"…what?…"

"…acid…you know lysergic di-…"

"…yeah I get the acid part but why are you talking about cake frosting?…"

"…last Tuesday…when you and Fergie went AWOL in the chairvan…"

"…and you thought you were air traffic control for Air Force One…"

"…yeah…" Blossom smirked and reddened. "…Tracy brought in that cake and we all had like three pieces of it…"

"…yeah it was awesome…I remember I kept thinking 'this would make awesome munchie food'…next thing I know…Fergie and I are drag racing a Yugo…"

"…and I'm pushing tin…you know…Tracy's kid goes to UMass…you know he knows about acid in cake frosting…"

"…because you went to UMass and you know about acid in cake frosting?…"

"…I got science credits for that knowledge…"

"…frightening…downright frightening…"

"…even more frightening…I think we all worked the last four hours of our shift trippin'…"

"…oooo…you mean we got slipped a mickey?…"

"…yeah I think so…"

"…cool…I always wanted to say that…"

"…of course you did…it's very *Charlie's Angels*…"

"…yes…"

"…four-thirty…dispatch…yeah you can put us out… MiddleCity Fire Basics on scene…hey are you awake back there?…" Paul slammed the truck into PARK and turned on the lights in the back of the ambulance…***weeee…back to the present…***Next the doors opened and both of them were grabbing bags and equipment. "…hey…if you want the tube…you carry the airway bag…"

"..got it…ooof…"The airway bag is easily the heaviest of all bags because it has an O2 cylinder in it but to get a tube I would gladly drag a rock with me.

"…Paul…this scene looks a little crazy…"

"…yeah…I'll go find the basics and see what they need… you…stay with Tracy…don't leave her side…" **boy this Paul guy sure doesn't act like he's younger than me.**

But after looking around I realized Tracy and Paul were right. This scene was a little crazy. We were on the backside of a twenty-four-unit apartment complex in a sleazy part of town. There were about forty people milling around a parking lot filled with a fire engine…five cruisers and now our ambulance. I love how the swirling red and blue lights dance on people and buildings and it can entertain me for minutes.

Paul disappeared into the crowd while Tracy and I hung back. I was confused and was wondering why we weren't getting in there. Then Paul's voice came on over Tracy's portable radio. "… yeah hey Tracy…you can leave the equipment…we just need the book…"

"…okay Paul…" Tracy looked at me. "…sorry hon…looks like you made the trip for nothing…"

"…why?…what do you mean?…what's going on?…"

"…come with me…let's get the paperwork and go inside…" So we ditched our bags…grabbed the paperwork book and headed inside. There was a steady stream of uniformed personnel leading to the appropriate apartment so we found our way with ease. When we walked into the living room I saw three guys standing around the couch writing in notebooks. Nobody seemed the least bit impressed that I was there so I felt comfortable getting right up close. When I did I saw an odd figure on the couch. An approximately 30 y/o woman was sitting on the end of the couch with her head in her hand. Her medium length blond hair was hanging down on her face and I remember thinking how sad she looked. I thought maybe she had gotten bagged for something and was stressing that all these cops were in her living room. Then I noticed that behind her hair she was a kinda purply color and not moving. Hey***…she's dead…***Whoa…wait a minute she's not sad***…she's dead…***well maybe she is sad but she's dead…on the couch. Now I'd seen plenty of dead bodies on scene before so that's not what was throwing me. It's just that I never saw a dead body sitting up like that. All the dead bodies I had previously met had the decency to respect tradition and lay down. There was something bizarre about how she had become like furniture. Then it struck me as odd that we were all there…twenty or so just hanging out in her apartment with her just sitting there***…dead…*** Detectives were looking in rooms and drawers and nooks and crannies…I assumed to find clues as to how this approximately 30 y/o died on her couch. Firefighters came in and out of the room anxious to see the crack whore.

"…MOM…I WANT MY MOMMMMMM!…" And just like that an 11 y/o girl tore into the room from the hallway. One of the cops grabbed her as she ran by while one of the detectives yelled "…**GET THAT KID OUT OF HERE!!!**"

"…oh Jesus…no…" Tracy took off out the door behind the cop who was now wrestling with the determined child.

"…NO GET OFF ME…LET ME GO…I WANT MY MOMMY…LET GO…" The cop dragged the kid down the hallway back outside and away from the crowd. I followed Tracy who had caught up with the cop.

"…Officer…let me take her…Officer…I got her…" The cop had no problem handing the kid over and Tracy scooped her up in her arms and sat down with her on the stairs. The custody transfer confused the girl momentarily and she stopped screaming. I stood by not quite sure what the paramedic thing to do now would be. "…honey… you can't go inside you have to stay here…" Tracy spoke in a reassuring tone.

"…but what about my mommy?…is she in trouble?… I wanna see my mommy…" The girl's voice started to escalate again but Tracy hugged her and rocked her. That seemed to keep her calm.

"Honey….you can't go inside because your mommy's dead…" Tracy looked at me and bit her lip. I couldn't believe she had said it like that but surprisingly the girl didn't freak out. Actually she got eerily calm.

"…she is dead isn't she?…I knew it…Joanne said she wasn't but I knew she was…"

"…who's Joanne?…"

"...our neighbor...I go over there when me and my mommy have fights..."

"...did you have a fight tonight?..."

"...yes..."The girl's voice trailed off and she started sobbing. "...my mommy was smoking crack again today..."Through the sobs she continued. "...and the last time she smoked crack I had to go live in foster care...and I yelled at her and I said 'mommy don't smoke crack...I want to live with you and they'll take me away'...she got really mad and started yelling at me and told me to go over to Joanne's house...I didn't want to but she was really yelling and her face got red...I told her I didn't want to go but she made me..."

"...it's okay sweetie...it's okay..."

"...so Joanne made me macaroni and cheese and I went home...and when I walked in the apartment I saw her hand hanging down on the couch and she was snoring and I yelled at her...'Mommy...Mommy wake up...mommy please wake up' and Joanne came over and she made me leave and she called the police and I knew she was dead and Joanne said no...but I knew...I knew..."

"...it's okay honey...it's okay..."

"...why did she die?..."

"...she stopped breathing honey..."

"...is it because of our fight?...is that why?...is it because I made her mad?..."

"...no honey...it's not..."

"...it is...it's because I made her mad and I shouldn't have yelled at her...but I didn't want her to smoke crack and I didn't want to have to leave again...and I'm sorry...I'm so sorry..."

"...it's okay honey...it's okay...it's not your fault..."Tracy hugged her tight and rocked her. She looked up at me and I felt my stomach grip in spasm and my eyes filled up with tears. I don't know what I was thinking but I ran around to the backside of the building and found the lone patch of darkness in the area. I started breathing really hard to keep myself from crying but in the process made myself gag and almost puke. I never felt so weak in my whole life but I couldn't help it. I started yelling at myself to pull it back together. I wiped my eyes on my stiff cuff hoping the scratching feeling would override the inconvenient pain I was feeling inside. I knew I only had two choices. I could get it back together or live the rest of my life behind this building. Somehow I managed to stuff it all back down and I met back up with Tracy who was now handing the girl over to social services. When the transfer was complete she looked back at me.

"...c'mon kid...let's go do paperwork..." **Tracy remained casual.**

I put my head down and walked back to the ambulance. I stoically climbed into the back and sat in silence almost not even noticing Paul was already up front writing his run form. There was a brief mumbled conversation between the two of them and then Paul got out and shut the door. I was never so happy to be sitting in the dark before...**how was I ever going to be able to do this?...**

"...**the medics see so much shit...you know?...and it's not the blood and guts stuff...**" Blossom's words came running back at me.

"...**no...that shit's cool...**"

"...**exactly...it's the sadness though...there's a lot out there...**"

"...**yeah...makes me wonder why we want to be medics...**"

"...**'cause we figure we can handle it and it's time for some fresh minds and souls to assist the burnt-out vets...**"

Yeah right...like this was handling it. I wonder what Blossom's doing right now***...probably some tragic cow-tipping incident...*** On the way back to the garage we stopped and got coffee. It felt good to drink the hot liquid as fast as I could and feel it burn all the way to my stomach. Still, I wondered what Tracy was going to tell people about me. The last thing I wanted was for it to get out that I was a wuss who cried on scene. There's no reason to get your skills signed off if you can't handle the emotion.

When we got back to the garage Paul muttered something about *Star Trek: Next Generation* being on and he flew upstairs. Tracy settled into dispatch and pulled out her knitting. I sat in the kitchen trying to get my head to stop spinning. Eventually I got really tired so I ducked out the back door and went home. I didn't really sleep that night but hell...I was getting used to the numbness of exhaustion. And who knows maybe someday I'll just get so numb I never feel anything again***...that'll be helpful...***

✲ ✲ ✲

Shifts went by but I couldn't stop thinking about that call. I thought about it when I saw the obituary in the paper and then I thought about it the day of the wake and then I thought about it the day of the funeral. I still think about it now...counting the years wondering how old that little girl is now. How did she turn out?***...has she overdosed in front of her little girl yet?...***

I never said anything to anyone about it but I thought for sure everyone could see on my face that I was a big giant loser who couldn't handle the job. And then one day I didn't think about it anymore. Other calls came and went and my ride time went on and I figured I was in the clear. Pretty soon I had all my skills checked off and I was ready to take my test. No other call my entire ride time challenged me anywhere like that one. Maybe I handled the hard one. I don't know...

...maybe I just think too much...

CHAPTER 10-
THE TRANSFIGURATION

...as soon as Jesus was baptized...he went up out of the water...at that moment heaven was opened and he saw the Spirit of God descending like a dove and lighting on him...and a voice from heaven said "...this is my Son the paramedic...I kept hoping he'd get a real job but this will do..."

Make no mistake...this job is not glamorous. To be a paramedic you must be able to tolerate shit...piss...vomit and people who smell like any combination of the aforementioned. To be a good paramedic you have to deal with it and show compassion. You can't judge by the color of skin...the size of the home or the dumpster you stand in. Your job is to provide treatment and transport to the sick and injured. To excel you must provide humanity and dignity in lands where it otherwise doesn't exist. Most days your partner is the only safe contact you have with the world. They provide sanctuary on dark nights. You break bread together...you sleep together...you become like blood. Occasionally you fall in love. Oh did I mention...*I'm a paramedic...*

I spent the next week getting slapped on the back by basics and medics and serenaded with a lot of kind words of encouragement and accolades. A few jealous people made some really dumb comments...*you all know who you are...*and even Blossom called to congratulate me. We spent some time catching up and he told me of his adventures as a new medic for a hill-town ambulance. He told me about doing calls involving tractor rollovers and I told him about my crack OD and he validated for me that yes the call did suck. I didn't tell him I had bolted around the corner to wretch and cry and he didn't ask so I let it go.

It felt weird having so much time on my hands now that I didn't have school filling up my schedule. I found I really didn't like the feeling of boredom so I started grabbing any shifts I could. The company was still in a transaction limbo so there weren't any solid rules yet on how new paramedics should transition from basic shifts to medic shifts. Everybody...including myself...agreed that I shouldn't be thrown to the wolves but with so many of the experienced medics gone there weren't enough left to train the flood of recently graduated newbies for 911 shifts. That meant another month of doing the same kind of transfer calls you did as a basic only now a person might have an IV or need the heart monitor for precautionary reasons. Say it with me...***Oooo Eeeee...***this was hardly the baptism of fire I yearned for but what are you gonna do?

Fortunately it worked out for me that rules in EMS are often just a good idea. Once you add reality into the mix best laid plans and stuff will go by the wayside. So one night I was home getting ready to bunk down with a healthy dose of *Nick at Nite* when the phone rang. One of the cool dispatchers was on the other end.

"...hey Casey...you busy?..."

"...nope...what's up Cathy?..."

"...Paul went home sick so I got an empty half a shift on a 911 truck..."

"...really?..."

"...yup...you interested?..."

"...yeah...who's it with?..."

"...Ariel..."

"...really?...and she's knows you're asking me?..."

"...yeah...she's right here..."

"...and she doesn't care that I'm brand spankin' new?..."

"...no..."

"…cool…I'm there…" And before anyone could change their mind or think better of it I threw on my uniform…bolted out the door and headed into the night for my first shift on a 911 truck…

…sorry Mr. Grant…I'll see you in the morning…

in which I work my first night on a 911 truck and we do a code…

"…we have to go back…" Ariel stated and I disagreed.

"…no we don't…" ***really I was afraid.***

"…yes we do…management frowns on us losing equipment and the laryngoscope counts as equipment…"

"…I can't believe we left it on scene…"

"…well…accidents happen but now we gotta get it…"

"…okay but what are we suppose to do?…sneak back in the house?…"

"…no…we'll knock on the door and hope the patient's husband is still home…"

"…and not at the hospital mourning his dead wife…oh yeah… we're exactly who he wants to see right now…"

"…it'll be okay…"

"…UGH…I don't believe you…"

"…don't worry about it…"

✡ ✡ ✡

we knocked on the trailer door…

…and a frail pale male opened it. From the confusion on his face I assumed he recognized us and that was when it hit me who we were. We were the two chicks who stormed through his front door an hour ago***…without knocking…***and paraded ourselves and our toys through his home to the back bedroom. Even though I was a scared newbie medic and Ariel was scared about working with a newbie medic we acted like there was actually something we were going to do to make things better and he was too naive to know different. His elderly wife laid in their bed...*cold and unmoving...*Three hours earlier she had excused herself from the dinner table saying she was full and felt like she needed to nap. Most likely she adjusted her covers and laid her head to the pillow hoping for rest. At some point she gasped her last breath and her heart quietly resigned defeat. She was covered in beef stew but even her carb-coated face was peaceful. She had passed nicely without much struggle...*what we all hope for...*Her muscles relaxed creating paths of least resistance and stew spewed out every available orifice. The natural pressure gradient that keeps our insides in and outsides out no longer applied. She was dead...*inside and out...*but we still gave her the twenty-minute workup and ride to the hospital that delayed the inevitable...*that's what we do...*

Somewhere in the ruckus one of our important toys got left behind. In my opinion...going back to retrieve it was asking for trouble because it forced us to enter a side of calls we don't need to see. Even as a new medic I had already learned that it isn't our fault when someone is dead before we get there and just because you see a dead body or two a shift doesn't mean you have to act like you're attending a funeral. What we do is more of a dog and pony show that we should never take too seriously. Put simply it goes like this...the family's all in a tizzy...neighbors are whooshing in and out and we breeze in with our buddies...do a quick sound check...*check one...check one...check...check...*tilt some lenses...light some flares and go...that's it...the end. Ariel however was more pragmatic and therefore hung up on the cost of the laryngoscope. As a newbie medic I had no choice but to defer to her ruling...*but that didn't mean I had to like it...*

✧ ✧ ✧

He let us in because Ariel told him we were there to help him clean up the mess we made. She made it sound like it was a service we provided for all our customers. When we got to the back bedroom we started thinking that maybe it should be. Furniture was moved...lamps were tipped over and buckets of puke were strewn about. That's where I found the laryngoscope... drenched in puke...stuck in a suction canister...*how lovely...*

As soon as our equipment was back in hand and all the lampshades were back in place I wanted to go. Finally we agreed on something and we made a beeline for the exit. As we passed through the kitchen though he stopped us.

"...I haven't made it to the hospital yet...I'm waiting for my daughter to call from California...can you tell me how my wife is doing?...she'll want to know..." *rats...*this is exactly the type of emotional exchange I wanted to avoid.

"...I'm sorry sir..." Ariel spoke softly. "...your wife's heart had stopped beating and we were unable to start it again...when we got to the hospital the doctor pronounced her dead...we're sorry...we thought you knew..."

Tears welled up in his eyes and he bit his lip. "...I guess maybe I did..." His voice dimmed. "...I was just hoping maybe..." He put his head down and began sobbing. Ariel reached over and hugged him. I didn't know what to do so I just patted him on his back. At one point Ariel's hand ran over mine and I looked up to see her staring at me. I knew what she was thinking because I was thinking it too...

...crap...this sucks...

✿ ✿ ✿

The rest of the shift was crazy busy and we did a bunch of cool calls. We had a severe conscious-but-confused subarachnoid bleed that we struggled with to keep an airway...a wicked car accident in a distant hill town...and a really good hypoglycemic with no veins. I was in heaven. As a basic I would have had to wait six months to see all this good stuff. Ariel saw it a little differently and kept calling the shift a horror show. Despite our differences by the end of the night we agreed that we liked working with each other. Ariel's partner had recently resigned in the paramedic exodus and she was worried about who she'd get stuck with. She let me know that if I was interested we could be partners. Didn't have to ask me twice. Ariel was a good medic...I'd always be on 911 shifts and she smelled way better than Blossom. Oh wait a minute***...did I say that out loud?...***

CHAPTER 11-
A BAPTISM OF FIRE

...now Moses was tending the flock of Jethro his father-in-law...and he led the flock to the far side of the desert...there the angel of the LORD appeared to him in flames of fire from within a bush...Moses saw that though the bush was on fire it did not burn up...so Moses thought "...I will go over and see this strange sight...why the bush does not burn up..."When the LORD saw that he had gone over to look... God called to him from within the bush "...Moses...Moses... do not come any closer..." God said "...and for God sake's...if your tunic catches on fire...stop...drop...cover and roll..."

So months went by and I knew right away that I liked working with Ariel. I saw patience and compassion in her little wiry self and she could read a monitor like nobody's business. I believed she could help me become a better paramedic...maybe even a better person. I wasn't sure at first what she thought of me. I mean right away I was a new medic and that was going to make me annoying to be around. I was constantly asking questions maybe even sometimes coming off like I was questioning her. It was all just so overwhelming at first. I knew I had Ariel to fall back on but who knew how long it would be before I'd have to work with someone else. The rumor was that NAA didn't want to pay for double medic trucks so they were going to pair medics up with basics. It pounds on the medics because they have to do all the patient care and paperwork but who the hell cared about that? Medics...*like paper towels*...are disposable. But bottom line...if I was going to have to work with a basic I wanted to be able to live up to the patch on my sleeve and be a whole paramedic.

One sunny spring Sunday…St Patrick's Day as a matter of fact…Ariel and I both showed up at work with wicked chest colds. It's no wonder we were both sick. We'd had pneumonia patients coughing in our face for a month. So there we were sitting in dispatch with our bottles of juice and Puffs tissues ready to face the day. We both agreed that we each looked like crap…felt like crap and didn't want to hear any complaining from patients who weren't as sick as us. Dispatch appreciated that we hadn't banged out and left them short a medic truck on the weekend and so in return promised not to beat on us if possible.

The morning went by and all we had to do was a few "Mrs. Fletchers." "Mrs. Fletchers" were the little old ladies or men who had fallen and couldn't get up. Our job was to pick them up…prop them up and make sure they were okay to stay by themselves. They never wanted to go to the hospital *and waste what little time I have sitting in that emergency room with winos and whores?* And since we really couldn't blame them or argue with them we usually just got refusal forms signed and we went on our merry way. In keeping with the day I called that Irish Dessert…*Piece O'Cake*…

At lunchtime we got designated dispatch's lunch picker-upper truck and that took us out of the rotation again. We headed up to Leonardo's to pick up the bulk order of grinders…onion rings and French fries. I pulled up to the door and Ariel ran in with the money. Five or ten minutes had gone by when this old style Mercury came barreling up into the parking space next to mine and screeched on the brakes.

"…are you working?…"

"…yes I am…" *great…now here comes the lecture about parking in the handicap spot*…I was about to begin my speech about us being exempt from the law and being able to park there. Besides…if you needed an ambulance would you want to have to wait for us to run across the parking lot to our legal parking space…*blah blah blah*…when she interrupted.

"…'cause this house up the street just exploded and there's people in there…"

My first reaction was to say "…oh my god are you kidding me?…" so it was a good thing Ariel had just come out with the order and caught what was going on.

"…what's the street address of the house?…" *oh my god… what a great question to ask.*

"…I don't know the number but it's up there on Scott Street… near the intersection with Clinton…"

"…okay…we got it…"Ariel sent the civilian along. "…call dispatch…let 'em know where their lunch is going to be…"

We knew right away where Clinton and Scott intersected but it wasn't as easy as you'd think to find the house on fire. The fire department wasn't there yet and it wasn't like there were flames blasting out the windows. We actually drove by it a couple of times before we noticed a small amount of smoke coming out of a back window on the third floor of a three-family.

Reports on scene indicated there were people inside and a cop already had tried to get in but intense heat beat him back. It's a good thing too because unlike in the movies where people run in burning buildings all the time without gear and the fire department thanks them, in real life you will absolutely get your ass handed to you for becoming a useless ball of human flesh that the firefighters now have to step over or carry out…*not a good career move at all…*

There wasn't any work for Ariel and me to do yet so we just stood by and watched as two engines and a ladder rolled on scene. Hose lines sprang full…ladders got thrown and a crew smashed down the front door and disappeared into the thick…brown… choking smoke. My heart was pounding a mile a minute. I had never been this close to a real house fire. I was actually standing so close to the captain that I could hear the guys on the inside of the house talking on their portable radios. They had commenced with a search of the first two floors while another crew who came in the backside of the house made their way up to the third floor and the assumed seat of the fire. The crew with the hose line reported intense heat coming from the third floor. The captain began to tell them to hold off and wait for external ventilation when all of a sudden the third floor window on the front of the house blew out. It made an awesome movie-explosion sound and spewed glass and wood splinters over everyone's head including mine and Ariel's. I got a strange sense of excitement and nearly lost my mind not having anything to do. I felt like running laps to get rid of the adrenaline that was building up inside me. I looked over at Ariel to see how much fun she was having. She had a nauseous look on her face and was ducking behind the ambulance...*she wasn't enjoying this much at all...*Immediately following the explosion there was some intense screaming over the radio. All I could make out was "...flashover..." and "...guys coming out burned..."

A quick second passed and a firefighter stumbled out the front door. He looked hurt so I rushed over to him. "...are you alright?...where are you hurt?..."

He ripped his facemask off and snarled at me "...get off me I'm fine...there's worse than me coming out..." His anger stunned me because I could see he was burned on his neck and ears but he wouldn't let me near him. He whipped his helmet off the ground and let himself fall to his knees while repeating **"...motherfucker..."** over and over.

Then I heard more ruckus by the front door and three firefighters appeared. They were screaming for us **"...medic... over here...medic..."** Two of the guys were actually holding up the third. He was holding his hands oddly in front of him and I noticed his gloves were hanging off in shreds.

"…oh my God…" I heard Ariel say as she ran up behind me "…those aren't his gloves…that's the skin off his hands…" And she was right. The skin had been burned right off and was hanging in strips. He was in tremendous pain.

"…what is it with us and hands?…" I thought back to that guy who had cut himself out of the tree that day in the region a hundred years ago.

Ariel half shrugged. "…I don't know…let's get his coat off…" We struggled to cut his thick firefighter coat off because we obviously couldn't pull his arms through but we had to start cooling the burns and step one was to get his hot jacket off. The sight of one of their own injured sent the usually calm and swaggering firefighters into a frenzy and they started crowding around us like an unruly mob. While Ariel and I struggled with cutting through the bulky jacket…trying to be efficient but also cautious of moving our patient's hands too much…they yelled and demanded to know why we weren't moving him to the ambulance yet. We had our reasons but there was no talking to these guys. A couple of times they even started dragging the poor guy by his half cut-off jacket inducing bloodcurdling screams and pleadings to knock it off. And I thought I got why they were upset but they still made an already difficult job much more difficult. Bottom line though was that they were firefighters and it wouldn't be cool or right to directly call them out. Fortunately Travis…our supervisor…rolled up on scene and got a cop to help us settle things down. Actually…all the cop did was get the captain to come over and remind these guys that they still had work to do behind them *…hey guys…remember that house that's on fire?…*

Once the jacket was off Ariel and I split up. She went to the ambulance to call for orders for morphine and I worked to continue the cooling process by cutting the tops off bags of IV saline and pouring them on his burns. His skin was so hot that when the saline made contact it made the sound of a sizzling fajita. I asked the firefighter what his name was and through his winces he said "…you wouldn't believe me if I told you…"

"…why?…"

"…my name is Pat…Pat Murphy and I usually love St. Patrick's Day…"

"…not so much today though…huh?…"

"…yeah…no…" **TA SSSSSSSSSSSSSSSSSSS** "….AHHHH BITCH…"

Travis helped us get Pat on the stretcher and into the ambulance and asked if we needed anything else. I barked "…bags of saline…" and Ariel said "…a basic to drive us to the hospital…I want Casey in the back with me…"

Ten milligrams of morphine later and Pat was still in enormous pain. I kept dumping bags of saline but there wasn't much more we could do. Sometimes the ride to the hospital is really long. Obviously it's far worse for the patients but it sucks when there just isn't anything you can do to make something better. In those cases the person driving is the true hero. I looked up front to see my old friend Bill navigating the city side streets and he was doing a fine job.

"…remember when you worked at Six Flags as a lifeguard?…"

"…yeah…" Ariel seemed puzzled at my segue. But the only explanation I offered was to point at the floor that was about two inches deep in saline solution.

"…wave pool…" Ariel smirked and drew up more morphine.

✿ ✿ ✿

Later at the emergency room Ariel and I got all the attention deserved by the two people who had done the best call of the day so far. Everyone wanted to know the story and we got to tell it over and over. Soon I found myself laughing with Mahan about almost crapping myself when the window exploded. I looked up and saw two basics scurrying by on their way up to the floor to do a transfer. And that's when it hit me...*I had arrived*...I was thriving post-adrenaline rush...I was talking shit while a basic cleaned my truck...

...I was a cowboy in the city...

CHAPTER 12 -
THE BOOK OF SKIPPY

...entreat me not to leave you...or to turn back from following after you...for wherever you go...I will go...and wherever you post...I will post...your people shall be my people...and your calls...my calls...where you die...I will die...and there will I be buried...when she saw that she was determined to go with her...she stopped speaking to her...

As you'd expect...the Patrick's St. Patrick's Day Fire taught me quite a few valuable lessons. For one thing...there are different ways to be a good medic and nobody is good at all of them. I may not have had the experience yet but I did have an aptitude for the thrilling. It's what I loved about street racing. But that was just a stupid and selfish way for me to feel it. Being productive while a window blows out over your head is much more mature.

Then there's the fact that I didn't have to be ready for everything. That was an impossible goal. I just had to learn to control my emotions and stay focused. If things get too crazy just go back to the basics. Think on your feet and keep your feet moving toward the hospital. My newfound revelations allowed me to chill out a bit with Ariel and it started to have a good effect on our relationship. I stopped acting like a flustered student and we became more like partners. I don't know...maybe we were even becoming friends.

✫ ✫ ✫

"...it's hard to describe...it was cold....it was snowing....it had already snowed seven days in a row...it was 2:30 a.m....we were driving through the center of the region....Ariel took a slow left turn and the truck decided to go 360 degrees..."

"...then what happened?..." Fergie sips her coffee.

"...I heard Ariel take a really deep breath and I said '...you just woke up... didn't you...?' and she said '...yeah...'...that scared me a little bit..."

"...I bet..."

"...yeah but then I fell back asleep...who knows...we may have done 360s all the way back to the office..."

"...wouldn't be the first time..."

...it's called careening and it can be fun...

✲ ✲ ✲

"...posting...what the hell is posting?..." I had read the memo six times and I still didn't get it.

"...they're taking away the garages and offices..."Ariel leaned on me while she tied her boot.

"...well who the hell thinks that's a good idea?..." I shift my weight to see if I can make her fall.

"...OOF..." ***she lists*** "...it's an NAA thing...they're going to have us stage strategically around the city so theoretically we'll always be closer to calls..."

"...because theoretical things always apply so well to emergency services...this should go well..."

"...yeah I can't wait to sit in the truck for a twelve-hour shift..."

"... great...like the truck seats don't already smell like ass..."

"...EEEEEEWWWWWWW..."

...and we're off to AppleBee's...

✲ ✲ ✲

"...I had a cool dream about us last night..."

BOMMMMMPPPPP Ariel hits the air horn. "...move ya stupid butthead..." ***the stupid butthead moves*** "...oh yeah?..."

"…yeah…it was 1920 and we were train robbers…and the government wanted to kill us because we were notorious.… so we're flying down the tracks at eighty miles an hour with all the booty we've robbed on the train…and we find out the government's laid another train car across the tracks up ahead.… and when we hit it we're gonna die…but we can't jump…"

"…because we don't want to lose the booty…"

"…yeah…and the train's going eighty miles an hour…what would you do?…"

"…I don't know…what did we do?.…"

"…I don't know…I woke up…" *BOMMMMMPPPPP*

…the world may never know…

☆ ☆ ☆

"…that was the stupidest call we ever did…" Ariel slams the truck in drive.

"…I hear ya…" I lean back and stomp on the dashboard with my right foot.

"…should I call clear from this fiasco?…"

"…nah…say brouhaha…it's less threatening…"

"…okay…four-ten…"

"…FOUR-TEN…" dispatch answers.

"…we're clear from this.." *snicker* "…brouhaha…"

"…whoa…" I slam the dashboard with my hand. "…you actually did it…"

"FOUR-TEN…YOU'RE WHAT?…"

"…we're clear…" she squeaks.

"…OKAY ONE-ZERO…COME BACK TO BIGCITY…"

AHHAHAHAHAHAHAHAHAHAHAHAHAHAHAHAHAHA
HAHAHAHAHAHAHAHAHAHAAHHHAHAHAHAHAHAHA
HAHAHAHAHAHAHAHAHAHAHAHAHAHAHAHAHAHA
HAAHHAHAHAHAHAHAHAHAHAHAHAHAHAHAHAHA

HAHAHAHAHAHAHAHAHAHAAHHAHAHAHAHAHAHA
HAHAHAHAHAHAHAHAHAHAHAHAHAHAHAHAHAHA
HAAHHAHAHAHAHAHAHAHAHAHAHAHAHAHAHAHA
HAHAHAHAHAHAHAHAHAHAHeeHAHAHAHAHAHAHA
HAHAHAHAHAHAHAHAHAHAHAHAHAHAHAHAHAHA
HHAHAHAHAHA **oh god** HAHAHAHAHAHAHAHAHAHA
HAHA **ahum**.....

> *...sometimes you just need to let it out...*

a conversation with an angel...

"...so what were we supposed to do?..." *I really wondered.*

"...we could have pretended that we didn't see it..." *She was in no mood to teach.*

"...oh come on...you're going to pretend you didn't see the kid with the bruised face...besides we're state-mandated reporters...."

"...he wasn't our patient..."

"...he was our patient's kid and he had a black and blue face and he told you his father kicked him...."

"...and now we enacted a system that will not only fail him in the long run but also will buy him the biggest beating of his life today...because when the social worker sends him back...or worse just stops by the house to chat and quickly leave...his father is going to beat him and demand to know what that kid said to get everyone so worked up..."

"...we did our jobs..."

"...we screwed up that kid's life..."

"...you can't lay that on me...that kid's life was already screwed up..."

"...well then we really screwed up his day..."

...some games aren't meant to be won...

✡ ✡ ✡

Ariel and I looked at the pale 45 y/o sitting in our stairchair. It was just another bravo sierra call on a sweltering hot July afternoon in the heart of the city. She had the flu***...big deal...***I had a headache. Ariel got the bottom and started slowly backward down the first wind of the staircase. Suddenly the woman gagged and by the look on Ariel's face I knew she saw it coming. The woman hurled violently and completely ignored the barf bag we had put in her hands. Ariel got covered. It was horrible because there was no way to put the woman down. By the time we made it to the bottom landing the stench made me gag. I tried to disguise it as a muted cough and then a feeble hum but Ariel knew. In desperation she managed a pitiful plea "...please don't hurl on me too..." I couldn't help but laugh***...but at least I didn't puke...***

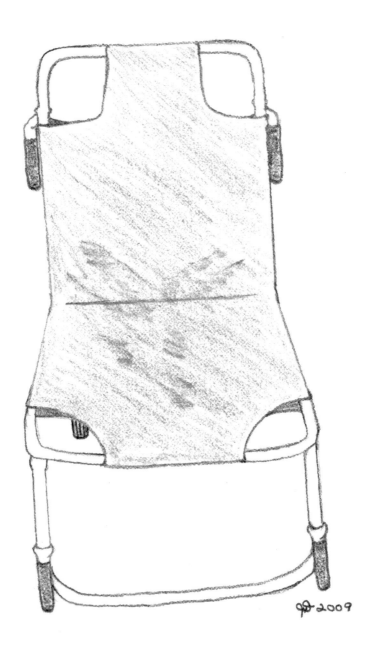

CHAPTER 13-
THE PRODIGAL SON WHO FORGOT TO COME HOME

...the older brother got pissed and refused to go in...so his father went out and pleaded with him...but he answered his father "...look...all these years I've been slaving for you and never refused a transfer...yet you never gave me even a Happy Meal so I could celebrate with my friends...but when this son of yours who has squandered your property with prostitutes comes home...you have a pig roast for him..." "...my son..." the father said "...you are always with me and so I can take you for granted...but we had to celebrate and be glad...because this brother of yours was dead and is alive again...he was fucked up but now he's in rehab..."

Lenny got out of the Taurus and slammed the door. "...fuckin' prick...**YOU COCKSUCKER!...**"

The Taurus driver rolled down the passenger window. "...Lenny...get back in the car..."

"...fuck you asshole...I'll fuckin' walk to asshole Alaska before I fuckin' ride with you again..." Lenny walked to the middle of the street...crossed behind an oncoming car and disappeared down an alley. The Taurus window rolled up...the driver paused and then drove away...

...

...

"...thanks douche bag..." Lenny mockingly saluted toward the ass end of the Taurus and lit a cigarette.

The douche bag was his older brother Dave. Dave was 32 y/o husband...father of two...living in the suburbs...good job...

nice house…clean pool…brother of dirtbag. Lenny was the 28 y/o smokin'…drinkin'…smackin'…nothing to nobody loser dirtbag brother. It is amazing how two people can grow up in the same suburban house and turn out so different. But if you asked Lenny he'd say it was simple…Dave got all the breaks…Dave was older…Dave was smarter…Dave was great…Dave was…Dave was…Dave was… **ahhhh fuck Dave…**Lenny was so goddamn sick of hearing how great Dave was that by the time he was sixteen he drank himself deaf to deal with the noise. A side benefit was that drinking was a lot of fun and people who like to drink are a lot of fun to hang out with. Certainly more fun than the teachers and students and all those other people who thought Dave was so great. So Lenny hung out and he drank and before long he smoked weed and not much longer and he was snortin' lines or poppin' pills or ingesting whatever got put in front of an orifice. And contrary to popular belief…they all made him feel good. That downside to drugs crap was all overblown. Yeah sure sometimes you come down hard or make your heart race too fast but there's always one way or another to reverse the trend. No matter what…another pill or another drink and you feel just fine.

Today however was all about one thing and one thing only… *scorin' some H…*Fortunately for Lenny…alcoholism is not just fun…it's a medical disability that comes with a monthly disability check. Dave cashed it for him and he was a car ride to the South End of BigCity away from scorin' big. He told Dave he needed a ride to his lawyer's office and picked a fight on the way so Dave would pull over and boot him out halfway there. Lenny could have cared less if Dave figured out that he was the one getting taken for a ride as long as Lenny was close enough to walk to his score. Pissin' off Dave on the way was just more fun for the ride.

Ariel held the door open for me and we cruised into Boston Bagel...

"...thanks man..." It was 11:00 and we had been running all morning. We hadn't done anything spectacular but we had burned the calories anyway and I was starving. Mmmm...the smell of rising yeast washed over my senses and I could already taste the egg bagel with olive and pimento cream cheese. I knew Ariel was hungry too because she was cranky. "...you going to the mandatory company meeting tomorrow night?..."

"...of course...it's mandatory..."

blank stare "...okay...I'll wait till you eat something before I talk..."

"...I don't know if I'm hungry..."

"...oh you're hungry and you're eating..."

"...FOUR-TEN...FOUR-ONE-ZERO..." Ariel's portable squawked.

"...no...no no no...c'mon I'm hungry..."

"...settle down...four-ten..." Ariel answered and I hung in the balance...

"...FOUR-ONE-ZERO...DO YOU HAVE FOUR-TWENTY'S GAS CARD?..."

"...ahhhh phewww...that was close..."

"...four-ten...we'll give you a landline..."

"...THANKYOU FOUR-ONE-ZERO..."

☆ ☆ ☆

...bullet dodged...we got our coffee and food and went back to the truck to snack...

☆ ☆ ☆

Lenny pulled his hoodie up over his head and stepped into the package store. A pack of smokes and a forty later and Lenny was back out on Main Street ready to roll. It was going to be a beautiful day...not that Lenny cared about warm air or clear skies. In fact...in another hour or so he hoped not to even be aware of the weather. But the sun was bright...the nippy morning air was warming up and Lenny was about to score a bag. All was well in Lenny's world and he owed it all to some guy he met in a bar last week who told him about this Puerto Rican dude who was selling high-grade shit for cheap.

"...he's getting it from his cousin in Hartford..."

"...Hartford...who the fuck cares about Hartford?..."

"...nobody asshole but Hartford is a hop and a skip from New York man...that's where all the primo stuff rolls in from... his name is Vega...you can find him here dude..." And the guy drew a little map on his Keno slip.

"...what the fuck is this?..." Lenny pointed at the slip. "...I can't read this shit..."

"...this is Main Street...this is Hoover..." The guy drew thicker lines with his stubby pencil. "...this is the third driveway on the left...there's a driveway here and a garage down the hill in the backyard...but hang out here on Hoover and he'll find you..."

Lenny was pretty sure Hoover was only a couple of streets up on the left. He kept working on the forty and sucked down a Newport...

...ah it's good to have a plan...

☆ ☆ ☆

Ariel and I were too hungry to try making it back to the office to eat in comfort so we spread our food out on the dashboard and dove in. Besides...grumblings were that posting***...whatever the hell it was...***was right around the corner. Might as well start getting used to it now.

I was sitting in the driver's seat and had to work around the steering wheel. Ariel got a good laugh when I dropped my coffee stirrer and it slid between the dashboard and windshield.

"...ahhhh...that's gonna come flying out at somebody at a hundred miles an hour..." I laughed too and secretly hoped it would be Mahan who got it.

SMACK SMACK SMACK Suddenly, there on a rap on the driver's side window that startled me. I turned to look and a Chinese dude was standing there with an angry look on his face.

"...can I help you?..."

"...roll your window down..." I heard his muffled request but played dumb.

"...what?..."

"...roll your window down..."

"...why?..."

"...roll your window down..." *okay...I slowly rolled it down about an inch.*

"...what?..."

"...why are you parked here?..."

"...we're eating our breakfast..."

"...you can't sit here..."

"...why?...we're just eating bagels..."

"...this is my restaurant ...you're sitting next to it and it looks very bad for business..."

"...what?..." I looked at Ariel. "...is he for real?..." Ariel shrugged her shoulders. "...look buddy...I've eaten in your restaurant and your food is bad for your business..."

"...oh...you have no right to say that...now move your ambulance..."

"...go away..."

"...I will call the cops..."

"...go ahead...here you can use my radio...it's channel seven..."

"...don't push me..."

"…all right all right….let's just go…" Clearly Ariel's blood sugar had not yet risen.

"…what?…"

"…let's go…so we can eat somewhere else in peace…"

"…fine…"

…and around the corner we went…

✲ ✲ ✲

Vega did indeed find Lenny and even though Lenny didn't speak Spanish he knew enough to follow Vega down the driveway to the garage. Some garage…it was a crap structure to begin with and sometime recently someone had set it on fire. It still smelled like smoke and patchwork plywood was nailed up to cover where the fire had burned through walls. What the fuck did Lenny care though? It was quiet and off the road and it didn't smell like puke and shit. That was much more than you could say for most of the places Lenny shot up in.

The only way in the building was through a hole about a third of the way up the back wall where a board had fallen off. Vega pointed and Lenny climbed into the hole. Vega followed him in. A brief negotiation occurred where Lenny thought cheap meant twenty dollars and Vega held firm to fifty. Lenny stayed pissed just long enough to get the needle in his arm. *Then there was the warm…then the rush…then the*………..

…………

…………

…………

✲ ✲ ✲

"…okay…this looks safe enough…" I pulled into the church parking lot. "…it's not Sunday so nobody should have a problem with us being here and everybody knows we're good for God's business…" Ariel agreed so we put it in PARK and unfolded our food again.

BRRRRRRRIIIIIIIIIIIIINNNNNNNNNGGGGG

Alas…a bell…and a door flies open. Next thing you know we're parked right in the middle of Christian Day Care and twenty-five 4 y/o's and a nun are barreling toward us with the kids screaming **"…COOL…AN AMBULANCE…"** and the nun glaring.

"…oh Jesus…now we did it…drive…drive…don't let her catch us…"

"…bad memories?…" I put it in PARK and juggled my coffee and shoved the last of my bagel in my mouth.

"…yes…eight years of Catholic school…"

"…oh…I'm sorry…" I chewed quickly. "…but boy that sure explains a lot…"

"…shut up…"

"…FOUR-TEN…FOUR-ONE-ZERO…"

"…four-ten on the run…"

"…FOUR-ONE-ZERO…CONTINUE YOUR RUN TO THE AREA OF 32 HOOVER STREET FOR THE UNKNOWN…"

"…four-ten…area of 32 Hoover Street for the unknown…" I stuffed my coffee cup into an open box of latex gloves to free up my right hand to work the siren. "…dispatch has a sense of humor today…I like it…"

"…do you know where Hoover Street is?…" Ariel was already reaching for the street guide.

"…south end of Main by the Laundromat…"

"…how did you know that?…"

"…I don't know…which brings me to my next point…how does someone call for an ambulance and not know why?…"

"…I don't know…pedestrian…"

"…got 'em…so the call must go like this '…hello…I need an ambulance but I don't know why…'"

I could see Ariel shaking her head in my peripheral vision**...**
which cracked me up...

"...pay attention to the road..."
"...got it...**WHOA LOOK OUT...**just kidding..."

We pulled on to Hoover Street and I slowed way down.
There were no cops on scene yet and we were in a not-so-good
part of BigCity. We also weren't even sure where we were going.
The "area of" an address can mean just about anything. It could
be the yard...the basement... across the street or even a few
houses away. Even when you have an exact address it can be off. I
remember one time when Blossom and I got sent to a "...PSYCH
WITH A GUN...at 57 DAVENPORT CIRCLE..."

Dispatch made a huge point of telling us to stage at 55
Davenport and wait for PD. Obviously Blossom and I thought that
was a no-brainer. Who would park in the driveway and approach
the house of a psych with a gun? So we pulled into the driveway
of 55 and waited and got into a lengthy discussion about techs
we knew who'd be dumb enough to approach the house without
PD. Soon enough the cops pulled up right behind us. I rolled the
window down and waved them back. "...it's not this house...
they're next door..."

The cop kept getting out of his cruiser and walked past
the ambulance door. "...no honey...it's this house..." That's
when Blossom and I looked up to see the psych opening the
front door of the house directly in front of us...waving a rifle
screaming **"...I WON'T TELL THEM...I WON'T TELL THEM
ANYTHING..."**
I was so shocked I never got mad at the cop for calling me
honey. Fortunately it turned out to only be a BB gun and nobody
got their head blown off that day but from that point forward we

always staged at the end of streets and followed the cops to the house.

This call was turning out to be a double doozy because not only was there the "area of" aspect but also there was the unknown part. See if you're looking for a specific incident it can **usually** narrow down your search. I say usually because there are times you find car accidents on porches or a man down could still be on the roof but the ambiguous "unknown" "in the area of" truly could be anything.

"...did that guy just wave at us?..." I asked and Ariel shrugged. The stocky Puerto Rican guy on the other side of the street seemed to motion again so I stopped and rolled down my window. "...did you call an ambulance?..."

"...yeah...my friend is sick..."

"...yeah...where is he?..."

"...in back of the house..." He motioned down a hill to what looked like a burned-out garage. I put the truck in PARK and got out and walked around to the passenger side door to get equipment. Ariel stayed in the cab to call dispatch and give them our true location. The guy came over and tugged on my arm "...c'mon...he's really sick...he's sweaty...I think he's got... what they called?...shakes...uh seizures...he got seizures..."

I grabbed for the first-in bag. "...so he's got a history of seizures?...he has them a lot?..."

"...oh I don't know..."

"...no...you don't know...okay..." The guy grabbed my arm again...this time with more of a pulling feel to it. I looked into the truck to see what was holding Ariel up. She was grabbing a pair of gloves but had to wrestle with my coffee cup to get them out of the box they were stuffed in. The guy kept pulling me so I waved at Ariel and got dragged off. I noticed she had a really puzzled look on her face...*as if to say* "...where the hell are you going?..." But even though the little voice inside my head kept telling me not to go without Ariel I didn't feel like I had a choice because the guy was really dragging me with him and goin' on and on about how his friend was breathing funny.

Then I looked back and realized that from the bottom of the hill you couldn't see the ambulance on the street. I also couldn't see Ariel. Just when it occurred to me that she might not have seen where I got dragged off to the guy started pointing at the back of the burned-out garage.

"...he's around there..."

"...in the garage?..."

"...yeah around there..." And he was pointing feverishly. Again...not such a great feeling about this but apparently this is what you feel like when you're doing something stupid and you just can't stop yourself. So I went around the back of the garage and there was a hole about a third of the way up the back wall where a board had fallen off. The guy pointed in it and when I stuck my head in I saw through the dark some guy lying prone on the ground breathing in drawn-out sonorous respirations.

I looked back again for Ariel. I didn't see her and then the guy gives me a shove through the hole. "...okay..." I figured "...I'm here...I might as well help the patient because he is definitely in distress..." I pulled out my mini Maglite and shined it up and down the patient. He was very sweaty and breathing about three times a minute and for the really big clue there was a needle sticking out of his arm. I pulled that out and put it safely to the side.

"...your friend's been doing drugs...was it coke?...meth?... heroin?...speedball?..."

"...I don't know...help him..."

"...I will...it's just easier if I know what kind of drugs he did..."

"…you don't need to know…"

"…okay…" And I continued my assessment. I checked his pupils and they were *reeeeeaaaalllllly tiny.* That meant heroin. Damn… *where the hell is Ariel?…*

"…I'm going to go get my partner…she has the oxygen…he really needs oxygen…" I was doing a bad job at coming up with an excuse to leave.

"…no …no es necesita…"

"…no I do…you see…"

"NO…NO ES NECESITA…" Damn…I am getting yelled at a lot today…*and in many different languages and accents…*

"…look…buddy…I wan-…"

"…NO HABLA MAS…" He interrupted. To emphasize his point he pulled his shirt back to reveal his big shiny gun…*and I don't mean the euphemistic kind.* **"…you're gonna fix him…right?…"**

Suddenly his English was dead on. Despite being a loner for my entire life I had never felt as alone as I did right then. I didn't even know if anybody knew where I was…and I was pretty sure this wasn't a BB gun. Great…just great…I've done some dumb things before but this was a new level of achievement. I pulled out my IV start kit…took a really deep breath and hoped the junkie had a good vein left. Amazingly he did and even in the dark I was able to hit it the first time. Those sixty hours being trained by ninja ER nurses was paying off big dividends…*I should buy them some donuts later…*Then I had to draw up "the antidote." In paramedic school you're taught to read the label three times to verify correct med…correct concentration and expiration date. They never quite got into doing these things in the dark so now with my hand shaking and my Maglite in my mouth I gave it my best shot. Unfortunately it occurred to me that even though the Narcan will reverse the effects of the heroin and that would make it look like I have "fixed" him…if the guy mixed the heroin with any other number of secret street ingredients…that could be just enough to keep the Narcan from being effective…*and then I will look like a big giant loser…*How disheartening to be judged by a drug dealer in my final moments…*goddamn him…*

Oh well…all I can do is push the Narcan and hope for the best. Point-four milligrams… point-eight milligrams…come on…breathe a little more…

CRRRRRRRAA*AAAAA*CCCCCC*CKKKKKKKK*… and sunshine poured in from behind me…*crap…did I just get shot and now I'm hurtling toward the light?…*Being a little jumpy I may have shrieked slightly only then to realize that it was the calvary coming for me. Two boots came kicking through the plywood and ripped a big sheet off to expose more sunshine… two cops and Ariel. I had never been so happy to see sunshine or cops in my whole life. Ariel was scaring me though. She had a look on her face boy…*kinda reminded me of the nun…*

The patient started coming around so the Narcan was working. The other guy magically disappeared as soon as the cops showed up. They helped Ariel and me walk the patient back up to our ambulance and carry our bags. We no sooner got the guy on the stretcher than he livened up enough to start being a big giant pain in the ass.

"…who are you?…I'm not going anywhere…"

"…listen…I'm in no mood…sit back…" *oh good…maybe Ariel will just take it out on him.*

"…where's my money?….hey…I had two hundred dollars in my shoe…where's my fuckin' money?…"

"…I don't know…maybe your friend took it…"

"…my friend?…"

"…yeah…your friend who called the ambulance…'

"…fucking Vega?…he ain't my friend…"

"…what'd you say?…" The two cops had been outside the open ambulance doors talking to each other but when they heard the name Vega they perked up.

"…nothin'…I didn't say nothin'…" The patient seemed to see the error of his ways.

"…ladies…may we have a minute?…"

"…absolutely…" Ariel and I jumped out the back door and switched places with the cops…only they shut the doors. That left me alone with Ariel.

"…Ariel…I'm sor-"

"…don't…we'll talk about it after the call…"

I wanted to say more but this time when my little voice spoke I listened…and it was telling me to shut up. Besides…as obvious as it was that Ariel was pissed at me…I could tell she was also post-scared. In fact…she had the same nauseous look on her face as she did at the Patrick's St. Patrick's Day Fire. So I humbly put my head down and kicked at the bumper. Damn…now that I thought about it…*I felt a little nauseous too…*

"…okay ladies…he's all yours…" The cops exited the back of the ambulance seemingly content with the info they had just acquired. One of them grabbed my arm on the way by "…be more careful next time…"

I acknowledged his advice…thanked them again and with a wave they were gone. My attention turned back to the OD. Despite his near-death experience the only enlightenment he received was when his bladder let go post-seizure…*great…now our truck was going to smell like dirtbag urine all day…* Our lovely guest continued his rant about his money being gone and seemed to believe that Ariel or I gave a crap. A perceptive dirtbag would have realized that we each had our own problems right now. Fortunately for us it was a short trip to the Valley Trauma and soon he would no longer be our problem. I did however genuinely feel bad for the ER staff as we were tossing him off our stretcher onto their bed. Ever since my ER time I had developed a very deep and solid appreciation for the ER staff. Not only could they do their jobs under the craziest conditions but they always stayed unflappable and treated us like comrades not competition... *today's experience just made the love grow exponentially...*

Anyhoo...turns out it was a good day to bring our buddy into Valley Trauma. See as a teaching hospital they are often overrun by interns and residents. Today was just such a day so the attending was in no mood to deal with a moron who was too stupid to know he shouldn't have overdosed on heroin with two hundred dollars in his shoe. So while the asshole screamed on and on about somebody better call his brother Dave to get him the hell out of here the attending conducted an informal poll.

"...hey...what's the grossest thing you ever threw up?..."

I looked up from my paperwork. "...I guess I'd have to go back to my screwdriver days and say orange juice..."

"...Kindergarten...I threw up my tuna fish sandwich...even with milk it was pretty bad..." Ariel made a face in reflection.
"...tuna and O.J....good combo..."
"...why...what's up?..."
"...your gentleman over there..."
"...yes...Mr. Bucket O' Sunshine..."
"...oh I didn't realize he was Irish..." The doc continued on talking slow and deliberate "...well he's really pissin' me off... demanding that we feed him if we're going to falsely imprison him...just being an absolute jackass and I got no patience today so when the Narcan that you so kindly gave him wears off and I got to give him more to keep his sorry smelly ass breathin'...I'm

gonna push it fast so he pukes and I'd like some say in what he tastes again..."

"...ah Doc...that's just nasty..." I fake gagged but I noticed Ariel looked at the OD guy and started sinisterly giggling. Coming from her innocent face it was quite disturbing...*and yet oddly enticing...*

✠ ✠ ✠

The rest of the shift was completely uneventful callwise but I did have to put up with Ariel telling EVERYONE about my misadventures. She never said another word about it to me directly but somehow got everyone else to scold me. Deep down though I knew she was right and that I was lucky to be around to get scolded so I didn't fight it and just took the lesson to heart. I also never mentioned the gun to anyone since that would have definitely added to the quantity of lectures. Overall though I'd say I made out better than the dirtbag. Last time I saw him he had orange juice and tuna chunks coming out of his nose...and a lovely nurse offering to put a tube down his nose to his stomach...if he thought it would help...

...gotta imagine that burns a bit...

CHAPTER 14-
THE DAYS OF KINGS

...blessed are you when the people insult you...persecute you and falsely say all kinds of evil against you because they are management...rejoice and be glad...because great is your reward in collective bargaining for in the same way they persecuted the ambulance drivers who were before you...

and then we had another company meeting...

...and all of a sudden I began to see what everyone was talking about. NAA was officially drawing their line in the sand and oh yeah since they owned the pen...the line and the sand...there would be no arguments. In single fell swoops they began to change a lot of what was really good about this job. They came armed with spreadsheets and figures that somehow could predict when there would be calls. This meant a whole new way of creating schedules. Gone were our awesome sixteen- and twenty-four-hour shifts that made it easy for us to work our hours and do things like go to school or have a life. Now there was only a few ten- and twelve-hour shifts that only a few would get and millions of crazy six-hour jobbers that could have you working 7 a.m. to 1p.m....off for a few hours and back that day to work 6 p.m. to midnight. And if you looked at the overall schedule there were tons of times when there were only the bare minimum number of trucks on. It didn't take a genius to realize that there was going to be a lot of crazy moments for us in the street. Oh yeah, they were going to realign all the partners too. Seems they didn't put too much stock into chemistry. A truck's a truck and a tech's a tech and we'll tell you what works. There were a bunch of other annoying new things. Like we all had to wear these ridiculous faux turtlenecks under our uniform shirts that were supposed to make us look more professional. All they did for me was remind me that I was probably hanged in a former life and did not like anything tight around my neck. Never mind having to do CPR while being choked by an annoying piece of fabric.

The pièce de résistance however had to be posting. Yes posting…the new concept that had been explained in a previous memo that I had to read six times to get. Actually it wasn't new to NAA… just us. Seems they had been posting in other NAA companies all along but they had to wait in BigCity for their new headquarters to be renovated. Gone were all the individual offices spread strategically around our coverage area. Now everyone would be centrally located in their ambulance. At the beginning of your shift you would get your truck assignment…medic gear and portable radio and then you'd have twenty minutes to check everything out and head for your posting assignment. Posting assignments were given numbers for ease of communication. For example 51 and 61 were the two spots considered to be the center of BigCity. They would be the posts that were filled first and then as other trucks were available they would fill other posts that spiraled out from 51 and 61. Great on paper…*not so great on your ass*…Imagine sitting in the front of a van-like vehicle for multiple consecutive hours while you stare at city parking lots. My legs ached just at the thought of it. Not to mention that going back to the office allowed you the privacy of a bathroom and the convenience of a microwave…*apparently the Borg was immune to human needs*…

Immediately following the meeting we all headed to Sully's and the bitching commenced. I felt good in knowing that I wasn't the only pissed-off employee. In fact I wasn't even the most pissed-off employee. As the alcohol flowed…talks of a revolution grew. We were still a union company after all…so there had to be something we could do to fight this. A couple of our stewards had a copy of the contract with them and at one table the three of them sat down to pour over it. I found this all interesting but didn't believe for one moment that we could fix any of it. They were the Borg after all…resistance was futile…

…I was beginning to understand why Blossom left…

Meanwhile the real work continued. It didn't seem to matter what was going on behind the scenes…once you got a call everything was the same. They called…you responded…you did paperwork…someone sent a bill and in the end that's all that really mattered.

One afternoon Ariel and I were lucky enough to have our truck pulled for some routine maintenance. Oddly Travis took kindly to us and didn't make us get in a spare truck. Instead we hung out…ate a meal in peace and sat with dispatch. Ariel sat and chatted with some of her friends from her medic class while I hooked up with the call-takers I used to work with. My buddy Kevin was working and he seemed glad to see me.

"…guess who starts the police academy first of next month?…"

"…you got in?…" Kevin nodded in the affirmative. "…that's awesome…now I got somebody to fix tickets for me…"

Kevin started laughing. "…I can't be promising that before I even do my first push-up…"

"…all right…I'll wait till graduation…seriously though… good luck…I think you're gonna make an awesome cop…" I gave Kevin a huge hug and even managed to pick his 6' 3" frame off the ground.

Ariel came over and broke up our lovefest with news of our truck's completed maintenance. After our midmorning of leisure we were being sent back into the workforce with a long-distance transfer to Boston. I wished Kevin luck again and Ariel and I headed out of dispatch and back to the garage.

"…since when have you and Kevin been so tight?…"

I kinda knew what she meant and smirked. "…what do you mean?…"

"…you guys didn't always get along so good…"

"…ahhhh…no…not at first…"

"…so what happened?…"

"…well…it's kind of painful to talk about…"

"…wwwhhhhaaatttt?…" Ariel was not buying it. "…spill it…"

"…all right…all right…have no respect for my feelings…"

reflections back to a chilly spring day in a homeostatic room…

"….so what are we doing for lunch?…" I spun around in my dispatch chair and waved the folder full of menus. "…I'm staaaaarrrrving…"

"…okay Casey at the bat…we'll let you eat…" Perky nicknames from cute twenty-two-year-old call-takers never got old.

"…thanks Jenna…" I passed the folder. "…what about you Kevin?… you ordering?…"

"…no I'm good…" Kevin held up a full brown bag with his left hand and with his right, keyed his mike to dispatch a chairvan to Valley Trauma Radiation…**a burn and return as they were called…**

"…hey Kevin…can I stay clear around three?…I gotta make sure my mom gets picked up at her doctors…" Jenna's roommate and chairvan driver Lana poked her head in the dispatch door.

"…Lana Fana Fo Fana…how are you?…"

"…good Jenna…how are you?…" Lana looked at me and laughed.

"…yeah Lana…I should be able to keep you clear…just call me at two to remind me…"

"…thanks Kevin…so hey…I saw you at Ca Rib & Beanz Friday…"

"...oh ribs...that sounds good..." **my hunger was all encompassing.**

"...yeah...me and my boys were goin' clubbin' so we had to carb up...I didn't see you...why didn't you say hi?..."

"..I was in quick for takeout and I didn't even see you till I was leavin'..."

"...I was undercover..."

"...I know...I hardly recognized you...you had your hoodie pulled up and your baggies..."Kevin put his head down and smiled."...hey...did you hear what happened to Richie Johnson?..."

Kevin looked up at Lana and his face got serious."...I was with Richie Johnson..."

"...you were?...when it happened?..."Lana was truly shocked.

"...yeah...he had met us out...we were all together..."

"...so what happened?...for real..."

"...it was bullshit..." Kevin waved his hand and turned his head in disgust. The phone rang and Jenna let me know MiddleCity Fire was looking for medics. I acknowledged and took the call.

back to the present...

"...that was when I sent you on that intercept for the guy who got his wanger stuck in the Shop-Vac hose..."

"...ah yes...the industrial accident..." Ariel laughed upon reflection. "...still don't know why they wanted a medic..."

"...moral support...that's why I sent you and Shirley B. Michaels and not a male crew...I could hear a quiver in their dispatcher's voice so I could only imagine what the guys on scene were like..."

"...yeah...their knees were knocking...but the guy waited a long time to call and it was really swollen and purply..."

"...too funny..."

back to the chilly spring day...

"...thanks four-two-nine...you're en route at 11:48..."I punched the dispatch card and started a new log entry for the MiddleCity call. Kevin and Lana were still talking.

"...so the bouncer at Gepetto's comes flyin' out the door and screamin' at us '...you fuckin' banger pricks...I said get the fuck outta here before I call the cops...' and you know Richie..."

"...yeah...he ain't shy..."

"...no he ain't...I mean...I was gonna leave...I don't need any trouble...I just took the Civil Service Exam...but Richie's pre-law...he lives for confrontation so he got all up in the guy's face '...you fuckin' Godfather Dago prick...you're callin' me a gangster...you neighborhood-bleedin' money-scammin'...' and he went on and on and then the cops showed up..."

"...did you get the hell outta there?...I woulda..."Lana looked at me and laughed and I nodded in agreement.

"...nah...I couldn't leave Richie..."I admired Kevin for his loyalty. "...so the cops were absolute asses and they frisked all of us and ran us for warrants and they cuffed Richie and threw him in the back of the cruiser..."

"...what the fuck?...'cause some old ladies complained that you were wearin' baggies?..."Lana laughed again. Kevin just kept shaking his head.

"...well then why wear them?..."I truly wanted to understand."...why purposely make yourself look like a gangster?..."

"...Timothy McVie wore blue jeans...you want your white ass searched for bombs every time you cross the street?..."

"...if I'm driving a U-Haul full of diesel fuel and fertilizer...sure..."

"...well we weren't cruisin' in a Lincoln hanging TEC-9s out the window..."

"...no I know...it's just you're trying to be a cop and your friend is pre-law...why not keep a low profile and avoid trouble?..."

"...wearing a hooded sweatshirt and baggy pants is asking for trouble?..."

"...yeah...if it makes it hard to tell you apart from a gangbanger..."

"...you think I'm a gangbanger?..."

"...no...but I know you...if I didn't know you and I saw you dressed like that I might not be able to tell..."

"...because I act like a banger?..."

"...no...because it's hard to tell..."

"...why is it hard to tell?..."

"...because it is...I can't explain why..."I noticed Lana and Jenna had gotten real quiet."...it's like when you see a black guy walking down the street in the region...you don't want to assume the worst but you gotta wonder..."

"...what's the black guy doing in the suburbs?..."

"...yeah..."I was relieved Kevin finally understood me.

"...my god you are a racist motherfucker..."Not content he continued. "...and I sure hope you don't take that attitude with you on the streets..."

"...WHAT?..."I felt his words poke me in the chest."...what the fuck did you just say?..."

"...you're racist...you're racist and ignorant..."

"...I am not...that's a horrible thing to call me..."I felt myself reeling and knew it wasn't just low blood sugar."...I don't hate you because you're black, and me and Lana hang out a lot..."

"...so that's it?...you smile at me and eat collard greens so you're not racist?..."

"...I don't believe this..." I felt my stomach rumble and I knew I shouldn't be having this or any serious conversation on low blood sugar but well...I had low blood sugar and wasn't thinking clearly."...this is why the races don't get along...because neither side can see when the other side is trying...how can I prove to you that I'm not a racist?..."

"…come hang out with me at my home…spend time with my family and friends…come to my church and meet my pastor…hell come listen to the Reverend Farrakhan speak and then tell me you can't tell the difference between a four-year college student and a gangbanger…"

I was speechless. Kevin had done the impossible and left me with nothing to say. Hell I didn't even feel angry anymore for him calling me a racist. I kinda had to think maybe he was right…

…what the hell was I supposed to do about that?…

☆ ☆ ☆

"…so is that how the conversation ended?…" Ariel switched out the monitor batteries.

"…yeah…that day…and then I had Trauma Rauma weekend in medic school and didn't work for awhile…The next time we worked together I got in first and was kinda nervous waiting for him to come in…"

"…I bet…so what happened?…"

"…I was dispatching a truck to a code and had my back turned when he came in…I didn't see him until he was standing next to me…"

"…I brought this in for you to take a look at…"Kevin took a paperback out of his lunch bag and threw it on the console next to me.

"…what's this?…"

"…some light reading…when you get the chance…"

"…A Torchlight for America by the Honorable Minister Louis Farrakhan…are you serious?…this is like those pamphlets those guys wearin' the black suits and skinny ties in Primus Square hand out at the light…"

"…yeah…."

"…they won't give them to white people…I've asked…"

"…you asked?…"

"...yeah...I'm curious but they won't even come over to the ambulance..."

"...it ain't about you...but here...before we get at it again read this...I'm letting you..."

I laughed and picked up the book. "...thanks man...I appreciate it... who knows...maybe someday the races will get along..."

"...that ain't gonna happen but read the book and maybe you'll be less of a cracker..."

"...ouch..."

"...did you read it?..." Ariel pulled the stretcher out of the back of the ambulance.

"...not all of it...I had a really hard time stomaching the attitude toward women...apparently we're just corn fields waiting to be plowed and seeded..."

"...oh my..."

"...yeah...that ain't happening..."

"...so did you read it?..." Kevin sat on the console next to me.

"...yeah...a lot of it..."

"...so what did you think?...was it everything you hoped the pamphlets would be?..."

"...are you a Muslim?..."

"...I didn't ask you to ask me what I think...I asked you what you think..."

"...you're a prick to have a conversation with...you know that?..."

Kevin laughed and put his hand on my shoulder. "...I love challenging your little white mind..."

"...okay homie...I think I understand the anger but I'm not going to tell you I do because then you'll tell me there's no way a white person can..."

"...okay...you're learning..."

"...and I do agree with reparations...it's no different than Volkswagen compensating victims of the Holocaust who were used as slave labor...nobody should get rich like that and yeah...there's a lot of rich white families who did it on the backs of slave labor...I'm not sure how you do it but I don't agree with anything getting done through violence or holy wars...I think we're better served as a country if we come together not rip apart and...like it or not...voluntary immigration or not...you are part of this country..."

"...I agree..."

"...he did?..." Ariel pushed the elevator button.

"...he did..." I put on my gloves.

"...you do?..." I was truly amazed. "...you mean we agree on something?..."

"...we do...and I'm not a Muslim..."

"...I knew he wasn't..." Ariel searched for the right room number.

"...you're not?..."

"...no...never have been...got some friends and family who are...but I'm not..."

"...then why did you give me this book to read?..."

"...'cause you were curious..."

"...yeah...but you didn't know that..."

"...yeah I did...maybe not specific to the Primus Square pamphlets but remember the first time we talked?..."

"...oh yeah..."

"...it got a little testy right?..."

"...a little..."

"...but you hung in there...I called you a racist and you didn't leave the room or the conversation...I've had that conversation a hundred other times and it usually ends different..."

"...how so?..."

"...well a lot of people who wear a uniform are power trippin' white boys so when someone like me comes along and challenges them it usually ends not so well..."

"...I'm a gay woman...I get that too..."

"...maybe that's why you hung in there...but whatever the reason I got the feeling you were trying to be open-minded...so I figured I'd help you crack it open a little bit more..."

"...okay but why this book...why not something by Oprah?..."

Kevin laughed. "...because you'll read Oprah on your own...you'd never find this by yourself..." Kevin held up the book. "...and right or wrong...this is another way to see things...I don't think the races will ever get along because there's just too much ignorance in the world...but I did think I saw enough heart in you to try pushing some of it out of your way..."

"...Awwww...that was cool of him to say..."

"...I know...and that's when we became so tight..."

CHAPTER 15-
THE TEACHER AND THE LESSON

...blessed is the basic who finds wisdom...the medic who gains understanding...for it is more profitable than silver and yields better returns than gold...it is more precious than rubies...but it doesn't do squat when you need a car loan or a month's rent...so make sure you learn how to suck up too...

For the most part I had been pretty damn lucky with partners. Except for the early days when it was partner du jour before I hooked up with Blossom I always had a rock-steady hardly-ever-out-sick partner. What I'm trying to say in a roundabout long-winded way is that I had pretty much steered clear of the horrors that is a crappy partner for any length of time. Still I knew the shoe could drop at any moment and I genuinely began to dread the day that I would have to work with a whoop...incompetent... or a lazy sexist schmo***...and you all know who you are...***

On our next to last day of our work week I kinda got the impression that Ariel was heartily considering calling out for our next shift. She'd fake cough really loud and say "...oh where did that come from?..."Then she'd talk about how much people were making her angry and whip Kling bandages of all sizes around the software supply cabinet during inventory. And it's not that I didn't understand. We had been working a buttload of overtime and people were driving me crazy too. Then we did a call where some miserable old lady tried to off herself by drinking lighter fluid. You gotta be pretty bad off to down that stuff but the kicker is it really works. Any chemical with hydrocarbons in it really messes up your heart rhythm and that in turn screws your whole body up leaving it to say ***"...what the fuck?...who ordered the hydrocarbons?..."***

By the time we got her out of the house and on our heart monitor she was in some funky rhythm that even Ariel didn't recognize. That blew me away because she always sees the rhythm. In fact I'd seen her argue with ER docs only to have the cardiologist say she was right. After running three separate strips and not being able to say anything but "...I never saw that before..." she told me just to drive fast. Even better...as fast as I wanted...*YES...I love this job...*

Unfortunately the miserable old lady started having second thoughts when she realized her plan might just be coming to fruition. This is the part where I figured out Ariel really did need a day off 'cause I was up front driving really fast and I heard the old lady shriek "...oh dear...am I really gonna die?..." In the rearview mirror I saw Ariel scrunching her forehead while gazing at the monitor "...yes...I think you are..."

I cracked up laughing and bellowed "...oh my god Ariel..." and the old lady started shrieking "...oh my god please tell me no..." and Ariel grabbed her mouth like the silent monkey and found me in the mirror. "...did I say that out loud?..." And then she started laughing...*yeah...she needed a day off...*

Still...selfish as I am...all I could think about was what loser I'd get stuck working with if she banged out. Oh well...it was better that way for all future suicidal old people so I'd just suck it up and prepare for the worse.

and so the next morning...

As I drove into work I pondered my options as they lay in front of me. First off...they could stick me with a basic and I'd have to tech all the calls all day. Or they could stick me with a loser medic and I'd feel obligated to do all the calls all day. Even worse...I could get stuck with someone who thought I was a loser and I'd know right away because they wouldn't let me do anything all day.

✩ ✩ ✩

Travis met me at the time clock...

"...so I guess you know your partner's out today..."

"...how would I know that?...we're not married..."

"...might as well be...anyway...you're working with..." *oh God...here it comes...* "...Kelly O'Brien..."

"WHAT!!!..." oh wait...that's a good thing. "...really?... does she know?..." Because this could have turned out to be the "stuck with someone who thought I was a loser and I do nothing all day" scenario.

"...yeah she knows...she suggested it...her partner's out today too..."

"...cool..."

"...yeah cool...she's comin' here from the south end office so get your truck checked out so you can be available as soon as she gets here..."

"...yes sir..."

When Kelly arrived I wanted to make sure I looked busy and competent so I signed out our radio and medic gear and headed to the truck to count baby aspirin. I saw her pull into the parking lot...punch in and go directly into the supervisor's office. They were talking awhile so I figured she had seen my Jeep in the parking lot and when faced with the true reality of her day she decided to back out of the shift. Then the two of them started laughing really hard and I figured they decided instead to have her work the shift and torture me all day long.

"...hey Casey...what's up?..." My daydream was broken and I realized Kelly was now standing next to me.

"...not much...hey thanks for working with me today..."

"…no problem…you need a coffee?…I gotta get one…I'm dyin'…"

"…coffee…I love coffee and will always accept coffee when offered…" Oh my god…how dumb did that sound? Fucking Blossom…he had built Kelly up so much like she's a living legend that I had no choice but to be nervous. In fact… yup…my lips were sticking to my teeth…*god damn it…*

"…Casey…are you getting in the truck or running alongside?…let's go…"

"…oh yeah…sorry…" *oh…I am so smooooothhhh…*

Fortunately I can drink coffee with the best of them so my awkward moments seemed safely in the past. Kelly fiddled with the radio and I cringed at what she might choose. Ariel and I started with the universally accepted rule that the driver picks but she continually chose yee-haw country music which made me choose "that god awful screechy stuff" as she called it. Finally we agreed on pop or classic rock and yup…I do believe that was what Kelly picked.

After we got our coffee and started back toward the office it dawned on me that this was my first shift with a true cowboy…*if only Blossom could see me now…*Ariel and I worked 911 in BigCity but we were merely posers. Nobody ever showed us the real city life. For example Carter preppies all tended to roost at the office. That's where you played Frisbee in the parking lot or cribbage in the kitchen or hung out in dispatch drinking coffee and watching Tracy knit. But the cowboys couldn't be tied to the ranch because they needed to roam the city. They had secret meeting places downtown where they watched the drunks and homeless during the day and the drunks and hookers at night…*and they knew all of them by name…*They'd drive around with their trucks covered in ketchup and mustard that they squirted at each other out of 50cc syringes during daylong condiment wars. Carter preppies were rule followers and Valley cowboys were lawless renegades.

As much as I wanted to feel like a cowboy I just hadn't yet. See where Blossom was highly motivated to be a renegade...Ariel just couldn't help but be a rule follower. But today I got to ride until sunset with a true legend of BigCity and maybe...just maybe some of the swagger would rub off on me.

Right away I picked up on Kelly's rule-bending ways when she didn't take the most direct route back to the office. Instead she took the long way back home...ziggin' and zaggin' down a whole bunch of side streets I'd never seen before.

"...you usually work with Ariel right?..."

"...yeah...since I got my medic...hey I didn't know this came out here..."

"...you like it?..."

"...yeah...we work well together..."

"...uh-huh...Ariel's a good medic...very patient..."

"...yup...especially with skittish new partners..."

Kelly laughed. "...you mean you?..."

"...yeah...I was a little edgy when I started..."

"....you don't say..." Kelly seemed to drift for a moment. "...well...we all were...it's not an easy job..."

"...FOUR-TEN...FOUR-ONE-ZERO..."

"...four-ten..." Kelly grabbed the mike.

"...WELL GOOD MORNING MA'AM..." Wow... dispatch called Kelly ma'am. "...I NEED YOU TO HEAD UP TO NEWTON AND CRANE FOR THE MVC POSSIBLE MINOR PI..."

"...received..." Kelly flipped on the lights and we were off.

"...do I need to look up Newton and Crane?..."

"…nah…I got it…" And she did because it was only a few lefts and rights and we were there.

As we pulled on scene it was immediately obvious that this wasn't a traditional motor vehicle crash. For starters the only collision seemed to be between the windshield of an old-style station wagon and a metal trashcan that was now resting gingerly on the hood. Kelly drove slowly past the car…eyeballing it up and down and then she proclaimed "…uh-huh…I'm not seeing it… let's find out what's going on…"

There was a cruiser parked a bit up the road and Kelly pulled up next to it. The cop was sitting in the driver's seat doing paperwork and some dude was in the backseat handcuffed with bloody gauze taped over his left eye.

"…Kelly O'Brien…what a nice way to start my day…"

"…I know you're lying so I'm not going to say thank you…" Kelly laughed and the cop grinned back. "…so why are we here Artie?…"

"…I don't know why you're here…I believe I told central to cancel you…"

"…oh maybe…messages get lost…so why are you here?…"

"…well…this fine gentleman got himself in a little jam this morning…" The cop pointed to a sad-faced middle-aged man in the backseat. "…seems he thought it would be a good idea to park in front of a school bus stop and watch the eleven- and twelve-year-old girls in an odd and peculiar way…"

"…ah nooo…"

"…yup and when one of the mom's didn't get the answer to the questions she was asking she picked up a metal trashcan and hurled it through the guy's windshield…"

"…okay so more of a trashcan crash…but I guess dispatch doesn't have a code for that…" Kelly looked at me. "…what a dumbass…huh?…" I sipped my coffee and agreed. The cop went on to say the guy had an outstanding warrant so they'd assume responsibility for his sorry ass and as soon as he was done with his paperwork they'd bring him down to the ER. Meanwhile they'd keep him in the cruiser...*mostly for his own protection...* because the mom was still spittin' fire and wanted at him. That was cool with us and we cleared ourselves with dispatch. As we continued down the street we drove by the second half of the scene of the crime. As we did it was impossible not to notice a rather large woman screaming and pointing and spitting and occasionally being held back by a small group of other women. It was obvious she still wanted at someone.

"...see that woman?..."

"...yeah...she is jacked up..."

"...I know...so remember that face and don't ever get in the way of a woman who looks like that..."

"...got it..." I laughed.

"...no I'm serious...some assholes try to get in people's shit and tell them to calm down and stuff...sometimes we are not in charge...we are in the way..." I looked at her again and I could tell she was serious. I nodded that I had heard her. It was a good point but so different from the typical bravado you'd see from other medics...*like LittleCity Medics...*I knew Ariel would never challenge someone like that but who would have thought a cowboy would back down?

We continued on to the office taking the scenic route but this time we made it back. Kelly pulled into a parking space and we moseyed inside to the kitchen. Kelly commented on how nice it was to have an office with an actual kitchen in it even if it was dank and cluttered. "...I can't stand making coffee with bathroom water..." She set her stuff up on the chipped Formica table and dove into her red cooler. After rustling around a bit she came up with a muffin.

"…oh my little muffin…you're all flat…" She held it up to me and laughed. "…that's a flat muffin…"

"…yes it is…"

It didn't take long for dispatch to find us again…this time for a man having seizures…so we packed up and headed out. I was busy running through all the differential diagnoses for seizures in my head but Kelly focused on the address. "…ever been to the Aspermont Motor Lodge?…"

"…no but I have always been curious as to why a motor lodge exists in BigCity…"

"…no idea…but here's the deal…it's roach infested so don't lean on the walls and don't put the bags down…we do not want to bring roaches back with us…" I nodded okay and she added "…and don't scream if you see roaches because you will…and they will be large…" *yes…there are all kinds of bravery…*

Once on scene we found an open door by a parked cruiser and followed it down a hallway to a really dark room. Kelly walked fast and with purpose. I had a hard time keeping up. The cops must have heard us coming as they opened the patient's door and hailed us in. We exchanged the customary grunts of acknowledgement as we passed by them to the patient. The room was dark and smelled really bad. I'm not even really sure what the smell was but it reeked. Ashtrays spilled over with crushed butts…newspapers were piled in sliding stacks and food-crusted dinnerware was hosting swarms of flies and yes…very large roaches. I fought off a shiver up my spine and turned my attention to our patient. He was a 50ish y/o male…very disheveled and smelling much like the room he was standing in. He wasn't seizing…which didn't surprise me. Patients usually aren't doing what we're told they're doing. But instead he was leaning on the kitchen wall with his body stiff and contorted. My mind immediately went to old stroke or new stroke but Kelly took a completely different tact.

"...do you take Haldol?..." The patient grunted out a yes through his clenched jaw. "...you ran out of your Cogenten?..." The patient grunted out another yes. "...pyramidal symptoms... let's go..."

Pyra-whatta-midal????? I was still swirling from the smell...the roaches and this term I'd never heard before but Kelly already had the patient shuffling down the hallway to the truck. No time to be dazed since I really just needed to keep up.

As they made their way out the door Kelly reassured the patient that she would help him. "...I got the medicine you need in my office...we're gonna help you out...can you get the door Casey?..."

I got a kick out of her calling the truck her office but I still had no idea what was going on or which one of our magic potions was going to do the trick so I did what I could and opened the door. Once in the "office" I fell back on an old standby and started hooking up the oxygen.

"...don't worry about that...draw me up some Benedryl..."

"...standard dose?..."

"...yeah..." I handed Kelly the syringe and she pushed it into the IV line she had established. The patient's hard...contorted arms and jaw loosened and the grip melted away. He actually sighed in relief.

"...thank you..." He smiled at Kelly.

"...no problem..." And she patted him on the arm. "...okay Casey...take me to Valley Trauma..."

I jumped out of the ambulance shaking my head. I still didn't know what had just happened and suddenly I felt like a civilian bystander bedazzled by the magic show. I did however feel grateful for the front row seat...

...Kelly the Great: Act One...

✣ ✣ ✣

At the hospital Kelly was again warmly greeted by name by everyone including the doctor in charge...*whom she called John...*She gave report on our patient and chatted with some nurses and I went off to clean the truck. I was surprised when a couple of minutes later she was out in the truck with me.

"...so Casey...what was up with our patient?..."

I wanted really badly to sound intelligent...hoping somehow I could still impress her. But the only thing I could think to say was "...I have no idea..." Kelly laughed and punched me in the arm.

"...I know you don't but I'm glad to see you didn't lie about it..." And then she went on to explain about pyramidal symptoms. "...I didn't expect that you would know because it's not something we learn about in medic school...I know because I went to BigCity College too..."

"...so where did you pick it up?..."

"...ten years on the job I've had a lot of time to be made to look foolish...good part about that is if you keep your mouth shut somebody who knows more will feel bad for you and teach you what you did wrong or show you what you missed..." I made an exaggerated gesture of closing my mouth hoping she'd continue. She laughed and did. "...there's a certain family of medicine that needs to be taken in conjunction with Cogenten...I call them the OLs because they all end in OL...haldol...respiradol... blah blah blah...for some reason patients tend to run out of Cogenten before their OLs...a day or two goes by and voila they end up with the tetany of certain muscles like our poor bastard patient...Benadryl...that wonderful little antihistamine...is the antidote..."

I wondered what else was out there that I didn't know about. Oh well...at least today I got to take something off that list. We cleared up from the hospital and went back to the world of BigCity. Dispatch may have called Kelly ma'am but they weren't shy about hammering her with calls. To say the least we were pretty busy for the rest of the twelve-hour shift.

Throughout the day though I couldn't squelch the feeling that something cool was definitely happening to me. Working with Kelly was taking an already great job and launching it to new heights. I know when I worked with Ariel I didn't mind being at work but with Kelly it even went a step further...*I didn't want the shift to end...*I remember thinking that it sucked not knowing when I'd work with her again. It was like having a one-day pass to sit in the dugout at Fenway. The game could go extra extra innings and it still wouldn't be long enough. And it wasn't even that we did anything extraordinary. There was a hypoglycemic at the court house...a 16 y/o delusional psych that we had to wrestle down and restrain and a couple of little old ladies with chest pain and shortness of breath. But it was the way Kelly handled the calls that I was in awe of. She just seemed to take the struggle right out of them. She clearly was in control of every scene because she didn't let it be any other way. But it wasn't like she bullied her way through them. She could effectively communicate with anyone no matter how diverse the crowd and get everyone on board with a successful mission. Even the mother of the 16 y/o psych seemed happy that we had restrained her child. Then I watched her work her magic with the most cantankerous of the cantankerous. A little old lady with chest pain who insisted on being a ball-bustin' complainer. She didn't like our pillows...the stretcher mattress...the color of my socks...nothin'. And I knew that she was just scared and reacting to her overwhelming stress but then she made a crack about me being very mannish...*OKAY BIG RED BUTTON PUSHED...*

Then just before I started bellowing at her...*and we all know how productive bellowing can be*...Kelly stepped in and redirected the situation. She took the bull by the horns so to speak and looked the old lady straight in the eye and proclaimed "...boy are you cranky old lady or what?..." At first the lady was as taken aback as I was but quickly she softened right up and even cracked a smile.

"...yes...I guess I am...I'm sorry..." And the rest of the transport was Irish dessert. I didn't know how or where Kelly learned what she knew but I knew I wanted to know too...*say that three times fast*...I was going to have to find a way to get closer to her. Even if it meant...*gulp*...cheating on Ariel.

Speaking of Ariel...following our days off she was back to work in a much less angry mood. She even brought me in a bag of trail mix with chocolate chips and I remembered how much I enjoyed working with her too. Still...I couldn't stop thinking about how cool it was to work with Kelly. I found myself repeatedly talking about her and asking Ariel what she knew about her.

"...did you ever work with her?..."

"...I've only worked at Carter...she's only worked at Valley... when would I have worked with her?..."

I ignored Ariel's tone. "...that's too bad...she's a wicked good medic...did you ever see pyramidal symptoms?..."

"...what symptoms?..." Ariel fiddled with the radio.

"...pyramidal...it's when you take OL meds without Cogenten..."

"...the OL meds?..."

"...yeah...Haldol...Respiradol..." I went on to describe the magic show to Ariel. She seemed mildly entertained.

As the day went on I started a new habit that I could immediately tell annoyed Ariel. Whenever we'd find ourselves at the hospital and I heard Kelly's truck radioing on the way in I would stall and find a reason to be there when she got there. And yes…I know how corny that sounds…it's just that I really wanted the chance for her to notice me and maybe I could get a little closer to the essence that was Kelly O'Brien***…and yes…I know that's the corny part…***

"…are you done yet?…" Ariel questioned.

"…hold on…I gotta get the mednec signed…"

"…I'll do it…"

"…no I got it…you relax…hey is that O'Brien's truck pullin' in?…"

"…hmmm…I don't know…is it?…"

"…yeah…cool…I'm gonna go see if they need a hand…"

"…need a hand?…they're bringing in a sprained ankle…"

"…well…never can be too careful…here…can you get this signed for me?….thanks…"

The way I looked at it…I owed it to myself to be friends with Kelly. It didn't mean I loved Ariel any less. I just thought Kelly was cool and I wanted to get to know her better. It seemed to be working too. Every time we ran into her she would talk and joke around with us. It was always such a good time. How could Ariel not see how great she was?…

…hold on let me get you a cup of Kool-Aid…

☆ ☆ ☆

Things with NAA were starting to get a little dicier. They had quite clearly articulated their position and so now we were forced to circle the wagons. They outwardly boasted that they were here to break up the cowboy mentality in EMS in order to engender a new professionalism *...insert sound bite of a coughing "... bullshit..."* Their changes were about one thing and one thing only: Them making as much money as possible off our talents and backs.

Not that this was a new concept in EMS but there's a big difference between a boss at the end of the hallway and a boss headquartered in Canada. When the boss down the hallway gets too carried away with crew cutbacks and other money-grubbing tactics you march down the hallway and pound on the door until he listens and reverses the changes. None of us had the means to march to Canada so they felt quite comfortable slashing away from their untouchable tower*...or so they thought...*

First off, a union meeting was posted for the end of the month. Word was the union was doing everything possible to keep as many of the new NAA policies from going into effect. For now at least...shifts would stay the same and partners wouldn't be changed. Unfortunately we had no choice but to accept posting because NAA had already given up all the leases on the buildings formerly known as our offices and gone ahead and opened up its Shangri-La of world headquarters. I think we were supposed to be real excited about our new digs but the meaning was lost on me. Our old offices may have mostly been dumpy rat holes but they were home. For years they had been our safe havens from the craziness we otherwise surrounded ourselves with. Then one day I showed up at work and got told we all had three days to get all our personal stuff out of the building because a muffler shop was moving in.

"...what?...a muffler shop?...are you kidding me?..." I protested to Travis who apparently was in no mood.

"...don't give me any shit Casey...just make sure all your personal stuff is out by Sunday..."

Personal stuff...right...like I really cared about my Gandhi poster and hand soap I kept stocked in the bathroom and the five extra pairs of socks I always had on hand after the Nor'easter of '93. It was the building that was personal stuff to me. It represented my whole coming of age that began the first time I walked through the front door in my new...crispy uniform and stiff boots...wondering if anybody else could tell my heart was beating five hundred times a minute. I remember Blossom and me ending our shifts parked in the corner of the parking lot late at night or early in the morning watching the trucks go in and out and past us. Calls beginning and calls ending***...our own little poetry at sun change...***

I kept thinking about the late nights in dispatch. Staying up way later than I should have and drinking far too much coffee but loving all the stories...jokes and new friends. New friends who understood without having to explain that they did. Then there was the night we all dropped acid...the Frisbee we played...the cribbage games that went on for twenty-four hours at a time...the night Mahan got ambushed with water balloons and dry chem fire extinguishers. It was really a sad day for me the last time I pulled out of the parking lot formerly known as Carter Ambulance but to NAA it all boiled down to "business is business and get the hell out."

The really sad thing was that I wasn't alone. Two companies totaling about two hundred people were all seeing their way of life trampled and discarded in the name of profit...

...this would not go down easy...

CHAPTER 16 -
ACTS OF POSTINGS

...cities are large and yet shall not go unwatched...
place yourselves so that you may see all around you...use
strategies...all along the watchtower...to stand diligent in
parking lots...hold fast sight to bridges and be vigilant in
your watch over light posts...poetry will be spun...jokes will
be hacked and it will never seem the same by the earthy hue
of morning...you will use all of your God-given strength to
fight your mortal nature...you will not sleep and you will
not pee...you will stare attentively to the windshield...for if
you sleep...you will drool and yes...even angels drool...

I think Ariel and I had spent about five minutes posting before I decided I hated it. There we were sitting in the Burger King parking lot...sipping our coffees...listening to the fleet sign on one by one and filtering throughout the city...when it struck me *"...this really blows..."*

"...yeah but it just started so let's not start the complaining now..."

"...oh sure...they'll be plenty of time for that ten hours from now..."

Ariel fought with her Scrunchie in pursuit of the perfect ponytail and I attempted to adjust my seat for maximum steering wheel clearance. Then I tried looking out the window. "...ahhhhh...this is so stupid...how are we supposed to occupy ourselves like this?...I feel incarcerated..."

"...would you relax?...it's not like it's going away..."

"...me relax?...how many times you gonna put in and take out that Scrunchie?..."

"...I tried a new conditioner this morning and I can't get my hair right..."

"…it's fine…wear a hat…or even better…it's just you and me don't worry about it…I won't tell anybody that your ponytail was fucked up for five minutes…"

"…hey is that four-twenty?…" I looked over and sure enough four-twenty was pulling up alongside our truck. I was psyched to see Kelly was driving.

"…hello ladies…having fun?…" She spoke over the whirl of the power window.

"…oh sure…this is great…" I answered while Ariel dove in her backpack to find her hat.

"…in all my years I've never seen anything so ridiculous…" Kelly was as disgusted as me. "…and this should go over real well with my aching back…"

"…oh yeah…so where are you guys supposed to be?…"

"…uhhh…I don't remember…where we are going…" Kelly deferred to her partner who was apparently lying down in the back of their ambulance.

"…81…" I heard a familiar voice answer.

"…is that Mahan?…" I started laughing. "…what's he doing back there?…"

"…he doesn't feel so good…him and the other stewards closed Sully's last night preparing for the union meeting…"

"…nice…"

"…yeah so we got a liter bag running through him and I'm doing my union duty and chauffeuring his draggin' ass around…"

"…good work union laborer…"

"…yeah well…all us bees gotta pull our weight…so the reason I'm here Casey…" Kelly lowered her voice and looked to the left and to the right to clear the perimeter. "…is the sisterhood has a mission for you should you choose to accept…"

"…yeah…really?…"

"…yeah…really…so you in?…"

"…uhhhhhh…I don't know…what's the mission?…"

"…NO QUESTIONS…either you're in or you're out…" I paused at the Patty Hearst treatment and Kelly started laughing. "…just kidding Casey…I have some furniture to move and I noticed your Jeep doesn't have a backseat…"

I took a breath and sighed. "…yeah I can move stuff in it…"

"…cool…meet me at the new building at 21:00…"

"…21:00…got it…"

"…excellent…over and out…" And just as quickly as she pulled in…Kelly pulled out.

☆ ☆ ☆

As the day unfolded…the calls began and soon we found ourselves at the ER. That's when it hit us. Let's just stay at the ER. There's a room with chairs and a microwave and a bunch of bathrooms and all our friends end up here eventually anyways. So we'll just wait and hang out. It was quite the glorious plan too until the supervisor showed up. Seems dispatch started to wonder where all their trucks were and realized the ERs had become huge sucking black holes that crews fell into and couldn't pull themselves back out of. Watching the supervisor roust us like pigeons off a roost I noticed for the first time the kind of stress the merger had them under.

They were in the unenviable position of middle management. They got crap from up above and down below and the sad thing was most of these guys were former road medics. They knew exactly what we were going through and they genuinely sympathized with us but we didn't sign their paychecks and they weren't protected by the union…*you had to wonder how the former comrades would hold up as the tensions mounted…*

☆ ☆ ☆

By the time the end of the shift came I was more pooped than I had ever been after a day that didn't include snow. I had time to go home before I was supposed to meet Kelly and unfortunately while lying down on my couch I fell asleep...

....
....
....

and I may have had an odd dream...

....
....
....

...but I woke up so fast that I shook it out of my head like a clearing Etch A Sketch screen...

Unfortunately my little snooze did nothing to make me feel refreshed and now I was running late to meet Kelly. I threw a Red Sox hat on my disheveled appearance...grabbed a coffee on the way and practiced my apology all while maximizing every gear my little four-cylinder Jeep could crank out. When I pulled down the long driveway of the new NAA building I saw Kelly's Saturn parked in the far corner. I pulled up alongside her and offered a meek wave.

"...hey...what's up?..."
"...not much...you ready?..."
"...yeah..."
"...okay...follow me..." Kelly whipped her car into reverse... quick three-point turn and then flew down the long driveway. I and my sleepiness struggled to keep up but once we hit the flow of traffic she slowed to an easier pace. In the customary manner of Kelly O'Brien she zigged and zagged down unknown side streets until eventually she came out at a very familiar point.

The gate outside of Carter. She pulled over and I pulled up next to her.

"…what are we doing here?…"

"…you'll see…" Kelly answered while she got out of her car and fiddled with a ring of keys and the gate padlock. I wondered whose keys they were. When she completed the task she gingerly opened the gate and directed me to drive through. Thoroughly confused…I saw no reason not to. Soon she followed behind me and we made our way to the old office. Kelly pulled up to the side door that once led from our kitchen to the parking lot. She directed me to back up to the door and she pulled her car over to the shadows. "…open up the back of your Jeep…" As I did Kelly walked to the door… again with the ring of keys in her hand. Now she was using them to unlock the door. "…this'll teach Travis to fall asleep on duty…"

"…you stole the supervisor's keys?…"

"…borrowed Casey…I'll give them back when our mission's complete…but yes…I lifted them right off his belt…" She laughed to herself. "…he sure is a sound sleeper…"

"…cool…" I tried to sound nonchalant. "…so we're breaking and entering…"

"…no we're just entering…see…nothing's broken…" And with that the door popped open and Kelly pushed me inside. "…head upstairs but don't turn on the lights…"

"…oooofff…my shin…"

"…c'mon…how many times you been up and down these stairs at night with your eyes barely open?…"

"…yeah true…you're right…" And with my newfound enlightenment I suddenly could see. Still I was grateful when Kelly pulled out a mini Maglite. As we quickly bolted up the stairs it struck me as cool that I was once again climbing the stairs I thought my feet would never touch again...*even if I had no idea why...*

When we got to the top Kelly shone her light around the room. "…all righty then…all in one place…I like it…" I looked around and all the creature comforts of our once proud office were in a pile in the middle of the room. Two TVs…a VCR…the microwave…a toaster oven…somebody's water pick…a raggedy couch and a bunch of beat-up chairs.

"…okay…so what's going on?…what are we doing here?…"

"…it's a people's liberation movement Casey…you ever heard of Robin Hood?…"

"…of course…I love Robin Hood…"

"…well tonight you are him…you see all this stuff?…"

"…yeah…"

"…well I have it on good word that NAA is planning on claiming it and doing whatever they want with it and that ain't right…didn't you guys buy all this stuff?…"

I looked at the pile. It was true. Management would have had us living in an empty box but slowly over time we all donated various items to furnish our pad. "…yeah we did…that's Fergie's TV and I think Jodi brought in the VCR and microwave…no idea who's water pick that is…"

"…that's okay…we're not worried about the water pick but Mahan told me when everybody put their claim in on their stuff NAA asked for receipts…I say fuck the receipts…let's get this stuff to the rightful owners…"

"…all right…" I felt a chill of excitement. "…I like it…"

"…I knew you would…so let's get busy…but we gotta be quick because Travis will be looking for his keys any time now…"

"…got it…what's first?…" And so one by one we grabbed the merchandise and loaded up the Saturn followed by the Jeep. The big TV was the last to go.

"…I never boosted a TV before…" I looked at the 36" screen. "…it looks heavy…"

"…it probably is…don't worry about it though…" Kelly threw me the keys. "….just get the door behind me…"

"…okeydokey…" I grabbed the keys while Kelly bent over to lift the TV.

"…ohhhh my achin' back…" Kelly strained under the weight.

"…you okay?…"

"…yeah…just get the door…" Kelly bellowed causing me to quickstep down the stairs. I made it down a lot quicker than she did and it gave me the opportunity to peek out and advance scout.

"…CRAP…HEADLIGHTS…" The sight of which panicked me and caused me to freeze in my tracks and close the door quickly. Unfortunately Kelly and the TV had way too much momentum to slam it in to PARK and she ended up running right into my back. I slammed into the door and she bounced directly backward and onto the stairs.

"…CASEY…WHAT THE FUCK?…" I looked over only to see Kelly's arms and legs flailing from under the TV like a flipped-over turtle…*I couldn't help but laugh*…Kelly yelled at me again. **"…CASEY… WHAT THE FUCK IS GOING ON?…"**

I slowly cracked the door open and peeked out. "…I saw headlights but they're gone now…coast is clear…" I reached back and helped Kelly to her feet and we each grabbed half of the TV. This time we were much more successful getting it out the door and to the back of my Jeep and now we were both giggling. I slammed the tailgate shut and Kelly locked up the building.

"…let's go…time is money…" Kelly hollered as she jumped into her car. "…keep up if you can…" And she meant it. Once she had the gate locked she floored it back into mainstream traffic. I stayed right on her tail though as I was too revved up to go slow…*I was alive…*

We ended up making our way to Sully's. I don't know if it was by design or just how it happened…but it was a pretty good idea. When we blasted our way through the barroom doors I imagined myself swaggering through the double doors of the Old Tyme Wet Your Whistle Saloon...*I was definitely a rule breaker now*...I almost ordered a double shot of whiskey but when Kelly ordered a beer I figured I'd keep it simple and stick with my trusty Sombrero. Hey...they're from Mexico...*that's part of the old west...*

Kelly and I only stayed for one but I made sure I soaked in the moment. It was so cool how we were going to give everybody back their stuff. "...it's like we totally snatched it from the talons of the bloodthirsty hawk..."

"...easy killer...it's pretty low-end swag..."

I leaned back on my stool and grinned. "...yeah...but we finally got one over on NAA..."

"...yes we did...but nobody can know we did...you got that... right?..." Kelly took a swig from her beer.

"...of course...absolutely...but how are we going to get everybody their stuff back?..."

"...we're going to give it to them...just not directly..." She took another drink. "...Mahan's going to serve as our fence... nobody'll know we were the actual liberators..."

"...Mahan's pretty cool..."

"...yeah he is..." Kelly turned and looked at me. "...he makes a pretty good cowboy..."

...oh god...the jig is up....

CHAPTER 17 -
NO GOOD DEED GOES UNPUNISHED

...in reply Jesus said "...a man was going down from Jerusalem to Jericho...when he fell into the hands of robbers...they stripped him of his clothes...beat him and took his cell phone...leaving him half dead...a priest happened to be going down the same road and when he saw the man he passed by on the other side...so too...a Levite... when he came to the place and saw him...passed by on the other side...but a Samaritan...as he traveled...came where the man was and when he saw him he took pity on him...he went to him and bandaged
his wounds...splinted his bones and provided transport to an appropriate facility...and he did all the paperwork and turned it in and it was a good thing...for the man recovered and sued the Samaritan...and the paperwork was all he had in court to justify his actions when clearly a wise and prudent man would have walked away like the priest and the Levite...
...dumbass...

The next morning I had a hard time not having a shit-eating grin on my face. Ariel knew something was up but all her poking and prodding couldn't get the secret out of me. I just kept denying anything was up and instead refocused on the tasks at hand.

As if we didn't have enough on our plate with all this merger crap going on, my landlord sent me a letter explaining that he was evicting me because he sold the house and the new owners didn't want tenants. Oh well...whatta ya gonna do? He was giving me sixty days notice and I was getting good at moving stuff. When I told Ariel she got excited and said we'd look for something while we posted. I wasn't quite that jazzed up but I was grateful for the help.

One side effect of posting was that the line between Carter and Valley was officially gone. The offices were our last islands of company territory and now we were all shaken up and spread all over the city. Ariel and I were definitely a Carter crew but other than a few other homogenous crews everyone else was a blend. When you added in that in the old days some people had routinely jumped back and forth over company lines you could actually forget who came from where or where they were the last time there was a line. Not to mention that with the exodus came new hires and**...*GULP*...**EMTs whose only affiliation was with NAA. There were some legitimate concerns that the new people could cause problems for the union. No ties...no loyalty... *no problem working for the man...*

As always though...the calls marched on and Ariel and I found ourselves more and more a dedicated city truck. We did a lot less driving to the suburbs and a lot more six-floor walk-ups. I loved the new scenery and felt really comfortable working with Ariel in the new land. Not that it came without its challenges. I remember one time we did a call for a diff breather in a huge apartment building on Main Street. It had four floors and at least forty-eight units but of course no working elevators. No worries though...we accepted our challenge humbly and prepared for the upcoming task by loading up our stairchair with equipment and humping it up to the deep ends of the building. We found our patient no problem and initiated treatment but it was when we tried to leave that the fun began. Somehow we got turned around and came out a door on a side street we didn't even recognize.

"...where the heck are we?..."Ariel scrunched up her forehead and stared down the street.

"...I don't know...I could have sworn we went in by the mailboxes..."

"...me too...there must be more than one set of mailboxes..." Ariel leaned down to the patient. "...do you know where we are?..."The patient just smiled under her O2 mask.

"...she's Russian...not deaf..."

"...I know I know...Let's just go back in and try a different door..."

"...'kay..." So we turned around and headed up the sidewalk. *BANGABANGABANGA* "...that's a locked door..."

"...okay...let's walk around the building..."

"...walk around the building?..."

"...yeah...the ambulance is somewhere around the building..."

"...this is a big building...we could be walking a while..."

"...we'll just have to walk the right way..."

Which of course we didn't. Once you walk around two sides and don't see your ambulance you know you went the longest possible way. Fifteen minutes and almost a whole bottle of oxygen later we made it back to our truck. In the meantime we looked ridiculous and I don't think we did a whole lot to instill confidence in our patient either. I don't speak a word of Russian but I do know a perplexed look when I see one and she had one for at least two sides of the building. You just didn't have these problems in suburbia.

Call natures were a lot different in the city too. One time we got called to the ubiquitous *man down*. I know I've run through the nuts and bolts of man down calls but this one came with a little twist. It started as a man fully clothed sitting in his car at a stop light. By the time it was done the man was stark naked and laying face down in the turn lane screaming for Jesus to come save him from his oppressors. Ariel and I asked the cops what they wanted us to do and their answer was for us to use our medical knowledge to identify appropriate handles to "...pick him up or otherwise get him off our road..."

At first we were a bit perturbed at the situation. Then as we knelt down next to the guy...stared at each other and recognized that medical knowledge was in no way helpful for the situation and in fact made it all the more depressing. Hilarity ensued and we broke into laughter. We wanted to help...*really we did*...but come on. The dude's naked...*what the hell would you want to use as a handle?...*

The cool thing was that everybody did cool stuff all day so whenever we met up...at the hospital or later on at Sully's...we all had funny stories to share. I loved being part of this fraternity. Everyone was hard working and just a little bit crazy so a lot got done and a lot of fun was had. And even though NAA was making a great effort to break up our way of life we didn't feel sorry for ourselves and cave. In fact the more they tried torturing the intelligent people with the minutia of corporateness the swifter the masses stirred the anarchy pot.

The first planned defiance demonstration was staged by Mahan and his partner Tom Richardson...or Rich as we all called him for some unknown reason. One Saturday afternoon they pulled their ambulance into the furniture store parking lot known as posting location Harbor Rd and Massachusetts Ave...*Harbor and Mass when you were in a hurry*...opened up the side doors on the ambulance and pulled out a hibachi...bag of charcoal... lighter fluid and **SPARKED IT UP BABY**...Mahan pulled out his stairchair and relaxed while Rich cooked up some dogs. The best part was when the furniture shoppers inquired as to what the hell they were doing and Mahan took the opportunity to educate the public on the concept of posting. A lot of people walked away scratching their heads but we heard rumor that NAA got quite a few phone calls wondering why a company wouldn't allow their employees an opportunity to eat or pee in a ten-hour shift. Shortly thereafter...NAA found a spot in Shangri-La to put in a break room with a microwave and bathroom.

✫ ✫ ✫

"...Casey...get over here..." I looked up from the coffee pot and Kelly was walking across the training center.

She was squinching her finger at me as if to pull me toward her. I eagerly accepted and got squinched in. "...I got an extra ticket to Melissa Etheridge and you're going..."

"...I am?..."

"...yes...I'll see you at my house 19:00 Saturday night..."

"...uh...okay..."

...strangely it never occurred to me that I already had a ticket...

✫ ✫ ✫

one day it was raining really hard...

"...so did you hear NAA reached out to all the local fire departments?..." I was tired of staring at the windshield.

"...you mean to cover our shifts if we strike?..." Ariel proved she's up on current events.

"...yeah and all the union departments told them to fuck off..."

"...well you can't blame them for asking...someone has to cover the calls..." Ariel's use of logic disturbed me.

"...I refuse to try to see things from their point of view..."

"...that would actually be the patients' point of view..."

"...dear God...WHAT DID THEY DO TO YOU IN THAT CATHOLIC SCHOOL?..."

"...calm down...you're fogging up the windshield..."

"...do you know how I've longed to hear you say that?..."

"...FORGET IT..."

"...now who's fogging up the windshield?..."

"...FOUR-TEN...FOUR-ONE-ZERO..."

"...oh thank god..."

"...and baby Jesus..."

...muted laugh... "...four-ten..."

"...FOUR-TEN...TAKE THE BIGCITY 911 FOR 27 ORCHARD HILL FOR THE MAN SHOT...PD ON SCENE..."

"...four-ten   received...***AH   COOL   MY   FIRST SHOOTING...***" Oh yeah...I am grace under pressure.

"...take it easy...do we need to pull over so I can drive?..."

"...no I got it...I'll relax..." I took a deep breath and turned on the lights.

"...good...suave chica..."

"...trying a second language?..."

"...yeah I think it'll help us blend in..."

"...AHHH no...you're way too WASPy to blend in..."

"...I'm Dutch Catholic...how is that too WASPy?..."

"...I don't know but I'll stay calm on shootings if you drop the Carmen Miranda *West Side Story* shtick..."

"...that was a good movie..."

"...so I hear..."

"...FOUR-TEN...FOUR-ONE-ZERO..."

"...four-ten..."

"...FOUR-TEN...PD ON SCENE STATE PATIENT SHOT IN HEAD...REQUEST YOU EXPEDITE..."

"...four-ten received..."

"...cool...the cops told me to drive faster..." *I could hardly believe my luck.*

"...don't you dare..." Ariel scolded me. "...we will get there when we get there...it's raining and these things roll you know..."

"…that would be cool…if we rolled and you landed on top of me…"

"…no it wouldn't…"

"…okay…if I landed on top of you…that would be okay too…"

"…that's not what I meant…"

"…whatever…" I smiled and she looked away in disgust…*I love yankin' her chain…*

As predicted…we arrived in due time. There were a boatload of cops and cruisers everywhere but nobody was with our patient. He was lying on the ground outside a large multi-unit apartment complex…upside down on the steep hill that is Orchard Hill. It was impossible to get the ambulance anywhere near him so I parked at the foot of the hill and Ariel and I prepared to trek up the incline with all our gear.

"…good thing we've been doing all that hiking on our days off…" I looked at Ariel who had three bag handles wrapped around her torso so her hands were free to claw at the muddy ground in front of her. "…although I don't recall having to do it with a trauma kit and longboard…**OOOF**"…And with that proclamation…

I slid back…

three…

feet…

When we got to the patient we noticed he was conscious but confused and trying to sit up against the grade of the hill. We dropped our gear and about half of it rolled back down toward the road. *"…god damn it…"* But I let it go figuring I'd just get it if and when I needed it. I turned my attention to the patient. Ariel was already at his head assessing the bullet hole. It was in the back of his skull and you had to move his hair out of the way to see it. There was hardly any blood and the hole itself was pretty small. Probably shot with a .22. Not that I'm a ballistics expert or anything but a cop told me once that the smaller the number the smaller the hole. The problem with the smaller calibers is they don't have enough kinetics behind them to penetrate and exit so they just rattle around your body cavity…or in this case his skull…and chew up tissue as they go. A protein pinball if you will*…cool…huh?…*

Back to our flailing antics in the mud which must have been quite the sight because about a dozen neighbors and family members became less interested in what had previously entertained them and they began to gather around us. The hill was muddy and Ariel and I were having a bitch of a time keeping our footing. We each fell a couple of times and by now our polyester pants and both arms from the elbows down were waterlogged and muddy*…this first shooting wasn't turning out to be nearly as much fun as I'd imagined it would be…*

Ariel and I were starting to get a sense that what we needed to do was get a handle on this extrication and get the patient to the controlled environment of the ambulance ASAP. Shootings by nature are violent and they attract a violent crowd. You are always much better off to get in and get out of the yellow tape zone as quickly as you can in your best ninja pose. Standing around looking for souvenirs may look like a good idea from the outside but not so much now. Unfortunately for us six inches of mud…a steep incline and the steady driving rain were quite counterproductive to the objective.

Goal number one was to get the patient secured to a longboard. Not only was protecting his c-spine a huge legitimate concern but it would also make it easier to carry him down the hill. I put a collar on him and the only purpose that served was to give him something to continually rip off while we struggled to get him on the board. We tried putting the board below him and using gravity to our advantage but I just kept on sliding down the hill. So then we tried pulling him uphill but he was freakin' heavy and fightin' us. That's pretty typical of head injuries. They can be a real handful. They get all wild-eyed and swing away at everything and you can't reason with them because they don't know what they're doing. A small minority of boneheads will just haul off and sock 'em…rationalizing that you have to settle them down and control the situation but you really should just roll with it and try not to be a flaming asshole in the process.

Understandably we were getting frustrated and concerned. This was an unstable scene and there were a lot of angry people around. Ariel stopped for a minute and looked up to see if a cop was nearby that could give us a hand. Quite to our dismay they were still a ways away and very occupied…*we were very much on our own…*

One of the neighbors saw Ariel looking around and got aggressive. "…what are you doing?…" Ariel ignored her. "…white girl…what are you doing?…help him…"

Ariel looked at me "…uh-oh…"

"…I told you you were WASPy…"

"…not now…"

"…LOOK AT HOW SLOW THEY MOVIN'…" The neighbor got others involved.

"…MAYBE THEY MOVIN' SLOW CAUSE HE'S BLACK…"

"…how about giving us a hand?…we need help in the mud…" I thought maybe if I involved the community in the solution they would embrace the process.

"…THAT AIN'T MY JOB…THAT'S YOUR JOB…HOW ABOUT YOU JUST DO YOUR JOB?…"

"…AND DON'T WORRY ABOUT HIM BEING BLACK… YOU JUST GET HIS BLACK ASS TO THE HOSPITAL…"

"…so much for conflict-resolution class…" I looked at Ariel. "…what are we going to do?…because I am about two seconds from laughing because really this is funny but…"

"…but not really right now…yeah…hold off on that…" Ariel scrunched up her forehead so I knew she was thinking. "…screw it…it doesn't need to be pretty…"

"…no…it doesn't…which is good because it's already not…"

"…lay the board the long way and let's roll him on it…"

We started making minor progress as the patient was now at least on the board. We just got going on the strapping-down part when mercifully a diversion was provided. Some guy came running out of the apartment complex carrying a huge TV and the angry crowd's attention turned from us.

"…ANTHONY…THAT'S ANTHONY JONES…HE GOT THE TV…"

"…HOW'D HE GET THAT TV…WHERE ARE THE MOTHERFUCKIN' POLICE?…ANTHONY…" *and they were off to the next shiny object…*

Ariel expressed relief. "…thank you Anthony…"

"…I wonder whose TV that is…"

The confused patient managed a groan. "…mine…"

"…he speaks…" Ariel leaned in. "…do you know where you are?…" Nothing but blank stare and another attempt to rip off the c-collar.

"…well…it looks like that dude just stole it…" The patient blinked slowly as I leaned in with sage advice. "…you outta get yourself some better friends…a good friend doesn't steal a TV from you*…he steals it with you…*"

☆ ☆ ☆

Finally we extricated off the hill and got him to the friendly confines of our ambulance. Other than him ripping out every IV we started the voyage was uneventful and our patient was alive when we got to the ER. I didn't even think about the call again until the end of the year when I read an article about the record-setting year of homicides in BigCity. It retold the stories of the mostly young male minorities who lost their lives to violence and there it was in black and white. ***"...Thomas Singleton shot in the head by neighbor Anthony Jones in dispute over television set..."*** There was no mention of me and Ariel's brilliantly choreographed Hill Side Story dance in the mud or the fact that everyone seemed to want to blame us for the mess. Looking back...other than the list of names and very brief histories...the article didn't say much of anything.

✡ ✡ ✡

"...so you're going to the Melissa Etheridge concert tonight?..." Ariel jumped into conversation as we pulled up to the stoplight.

"...yeah...I guess Alyssa ended up with a couple of extra tickets and sold them to Kelly...she asked me to go last week..."

"...that's cool..." The light changed and Ariel slowly accelerated.

"...I'll say...I've been knocking myself out to get her attention..."

"...no way..."

"...anyway..." I deflected her sarcasm. "...now I can't believe I actually get to go to her house and hang out with her..."

"...and her girlfriend..."

"...her what?..."

"...her girlfriend..."

"...she doesn't have a girlfriend..."

"...she doesn't?..."

"...no..."

"...who's that Rickie chick?..."

"...it sounds funny when you say 'chick'..."

"…'woman' then…who's that Rickie woman?…"

"…that Rickie woman is just her roommate…I don't even think Rickie's gay…"

"…really?…"

"…really…I didn't get an official memo or anything but I'm pretty sure she was dating some guy in our medic class…"

"…really?…"

"…yeah…I worked an overtime shift with Mahan last year and we were at the Randall Street office with Rickie…that guy showed up off duty and they took off for an hour together…even dispatch couldn't find them…when she came back Mahan and I definitely thought she looked tussled…."

"…tussled…hmmm…"

"…yes…the chick was tussled…"

☆ ☆ ☆

The day of the concert found me extremely nervous…in fact way more nervous than I expected to be. I believe most of it stemmed from the fact that because I knew myself and my history well I feared that I would find at least one way out of a possible hundred to make a fool out of myself around Kelly. I mean I had put a lot of work in to making my way through the adoring crowd just to get her attention. The important question remained that now that I had it what was I going to do with it? It was not that inconceivable that somehow I'd manage to trip and fall down every stair from the nosebleed seats to a point on the arena floor where it would just be best for me to curl up and die. I have no idea where the rest of it came from but it reminded me of the night I met her and the way Blossom was acting…*maybe she just brings it out in people…*

Unfortunately for Ariel she was stuck with me all day and had to put up with my angst. Time couldn't pass fast enough and as the end of the shift approached I obsessed about getting held over.

"…four-ten…clear of Valley Trauma…" I radioed in. "…c'mon…c'mon send us somewhere out of the loop…"

"…will you relax?…"

"…I'm trying…I just don't want to get held over…I'm on a very tight schedule…"

"…tight schedule?…what time's the concert?…"

"…nine but I gotta go home…get ready and be to Kelly's by seven because we're hanging out first and I don't want to miss it…"

"…the hanging out?…"

"…yes the hanging out…"

"…FOUR-TEN RECEIVED…"

"…okay and the winner is…"

"…FOUR-TEN I HATE TO DO THIS TO YOU BUT I NEED YOU TO HEAD TO THE REAR OF THE BUS STATION ON MAIN STREET…SEE SECURITY FOR A POSSIBLE OD…"

"…FUCK ME MOTHERFUCKER…"

"…easy…"

"…four-ten received…taking it in the rear…"

"…ahhhhh…you should not have done that…dispatch will remember attitude…"

"…he's a fuckin' cocksucker anyways…like I could be nice enough…"

"…oh no…there's no way you could be nice enough…"

"…shut up Skippy…"

"…SKIPPY?…"

"…yeah…Skippy…I don't know why…it just is…"

"…oh brother…" Ariel rolled her eyes. "…that better not stick…"

When we got to the bus station Ariel grabbed the mike and called off. Then she mumbled something about dispatch being soothed by a calming voice. Whatever…by the time we found security all I was thinking about was knocking this call off in a hurry and goin' home.

I should have known better though. There is just no negotiating with the gods. The likelihood of getting held over is directly proportionate to your desire to get out on time and the likelihood of a call going smoothly is inversely proportionate to you demanding it…*and you thought you'd never need that math…*

I was among friends though because the security guard we hooked up with looked like he was having as much fun as I was and Ariel had long since grown tired of dealing with me.

"…this chucklehead came in on a bus from Hartford…he hasn't been in the terminal for more than half an hour and he's stoned out of his gourd…"

"…heroin?…"

"…yup…here he is…" The security guard opened the men's room door and the stench immediately hit us. Ariel and I both pre-gag coughed and covered our mouths and noses with our forearms.

"…oh god that's wretched…" I felt my eyes getting watery. The security guard nodded and opened the stall door for us. A 20 or so y/o male was lying on the floor covered in shit. "…is that his?…" I'm not sure why I asked.

"…that'd be my guess…" the security guard offered. "…not that I checked or anything but sometimes they cut heroin with a lot of laxative…they'll shoot up and shit diarrhea at the same time…"

"…so you're a multitasker…" Ariel's sarcasm toward the patient cracked me up. "…all right let's carefully check him for needles and then get a bunch of blankets and wrap him up like a burrito…"

The weird thing was that the patient didn't seem to mind being covered in shit. The whole time we struggled with wrapping and extricating him he laughed his ass off. There was nothing wrong with his breathing so Ariel suggested we not give any Narcan since Narcan can cause vomiting and that was the last ingredient we wanted to add to this mixture. I was all in favor of doing absolutely nothing and didn't even attempt a blood pressure. Kelly said anybody that nasty just has to meet one criteria...are they breathing? Anything else is just fluff and fluff can wait until they can be hosed off or whatever they do for them in the ER. I just hoped it was one of the cranky nurses who'd get stuck with him.

I called the hospital and told them we were coming in with a possible OD but vitals were stable. In fact...the patient was having a pretty good time. Trapped in the back of the ambulance with him left me fighting for breathable air but he was laughing and singing and lovin' life...*I was so happy for him...*

"...oh what have you girls brought me?...you're usually so nice to me..." Damn...it just had to be the nicest of the nicest nurses.

"...I know Chris...we're sorry..." I let Ariel do the talking and I stayed in the background offering sympathetic looks.

"...okay...so what's up with this gentleman?..."

"...well Chris...it goes like this..." Ariel filled in Chris while I helped her cut the patient's clothes off so they could be removed with the now shit-soaked blanket. The whole time I couldn't get over him rolling around laughing his butt off.

"...what's so funny?..." He stared back at me and I could only imagine what I looked and sounded like to him. *"...do you know where you are?..."* More giggling. *"...you do realize you're covered in shit of some sort... don't you?..."* Even more giggling.

"…wow…" I mumbled. "…I gotta get me some of this drug…that is one righteous buzz…" I looked up to see Chris and Ariel staring at me…

…well not today…

CHAPTER 18-
THE NEW TESTAMENT BEGINS

...and man SHALL lie with man and woman SHALL lie with woman...and Kelly O'Brien will make the snacks...

the night we went out may not have seemed like much at the time...but in retrospect...it made for one hell of a turning point...

Despite my earlier fears I got out of work in plenty of time to do everything I needed to do to be on time for the hanging out... including getting the smell of our last patient out of my nose... *lots of incense and breathing deep in a steamy shower...in case you're wondering...*

I got to Kelly's house around seven and she was the only one home. She offered me a beer and introduced me to her cat and dog...*pet pet wag wag...*I declined the beverage because I brought my own...and she gave me the mini-tour.

The house was very cool. It was a completely restored Victorian nestled in a mostly female college town and Kelly and Rickie had it decorated in modern frat house. There was a huge movie poster of *Thelma & Louise* in the living room that hung over a very comfy looking sectional couch draped with afghans and fluffy pillows. The center piece of the room was a kickass recliner that Kelly let me try out. On the coffee table was a coaster that asked **GOT POT?** and a white porcelain bong was discreetly tucked underneath so I knew I was amongst friends.

The kitchen was clean and came with the requisite Gumby and Pokey salt and pepper shakers. The upstairs had four huge bedrooms. Rickie's was painted in earth tones and her futon was a quilted mess of uniform parts...jeans and work-out clothes. Turns out she got to live here the whole time we were in medic school...*I was instantly jealous*...Imagine coming back from class every night and getting to brainstorm with Kelly.

Kelly's room was at the far end of the hall and we walked past two empty rooms to get to it. "...this was Allie Blomquist's room...did you know her?..." I shook my head. "...she was a medic at Valley..." Kelly continued walking. "...she just left for medical school in Texas...good egg...we're gonna miss her..." Kelly laughed. "...and her rent money..." She pointed to the next room. "...this is where I iron my uniforms..." She flipped the light on and off and I barely made out the shape of an ironing board. "...and now on to the pièce de résistance..." Kelly spoke with an exaggerated bravado. "...MY ROOM..." She boldly pushed the door open and I timidly peeked in. She walked in and headed for her bureau. I followed...wisely resisting the urge to run and jump on the bed à la Warren Beatty.

Unlike Rickie's...Kelly's room was very neat but it definitely carried on the theme of the house. A trippy lava lamp was oozing on the nightstand and incense was burning in strategically located points. Kelly motioned for me to sit on the bed as she reached into her bureau pulling out a bamboo tray. "...would you like a little herbal essence before the show Casey?..."

My ears perked up. "...why yes I would..."

"...Rickie will be mad we didn't wait for her but who knows when she'll be home..." Kelly filled the bowl and offered me the first hit. "...I love weed...I swear I have ADD and this stuff helps me relax..."

"...I rather enjoy it myself...I had no idea you did..."

"...oh yeah...I'm a stoner from way back..."

"...from way back?..."

"...yeah...from way back when you could smoke it in the ambulance and nobody cared..."

"...for real?..."

"…oh yeah…those were crazy days…*Mother, Jugs and Speed* was not an exaggeration…"

I laughed. "…*Mother, Jugs and Speed*…"

"…you seen that movie?…"

"…yeah…they showed it to us the first night of medic school…"

"…oh yeah…Rickie told me that…interesting choice… anyhoo…Bill Cosby's funny with the cooler and blastin' the nuns with the airhorn…EHH EHH…or as I like to call it…the Pee-wee Herman horn…HAA HAA…" I laughed some more.

"…sometimes I like to imagine Ariel as Raquel Welch…"

"…sure yeah…but Ariel's all right…" Kelly elbowed me. "…right?…" I smiled and nodded my head. "…she's definitely worth a slap…" I laughed even harder. "…is she?…" Kelly motioned left or right with her hand. I stopped her right away.

"…no…no…she's straight…definitely…definitely…but I like to kid her anyways…"

"…uh-huh…uh-huh…" Kelly absorbed the info and we continued on until she declared "…well this is spent…let's go wait for Rickie…" Kelly jumped up…stashed the tray and I dashed for the door.

We had just settled back into the living room when the door flew open and the dog raced to it. Cold air blew and Rickie stumbled in wrestling bags…a pair of sneakers and a CD case and now the dog jumping up and down barking. She laughed and made a decent recovery.

"…close the door Loser…" Kelly scolded.

Rickie pulled herself up and kept laughing. "…I picked the wrong time to clean out my car…"

Kelly shook her head. "…unbelievable…do you have my change?…"

"…yes…it's in my pocket…" Rickie pulled a beer out of the bag and walked over to us. "…hey what's up?…" She looked at me and smiled.

"…not much…how you been?…"

"…good…you're comin' to the concert tonight?…"

"…yeah…you too?…"

"…yup…"

"…hello…my change…" Kelly interrupted us and this time Rickie actually pulled the money out of her pocket and handed it over to Kelly. They exchanged some more playful banter while we had one more drink and then we hit the road…

…I was having fun…

☆ ☆ ☆

in which we go to the concert and have to drive through LittleCity to get there…

Kelly was driving and Rickie was reclining so far back in the passenger seat that she might as well have been in the backseat. The two things I most remembered about Rickie from medic school were how young she was…as in barely twenty-one…and that she was pretty damn hot. Turns out she was actually pretty funny too. I was starting to think I really missed out in medic school. I was so consumed with maniacally ingesting knowledge and information I tuned out any social activities. I completely missed Rickie's performance. Not to mention when school started we were on opposite sides of a long existing fence. It seems like forever ago that that was even important.

"…Kelly…make sure you drive very carefully through LittleCity…" Rickie exhorted.

"…don't you try to drive careful every where?…"

"…not really…" And to prove her point Kelly swerved wildly into the oncoming lane causing Rickie to holler.

"...come on...I'm serious...we do not want the LittleCity medics responding to our motor vehicle..."

"...that's a big affirmative..." I felt my buzz beginning.

"...no shit..." Kelly continued. "...as soon as they saw it was the three of us they'd have us stripped down and tied to longboards in the middle of the street..."

"...you guys aren't fans of them either?..." I was kind of surprised. Since Carter covered LittleCity and Valley covered... well... BigCity...I thought for sure the LittleCity medics would have very little interactions with them and at the very least have to respect their work in the tougher zip code.

"...a fuck's a fuck Casey..." Kelly looked at me from the rearview mirror. "...doesn't matter where you work..."

I just shook my head and then got startled when Rickie grabbed my arm and hollered "...WE CLEARED THE CITY LINE...WOO-HOO..."

"...all right...welcome to the fuck free zone..." Kelly beeped her horn and gave her best Pee-wee laugh...

...Melissa Etheridge here we come...

✪ ✪ ✪

"...there are our seats...over there Casey..." Kelly pointed up toward the section. Preconcert hum throbbed through the arena.

"...cool...yup..." I stared at my ticket. "...those are them..." I tried hard to be nonchalant but I'm not...

...ever...

"...here Casey...sit next to Rickie..." Kelly pointed and I followed. I scored the middle and realized Kelly was right behind me...we sat...Kelly's leg brushed mine...she didn't notice...*I was buzzed enough to make it last an hour...*

✪ ✪ ✪

The concert was over by 23:30 and none of us felt like calling it a night yet. Kelly suggested hitting a bar on the way home and we agreed. I assumed we'd hit Sully's or Murphy's but Kelly drove straight to "the girlie bar" as she called it.

Now I've never been much of a "girlie bar" person. Other than rare social and union gatherings at the usual spots I don't go out a lot. I also don't drink a lot and when you're sober bars...*as it turns out...*are actually nothing more than dark stinky rooms where a lot of depressed people hang out instead of going out into the world and forming real relationships. The girlie bars also boast a higher than average clique ratio and I am anything but cool and in style. I know a lot of gay people see the bars as safe havens from the straights and sanctuaries in which PDAs are not met with groans and chants of "...there ought to be an island...blah blah blah..." but I've always been at peace with the straights and never felt I needed such a refuge. Still the chance to walk in with Kelly and Rickie on each side of me tantalized my scandalous side.

On our way through the parking lot my curiosity got the best of me and I interviewed Rickie. "...so are you gay?..."

Rickie paused. "...uhhhh...I don't really like labels..."

"...labels?..."

"...yeah...gay straight bi...who cares?...let's just have fun..."

"...okay..." I looked at Kelly and she shrugged.

"...this younger generation..." She smiled. "...they're so at ease..."

As we got closer to the door the pounding bass of a dance track came into focus. Rickie let out a "...awesome...let's do some dancing..." and broke into a light jog. She dusted Kelly and me and by the time we entered the bar she was lost in the sea of grateful lesbians who could not believe their luck that this gorgeous chick was adorning the crowded dance floor.

Kelly shook her head as she watched. "...she's a nut..." I agreed. "...let's get a drink..." I agreed again.

Kelly flirted with the bartender and I made the cursory scan of the room. It's important to identify right away if any of your exes are present so as not to get blindsided as the evening wears on. In typical fashion following a Melissa Etheridge concert the room was filled with smiling lesbians sporting new T-shirts splattered with tour dates and album covers...*so far no exes spotted...*

Kelly and I gathered our drinks and found a small table in the corner of the room. Rickie took occasional breaks from dancing to come by and gather up her beers. We all took turns buying rounds and this is where the blur really set in. I remember laughing a lot and enjoying the scenery on the dance floor. Kelly mumbled something about having to drive home and switched to ice water. Just as the lights flickered for last call Rickie came two-steppin' back to the table.

"...let's hit the parking lot and smoke some weed..."

"...let's hit the parking lot and go home..." Kelly was done with the night.

"...ah mother Kelly...getting everybody home safe...look at you with your ice water..." Rickie was also pretty buzzed. "...will you make grilled cheese squares when we get home?..."

"...sure...let's go..."

"...grilled cheese squares?..." Mmmm...sounds good...*I'm hungry...*

"...yeah...Kelly makes the best grilled cheese squares..." Rickie stressed "best" and gave her a big hug...*or maybe she was leaning on her...*

"...what are grilled cheese squares?..." I prepared to be amazed by yet another of Kelly O'Brien's talents.

"...you make a grilled cheese and cut it into squares...usually four..." Kelly wasted no time sharing her culinary secret.

"...that's it?..."

"…yeah…but they're the best…" Rickie raved on…*clearly she had drunk the Kool-Aid…* Kelly gave a shrug. It was all just in a day's work for her to be worshipped and adored.

✵ ✵ ✵

on the way home…

"…who'd of thought at thirty-five I'd still be drinkin' and smokin' pot…" Kelly drove casually up 91 with one hand on the steering wheel. I lied in the backseat living dangerously…*I didn't have a seatbelt on…*

Staring upside down out the rearview window at the stars and passing streetlights provided poetic back lighting.

"…and on a Monday night no less…" Rickie handed the joint to the backseat. "…'ere Casey…"

"…life is a series of continued repeating patterns…" I slurred and no one heard…not even a word. "…WE'RE ALL WALLPAPER…" I yelled loudly from my haven.

"…easy Scooter…" Kelly counseled coolly. "…I think Casey's shut off…" Then she turned around and smiled. "…now would that be flowers or plaid prints?…"

…bitch…

✵ ✵ ✵

When we got back to the house it was agreed that I shouldn't drive home. Hell it was pretty much agreed I couldn't walk up the driveway without an assist. The blur ends with me flopping on the couch and Kelly throwing a blanket on me. If I had died right then and there I would have died a happy person. I had scaled the highest mountain. I had not only gotten Kelly's attention at work but I had made it to the inner sanctum…*if only Blossom could see me now…*In fact there truly was only one thing left to do…find the bathroom…

…quickly…

✵ ✵ ✵

two days later at work...

"...so the concert was wicked good..." I offered as we pulled into the parking lot known as 81.

"...yeah?..." Ariel pulled a yogurt out of her cooler.

"...yeah...Melissa Etheridge was awesome...and there were hot chicks everywhere..."

Ariel smiled and shook her head. "...you're funny..." She offered me a nectarine.

"...it looks a little soft..." I squinted at the fuzzless fruit.

"...yeah...I cleaned out my fridge yesterday...if you eat it fast it should be all right..." Ariel laughed.

"...ah...no thanks...I'm good..."

"...I called you Tuesday morning to see if you wanted to have breakfast..."

"...you called me the morning after a concert?...you're lucky I wasn't home..."

Ariel took a big mouthful of yogurt. "...you weren't home?..."

"...uh-uh...I stayed at Kelly and Rickie's..."

"...so are they a couple?..."

"...no...they're both single..."

"...so who did you stay with?..." Ariel stared at the bottom of her yogurt...stirring what little remained. I was shocked at her question and yet very complimented.

"...both of them...I just went back and forth until they smartened up and joined me in one bed..." She stopped stirring. I stared at her waiting for her to look up. She did.

"...really?..."

"...no...I slept on the couch...but thank you..."

Ariel sheepishly smiled. "...you're welcome..."

...I do believe she was worried...

✻ ✻ ✻

"...Casey...get over here..." I turned around in the ER to find Kelly summoning me...*obviously I obeyed* "...what are you telling people about me?..."

I'm truly puzzled. "...what are you talking about?..."

"...well I got Fergie trying to touch my state patch...Alyssa calls me 'Kelly the Great'...and you got Jodie convinced she has to carry my cape up the stairs on calls..."

"...Blossom thinks you really do have a cape..."

"...I do..."

"...I know..."

"...but I carry it myself on calls...it's part of my mystique..."

CHAPTER 19-
TO THE ROOT OF ALL EVIL

*...no one can serve two masters...either he will hate the
one and love the other or he will be devoted to the one and
despise the other...you cannot serve both the God of
EMS and money...*

Did I mention that posting sucked to no end? Sitting in a
truck all day...staring at the same parking lots over and over and
arguing with the same dumbass convenience store managers who
just didn't get it that we didn't really want to use their smelly
swamp gas restrooms***...but we had to...***

And Ariel may have tried playing it off like there was no good
reason to complain but over time she also started to crack from
the confinement of it all. I remember one night we got posted at
the bridge just outside of BigCity. It was a good posting location
because it got you out of the BigCity rotation. Kindhearted
dispatchers would put you there toward the end of your shift to
lessen the chance of you getting one of the more available BigCity
calls and being held over. The timing was perfect for us because
Ariel and I were done with people for the day and we just wanted
to hide***...something we used to be able to do at the office...***

On the other side of the bridge was the famous North End
Rotary where Blossom and I had been positioned perfectly to get
sent to the "Great Crash of '93" that had been precipitated by the
Nor'easter of '93. To avoid the crazy flow of rotary traffic and
accomplish our hiding we pulled around to the back parking lot
of a pizza place. Initially we sat quietly with our eyes closed and
our heads back to rest. Then a cool dance tune came on the radio
and I started singing. To drown me out Ariel turned the radio
all the way up. I thought that made the tune sound even better
which inspired me to think I could pull off a cool disco effect

if we turned the lights on which bounced back off the building walls and the next thing you knew we were totally truck dancing. Even Ariel threw caution to the wind and kicked off her boots and started trying to stuff her foot in my mouth so I couldn't sing anymore. I responded by grabbing her socked foot and singing into it like a microphone. Of course all this action got the truck totally rocking to the beat. Naturally timing being what it is that's when some dude working at the pizza joint came out the back door to dump the trash***...so much for hiding...***He stopped as soon as he saw us...put down his bags of trash...leaned back and gave us the cool two thumbs up. I thought it was funny because we just got totally bagged being goofy but Ariel got real embarrassed and turned everything off.

"...hey...the song's not done..."

"...I know but let's get out of here..."

"...oh my god Skippy..."

"...I'm not kidding...let's go..." Ariel fumbled around to find her boots. "...and leave the lights on so we can get out of here fast..."

I couldn't stop laughing but I did manage to get us safely and anonymously to another parking lot. I would imagine that if a public vote was taken...pizza guy would probably vote yes for more posting...

...ah snap...what is it they say about rhythm?...

✲ ✲ ✲

Meanwhile NAA kept up its March toward world dominance leaving we the underlings to come together to fight the tyranny. As I've said before...we may be dysfunctional but we're also very intelligent and there are many ways to stage a protest and many ways to clog the wheels of the unrelenting corporate machine. I like to think the diversity of our ranks meant we covered them all.

Some were content with letting the union handle the process...
others staged work slowdowns and a select few just became
overly defiant whenever anything was asked of them. They didn't
wash their trucks...they didn't wear their uniforms correctly...
they'd turn in incomplete paperwork so calls couldn't be billed
for. Pretty much everything just short of affecting patient care.
We all knew and respected the code that the patients had to be
left out of it. This was about one thing and one thing only and that
was the fight of the little guy verses the large corporate monster
hell bent on destroying our way of life.

One of the medics had T-shirts made up that said **NAA
bought my company and all I got was this lousy T-shirt** on
the back and on the front was a list of all the companies bought
locally and crushed with their names crossed off to illustrate the
pulverizing nature of the acquisitions. There it was in black and
white...right at the type of the list...Carter and Valley...together
as fallen sisters. We all bought them and wore them under our
uniforms. When the light hit your uniform shirt just right...like
say if you were bent down at a car accident...you could read the
message. That always started conversations with the other union
members on scene. You know...the cops and firefighters. Pretty
much everybody who worked with us sympathized with our plight
and we knew that would be important if things got really ugly. You
know...like if nothing got resolved and we ended up going on
strike. It would be helpful to say the least to be friendly with the
cops and firefighters when we started tipping over ambulances
and setting them on fire.

Speaking of the union...the night of our big union meeting
finally arrived and as expected just about everyone showed up for
it. Even on-duty crews made the effort to drive by. Not only were
we addressing some weighty topics but all the bigwigs from the
district office were supposed to be there to explain our options.

Most of us were hoping we could start getting some resolution to some of the things hanging over our heads like shift changes and partner shakeups. The union manager and business agent seemed to understand our priorities and dove right in to the laundry list of company policies we could and couldn't do anything about.

Unfortunately what most of us was hearing was there wasn't anything we could do about any of them. The union made it sound like NAA had done everything by the book so we had no recourse. Personally I wasn't buying it. We knew our contract was about to be up and a lot of these issues could be considered "change in working conditions" that had to be negotiated. I couldn't understand why the union was talking about rolling over so easily. So what if NAA said they had no plans to negotiate any changes? Isn't union representation all about legal recourse to effect negotiating in good faith? What did we care if NAA was busy with other mergers and acquisitions and didn't want to be held up with the loose ends of our merger and acquisition? It's not like we wanted to be merged and acquisitioned in the first place. Hello...*people here*...people with lives...people who don't care if you make a buck just don't trample the people to make two.

The union tried selling NAA's promise that if we gave them an easy negotiation they'd make it worth our financial while. Apparently the underpaid people are supposed to be thrilled to be just a little less underpaid...*how's an extra dollar an hour sound?...huh...huh...want some candy too?...*Otherwise if we chose to make a big deal out of it they would legally out-manpower us and punish us financially for as long as possible. And the union agent threw in a "...and they will..." just to drive the point home...*this all just seemed so wrong...*

Our chief steward opened the floor up for discussion and that's when the unspoken was spoken. Mahan stood up and said we should tell NAA to shove it up their ass and if they wouldn't negotiate in good faith we should take legal action. Our union agent...*who didn't really seem to be on our side*...repeated that that was a battle we probably wouldn't win and her suggestion was to take the money they were offering and learn to live with the other changes. The room started to stir. The agitation started to simmer and you could sense the bubbling under the crust... *this was bullshit...*

"...*THIS IS BULLSHIT*..." Hey was that my outside voice or inside voice? Wait a minute...*that wasn't my voice at all...*

"...excuse me Kelly..." The union agent peered over her bifocals.

"...no...I won't excuse you...what are we paying union dues for if when it's time to fight you guys aren't behind us?..." Kelly was standing up pointing at her and everyone quieted down to hear her.

"...it's not that we're not behind you...we just don't think this is..."

"...it doesn't matter what you think...**THIS IS OUR UNION**..."

"...**YEAH..**" Mahan yelled out from the back of the room.

"...**AND THIS IS OUR DECISION...**"

"...**YEAH...**" The whole room cheered.

"...**AND WE WANT TO FIGHT IT...**"

"...**YEAH...**" And the whole room went crazy wild. People started high-fiving each other...somebody yelled out **ATTICA**... the union agent shook her head in defeat as if to say "...all right okay...you win..." Rickie jumped up and hugged Kelly and I picked Ariel up and spun her around...Ariel yelled "...**PUT ME DOWN...**" and we both went over and hugged Kelly.

"...you fuckin' rock O'Brien..." Rickie yelled.

Kelly just laughed. "...who the fuck do I think I am?..."

✭ ✭ ✭

The whooping up of a revolutionary frenzy is one thing. Actually planning a revolution and seeing it through to its conclusion is a whole nother world. Kelly remained convinced that it could be done.

This time when we headed to Sully's after the meeting I drove up with Kelly and Rickie. All the way to the bar Kelly expounded on how disappointed she was in the union.

"…Margie O'Connor has always been an arrogant fuck but I have never been told the union is powerless…what the fuck?…"

"…no shit…" Rickie agreed. "…can't we have a vote of no confidence for her?…"

"…we could but not now with this going on…" Kelly stared through the traffic. I sat quietly in the backseat pissed off but unsure how to express it.

"…what the fuck Casey?…" Kelly was now staring through the rearview mirror at me.

"…I know…I'm pretty pissed off…"

"…so what are we going to do?…"

CRAP…serious pressure. "…I don't know Kelly…I was kind of hopin' you knew…"

"…so you're in for whatever I decide?…"

"…sure…I trust you…"

"…me too O'Brien…what are we setting on fire?…" *Rickie scares me sometimes.*

When we walked in the bar the union stewards called Kelly over to join them at their table. That was pretty impressive because the stewards were somewhat of a secret society. Discretion is vital when planning a revolution because nothing brings down a movement faster than baseless rumors.

Kelly acknowledged them and turned to me. "…can you get me a beer and bring it over?…"

"…yeah sure…"

When I brought the beer over Kelly stunned me by pulling out a chair and telling me to sit down. "…you guys don't mind if Casey sits in…"

I could tell from their faces that two of them did mind but Mahan beat them to the punch. "…no…Casey…sit down…maybe you'll learn something…" Mahan patted the back of the chair.

"…thanks guys…" I smiled at everyone as I sat down and then I shut up and didn't talk again.

"…so how about those mealy-mouth union fucks?…" Kelly pulled no punches.

"…yeah…I don't know…" Mahan chewed on his swizzle stick. "…we're going to have to cattle prod or set some asses on fire…"

"…well leave Margie for me…" Kelly curbed her anger. "…she may not want to be on board but she will be…we go back a ways…I guess I'll just have to remind her of a few things…"

"…I'm not worried about Margie…" One of the two spoke. "…it's keeping the ranks focused that scares me…"

"…I don't know…everyone seems pretty fired up…" The other of the two offered.

"…yeah tonight…" The first countered. "…but let a little time go by and everybody could start getting used to things…"

"…used to six-hour shifts and getting fired for calling in sick more than three times a year?…" Mahan retorted. "…are you going to get used to that and all the other shit they're coming up with?…"

"…no…"

"…all right then…the issues will keep people focused…" Mahan spun the rim of his rocks glass. "…and when the ranks need a kick in the ass we'll let Kelly at them…"

Kelly coolly nodded her head in the affirmative while all the other stewards chimed in with "…yeah Kelly you were awesome…" and "…you had me ready to kick some ass…"

"…okay…so then what we gotta start preparing for is the reality of a strike…" I tried hard not to look shaken when Mahan dropped the S-word.

"…agreed…" One of the two chimed in. "…we have to let NAA know we're ready…otherwise they'll never take us serious in negotiations…"

"…and there's nothing more pussy than throwing the strike word around and not meaning it…" the other of the two offered.

"…we'll mean it…" Mahan stared at me. "…right Casey?…"

"…right…"

...and I spoke no more...

CHAPTER 20-
A SOBERING EVENT

...Noah...an earthy crunchy kinda guy...proceeded to plant a vineyard...when he drank some of its wine...he became drunk and lied uncovered inside his tent...Ham saw his father's nakedness and told his two brothers outside that the old guy was soused again...but Shem and Japheth took a garment and laid it across their shoulders...then they walked in backward and covered their father's nakedness... their faces were turned the other way so that they would not see their father's nakedness because that was not a sight to behold...when Noah awoke from his wine and found out what his youngest son had done to him he said "...cursed be Ham and where the hell are my teeth?..." He also said "...blessed be the LORD...the God of Shem...and get me another glass of wine...'kay?..."

The next morning at work I was somewhat dragging from my previous night's extracurricular activities. Ariel had gone to the union meeting too but didn't join us at Sully's. Therefore she felt no pity for me in my vulnerable state. Not that I was looking for it but this is no easy job to have a hangover on.

Fortunately our morning started fairly easy so I had the opportunity to lie on the stretcher while we posted. That seemed to mean to Ariel that it was time to crank country music on the radio and...*oops*...occasionally pipe the Grand Ole Opry through the back speakers. When I asked her to start a line on me so I could do a rapid rehydration she got such an evil and sinister look on her face I decided against letting her jab at me with an eighteen-gauge needle. At one point I was just starting to doze off when I thought I heard her call dispatch and ask them if they had any calls we could do. I spun around on and scurried up the stretcher poking my head through to the cab. "…what the hell are you doing?…"

"…just kidding…" And she showed me her hand wasn't keying the mike.

"…no matter what I do you're going to torture me…aren't you?…"

"**…YES…**" she hollered "**…IT'S CALLED TOUGH LOVE…**"

"…I HATE YOU…" I tried to yell back but could only fall back. "…oh my head…"

"…FOUR-TEN…FOUR-ONE-ZERO…"

"…oh thank god…a call…something to divert your attention from abusing me…"

"…we'll see…four-ten…area of Harbor and Mass…"

"…FOUR-TEN TAKE THE PRIORITY ONE TO AREA IN FRONT OF AUDREY'S RESTAURANT 1876 MASS RD… ONE CAR MVA WITH PI… ADVISE IF YOU NEED SECOND TRUCK…"

"…four-ten received…" Ariel answered. "…huh…that's right up the road…"

"…yeah…" I wiggled myself through the cab over the glove boxes into the passenger seat making sure to move myself along by planting my hand on Ariel's shoulder and pulling. "…that's a lot of traffic for it just to be a one-car…"

"…ugh…easy…I'm fragile…"

"…oh please…"

We were literally right up the road yet oddly we didn't see traffic backing up like you'd expect. Mass Road is a really long four-lane street that runs through the BigCity business district and continues into some of the other local communities. Motor vehicle accidents usually instantly clog things up for miles. As we approached though it all became clear. It was a single-vehicle accident because the road and all its traffic curved and this single vehicle didn't. Instead he took the path directly through a fire hydrant and into a telephone pole. Amazingly he didn't knock the power lines down to the street because even after clearing out the hydrant he still hit the pole with so much amazing force that his body ended up thrown from the driver's seat...up and over the steering wheel and through the windshield. All of which left him lying bloody...twisted and prone on the hood of the car. Only his feet getting caught in the steering wheel kept him from completely clearing the passenger compartment of the vehicle.

"...ah...this isn't going to be a refusal..." Ariel moaned as we approached the carnage.

"...no...it's a transport..." I looked at the tipped-over hydrant and telephone pole bent and leaning. "...and we might want to get fire here for the hazards..."

"...I'll let dispatch know...go see if he's breathing..."

I gloved up...grabbed the O2 bag and approached the patient with extreme caution while four lanes of traffic continued to whirl by me...*I've come to fear a rogue hubcap flying off a car and decapitating me...*

"...he's breathing..." I yelled back to Ariel who was grappling with the longboard and collar. "...pulse is pretty thready though..." I snapped the O2 mask on him and turned the tank on high. It was a pretty easy extrication since kinetics had done most of the work for us. The hardest part was avoiding all the broken glass surrounding his broken body.

In the ambulance Ariel checked his blood pressure...*which was really low...*and I put him on the monitor.

"...he's gonna need two large lines..." Ariel scoped out the arm she was using for the BP. "...anything good on that side?..."

"...yeah...I see one..."

"…okay…I see one too…hand me that start kit…" Ariel re-inflated the BP cuff and used it as a tourniquet to start an IV on her side. I leaned over her to reach his left arm. It was something we felt very comfortable doing...*working much closer than most partners...*

"…is that you or the patient that smells like a gin mill?…" Well so much for closeness.

"…and what the hell would a proper Catholic girl like you know about the smell of a gin mill?…"

"…okay…who smells like the Brewery?…I've had lunch there…"

"…I get it…I don't know who…why don't you tell me…"

"…maybe it's William Parsons…" Ariel had discovered the patient's wallet while cutting off his pants. "…I'll give you the benefit of the doubt…"

"…thanks oh gracious one…how old is he?…"

"…birthday's in '45…" Ariel scrunched her forehead and subtracted. "…52…he's an organ donor…"

"…not yet…"

"…no…true…oh man his pressure is low…what's the rhythm?…"

I stared at the monitor. "…sinus tach about 150…154…160… yeah call it 160…"

"…he's pretty crunched in the lower extremities…let's put the trousers on him…"

"…for real?…are you kidding?…" I cringed at the thought of having to pull out the trousers from the bench seat compartment. The trousers or MAST pants…Military Anti-Shock Trousers…as they were also known…were a very little used device that the state mandated we keep on the rig...*kind of the appendix of ambulance equipment...*They were designed in the tradition of the fighter pilot pants that adjusted for g-forces and kept the pilot from passing out. They work by inflating and constricting blood flow in the lower extremities thereby keeping more blood in the body's core and cerebral areas. That stabilizes the pilot's blood pressure and prevents syncope. Back in the day someone thought that concept would translate well for trauma patients who had low blood pressure or hypotension because of massive blood loss. The idea was to squish what was left to the vital organs. Unfortunately over time nasty side effects were discovered...*and by discovered I mean some poor asshole had to suffer from them so they could be noted and passed along...*when the pants were left on for any length of time. You see...sometimes with trauma patients things are so bad you have to make some ugly choices. What we do for you today will save your life but very well may leave you with untoward effects. In keeping with that theme...the MAST pants could cause compartment syndrome in the patient's compressed tissue of the lower extremities. Then they have to have an escharotomy or in other words be surgically cut to keep their skin from exploding. Those nasty side effects mean you don't just casually throw the trousers on anyone. You wanna make damn sure there's a good reason you're going to make someone's skin explode.

"...no...we can inflate till they crackle for pelvic stabilization and they'll be on if his pressure drops much more..." Ariel was right. This probably was the one good use left for MAST pants. Inflating just until the nylon started making a crackling sound would make a lower extremity air splint that would help us manage his crushed bones more efficiently and if his pressure dropped much more ruptured skin would be the least of his problems. I dove in the bench seat and came out with the dusty box. Ariel cleared away what was left of his cut-off clothes and we slid the Velcro nylon pants under his waist. I opened all the leg flaps while Ariel adhered the pelvic portion.

"…how are we supposed to get his legs in here?…" I was perplexed by the many angles in the lower limbs.

"…you're gonna have to straighten them out a bit…"

"…WHAT?…straighten them out a bit?…" I was sure she was kidding.

"…yeah…grab 'em…straighten them out…not a lot…just enough to get them to fit…"

"…you're serious?…"

"…yeah…" Normally the thought of it all may have been fun but on a hangover I was not looking forward to the quiver that would run up my spine. Oh well…I couldn't look weak in front of Ariel. I reached down and grabbed behind the patient's left knee and ankle and pulled slightly…the bones crunched and grinded in my hands…waves of nausea rolled through my body***…oh god…***The patient was mercifully unconscious so I truly had the worse end of it. But I learned a long time ago that you can't puke if you hum.

"…hum hummm hum hum…"

"…how's that feel?…" Ariel started laughing because she knew why I was humming *The Smurf's* song. "…now do the right…"

I repeated the process again still maintaining my will not to let her see me squeamish. In fact I just kept smiling and saying how cool it was***…didn't she want to give it a try?…***

"…no…not at all…and if you're all set…I'll drive to the hospital now…"

"…I'm good…" And as soon as she was up front I broke open two ice packs and smacked them on my face***…ahhhh…nausea relief…***The one good thing about nausea though is it makes you sweat and sweating helps pass a hangover. As soon as the call was done I downed a thirty-two-ounce Gatorade and a Milky Way and felt much better. Ariel still gave me a bunch of crap for the rest of the day but it just didn't sound as loud. And as luck would have it the end of the shift allowed me the opportunity to see Ariel get some of her temperance comeuppance.

Right around dusk we got sent to another of the long four-lane streets that runs through the city for a guy hit by a car. Once again we found ourselves dodging crazy drivers to help some poor slob who got biffed by a Cadillac. Seems the dude had lost his driver's license to a DUI a few months ago so he was reduced to running across the four-lane street from his apartment to the closest package store. It was dusk…he was wearing dark clothes and the driver of the Caddy had already been to his package store…*bad trifecta…*

So while the cops walked the Caddy driver through the field sobriety test we evaluated our patient. He was actually pretty lucky because the Caddy had started to stop and barely clipped him below the left knee. He was fairly scraped up but the only significant trauma was to his left leg. Ariel had cut the shoelaces off his construction boots but got an uneasy feeling when she tried taking it off.

"…he's got a pretty significant fracture…" She pulled her gloved fingers out of his boot covered in blood. "…let's pad it with some gauze and use the boot as a splint…"

"…sounds good…here's some gauze…" I handed Ariel a wad. "…how about morphine?…"

"…uh…not so sure…" Ariel looked at the patient. "…how much have you had to drink today?…"

"…just a six-pack…" The guy answered unabashedly.

"…oh…just a six-pack…" Ariel looked at me and shook her head. I agreed. We pulled the stretcher out and got the guy loaded up but when we started rolling toward the ambulance he got agitated.

"…hey my beer…"

"…your what?…" Ariel spoke from the foot of the stretcher.

"...my beer...I just bought a case...I only had one..." And the guy started flailing around like he was going to roll off the stretcher and keep going until he reached his beer. "...don't leave my beer..."

Ariel did not seem the least bit interested in the detour but I figured what the hell...the guy did pay a pretty good price for it. He should at least get to enjoy it later. "...I'll get it...just let us get you in the ambulance first..."

"...thanks man...I appreciate it..."

"...no problem..." So we got him secured and I went back and found the case of cans resting against the sidewalk. They too had sustained significant trauma as the cardboard box was fractured and one beer had bled all over the others secondary to a penetration injury. I scooped them up as best I could and tossed them on the floor of the ambulance at the foot of the stretcher. Ariel helped me button up a few details with the patient and then she scurried off to drive.

My good deed guaranteed I was the patient's new best friend and he really was feeling no pain so I settled in for an easy transport and started my paperwork. We were casually chatting away when Ariel got to the part of the four-lane street that narrowed quickly to two lanes and a sharp right turn. She took it just a wee bit too fast and everything in the ambulance shifted hard to the left. The monitor slid...the BP cuff landed on the floor...I shifted hard on the bench seat and the patient's foot fell off the end of his leg. Well... *not completely off...* There were still some tendons...muscle and a shoelace holding it together but that's about it. I was sober and it took a moment for it to sink in. Fortunately the patient was a little farther behind and I had a chance to get Ariel's attention.

"...uhhhhhhh Aire..."

"...yeah?..." She adjusted the rearview mirror to see me.

"...can you pull over?..."

"…hey my foot…"

"…yes sir…I know…"

"…I'm on the highway…"

"…I don't care…"

"…but my foot fell off…"

"…yes sir…**BUT MY PARTNER'S GOING TO PULL OVER AND WE'RE GOING TO PUT IT BACK ON…**" I made eye contact with Ariel and she got it. Unfortunately we weren't just on the highway. We were also on the part of the highway that ran parallel with Orchard Hill so when Ariel came around and opened the back doors of the ambulance all the beer cans that had also shifted in their fractured cardboard came rolling out into her arms. It was quite the sight to see her trying to catch and juggle a case of beer pouring out of the back of our ambulance in the breakdown lane of a busy highway. Several carloads of young males took the time to beep their horns in approval and hang out the window of their cars waving at her…*hey babe… we're partying too…*She was clearly mortified but still did an admirable job of beer can recovery. Eventually she climbed back in to the ambulance with her arms full of brew and we were able to flip the patient's foot back up where it belonged and better secure it. The humorous consequence of Ariel's rescue was her getting covered in beer from head to toe. I didn't have to say a word. Everybody at the Valley Trauma noticed right away and all of them took the opportunity to turn Ariel an ever deepening darker shade of red. I got a particular charge out of it when Kelly wheeled by the door with her patient and yelled "…damn Skippy…you smell like a brewery…"

Ariel whipped around and shrieked at me "…I told you that name better not stick…"

I threw my hands up awash in laughter…

…I control no one…

CHAPTER 21-
A SHOT IN THE DARK

...blessed are the peacemakers for they will inherit the earth...

one day Ariel and I were hanging out in the ER enjoying free air-conditioning...

"...we should clear up...other trucks are coming in..." Ariel leaned back in her chair which did little to convince me she was serious.

"...there's plenty of coverage..." I reassured her. "...besides... they need to get used to the idea of minimal trucks if we strike..."

"...what?..." Ariel spun around. "...nobody's going to strike... we can't afford it..."

"...I don't know..." I shrugged my shoulders too tired to argue. Then Fergie and Jodie came in with a patient and soon joined us in the tech room.

"...hey guys...what's up?..." Fergie pulled up a chair at the table and set down her paperwork book.

"...Casey...Skippy..." Jodie patted me on the back and Ariel scowled.

"...what's up?..." I playfully swung at Jodie.

"...did you guys hear about Mark Tucker?..." Jodie spoke while Fergie wrote.

"...no...what happened?..."

"...he got fired this morning..." Jodie sat on the counter.

"...what'd he do?..." Ariel asked.

"...he decked a patient..."

"...what?..." I sat forward. "...who'd he hit?..."

"...some asshole drunk he was c-spining who kept grabbing at his face..." Jodie continued.

"…he hit some guy that was tied to a board?…" Ariel was perturbed.

"…no…he hit some dirtbag that wouldn't let him secure him to the board…" Jodie fired back.

"…I didn't think you got fired for hitting a patient…" I sarcastically offered.

"…what?…are you high?…" Ariel missed the sarcasm.

"…no…actually I've seen a bunch of patients get smacked… nobody ever got fired…"

"…that's because nobody got videoed by the local news…" Fergie picked her head up from her paperwork. Ariel and I just stared. "…yeah…that's why he got fired…he got bagged…"

"…well I guess we should make sure we watch the news tonight…" Ariel laughed.

The funny thing was you didn't have to watch it that night. It was on many times that week and twice in a super spotlight news highlight on the weekend. It didn't take a genius to realize this would have some consequences for everyone. Obviously it was the talk of NAA and it didn't take long for the community to chirp in. The good news was that all he did was punch a drunken white boy so the race issue never came up but it did still stir quite the controversy. It got editorial coverage in the newspaper… community leaders made statements and NAA announced immediately that the paramedic had been fired. Somehow all the homeless people who regularly called for ambulance transport saw the clip. For about a week every time you approached one on a scene they would roll around on the ground and start screaming "…oh please ambulance driver…don't hit me…" Since the homeless usually congregated on the court house lawns by the benches where all the lawyers ate lunch it was usually worth a good laugh from the crowd.

The controversy also extended to our truck where it turned out Ariel and I disagreed on the overall issue at hand. Should we ever hit patients? I know it sounds simple enough but think about it. Would you go to work and let someone hit you...spit at you... pinch you...swat at you...not to mention the plethora of names we get called...and not feel tempted to swing back?

Plus I knew I wasn't completely innocent. One time Blossom and I did a call at a sleazy hotel in LittleCity. Some dirtbag crackhead had fallen and split his head open on his nightstand. When we got to the room one of his other dirtbag friends was kind enough to let us know he was HIV positive. I always protected myself on calls like everybody in the world has HIV because you really can't tell by looking but the heads up is a courteous move. The patient wasn't so friendly though and despite my best efforts to establish diplomatic exchanges he just kept telling me to fuck off. Well... normally I would have loved to have just fucked off but he was drunk and bleeding from his head so it wasn't just about my innate desire to serve humanity. There would also be some serious legal ramifications if I just fucked off so I opted for the "let's move this thing along" option. When I went to help him stand up he screamed "...FUCK OFF CUNT..." and whipped his head around...*I believe*...with the intent to spray me with his HIV infected blood. That really pissed me off and without thinking I lunged at the guy. It was only Blossom's quick response to pull me back that kept me from actually commencing a beating. And how smart would that have been?...*making an HIV person bleed more..*

I don't know if I was right or wrong for that but I do know for certain that I never really thought about it at the time. It was just a reaction from a perceived threat and who could be held liable for that?

Ariel saw it completely different. You just never ever had a good reason to aggressively touch someone and if you did your job right you would never even think you had a reason. I don't know…but she seemed very convinced.

Word around the ranks was pretty consistent…a dirtbag's a dirtbag and sometimes you gotta pop 'em. What Tucker did wrong was not clear the perimeter first to make sure he wasn't being watched by the wrong eyes. For example…the eyes of a local news crew or neighbors peering through their windows. The cops and firefighters didn't care though. Hell…we covered for them enough. One time Ariel and I took a patient out of a bar fight. He was pretty lumped up and the cop who was first on scene to the bar fight had corresponding divots in his knuckles. I didn't ask questions and I didn't pass judgment but I did take care of the cop before the lumped-up guy and I told the lumped-up guy to shut up every time he yelled police brutality and who knows…maybe the cop was wrong. Sometimes the cops were wrong but I still trusted them a whole lot more than the dirtbags and like Jodie says…if you want the cops to back you up you gotta back them up.

☆ ☆ ☆

Later that week I ran into Kelly in front of an ER vending machine. She pulled three quarters out of her pocket and stared at the choices. "…what's up Casey?…"

"…not much…crazy day…" I secretly voted for M&M's and a potential sharing.

"…I was talking to Fergie last week…"

"…she still trying to touch your state patch?…"

"…I cut one off an old uniform shirt and gave it to her…" *she chose C6.*

"…very good…" *damn…Fritos.*

"…so she told me you are about to be homeless…"

"…yeah…landlord's selling the house…blah blah blah…"

"…that sucks…"

"…uh-huh…"

"…so why don't you move in with me and Rickie?…"

"…really?…"

"…uh-huh…"

"…FOUR-TWENTY…FOUR-TWO-ZERO…"   Kelly's portable squawked and she answered.

"…four-twenty…"

"…FOUR-TWENTY…FOUR-TWO-ZERO…TAKE   THE PRIORITY THREE TO COURT SQUARE AREA OF FOR THE WOMAN YELLING AT PEOPLE…"

"…oh for fuck's sake…spring is in the air…" She keyed the radio. "…four-twenty received…" She clipped the radio back on her belt. "…I gotta go…but we'll talk…"

…sa-weet…

☆ ☆ ☆

The union faced a serious dilemma with the Mark Tucker situation. NAA fired him without hesitation even though rumors swirled that he had never actually hit the patient but punched the board next to his head. The video was just vague enough that maybe you could see that as plausible. General consensus however remained that he clocked the guy and from that moment forward a blow to the head was forever known as a Tucker and a patient receiving a blow to the head became Tuckered out.

Unfortunately though…the union was already faced with the potential PR nightmare of a strike…it was in no position to deal with more bad press. Still they had no choice. No matter what the videotape showed they had to grieve the termination or risk being cited for failure to represent. Fighting it though would be an ugly battle while we had the bigger fight for legitimacy raging.

Then about a week later Ariel and I were eating dinner in a D'Angelos with a TV. We were munching away on turkey wraps and the local news played in the background. I had my back to the TV and hardly noticed and Ariel barely gave it more than a passing glance. I got on one of my kicks about the government not being able to handle simple drug laws so how could we possibly trust them with the death penalty when I noticed Ariel's eyes drift upward.

"…don't roll your eyes at me Skippy…just because you good Catholic's like to strap a human down and juice them…"

"…the Pope is opposed to the death penalty…"

"…don't try to defend him…and I gotta think Jesus has his issues with it too…"

"…isn't that Kelly O'Brien?…"

"…where?…in the parking lot?…" I strained to look out the window.

"…no…on the news…"

I turned to look. "…yeah…that is…and she's not doing a call…"

We got up from our table and stood closer to the TV. Ariel reached up and turned up the volume.

"…Paramedic Kelly O'Brien answers these questions… Kelly…how long have you worked in BigCity?…"

"…fifteen years…"

"…she looks good…" Ariel observed.

"…yes she does…"

Ariel rolled her eyes.

"…what's important for people to understand is that this is a poor representation of the work being done every day in the city by very talented dedicated people…"

"…this has got to be in response to Tucker…" I offered and Ariel agreed.

"…working in the city providing life-sustaining services is extraordinarily challenging and every day hundreds of people receive these services in safe and efficient ways…"

"…she makes us sound pretty awesome…"

"…unfortunately the actions of one can overshadow the actions of all but I would hate to see people lose sight of the great work being done by the emergency services providers in BigCity…"

Kelly's segment wrapped up and we went back to our sandwiches.

"…that was good but I don't know if it helps…" Ariel picked up her pickle.

"…it's gotta help…" I adjusted my wrapper. "…I don't know if it's enough but it helps…"

☆ ☆ ☆

later that night I had another strange dream…

*I was riding my bike with some chick that I don't know. It was beautiful out. The sun was warm and shining on our faces and the spring air was freshly laced with honeysuckle and hay. The chick was riding next to me and we were cruising down the bike trail. She was beautiful…a female Adonis…She didn't talk much though and seemed content just looking at me and smiling occasionally. That was okay though…**she was hot…***

*Together we rode into a tunnel where the white cement walls were dotted with yellow recessed lights and the dimly acoustic walls held the hypnotic pedaling and occasional click of derailleurs. The tunnel lasted a while and my eyes began to focus to the darkness…**THEN IT GOT REALLY BRIGHT…**I had to close my eyes…it hurt so bad…and when I opened them the light was gone. Relief flooded my retinas and as the disorientation passed I realized the chick was riding her bike in front of me. At least I assumed those were her white socks pedaling up and down…**that's all I could see…***

For some reason the chick pulled out of her lane...**maybe to leave me behind**...but little did she know there was someone coming the other way. Oh well...it didn't come to affect her because she abruptly cut back into our lane and left the other person to react...and react they did...**right into me**...Our front wheels rubbed and the following chain reaction was explosive. I hurdled over my handle bars...the other biker was pitched off-road...

You never really appreciate how hard asphalt is until you smack it and skid three feet...I couldn't move...I couldn't scream...Hell...I couldn't even breathe...I just lay there hoping the chick would help...she just rode coldly into the darkness...

...I think she was over me...

CHAPTER 22 -
A GOOD MOVE

...when Jesus came into Peter's house he saw Peter's mother-in-law lying in bed with a fever...he touched her hand and the fever left her and she got up and began to wait on him...this has never happened to me...

"...therefore...anyone who turns in three or more incomplete run forms in a three-month period will be subject to the progressive disciplinary process..." The Borg representative stood before us in the training room. "...and by complete you are to include a patient's signature on all run forms...no signature... incomplete paperwork...incomplete paperwork...progressive discipline..."

"...and when our patient is dead?..." Jodie looked to be in a feisty mood.

"...I'm sure there would be a family member present who could sign..."

"...really?..." She adjusted her posture. "...so the next time I code some squeazy OD in an alley off Main Street I should find a parent or legal guardian to sign?..." *the Borg stuttered.* "... because in all your relevant street experience that's how it is?..." *the Borg stammered.*

"...Casey..." I heard someone call my name. "...Casey...get over here..." I turned in my chair to see Kelly calling me from the back door of the training room...*of course I obeyed...*

"...hey....what's up?..." I slid through the door. "...why aren't you in the training class?..."

"...please..." Kelly mocked annoyance. "...who am I if not someone who gets out of stupid training classes?..."

"...I wish you'd write a book..."

"…maybe someday…a manifesto at least…" Kelly laughed. "…so I have a key for you…"

"… a key?…"

"…yeah…a key that unlocks the doors to our house…" She pulled it from her pocket and handed it to me. "…you're moving in…right?…"

"…ahhhh…" I spoke eloquently for a moment and then Kelly interrupted.

"…what's the holdup Casey?…"

"…well we never talked details…like the rent or parking…"

"…we have a driveway…and here's your part of the rent…" Kelly took out a pen and paper…wrote something down and slid it on the counter to me.

"…wow…this is less than I'm paying now and I park on the street…"

"…so you're in?…"

"…yeah…when can I move in?…"

"…how fast can you load your Jeep?…"

"…see ya Saturday…"

✫ ✫ ✫

scenes from a parking lot…

"…I think we might have finally helped one…"

"…you think so Aire?…"

"…yeah she's a smart girl…she doesn't want her baby's father doing drugs and she's out of the house now…"

"…yeah…but who says she'll stay out?…"

"…she will…I feel it…the ER's going to help her…they're going to hook her up with the right people…"

"…I hope so…I hope you're right…something about 18 y/o pregnant girls who want to kill themselves because their boyfriends smoke crack and beat them depresses me…"

✿ ✿ ✿

"…Casey…wassup?…" Rickie glided between the parked ambulances.

"…not much…wassup with you?…" I paused from my inventory.

"…is that Rickie?…" Ariel stuck her head out of the truck.

"…oh hey Ariel…" Rickie greeted her. "…so Casey…"

"…yes Rickie?…"

"…I hear you're moving in…"

"…yeah…sometime this weekend…" I felt Ariel's eyes upon me.

"…awesome…well I got Sunday off if you want a hand…"

"…yeah…that'd be great…I'll give you a call…"

"…cool…see ya chicas…"

"…bye Rick…"

"…later…"

✿ ✿ ✿

"…so I heard the union dodged a bullet…" Jodie joined us at the time clock.

"…why won't this damn thing ever acknowledge my employee number?…" I swiped and swiped again.

"…what bullet was that?…" Ariel was punched in and calm.

"…Mark Tucker decided to accept his termination and not ask the union to grieve it…"

"…MOTHERFUCKER NOW I'M GOING TO BE LATE…" Ariel and Jodie ignored me.

"…turns out he was going to engineering school in the fall anyway so he made it simple on everyone and agreed to go away…"

"…good…that saves us some huge embarrassment…"

"…got that right…now we can focus on negotiations…"

"...THAT'S IT...WHERE'S THE GODDAMN SUPERVISOR?..."

"...CALM DOWN..." Ariel bellowed.

"...CALM DOWN?...THIS HAPPENED TO ME TWICE LAST WEEK AND THEY DOCKED ME TWO HOURS OF OVERTIME...I'M NOT CALMING DOWN..."

"...I know you're perturbed and all but don't feel too bad..." Jodie offered. "...Diane in dispatch hasn't been paid in two weeks..."

"...what?..." Ariel leaned forward.

"...yeah..." Jodie continued "...she's supposed to have direct deposit but her checks just don't show up...supervisor's probably on the phone with corporate trying to find them..."

"...unfucking believable..." I threw my hands up. "...well then I guess my two piddly hours don't mean much..."

"...only to you..." Jodie smiled and walked away.

✲ ✲ ✲

so there we were in a parking lot...

"...so you found a new apartment?..." Ariel broke in to conversation.

"...huh...what?...four-ten...we got a call?..." I was asleep***... or at least had been.*** "...what?..."

"...apartment...you found a new apartment..."

"...yes..." I wiped drool from the corner of my mouth. "... no...not an apartment...I'm moving in with Kelly and Rickie in their house..."

"...which room?..."

"...my room..." I struggled to focus. "...you woke me up for this?..."

"...yes..."

"...why?..."

"...I'm worried about you..."

"…I'm touched…but really…why?…"

"…I'm worried about you…you're fairly impressionable and they party a lot…"

"…fairly impressionable?…" I sat up straight wondering if I was still asleep and dreaming. "…what are you talking about?…"

"…I'm worried about you…let's just leave it at that…"

"…okay…" I stared at the windshield for a minute. "…what are you afraid is going to happen?…"

"…I just don't want to see you get hurt…"

"…from partying too much?…"

"…no…from partying too much while you have the feelings you have for Kelly…"

"…I'm okay with that…"

"…you are?…"

"…yeah…I'm used to being around someone I love and can't have…" Ariel looked puzzled. "…you…I'm with you all the time…in fact even after I move in I'll still be around you more than Kelly or Rickie…"

"…you love me?…"

"…duh…you love me don't you?…"

"…yeah…but not like that…"

"…I know…I get it…that's why I'm used to being around someone I love and can't have…"

Ariel got quiet for a minute…I shifted in my seat attempting to get comfortable and then she blurted out "…so who do you love more?…me or Kelly?…"

"…are you kidding me?…" Ariel just smiled. "…you…of course…"

"…good answer…" She seemed pleased with herself.

"…oh sure…like there was a choice…"

…this being the cross I bear…

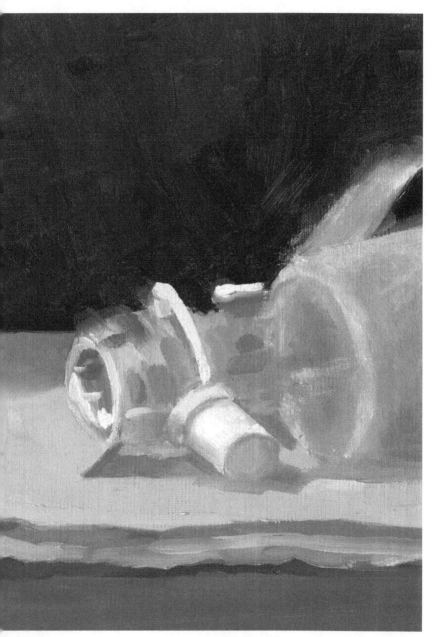

...still life...

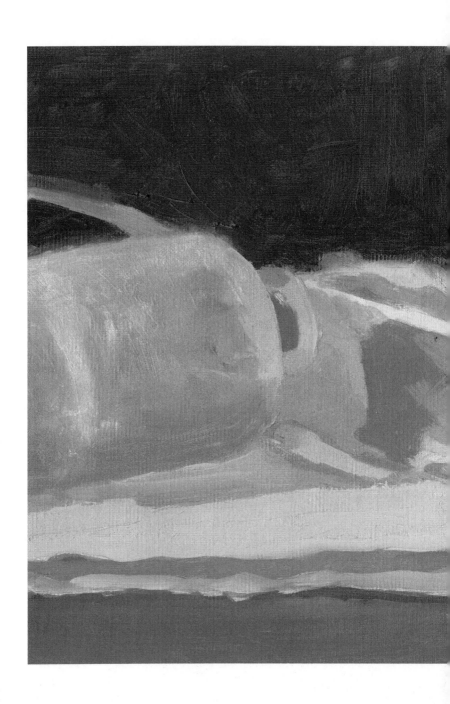

CHAPTER 23-
THE LAND OF SODOM AND GOMORRAH

...early the next morning Abraham got up and returned to the place where he had stood before the God of EMS...he looked down toward Sodom and Gomorrah...toward all the land of the plain...and he saw dense smoke rising from the land...like smoke from a furnace...like some righteous weed dude...

and so I moved in...

"...so is there anything I need to know about living here?..." Rickie made couscous through the inquisition.

"...uhhhhhh...." She stirred...thought and stared up. "...no... nothing I can think of..."

"...you sure?...no hidden shower quirks or rules about forbidden spoons?..."

"...forbidden spoons?..." She was truly shocked. "...well actually...when I first moved in I thought there'd be more sex..."

"...more sex?..." I was truly shocked.

"...yeah but living with two lesbians hasn't made a difference..."

"...no?..."

"...no...and it's been disappointing..."

"...well...you know us lesbians..."

"...I thought I did..." she stirred some more. "...turns out... not so much..."

...is it hot in here?...

☆ ☆ ☆

...and together we smoked a lot of pot...

"...okay...here's one..." My eyes were squinty red. "...what are you gonna do if NAA decides to drop the ol' whiz quiz on us?..."

"...surrender and beg for rehab..." Kelly picked up her lighter. "...you know... the ol' 'I'm sorry...I'm sorry...please let me go clean...'" Kelly believed she meant it.

"...this is my favorite show..." Rickie stared at the third rock.

"...nah...'cause then you gotta really go clean...." I accepted the bong from Kelly. "...because then they are going to pop test your ass...every week..."

"...is that the chick from *Saturday Night?*..."

"...sit a little closer to the TV why don't ya..." Kelly whipped a pillow at Rickie's head.

"...man...the government sucks..." I felt my communism rise. "...first they ban the shit and then they make it practically impossible for decent people like us to enjoy it.....................
...."

Rickie turned to Kelly…

"………………………………………………………………………we got any chips?…"

"…WOOWWW…that was intense…huh?…" Kelly slapped my leg and laughed.

…uh-huh…

~~~~⋀⋀⋀~~~~~~~~~~⌃~~~~⋀~~~⋀⋀⋀~~~~~~~~

"…so me and Rickie went to a movie last night…" I grabbed a towel and gave Kelly a hand with the dishes.

"…yeah… what did you see?…"

"…she wanted to see *The Birdcage*…"

"…really?…" Kelly shook her head. "…I can never figure her out…"

I continued drying. "…it was a good movie…"

"…oh I'm sure…hand me that Brillo pad…" She continued scouring.

"…and it was nice 'cause after we got to hang out and talk… and we've never really done that before…"

"…uh-huh…"

"…I like her philosophy…"

"…which one?…WAHOO let's party?…"

"…well…yeah that one too…but I was referring to her philosophy on stress…"

"…and it is…"

"…she doesn't have any…she can't be bothered with it…"

"…hmmm…"

"…yeah…she figures not much happening today is going to mean anything in ten years so why stress about it now…"

"…I see…" Kelly stopped scrubbing for a second. "…you know…she also smokes a lot of pot…"

"…well yeah…there's that too…"

✧ ✧ ✧

"…Casey…this is an awesome ceiling…" Rickie popped in my room on her way from the bathroom. "…are those fluorescent paint stars?…"

"…yeah…I got a kit at the A to Z Science Store…" I was laying on my futon with my room lit by the glow of my television. "…it comes with a stencil you tack up to the ceiling and fill in with the paint…this is a summer sky…" I stared at the many constellations.

"…this is fucking awesome…" Rickie came in and lied on my futon. "…turn the TV off…"

"…but it's *Xena*…"

"…please…"

"…all right…" I clicked the remote and the room got very dark except for the glowing luminaries.

Rickie stretched out and crossed her legs. "…this is fuckin' cool…"

"…Casey I brought up the socks you left on the laundry table…" Kelly knocked and entered quickly. "…boy it's dark in here…"

"…hey O'Brien…" Rickie chirped from the darkness. "…close the door…"

"…oh my god I'm sorry…" Kelly seemed very startled and in the shadows I saw her cover her eyes and bolt. She closed the door behind her.

"…I meant stay on this side…" Rickie yelled but Kelly was gone. A minute went by.

"…I think she thinks we were fooling around…" I offered.

"…yeah?…"

"…yeah…"

"…AHHAHAHAHAHAHAHAHAHAHAHAHAHAHAHA HAHA…"

"…you don't have to laugh so hard…"

"…sorry Casey…" *pause* "…awesome stars…"

…thanks…

✲ ✲ ✲

"…Kelly…" I rustled around the papers on the kitchen table.

"…yes Casey…" She poured herself a coffee.

"…do you have that paper we were writing on last night?…"

"…no…I threw it away…"

"…what?…you threw it away?…why?…"

"…because I read it this morning and it was not funny…"

"…we laughed last night…"

"…we were very drunk last night…"

"…oh…I thought we had something…"

"…I know…." She sipped. "…but we didn't…"

…damn that just doesn't seem fair…

✲ ✲ ✲

"…so I'm thinking of writing a book about our place…" I grabbed my notebook out of my backpack.

"…what place?…" Rickie argued with the toaster oven.

"…our house…"

"…oh yeah?…am I in it?…"

"…absolutely…you'd be Stacy…the wonton chick…" Rickie laughed and I continued. "…*La chica de Amor*…"

She   laughed   harder.   "…*la   chica   de   Amor*….
A H H A H A H A H A H A A H A H A H A H A
HAHAHAHAHAHAAHAHAHAHAHAHAHHA…hey…can my name be something else besides Stacy?…"

…oh sure…

✼ ✼ ✼

"…you know what?…" Rickie spread the jam on her potato bread. "…my neck never gets any rest…" *so far she appeared serious.* "…because it always has to hold my head up…"

"…AH HAHAHAHAHA AHHHH HAHAHAHAHA HAAA AAAH HAAA HAHAHAHAHA HAHAHAHAHAHAH AHAH AHAHAHHH…are you serious?…"

"…well yeah…"

"…what do you think my neck does all day?…"

"…oh yeah…yours must be tired too…"

…and they give her a drug box…

✼ ✼ ✼

so one night Kelly made pot brownies…

"…hurry up Casey…*The X-Files* is starting…" I hear Kelly open and close the oven door.

"…coming…" I fly down the stairs and slide across the floor to the couch. "…I love it when Scully yells for a medic…and I imagine she waits for me…"

"…of course you do…here…they're still warm…"

"….wow…that's huge…" I stared at the chocolate mass. "…I've never done this before…should I only have half?…"

"…you're not mainlining heroin Casey…you'll be fine…"

"….okay…" I gobbled it up. "…oh man…this tastes awesome…"

"…extra chocolate chips…" Kelly partook herself.

"…when's Rickie getting home?…"

"…her shift was over at 20:00…she should be home anytime now…"

"…well hopefully she gets one while they're still…………………"

"…hey…can I have a brownie?…"

"…Rickie…when did you get home?…"

"…just before *The X-Files*…."

"…no way…"

"…yeah…I said 'helloooooo…I'm home…' and nobody heard me…"

Kelly and I looked at each other. "…. AHH HAA AHAAHAHAHAHAHAHA HAHAHAHAHAHA HAHAHA HAHAHAHAHAH…"

…maybe Ariel was right to be worried…

✷ ✷ ✷

"…you know…" I rolled on Rickie's futon. "…people at work think it's scary we all live together…"

Rickie's eyes got big in the wall mirror and she applied her mascara… "…it is scary" *she hummed a little tune.* "…owww I poked myself…" I rolled off the futon laughing…

…how did I get so lucky?…

CHAPTER 24 -
JUST DON'T TRUST THEM

*...you have heard that it was said "...love your union and
hate management..." But I tell you "...love management
and pray for those who will not negotiate in good faith with
you that you may be sons of your Father the God of EMS...
he causes his sun to rise on the evil and the good and sends
rain on the righteous and the unrighteous...if you love those
who love you...what reward will you get?...is not even the IRS
doing that?...and if you greet only your union brothers...what
are you doing more than others?...do not even scabs do that...*

Contract negotiations with corporate began and once again
hope sprang eternal that resolution was on the horizon. Well...
maybe nothing that optimistic. Negotiations began and we all
hoped that at the very least NAA would meet with our team and
sit down for reasonable conversation. I was in the NAA break
room when the negotiating team gathered to carpool to their first
negotiating session. They all looked sharp in their suits and ties
but they also had a hint of terror subtly running through their
countenance. Even Mahan was a little bit quieter...not much but
it was still pretty eerie. I wished them all luck and they thanked
me. Then Kelly came in and pulled Mahan to the side. They talked
quietly...laughed pretty heartily and parted ways. The guys all left
and Kelly turned to walk down the hallway to the admin wing.

"...Casey...get over here..."

"...what's up?..." I scurried to catch up with her.

"...what's your status right now?...you working?..."

"...no...my shift just ended..."

"...excellent..." She opened the door and we entered
the admin wing. "...I'm doing a little recon work and I need a
lookout..."

"…a lookout?…"

"…yeah…I gotta get something from Sommers' office and he's probably on his way in…"

"…and you don't have an appointment?…"

Kelly broke toward the operations manager's office. "…no…I didn't make an appointment to rifle through his desk…"

"…oh…" It came into focus. "…yeah…that makes sense…"

"…stay here and keep an eye out…" She positioned me ten feet from the office door leaving me a full view of the front door. "…have an excuse ready for being here and talk loud enough so I know the jig is up…you good?…" I barely digested it. "…good… remember…loud…" And she was off into the dark doorway.

Naturally my heart raced immediately and the corresponding sympathetic nervous system response was for my lips to dry and stick to my teeth. That made it even trickier to talk to the non-Sommers management people who walked by and wondered if I was lost. I didn't want to talk too loudly and give a false tip-off so that led to cotton-mouth-mumbling followed by a bellowed "… oh hey…there's Jim Sommers…" when he appeared at the front door. How that didn't buy me an instant piss test is beyond me.

"…Ms. Casey…how are you today?…" Jim was his usual professional self.

"…not bad Jim…how're things for you?…" I attempted to maneuver my body between him and his door.

"…good…can't complain…" He looked puzzled and darted around me.

"…so I was wondering if you have a minute…"

"…sure…just let me get in my office and settle in a bit…" And just like that he was in the door.

Crap…there was only one door in so Kelly had to still be in there. I paused for a second waiting for Jim to start questioning a discovered Kelly…*but nothing happened*…I was confused and really unsure what to do next. Then it hit me...a truly inspired thought.

"...JIM...JIM COME HERE..." I started moving toward the front door.

"...what?...what is it?..." Jim was a bit perturbed as he came back to the hallway.

"...I think you left your headlights on..." I continued toward the front door.

"...my headlights?..." His tone softened.

"...yeah...isn't that your car?..." I pointed to the far end of the parking lot where unfortunately there were no cars with headlights on.

"...no...my car's parked down there..." Jim pointed to the other end of the parking lot and never noticed.

"...oh...okay...sorry..." I sheepishly laughed. "...I'll go check in dispatch..."

Jim gave me a weird sideways glance and continued back to his office. Kelly was now walking down the hallway. "...hey Kelly what's up?..."

"...not much Jim..." *she was amazingly casual.* "...you look tired..."

"...first thing in the morning and your buddy Casey's wearin' me out..." Jim shot a distrustful look my way. I smiled back and looked at Kelly.

"...someone in dispatch left their lights on...I'm gonna go check it out..."

Kelly shook her head up and down. "...sounds good Casey... good luck with that..." and I was off. To make it look good I actually walked through dispatch...said hi to everyone and then bolted out the back door that cut through the training room back to the break room. When I got there Kelly was waiting.

"…good fucking job Casey…" She was smiling. "…we got what we needed and it went off without a hitch…"

I smiled from ear to ear...*also quite pleased with myself.* "…so what did we risk life and limb for?…"

"…statistics for negotiations…" She held up sheets of computer paper.

"…statistics…as in math?…" I paused. "…I risked my life for math?…hmmm…"

"…you didn't really risk your life…and yes…for math… math that we're going to need when they pull out their load of crap numbers in negotiations…these are the numbers they don't want us to have…" She tucked the papers in her backpack and pulled out a bottled water. "…you want some?…you look a little parched…"

"…thanks…" I took the bottle and we walked out to the garage to leave. "…so how did Sommers not see you when he went in the office?…"

"…I ducked in the closet…" She laughed. "…and I was ready to spend the day there until you pulled out the headlight gag… good thinking…that was really quick on your feet…"

"…well…" I tugged on my collar. "…I am a paramedic…we're kinda smart…"

"…kinda…"

☆ ☆ ☆

"…so your girlfriend was hittin' on your best friend so you threw the television out the window of your fourth-floor apartment?…" I sat on the bench seat talking to my pissed-off patient.

"…yeah…I spent four hundred bucks on that box just so my cunt girlfriend can put the moves on my…"

"…all right…all right…I get it…your girlfriend's a cunt…so how did your head end up split open?…"

"…the motherfuckin' nigger neighbor called the…"

"…hey…asshole…language…"

"…fine…the nice nigger neighbor called the cops and they bashed my head in…"

"…so you fell…"

"…I fell?…no I didn't fall…you fuckin' bitch aren't you listening?…"

"…yeah…I got no choice…I'm hearing it all…"

"…FUCK YOU…"

"…FUCK YOU…"

"…**YEAH WELL FUCK YOU**…" And he spit at me. So I spit back at him.

"…hey…you spit at me…" He whimpered while wiping goo from his nose and cheek.

"…yeah…I got you good too…'cause see I thought we were playing a game…you spit at me…I spit at you…wanna go again?…"

"…fuck you…get away from me bitch…"

"…I'm not cleaning that…" Ariel peered at me from the rearview mirror.

"…oh don't worry…" I threw a towel on the floor goo. "…it will be my pleasure to clean this mess…"

…most of it was on him anyway…

✿ ✿ ✿

"…you guys called for an ambulance?…" Ariel and I rolled the fully loaded stretcher up to the nurses' station.

"…yeah room 306…cardiac arrest…"

"…that way?…" I pointed left.

"…yes…three doors down…"

"…thanks…"

"…so I'll get the tube and you take the monitor?…" I offered up a work partnership.

"…sure…" Ariel nodded while she pushed. "…hopefully dispatch has a basic truck rolling this way…"

We rolled into the patient's room and found four staff members of various levels swooshing around the patient's bed. Some impressionistic form of CPR was being performed and a lot of yelling was happening. In other words…the usual ballet of a skilled facility cardiac arrest. The only ingredient left to be determined was who was going to start cracking on the medics first.

"…so which one of you thinks you know how to read that?…" Okay…question answered. It was going to be the short dumpy gray-haired one who pointed her query to the monitor Ariel was taking off the stretcher.

"…that'd be her…" I pointed at Ariel. "…but don't feel bad…I've seen cardiologists argue with her and lose so I wouldn't expect a nurse to do any better…" I looked at Ariel and smiled. She smiled back while hooking up that new fangled contraption she's been monkeying around with. I grabbed the tube kit and moved to the head.

"…how about we put a board under the patient so we're not just doing squishy mattress compressions?…" Ariel's request appeared to be the final straw in failed nurse/paramedic communications and the room cleared out. "…oh thank god…I thought they'd never leave…"

"…all that flapping…do I have feathers in my hair?…" I turned my head to show Ariel a better angle.

"…no…" She laughed without looking. "…fine v-fib…get ready to clear out…"

"…and the tube's in…go ahead…" I cleared off the bed to avoid getting zapped. I've never had the pleasure but I've heard first hand that it does hurt like a bitch. Back a few years ago Jodie was intubating a code while working with a new medic. Jodie said she was just getting ready to pull the laryngyscope blade out when she felt a sharp pain race through her body and both her arms went numb. When she was finally able to pick her head up she looked at her partner who could do no more than offer a weak "…oh…did I forget to say clear?…" Jodie was totally pissed and on a good day probably would have maimed the idiot but instead was left helpless in the wake of two numb arms.

Ariel proceeded through the stacked shocks and we watched the fine v-fib progressively get finer and finer. This was going in a bad direction.

"…hey guys…what's up?…" *well surprise surprise* Fergie and Jodie arrived in the room.

"…Jodie…I was just thinking about you…"

"…really?…"

"…yes…the time Siano defibbed you…"

Jodie winced in reflection. "…asshole…I still owe him a smack in the head for that…"

"…what did Casey do to get the nursing staff all riled up?…" Fergie started compressions.

"…it was a mutual effort…" Ariel screwed an epinephrine in a Bursta Jet.

"…they started it…" I guarded my tube and bagged away. "…they wanted to know which one of us thought we could read the monitor…"

Jodie started the IV and snarled. "…yeah…thanks for coming…go get my paperwork…"

"…hopefully that's what they're doing…" Ariel administered the epi and lidocaine.

Fergie continued to straddle the patient on the bed. "…we good to move him and get out of here?…"

"…yeah…tube's secure…"

"…lines taped pretty good…"

"…first round of meds is in…yeah let's do it…" And on a one-two-three our patient was transferred to our stretcher. All pertinent lines and objects were secured to the patient and/or stretcher and Fergie hopped on the bottom rail to ride along while she continued compressions. Ariel stopped at the nurses' station to gather the necessary paperwork and then Jodi and I steered the stretcher...proceeding directly to the ambulance. There we shuffled equipment...readjusted the patient and got everything battened down for the transport. A few minutes later Ariel climbed in the side door of the ambulance and sat on the bench seat. She had the face sheet from the patient's chart on top and was staring at it and then at the patient.

"...what's up Skippy?...you look perplexed..." Jodie had noticed too.

"...you know who this is?..." Ariel looked at me.

"...the current dead guy in our ambulance?..."

"...you're a poet Casey..." Fergie laughed.

"...this is William Parsons..." Ariel was clearly impressed but the name meant nothing to me.

"...who?..."

"...William Parsons...remember the guy lying on the hood of his car?..."

Suddenly it came back to me. "...dude with the messed-up legs..." I moved the sheet covering them now. "...wow...that's a lot of pins and screws..."

"...holy crap..." Fergie was also impressed by the hardware.

"...so you guys have already met?..." Jodie backed up to the rear doors.

"...I thought we killed him off a month ago..." Ariel took over compressions from Fergie.

"...well it looks like you succeeded today..." Fergie headed for the side door. "...you drive them...I'll drive our truck..."

"...sounds good...see ya guys..."

"...later...thanks for the assist..."

...and they were gone...

✵ ✵ ✵

later that evening...

I got home around 20:00 and as expected Kelly and Rickie's cars were in the driveway and the porch light was left on for me. The downstairs was completely dark though except for a small light in the hallway and the light over the stove so I wondered where everyone was as I traversed my way to the kitchen. I knew Rickie was somewhere because her traditional trail of uniform parts and backpacks and water bottles and debris from her car led to the refrigerator where I noticed a new supply of humus had been deposited. Kelly was somewhere too because the laundry basket had been moved.

"...CAAAASSSSSEEEEYYY..." Ah-ha...voices from above. I slid to the bottom of the stairs and called back up.

"...HELLOOOOO..."

"...BBBRRRRIIINNGG USSSSSS UUUPPP SSSOMMEEE BEEEEEERRRRRS..."

"...'KAY..." I slid back to the kitchen...grabbed some beers and headed upstairs. Rickie's room was empty...I stopped in mine to shed some uniform parts of my own...*particularly the stupid faux turtleneck...*and then I made my way to Kelly's room. Kelly was sitting up on her bed leaning on the headboard and Rickie was on the floor balancing on her workout ball.

"...wassup Casey?..." Rickie took the first beer.

"...not much Loser..."

"...here...I'll trade ya..." Kelly extended the bong as I passed the brew.

"...ah thank you..." *bubble bubble bubble.* "...so what are you guys up to?..."

"...Kelly's filling me in on negotiations and I'm doing my ab workout..."

"…cool…so what's new in negotiations?…" I sat on the bed up against the headboard next to Kelly.

"…in a nutshell…they're not going anywhere…" Kelly looked frustrated. "…NAA is truly bent on our complete submission…"

"…which is complete bullshit…" Rickie banged out some crunches.

"…I'll take that back…" Kelly reached out. "…it is but it's also a strategy that they're well within their rights to employ…we just hoped they'd be bigger than that…"

"…so what's next?…"

"…oh a few more back-and-forth bullshit sessions and then the negotiating team will come back with a contract proposal… the body will have to vote whether or not to accept it…"

"…it'll suck if people act stupid just because they don't want a strike…" Rickie leaned back on the ball.

"…we'll make sure nothing stupid happens…" Kelly grabbed the remote and turned on *M*A*S*H*.

"…why do they have to be such pricks?…" I pulled my knees up to my chest. "…all we want is to do our jobs and enjoy them a little bit…why do they have to fuck with it so much?…"

"…no idea…" Kelly drank from her beer. "…my best guess is that they're evil fucks…but what are you gonna do?…"

"…UMMMM guys…"

"…I know…it really only bugs me when I'm tired…"

"…guys…"

"…it bugs me all the time but we gotta stay focused…"

"…GUYS…I'M STUCK…HELLO HELP ME…" Rickie kicked a leg up and down and got our attention.

"…what the fuck are you doing Loser?…" Kelly swung off the bed and came around to the workout ball. Then she started laughing hard. "…what is wrong with you?…Casey…come here…"

"…what?…" I joined them at the end of the bed and I started laughing hard too. "…hey…you are stuck…HA HA AHAHAHAHAHAHAHAHAHAHAH…"

"…yeah very funny guys…get me out…"

"…how did you manage to roll the ball over your hair?…" Kelly was near tears.

"…I don't know…I think I leaned too far…"

"…you look like a hyperextended crab…"

"…yeah I kinda feel like one too…"

"…what the hell are we supposed to do?…" I asked because Kelly was now kneeling on the floor laughing so hard she could hardly breathe.

"…help me flip over…"

"…wait…I'll get a spatula…" Now I was kneeling on the floor in hysterics. Even Rickie was laughing hard which seemed to make her more stuck.

"…c'mon….help me…" She whimpered.

"…oh my god you Loser…" Kelly was making her way to grab one of Rickie's legs. "…Casey grab the other one…"

"…'kay…AH HAHAHAHAH AHA…okay…I'm good…"

"…FLIP…"

"…OOF…" Rickie's legs flew over her head sending her backward and into a heap. "…thank you…I'm free…"

"…thanks again for the show Loser…" Kelly whipped the ball out of the room and we heard it bounce all the way down the hallway. "…but you are banned from ab workouts in my room…" Kelly looked at me and laughed. "…for fuck's sake…"

…tee hee…that was funny…

CHAPTER 25 -
A DAY IN THE LIFE

...as Jesus read the news he sighed "...oh boy..."

Just as Kelly had predicted the supposed negotiating sessions were just a load of hooey most likely designed to waste our time. The stewards did a good job keeping a lid on things but word still got out that NAA was being ridiculous and progress was not happening. Another union meeting was scheduled for the end of the month at which point it was expected that whatever tripe NAA was offering would be presented in contract form and we would vote to ratify or turn it down. The buzz around the city was that we would have to tell NAA to shove their offer and we'd hit the picket line running. Right on down the line to a person nobody wanted to strike. Besides the many gray areas of ethical considerations was the very black-and-white issue of financial solvency. Most of us lived overtime-laden paycheck to overtime-laden paycheck. It was stressful enough to have to choose between sleep or taking one more eight-hour shift to fill out the pay week never mind the thought of having no pay at all. To a person though it was agreed that we had no choice. If we let NAA come in and destroy our way of life without a fight there'd be no telling how far they'd keep pushing us. It was fight now or resign ourselves to becoming corporate wheel fodder.

✯ ✯ ✯

"...HELLOOO...PARAMEDICS..." Ariel yelled into the open first-floor window. No one answered. "...I hate doing these calls..." She turned her attention to me. "...now we gotta go creeping through the house looking for the dead body..."

"...would it help if I narrated like Marlon Perkins?..."

"…who?…" Ariel scrunched up her forehead while she popped the window screen.

"…Marlon Perkins…you know *Wild Kingdom?*…he'd fly around in a helicopter and tell his partner Jim to poke ferocious animals with sticks…"

"…and he would?…"

"…well…he wasn't smart enough to be in the helicopter so…"

"…how does this apply to this call?…"

"…I don't know…I guess because we're going into a jungle-like zone to hunt for a dead body…" Suddenly I wondered why I saw a connection and Ariel didn't. "…I guess I forget how much younger you are than me…"

"…yup…three whole years…" Ariel didn't care to comment further and just shook her head. "…it's your turn to climb in the window…"

"…**ADELANTE**…" I loved climbing through windows to do well-being checks. True…I liked kicking doors down a lot more but in the spring when windows were left open it was the more sensible route.

Well-being checks themselves could also be mini-adventures. Usually they were initiated by neighbors who hadn't seen a resident for a while or sometimes mail carriers or Meals-On-Wheels drivers notice food…mail or newspapers piling up on a doorstep and get suspicious. They'll call 911 and then it's our job to gain entry to the residence and find the person. Sometimes the person isn't even home. Many a time they're wintering down south or out west and have no idea two highly trained medical personnel are stomping through their home searching for signs of life. Sometimes they're dead and you search room to room looking for where the last of their life played out. Kelly told me she did a well-being check once and they found the woman on the floor holding the phone with her finger on the 9...*sad...so close...*

Sometimes they're not that lucky. Seniors will fall...really hurt themselves and not be able to get to the phone. Imagine lying on a broken hip for days...unable to get to the bathroom or eat or drink. It can really get ugly and it's why I always encourage seniors who live alone to get a Lifeline or Life Alert or some kind of electronic system they can activate if they fall. One time I dispatched Paul and Tracy for a well-being check and they found a guy who was still conscious but had been on the floor so long his face fused to the carpet. I'm not making that up and I'm not exaggerating. They actually had to cut a huge square of the carpet to get the guy up and make him transportable to the hospital.

"...HELLLLOOOO PARAMEDICS..." This time it was me yelling as I slid headfirst through the window and onto the floor. You always want to announce your presence loudly because some old people do have guns and some old people have been known to shoot paramedics who surprised them.

"...you smell anything yet?..." I had made my way across the room to let Ariel in and she came in the door sniffing.

"...no...no rotting flesh..." I sniffed too. "...but I'm getting a strong whiff of BENGAY from the front room..."

"...let's start there..."

"...ANTICIPATING THAT THE SNOW LEOPARD MAY LEAP OUT OF HIDING JIM WILL KEEP HIMSELF CLOSE TO SHELTER..."

"...why are you talking like that?..."

"...I'm Marlon Perkins..."

"...I still don't get it..."

"...oh...I thought playing it out would help..."

"…no…not so much…hey what's over there?…" Ariel pointed across the large front room to a shadowy figure in front of the couch.

"…let's check it out…" We stroll over and sure enough it's our person of interest. Ariel checked for an apical pulse and after a minute or so confirmed what we pretty much already knew. "…I'll call dispatch and let them know we'll need PD to take custody of the body…"

"…I'll go check the bedroom for ID…"

Ariel got on the radio and I headed off to find more information. I rustled around the bedroom and bathroom and found a name and list of meds. Ariel was already doing paperwork when I came back.

"…did you look for potential cause of death?…you know… rule out shooting stabbing or strangulation?…" I surveyed the small-framed elderly woman kneeling in front of the couch with her face planted on the couch cushion. "…the cops will want to know…"

"…I'm pretty sure it was something less dramatic…"

"…did you notice this orange light by her ear?…"

"…are you being Marlon Perkins again?…"

"…no…" I laughed. "…there really is an orange light… EEWWWWW…"

"….eeeeewwwww what?…" Ariel stopped writing and looked over.

"…however she ended up facedown on the cushion she landed on her heating pad…" I pulled the cord up. "…and it's turned on…look at her face…" Ariel peered over my shoulder.

"…oh my god…" She winced. "…it's melted…"

"…like a wax candle…" I walked away temporarily grossed out. "…a big giant BENGAY wax candle…"

…paperwork…

✵ ✵ ✵

"…this weather is absolutely beautiful…" I proclaimed.

"…it's the perfect day for a bike ride…" Ariel agreed.

"…or rollerblading or hiking or anything…" I continued.

"…anything but this…"

"…yes…but at least we're prepared…" Taking a page out of the Mahan book of posting etiquette Ariel and I brought supplies for this gorgeous spring day. At the present time we were setting up our lawn chairs in the Bess Eaton parking lot. "…we shouldn't get run over back here…"

Ariel laughed and handed me my bagel in a bag. "…you never know but I'll take my chances for the opportunity to stretch my legs…"

Just then one of the more well-known homeless guys walked by our patio. "…hey…lookey lookey…a party…"

"…hello James…" I forget names but Ariel always remembers.

"…and it's the best kind of party 'cause the hot chicks are already here…" James let rip a belly chortle through his broken-tooth grin. We were not amused.

"…what do you want James?…"

"…how come you're always the bitchy one?…" James asked me as he plopped himself down. An odiferous aroma escaped from his dirty multi-layered stack of clothes and I no longer wanted my bagel.

"…I'll give you half my bagel if you'll keep walking…" Ariel was always the diplomat.

James smiled and extended his smudged hand in acceptance. "…now see….that's how you talk nice to people…"

"…thanks for the life lesson James…" *we exchanged smug smirks.* "…I feel so enriched…"

"...FOUR-TEN...FOUR-ONE-ZERO..." Our cultural enlightenment was interrupted by dispatch squawking out the ambulance window.

"...I got it..." I volunteered to get up since I no longer had an appetite and it would put some distance between me and James.

"...well...I'd say you might as well just give me the whole bagel..." James continued charming Ariel.

"...why would I do that?..."

"...you'll see when your girlfriend gets back..."

"...get in the ambulance James..." I strolled back from the truck.

"...what?..." Ariel was perturbed.

"...hot dog..." James was happy. "...want your bagel back?..."

"...no..." Ariel was disgusted. "...what's going on?..."

"...seems James here is feeling suicidal today..."

"...yeah...I been real down..."

"...are you kidding me?..." Ariel folded her chair. "...you saw us sitting here and you called 911?..."

"...posting brings me down..."

"...I wasn't sure of the proper procedure...should I have just told you?..."

"...get in the ambulance James..." I held the back door open and waved with my chair. "...and don't sit on the stretcher..."

"...but I'm a patient..."

"...DO NOT SIT YOUR SMELLY ASS ON THAT STRETCHER JAMES..."

"...talk nice to me I'm suicidal..."

"...let me see if I can't help you along with that James..."

...paperwork...

✧ ✧ ✧

"…so this car hit that car?…" Ariel attempted to recreate the motor vehicle choreography with the MiddleCity firefighter. "…and that car spun around so hard it hit that telephone pole and knocked it down?…"

"…yeah…that's what we're figuring…" The firefighter shook his head and scanned the scene. "…our guys got the two patients out of the first car…they're very minor injuries…"

"…okay…we'll check out that car…" Ariel turned toward the car and I followed dragging with me the longboard and c-spine bag.

"…for all that force there doesn't seem to be a lot of damage to the car…"

"…ahhh…the front end's pretty crunched…" Ariel pointed ahead. "…and I'm wondering what the door on the other side looks like…"

"…I don't see anybody…are they out of the car?…"

"…I don't think so…" Ariel and I approached the midsize Buick from opposite sides. I got to the passenger side and she made it all the way around to the driver's side. As she expected the driver's side door was crunched pretty badly from whacking the telephone pole and Ariel couldn't get it open. She came around to the passenger side just as I got my door open.

"…you see anyone yet?…"

"…uh-huh…she's right here…" She being an approximately 60 y/o female kneeling on the front passenger floor of her car. "…ma'am are you alright?…"

"…oh yes…I'm very good…how are you?…"

"…oh I'm fine…thank you for asking…are you hurt anywhere?…"

"…oh no really I'm fine…and how are you?…"

"…oh boy…" Ariel noticed she was repeating herself…*that's never a good thing…* "…let's get the collar on her…"

"…got it…Ma'am I'm going to put this collar on you to protect your neck…"

"…oh sure…and how are you?…"

"…I'm good thank you…now it's probably going to be a little uncomfortable but let us know if it makes it hard for you to breathe…"

"…oh sure…that's fine…" And she let me put the collar on. "…can I ask a question?…"

"…sure…anything…"

"…what are you lovely girls doing here in my living room?…" I looked up at Ariel.

"…I'll go call the trauma room…"

"…good idea…" And Ariel was gone.

…paperwork…

✡ ✡ ✡

"…FOUR-TEN…FOUR-ONE-ZERO…"

"…four-ten…area of 61…"

"…FOUR-TEN I NEED YOU TO DO ME A FAVOR… COULD YOU PLEASE TAKE THE PRIORITY THREE TO MERCY THREE-OH-SIX FOR THE PATIENT GOING TO ROSE MANOR EAST WING?…NO SPECIAL REQUIREMENTS…"

"…four-ten received…"

"…wow…a basic transfer…" I put the truck in DRIVE. "…I haven't done one of those in years…"

"…they sound backed up…at least they gave us a quick one…"

"…oh yeah…I don't mind…" I turned into traffic. "…they're fairly mindless…" We made our way through traffic and turned into the Mercy parking lot. Ariel called us off…we grabbed the stretcher and made our way past the ER to the elevators. "…you know what I've always wondered?…"

"…what?…" Ariel pushed the elevator button.

"…if Wonder Woman's plane is invisible how does she find it in the parking lot?…"

"…what parking lot?…"

"…the parking lot where she parks it…" The elevators opened and we entered.

"…what do you mean where she parks it?…" Ariel pushed the third-floor button.

"…when she lands it she puts it in a parking space…"

"…yeah…"

"…and she gets out and fights crime and then has to get back in it to go home…"

"…okay…"

"…how does she find it if it's invisible?…" The doors opened and we were on our floor. "…does she just walk around until she bumps into it?…"

Ariel laughed. "…I really don't have an answer for you…"

"…great…and the mystery lives on…" We approached the nurse's station and Ariel accepted the paperwork from the RN. I wandered off to explore.

"…hey…you…nurse…" I heard a voice calling from a dark room. I had no problem ignoring the voice since they called for a nurse and I am not one. "…c'mon…hey you…" Okay…so then like a cat who didn't get the memo my curiosity got the best of me and I approached closer. Through the shadows I saw a frazzled middle-aged woman restrained in her bed.

"…what's up?…"

"…nothing's up…untie me…"

"…can't do that…"

"…c'mon…they made a mistake…untie me…" I smiled and backed into my exit while she continued to plead. "…c'mon… let me out…"

"…gotta go…" And like the moon at dawn I was gone. Unfortunately though she had me honed in her sights and the patient we were there for was in the room directly across the hall from hers. She didn't miss a beat when I walked back and was forced to stand in her line of vision.

"…hey you…over here…I know you hear me…"

Ariel stared at me. "…made a friend did ya?…"

"…yeah…"

"…hey…you what's your name?…c'mon…just tell me your name…I know you can hear me…" And she went on and on and I tried hard to ignore her but Ariel got ruffled.

"…would you just answer her already so she'll stop?…"

"…for real?…like answering her is going to help…"

"…hey you…c'mon…what's your name?…just tell me…"

"…just give her something else to say…"

"…hey you…what's your name?…c'mon tell me…"

"…alright…I will…" I leaned into the hallway. "…Jodie… my name's Jodie Twist…"

"…oh thank you Jodie…you're so kind…can I have some lemonade?…"

I came back into the room and Ariel was laughing. "…you should not have done that…"

"…I know…but I couldn't give her my name…and you didn't want me to give her yours…right?…"

"…oh no…that's for sure…but you better hope Jodie doesn't find out…"

"…how could she?…"

…paperwork…

☆ ☆ ☆

"…I am pooped…" I reclined the driver's side seat back as far as it would go.

"...were you up late partying last night?..." Ariel began the inquisition.

"...yes...last night we decided to try crack party favors so as you can imagine I got absolutely no sleep..." I kept my eyes closed and head back refusing to even look at her.

"...really?..."

"... ..."

"... ...."

"... ..."

"...really?..."

"...Ariel I am not answering that question so stop asking it..."

BEEP BEEP I heard an air horn and looked up to see an ambulance pulling up alongside us **"...CASEY WHAT ARE YA DOIN'?..."** Kelly was driving...rolling down the window and calling my name.

"...CASEY WHASSUP?..." I was surprised to see Rickie in the passenger seat.

"...you guys are working together?..." I asked out my window.

"...yeah...my partner went home sick so Loser came in to finish the shift..."

"...awesome..." *but really I was jealous.*

"...yeah well this way I don't have to finish off my shift cleaning trucks..."

"...remember the old days when they'd just let you sleep if your partner went home?..."

"...yup but now those days are gone...gone for good..." Kelly shook her head in reflection. "...so do you have plans for dinner?..."

"...nothing special..."

"…cool 'cause Loser and I are cooking out…we're gonna grill it and burn it…you in?…"

"…absolutely…I love grillin' and burnin' it…what time?…"

"…19:30…you bring the rolls…"

"…got it…"

"…how about you Aire?…you up for some burgers and dogs?…"

"…yeah Aire…how about you?…" I smiled and turned to a very surprised Ariel.

"…me?…uh?…"

"…I'm having turkey burgers so it won't just be junk food…" Rickie offered.

"…c'mon Ariel…you gotta eat…" I kept the pressure on.

She broke into a smile. "…yeah…sure…I'll come by…"

"…ALL RIGHT…" Kelly and Rickie broke into cheer…hit the air horn again**…BOMP BOMP…**and said goodbye…

✫ ✫ ✫

"…four-ten on arrival 1545 Main…"Ariel signed us off.

"…no cops yet…great…" I tapped on the steering wheel.

"…they sound pretty busy on the scanner…"

"…maybe I should pull up the street a little bit…"

"…yeah…good idea…"

"…AMBULANCE DRIVERS…AMBULANCE DRIVERS …STOP…HELP…"

"…where's that coming from?…"Ariel looked around.

"…up there…the third-floor window…"

"…oh crap it's a kid…"

"…yeah…so?…"

"…it's a kid screaming for help…"

"…we're here for a suicidal male…"

"…but it's a kid screaming for help…"

"…okay…so what should we do?…"

Ariel thought for a second. "…go…just go…"

"…you got it…" And I started to pull away from the curb.

"…WAIT…STOP…AMBULANCE DRIVER…STOP.."

"…OH CRAP.." Now it was a different kid running in front of the ambulance. "…where did she come from?…" I jammed on the brakes.

"…I'm gonna guess the third floor…" Ariel leaned forward on the dashboard and picked up the mike. "…four-ten…four-one-zero…can we get an ETA on PD for this scene?…"

"…HELP US…HEY HELP US…" Now the young girl was banging on the hood of the ambulance while the other kid continued screaming out the window.

"…FOUR-TEN…FOUR-ONE-ZERO…YOU'RE   ON YOUR OWN…PD TIED UP WITH MULTIPLE CALLS…"

"…CRAP.." I'd never heard Ariel use such language. "…put it in PARK…we'll have to check it out…"

"…you sure about this?…"

"…yes…but we stay together…no getting pulled away…"

"…got it…believe me I'll be close…and if we run into trouble I'll just pick you up by the ankles and hit people with you…"

"…what?…"

"…nothing…" And with that Ariel and I exited the ambulance. The girl ran back around the truck and walked fast in front of us but kept an eye on us the whole time.

"…so what's going on?…" Ariel asked her while we took large strides toward the building door.

"…my brother Willie drank alcohol and now he's yelling and breaking shit…"

"…what kind of alcohol?…beer?…whiskey?…"

"…no…the white kind…" She opened the door and we began climbing the dark…dirty…urine-smelling stairs.

"…rum…vodka…" I'm impressed that Ariel knows the white kinds of alcohol.

"…no…the white kind…like when you cut your leg and your momma pours it in it…"

"…rubbing alcohol…" **oh no…HYDROCARBONS!** "…how much did he drink?…"

BANG "…MOTHERFUCKER….MOTHERFUCKER…" BANG BANG

Ariel and I cowered in the stairway under the sounds crashing above us. The little girl seemed unfazed. "…that's just Willie… he's breaking shit…"

Ariel and I looked at each other and without words knew what the other was thinking…*this is no place for a paramedic…*

"…who else is up there?…" **BANG BANG**

"…my brother David…"

"…anyone else?…"

"…no…my momma's workin'…"

"…how old is David?…"

"…he's seven…"

"…yeah that was the kid hanging out the window…"

"…we gotta get David out of there and beat feet…" I spoke and Ariel shook her head in agreement.

"…honey…can you get your brother David to come down here?…" **BANG BANG**

"…he won't leave Willie…Willie keeps saying he's gonna kill hisself…"

"…okay…we're going to help Willie but we gotta get you and David downstairs first…all right?…"

"…no…he won't come…"

"…well we gotta try okay?…come on…" **BANG BANG**

Ariel and I started creeping up the stairs toward the third floor. The banging and screaming got louder and louder and I was starting to have the same funny feeling I had just before I got shoved into the burnt-out garage. Oh well…at least this time Ariel was by my side and not getting progressively smaller on the horizon. When we got to the top of the stairs they opened directly into the apartment. Willie had locked himself in the bathroom and sounded like he was hurling himself and other objects off the walls. **BANG BANG**

"…where's David?…"

"…he's in the bathroom with Willie…"

"…what the hell?…" I didn't see that coming.

"…you said you'd help him…" This kid was relentless.

"…I know honey…" Ariel scrunched up her forehead. I knew she was torn.

"…fuck it…" I stood up. "…let's do this…" I got up and headed for the bathroom door. "…David…are you in there?…"

"…what are you doing?…" Ariel tore after me. "…don't stand in front of the door…" And she pulled me back.

"…David…are you in there?…" I knocked on the wall since I wasn't standing in front of the door anymore.

"…MOTHERFUCKER….WHO IS MOTHERFUCKIN' OUT THERE?…" BANG BANG Now it sounded like Willie was trying to break down the bathroom door…almost like he didn't realize he was the one who locked it.

"…PARAMEDICS…we just want to help you Willie…" I tried my best to make friends.

"…WILLIE…LET THEM HELP YOU…" The young girl pleaded.

"…GET THE FUCK OUT OF MY HOUSE… MOTHERFUCKERS…" BANG BANG

"…we will Willie…just send David out here…"

"…NO MOTHERFUCKERS…NOW GET OUT…" And with that a young boy screamed and a fist came punching through the door. **" ...GET OUT..."** And then a foot came breaking through...and the yelling got louder and louder.

"...ah crap Aire...she's gonna blow..."

"...let's get out of here..." And with that Ariel grabbed the girl and we bolted down the stairs. The girl started screaming but she let herself be dragged away. Ariel was ahead of me going down so I got to see Willie actually break through the door. That meant I also was the one to feel his hot breath breathing down on me.

"...run faster Aire...he's gaining on us..."

"...I'm going as fast as I can..." We were so close to being out of the building but I was sure Willie was about to grab me so I turned around and chucked my portable radio right at his head...***BOINK...excellent...dead on...*** Willie crumpled up in a ball holding his forehead and me and Ariel made a clean break to the light.

When we got back to the street we saw the most beautiful sight...a cruiser parked behind our ambulance. The two cops looked surprised to see us running...out of breath and dragging along a kid.

"...ladies...what's going on?..."

While coughing up a lung Ariel and I spit out our story. The cops wasted no time radioing for backup and heading into the building. A few minutes later a handcuffed Willie was on our stretcher and a crying David and little girl were seat-belted in for the ride.

"...I think this is yours..." The cop handed me my portable.

"...thanks..." I gratefully accept it. "...I'm glad you found it... that would have been a lot of paperwork..."

"...you know...you ladies are just a little crazy..." I smiled while I wiped the blood off the corner of the radio.

"...no higher praise from a cop..."

...paperwork...

CHAPTER 26 -
A NIGHT IN THE LIFE

*...late in the afternoon the Twelve came to him and said
"...send the crowd away so they can go to BigCity and find
food and lodging...because we are in the region...and there
is none..." He replied "...you give them something to eat..."
They answered "...we have only five loaves of bread and two
fish and no propane..." But he said to his disciples "...have
them sit down in groups of about fifty each...and spark up
the grill..." The disciples did so and everybody sat down...
taking the five loaves and the two fish and looking up to
heaven...he gave thanks and broke them...then he gave them
to the disciples to set before the people...then dispatch broke
in and sent everyone on a call and nobody got to eat nuthin'...*

...later on at the house...

"...go ahead...just park in the driveway..." I motioned for
Ariel to pull the Subaru into the driveway and she maneuvered
into a spot.

"...hey guys...wassup?..." Rickie strolled around from the
backyard with a beer in one hand and waving with the other. She
walked over to Ariel first and gave her a big hug. "...what took
you guys so long?..."

"...couldn't find hot dog rolls..." I held up my bag of groceries.
"...everybody must be cooking out tonight..."

"...I stopped home to get a change of clothes..." Ariel chimed
in.

"...aw...I could've lent you something..." Rickie offered.

"...you're two feet taller than her...we wouldn't see her all
night..."

Rickie and Ariel laughed and I turned to Ariel. "...I'm gonna
go change too...you wanna use the bathroom?..."

"…yeah…"

"…okay chicas…well I'm supposed to be watching the grill…"

"…oh boy…" I laughed. "…is Kelly inside?…"

"…yeah…making her awesome potato salad…"

"…excellent…I'm starved…"

Ariel and I darted into the house and I pointed up the stairs to where the bathroom was. Ariel nodded in acknowledgement and as we headed up Kelly yelled from the kitchen "…Casey…is that you and Ariel the flirtin' Guertin?…"

"…yes…we're going up to change…"

"…'kay…"

Ariel and I continued up the stairs and I gave her the quick tour. "…there's Rickie's room…don't look it'll only raise questions that can't be answered…my room…where I get away from it all…Kelly's room or the inner sanctum as we like to call it and the bathroom…light's on the wall on the right…"

"…got it…thanks…"

I went to my room to change and ten minutes later we both ended up back in the kitchen. Kelly was at the counter chopping eggs and through the window we could see Rickie manning the grill.

"…Casey did you get rolls?…"

"…yeah I left them outside with Rickie…" I looked out the window. "…boy that looks like a lot of smoke…"

"…very good…" Kelly continued chopping. "…hey Ariel…want a beer?…"

"…oh no…I'm good…thanks…"

"…how about some wine?…" Rickie entered the kitchen through the back door. "…there's a bottle in the fridge…"

"…shouldn't you be with the grill?…" I quizzically asked.

"…no it's good…"

I looked out at the puffs of smoke. "…uhhh…okay…"

"…reeeeeelax Casey…so Aire…how 'bout some wine?…"

"…uhhh…yeah…well…what do you have?…"

"…let me show ya…" Rickie headed to the fridge. "…I have a Riesling…" She rustled around. "…oh…and I have some zinfandel…"

"…white?…"

"…no blush…"

"…hmm…let me try the Riesling…"

"…sure…I think I'll have some too…" She paused. "…do I want some?…"

"…don't answer…it's just her process…" I instructed Ariel. She nodded and laughed.

"…yes…I think I will…" And so Rickie pulled two wine glasses out of the cabinet. "…you want some O'Brien?…Casey?…"

"…got my beer…"

"…don't drink wine…"

"…good…" Rickie smiled at Ariel. "…there'll be plenty for us…"

…oh boy…

✫ ✫ ✫

"…so everything's covered in ice…remember Aire?…"

"…oh yeah…" Ariel munched on a turkey burger.

"…I mean everything…cars…telephone poles…trees…houses…everything…it was like working in a snow globe…" Rickie laughed and Kelly nodded her head in acknowledgment. "…and Ariel's driving…"

"…don't say it like that…" Ariel shrieked a bit.

"…c'mon Aire…you're not a good dry-road driver… remember when that guy's foot fell off?…"

"…what?…" Ariel shrieked louder.

"…you took the corner too fast…"

"…his foot fell off?…" Rickie crunched a cucumber.

"…it was nearly severed to begin with…" Ariel defended herself.

"…AND IT WAS ICY…" Kelly was frustrated by the diversion.

"…yes…it was icy and Ariel was driving and we get a call for a suicidal male on that street behind the Dunkin' Donuts at 81…"

"…yeah…Randolph…" Kelly recognized the spot.

"…that's a decent hill…" Rickie also recognized it.

"…yes it is…" Ariel continued. "…and the hill was covered in ice…at least a half an inch thick…"

"…oh no…" Kelly saw where we were going.

"…so we get to the top of the hill and Ariel stops before the incline…"

"…at least I thought I did…" Ariel laughed in retrospect. "…I must have gone just a little too far over the crest because when I put the truck in PARK it kept sliding…"

"…down the hill?…" Rickie started laughing.

"…in a perfect tact formation…" Ariel illustrated with her finger. "…into the parked car on the left then into the parked car on the right…back to the left…"

"…so we get into a fight because I think she's still in DRIVE and I'm telling her to hit the brake…"

"…and I'm screaming '…I'm in PARK… quit giving me useless advice'…"

"…and then the cops show up behind us and manage to stop in time so they get out of their cruiser…see and probably hear us yelling at each other so they go in the house…"

"...finally the truck stopped sliding but we kept arguing all the way out of the truck...down the sidewalk into the apartment building down a flight..."

"...to where we come upon the cops...in the defensive position with their guns drawn on our patient..."

"...and he's in the doorway of his apartment...stark naked... holding the cops at bay waving an authentic samurai sword at them..."

"...we were both just like '...whoa...okay...good time to end the argument...'"

"...good move..." Kelly opened her beer.

"...yeah our first fight as partners and it probably saved our bacon..." I dug in to the chips.

"...none of our other fights since have been nearly as productive..." Ariel smirked at me.

...all right Skippy...you're cut off...

✫ ✫ ✫

After we ate we sat around the table for awhile talking and sipping beverages. As you might imagine...amongst the four of us there were a lot of funny stories to tell. The warm spring air had brought out the best in everyone and it felt good to relax after a semi-crazy day.

I was also really glad Ariel was getting to experience me and my housemates in our natural habitat. Maybe now she could see that we weren't the second coming of the Chicago Seven and relax a bit.

Once it got dark we all chipped in and started moving things back in the house. Ariel...Rickie and I started putting stuff away and while we were laughing and cleaning Kelly ducked out and went back outside. Rickie noticed and got excited.

"…is she?…" She leaned toward the window. "…yes…she is…she's pulling out the fire pit…" Ariel and I came over to the window and saw Kelly dragging half a metal drum to the middle of the yard.

"…you guys do fires?…" I started getting excited too. "…all right…I love fires…" I turned to Ariel. "…more wine Skippy?…"

"…sure…we're not working tomorrow…"

"…wahoo…it's a party…" Rickie celebrated as she poured.

…and suddenly I felt like dancin'…

✷ ✷ ✷

By the time we cleaned up…grabbed sweatshirts and headed back outside Kelly had a nice fire started.

"…this is so awesome…" I plopped my beach chair close to the flames.

"…yes…thank you Mother Kelly…" Rickie pulled her chaise lounge close.

"…anyone mind if I take the hammock?…" Ariel asked.

"…no…I'm good…" Kelly was already sitting in her beach chair poking at the fire with her stick. Rickie and I waved okay so Ariel hopped in and started swinging. Nobody said anything for awhile as we all kicked back and enjoyed the crickets and fire sounds.

"…I wish Yankee Candle would make a candle that smells like a smoky fire…" I broke the silence.

"…they could call it 'Campfire'…" Rickie suggested.

"…or …'Arsonist'…" Kelly laughed.

"…wouldn't that need a hint of gasoline?…" Ariel swung back and forth.

"…I guess so…" We all pretty much agreed and then it got quiet again. I was in my own world staring at the flames dancing on the charred wood when from behind I heard the familiar flick of a lighter followed by the traditional pungent aroma. **CRAP** So much for Ariel not thinking we were the second coming of the Chicago Seven...*I felt my face get warm from the inside out...*

I wasn't prepared yet to deal with the issue of smoking pot in front of Ariel. Up until now these were just two worlds that never met and I would have been just fine if they didn't ever meet. But here they were...staring each other down and ready for the collision. I'm pretty sure she knew I got high but I knew she definitely didn't approve. It was like my smoking pot to her was like her sleeping with men to me...*we both just didn't get it...* Obviously I didn't see the evil monster in marijuana but I knew if I exercised my liberal rights I risked pissing off Ariel or even worse...*losing her respect...*

I thought about politely declining when the time came around but that didn't feel right either. Kelly and Rickie knew I smoked every time it was offered and in more imbibed states I carelessly proclaimed that I felt so comfortable in my stoner skin that I didn't care who knew. Passing now would clearly be seen as a ploy to pacify Ariel. I could hear the chants now. They'd go on and on laughing about how I was whipped and Ariel didn't even have to use anything to whip me.

I continued staring at the fire waiting until the last possible moment to decide. Then I don't know if it was by design or not but Kelly bailed me out. Rickie had passed the joint to her and then she did the completely unexpected thing and offered it to Ariel.

"...oh...no thank you...I don't smoke..." Ariel was surprised. Kelly handed it off to me and while Kelly kept Ariel distracted I took my hit and passed it off to Rickie.

"...no?...have you ever?..."

"...ahhh...well a long time ago..." Ariel's admission floored me. "...I dated a guy in college who smoked and one time I tried it..."

"...didn't like it?..." Kelly quizzed.

"...no..." Ariel shook her head. "...not so much...and I thought it made my boyfriend lazy..."

"...maybe he was just lazy..." Kelly reasoned.

"...yeah...because it makes me wanna get busy..." Rickie chimed in. "...I loooooove cleaning stooooned...."

"...I like doing projects..." I joined in. "...like painting or sanding..."

"...I've never seen you sand anything Casey..."

"...I've never seen you clean anything..."

"...touché..." And Rickie and I giggled for a minute or so.

"...do you mind if other people smoke?..." Kelly jumped back in.

"...you mean like you guys?..." Ariel laughed.

"...well...yes...now that you mention it...like us..." I sat back happy to be out of the line of questioning.

"...it's your house...you should feel comfortable doing what you want...but I wouldn't want you to smoke in my house..."

"...that's fair..." Kelly poked at the fire. "...I'm glad you didn't insult me and say you wouldn't want me to do it at work..."

"...I've seen you work...I know you take it serious and I know you're very good at what you do...there's no doubt in my mind you keep it separate..."

Kelly seemed taken aback a bit by Ariel's praise. "...thank you...I appreciate that..." I remained focused on the fire. "...maybe someday the law will catch up and realize that it can be kept separate and that it's not worth the time and dollars it takes to keep it illegal..."

"...I wouldn't have a problem with it being legal..." Ariel surprised me yet again. "...it's no worse than cigarettes being legal..."

"...actually I think it's much different from cigarettes..." Rickie commented. "...this is a plant...pulled from the ground... dried and wrapped in an all-natural wrapper...if you have a problem with the smoke part you can eat it in many different foods...cigarettes get treated with all kinds of crap..."

"...yeah...basically all the ingredients you'd find at your worst hazmat..." I interjected.

"...yes..." Rickie continued "...and then they stick an asbestos filter on it...and then they add addictive nicotine ...when I went to Vegas I didn't want to fly with pot so I went my whole ten-day vacation without it...I was fine...can you imagine going on vacation with someone who just quit cigarettes cold turkey?... that day?..." We all groaned at the thought.

"...in my fifteen years of EMS I've never dealt with an out-of-control stoner..." Kelly recounted. "...it's usually booze...the legal stuff that gets people most consistently crazy..."

"...or assholey..." I added.

"...you certainly can't overdose on it..." Rickie jumped in.

"...we've tried..." Rickie and I said in unison and then burst out laughing. Ariel just rolled her eyes.

"...I think they should legalize it and use the proceeds to fund the war on the real drugs...coke and heroin...that's the shit that fucks people up..." I squeaked through my giggles.

"...and that synthetic crap like acid and ecstasy..." Kelly continued.

"...yeah we don't find people lying in their own shit and vomit with roach clips in their hands..." Rickie stared at the flames.

"...and it's your caffeinated drugs that make people violent and psychotic..." I theorized.

"…caffeinated?…" Ariel asked.

"…yeah…your cokes and coke like products…crack… meth…dust…"

"…true…I see…" *I still didn't think Ariel wanted a hit.*

"…how about kids huffing legal chemicals?…remember that call you and Paul did in the region?…where was it?… MiddleTown…" I continued with Ariel.

"…oh yeah…" Ariel winced in reflection. "…that was awful…"

"…what happened?…" Rickie refilled the wine glasses.

"…a couple of kids ditched school and sat around in the basement huffing gasoline…one of them ended up taking off leaving the other behind…he decided to kick back and smoke a joint…"

"…uh-oh…" Rickie grimaced.

"…yeah…" Ariel went on "…he inhaled and the hot smoke ignited an explosion in his airway which precipitated an explosion in the basement…"

"…oh Jesus…" Kelly stabbed at the fire.

"…he was crispy inside and out and the worst part was he was still alive…"

"…shut up…" Rickie snapped.

"…Paul was trying to start an IV…" Ariel started to laugh. "…and every time he wiped with the alcohol prep layers of skin flaked off…"

"…sometimes you just gotta wing it and jab…" Kelly tossed a log on the fire. "…with that much skin gone an infection is inevitable…you can't wipe all the way down to tendon…" *we all laughed at the thought.*

"…he ended up dying a few days later in Boston…"

"…mercifully…" Kelly sat back down. "…I did a call once where a guy tried killing himself by breaking a gas line in his house figuring he's asphyxiate…he didn't plan on the furnace kicking on and blowing his house off the foundation…" Kelly started laughing. "…the poor bastard came stumbling out of his house with all his clothes blown off except for the bands on his underwear…" *now we were all laughing hard.*

"…you know…" I interjected. "…all this talk has me craving toasted marshmallows…"

"…yeah Casey…dead on…" Rickie was with me.

"…I'll do you one better…" Kelly got up. "…I bought fixin's for S'mores…"

"…oh yeah…" *and a cheer went up from the crowd.*

"…Kelly always makes the best snacks…" Rickie lauded.

It just didn't get any better than this…dinner…stories and S'mores with friends…

…and no paperwork…

✵ ✵ ✵

So the evening/early morning ended with Ariel in no shape to drive and she knew it. Rickie and I weren't quite ready to sleep so we decided to go upstairs and stare at my stars for awhile. Somehow though Ariel beat us up the stairs and passed out in my futon. Not that I minded but it left very little room for both me and Rickie. So we started a new tradition. We climbed out the window in Rickie's room…sat on the porch roof and looked at real stars.

"…this is quite the view…" I lit the joint and handed it to Rickie.

"…yes it is…I could be happy sleeping out here…" Rickie leaned back.

"…but you know that's not really a good idea…right?…"

"…yes of course…" She took a hit. "…I just mean it's beautiful…that's all…"

"...okay...I don't mean to sound condescending...I just wouldn't want to not say anything and have you land on my Jeep... wreck my soft top...blah blah blah...it's all about me..."

"...got it..." We got quiet for a moment. "...so Ariel's passed out in your futon?..."

"...yeah...but she's small...I'll just slide her over and have plenty of room..."

"...too bad she's passed out..."

"...why?...it's the only way she'd ever be in my bed..."

"...so you two never really?..." Rickie's voice trailed off.

"...no...she's straight...and I'm pretty sure she's into labels... very specific labels..."

"....hmmm...maybe...you never really know..."

I pulled my knees up to my chest. "...you live a very different life than I do..."

"...nuh-uh...not that much different..."

"...maybe not...I don't know but I do know I don't let myself think about Ariel like that...I really love our friendship and I don't wanna do anything to weird her out and screw it up..."

"...there's nothing wrong with that..." Rickie looked up at the stars. "...you guys'll probably be friends for a long time..."

...I was hoping...

CHAPTER 27-
MAY I HAVE YOUR ATTENTION PLEASE?

*...he went down with them and stood on a level place...a
large crowd of his disciples was there and a great number of
people from all over BigCity and LittleCity and MiddleCity
and from the Region comprised of SmallTown...MiddleTown
and RichTown who had come to hear him and to be healed
of their diseases and be transported to external triage...
those troubled by management and the people all tried
to touch him...because power was coming from him and
healing them all...it's good to have a God you can touch...*

the following Monday...

"...okay everybody...if we could get started..." Mahan talked
into the microphone on the podium. At long last our union
meeting had arrived and we all assembled for the gathering
storm. "...just to get everybody up to speed...we're here tonight
to go over the proposed contract offer from NAA and vote on
whether or not to accept and ratify...I know word's gotten out
that the offered deal is less than what we hoped for...I'd have to
agree that it's much less than we hoped for but we need to be
clear with what's at stake...if we don't ratify tonight we go back
to the tables for one more window of negotiations....our union
reps tell me that it would probably be a sixteen-hour window...
if an agreement isn't worked out at that point we need to vote
tonight whether or not to proceed directly with a strike vote..."
There was a murmur stirring through the room. "...and all I want
to say about that..." Mahan spoke over the buzz "...is that non-
ratification without a strike vote is a ball-less stand...it won't say
anything to NAA except '...oh please...oh please give us what
we want...okay never mind...' I'd like to think we're going to

say a little more than that...all right...let's go over the contract proposal and then we'll open the floor for discussion..."

Mahan went over the contract...article by article...explaining what it had been and what it would become. Pretty much every dreaded change was now in black and white there for all eyes to behold and fear. Shifts would be changed to six-hour blocks. Everyone...regardless of seniority would have to work two blocks on the weekends. Weekends would begin Friday at 18:00 and end Monday at 08:00. Shifts would be put up for bid according to seniority and then assigned for a period of one year at which time they would be put back up for bid and reshuffled. A whole bunch of new reasons to fire people were written in. Like losing your gas card or not reporting damage to equipment...*for which you would be fired...*or sleeping on duty...including the overnights... or backing up without a spotter...regardless of the circumstances. The big money considerations worked out to be $1.50 an hour for medics...$1.00 an hour for intermediates...$.75 an hour for basics and $.50 an hour for the chair van drivers. Dispatchers and supervisors weren't part of the union so it was pointed out that they were all being given $2.00 an hour raises...*presumably because they weren't rabblerousing...*

The floor opened for discussion and people wasted no time expressing themselves. One intermediate suggested we tip over a few ambulances and set some stuff on fire...*I was surprised it wasn't Rickie...*another reminded us that it would be okay to get other jobs while we striked. As Mary Ann so eloquently put it "... practice it with me...'paper or plastic?' and 'would you like fries with that?'...either one will pay your bills...if you're scared...I get it...I'm a single mom...you think I'm not scared?...but we gotta do this...we gotta do it for ourselves and our kids because NAA doesn't care about us and anything they do has nothing to do with our survival...it's there's and don't forget it..."

Finally Kelly got up...*I wondered if she would...*and tied it all together. "...I'm really glad to see so many people here tonight...this turnout is great and it shows that we care...we care about our jobs and we care about the work we do...NAA tries to tell us that we're cowboys and we're reckless and we're no good for risk management and we present all kinds of problems for their successful business so they have to put in writing protections from us...to guarantee we will behave and we will follow the structured order...but I'm looking around the room and I see a lot of people who I've worked with and that I've been with in tough situations who have repeatedly shown me that they know what they're doing when it really counts...when we're out in the streets with nothing around us but crazy people and a problem we're entrusted to deal with...we care enough about our jobs to stay trained and relevant so that when it does get ugly we know we have each other's backs...there's a lot of hard-earned trust in this room and that's something an office manager is just never going to understand...but I also look around this room and I see a lot of faces gone...our friends who preferred to leave the job they loved rather than watch it be destroyed...that makes me pretty sad because so many of them were good people who did this job well...and I think the watering down of the experienced talent is what's really bad for the integrity of our job...I know this is supposedly a transient field and we're not supposed to want to do this work beyond the age of thirty but I'm still here and I can tell you...you should want to keep doing this work...we shouldn't want to keep seeing good people leave all the time...we have the opportunity to make this a legitimate career...something experienced people stay for...this contract is a turning point for us and if it's done right...its impact will be far reaching to people who aren't even here yet to understand what's being done for them...so I say we tell NAA to shove this horseshit up their ass and we're going to fight and work and demand that they honor us with the contract that we so deserve..."

...and the crowd went wild...

☆ ☆ ☆

After the vote the stewards stayed behind to count the ballots but we all already knew the results as we headed off to Sully's. It was a resounding fuck you and watch us walk if you feel the need to push it. I don't know about anyone else but I was scared out of my mind. I wondered how long my heart could keep up the pounding.

We were all circled around the bar when the 11:00 local news came on. Someone yelled quiet when they saw the NAA logo up on the screen and the bartender turned up the volume for us.

"...NAA employees voted tonight to turn down the proposed contract offer from North American Ambulance...most of NAA's employees involved in negotiations are trained emergency medical technicians including the forty or so paramedics responsible for covering BigCity 911 ambulance contracts...union officials say they will return to the negotiating table on Wednesday to continue negotiations for a sixteen-hour window...if an agreement cannot be worked out at that time the union has already ratified a strike vote... NAA officials could not be reached for comment at this time..."

"...that's fucking awesome..." Rickie was next to me at the bar.

"...pretty intense too..." I sipped my Sombrero.

Rickie sensed my angst. "...don't worry Casey...we'll find some fun jobs..."

"...fun jobs?..."

"…yeah…fun jobs like at the movies or a car wash…"

"…a car wash?…a car wash is not a fun job…"

"…sure it is…we can get stoned and have water fights…"

"…you're not planning on having this fun job for long are you?…"

"…well hopefully we'll be coming back to our real fun jobs sooner than later…"

"…I'll drink to that…"

"…I'll drink to anything…let's do shots…"

…eat drink and be merry for tomorrow we may picket…

✵ ✵ ✵

"…can you believe this heat?…" I tugged uncomfortably at my polyester waist.

"…this is great beach weather…" Ariel changed the battery in the portable.

"…you know what I've always wanted to do?…" I counted milligrams of Valium.

"…fly?…" Ariel had amused herself. "…at the speed of sound…"

"…well that too I guess but I was thinking of something more mortal…"

"…oh…do tell…"

"…okay…well…wouldn't it be cool to clean out the bench seat…fill it with ice and head to the beach?…then we could hit a seashore fish store and fill it back up with steamers and lobsters and have ourselves a big ol' clambake…"

"…you mean instead of our traditional posting location?…"

"…we're only told where to post…not necessarily how to get there…"

"…I think we'd be missed…"

"…isn't that supposed to be a good thing?…"

"…usually…"

"…posting skews everything…" I closed the narc box. "…god it's hot…"

☆ ☆ ☆

"…okay…here are our options…" I leaned on the steering wheel and stared at the fifteen-story building. "…we can walk up to the eighth floor and risk evaporating before we get there…"

"…lovely option…" Ariel pressed her face against the air-conditioning vent.

"…especially since it's only ten o'clock and my underwear has already sucked itself halfway up to my transverse colon…"

"…thanks for sharing…" She opened her collar and the a/c puffed out her shirt.

"…or we can confine ourselves in the tin can called the elevator and suck in all the lovely heated vapors of urine and crack fumes and baby laxative induced…"

"…enough…I got it…"

"…so what are we doing?…"

"…how about we buddy-breathe a non-rebreather off an O2 cylinder and ride in style?…"

"…for real?…"

"…yeah what the hell…desperate times call for desperate measures…and I threw an extra bottle in the house O2 compartment…"

"…you know…you're all right Skippy…" I patted Ariel on the back. She smiled and we moved onward.

☆ ☆ ☆

"…well I'm no coroner…" I looked at the decaying male prone on his linoleum kitchen floor.

"…oh boy…here we go…" Ariel swatted at a flock of swarming flies.

"...no...really...hear me out..." I did my best Dana Scully impression. "...I'd say he probably died of a GI bleed..."

"...and how did you come to that conclusion?..." I could tell Ariel was having a hard time trying not to breathe too deeply lest she smell anything.

"...look by his mouth...there's a trail of blood coming out..." I pointed from a distance with my pen.

"...there...where all the maggots are hanging out?..."

"...yeah..."

"...that's not blood..." Ariel shook her head. "...he's decaying and that's what decaying flesh looks like..."

"...we turn to liquid?..."

"...among other things..."

"...interesting..." I looked around. "...where the hell is a cop with a cigar?..."

"...wanna wait in the hallway?..."

"...and be mistaken for crack hos?...no thanks..."

Ariel laughed. "...I don't think anyone's going to think we're crack hos..."

"...my point exactly...we're not going to blend in..."

"...how much is left in that O2 tank?..."

"...1,000 PSI..."

"...let's hit it..."

"...WAHOO...it's a party..."

✿ ✿ ✿

"...isn't there some big country music doin's goin' on at the fairgrounds today?..." I taunted Ariel with a twang.

"...yes...I thought about getting a ticket...It's a daylong concert with a lot of big acts..." We moved up in the frozen yogurt line.

"...Kenny Rogers?..."

"...no..."

"…Alabama?…"

"….no…"

"…Oak Ridge Boys?…"

"…no…"This time Ariel cracked up.

"…well then who the hell else is there?…"

"…there's a lot more than Kenny Rogers…Alabama and The Oak Ridge Boys…" Ariel laughed and I ordered two cones. "…Trisha Yearwood…Kenny Chesney and my personal favorite…Clint Black…who's headlining today…"

"…these people mean nothing to me…"

"…well the three thousand people who bought tickets to the concert today know who they are…"

We get our cones and head back outside to the ambulance. Despite the heat we both dart to our respective doors to get in as fast as we can before our yogurts melt. "…so why didn't you get a ticket?…"

"…I don't know…I didn't want to go alone…"

"…you wouldn't be alone…three thousand of your tone-deaf brethren would have been with you…"

"…you know what I mean…"

"…no…actually I don't…" *I mixed in some licks.* "…I'd go to a concert by myself…in fact I have…"

"…really?…"

"…yeah…I go to movies alone and the planetarium…what the hell…I'm not going to waste my good years waiting at home for somebody else who for all I know is waiting at the concert for me…"

"…that's very profound…" Ariel was serious and stared out the windshield for a moment. "…now I wish I had bought a ticket…"

"…just make sure you buy the next one…"

…holy crap…I think I was just the wise one…

✫ ✫ ✫

"...OH MY GOD...I NEVER WANT TO LEAVE THIS ROOM..." My paperwork was done and now I swiveled in my chair and reveled in the tech room cold air.

"...well don't get too comfortable...on the way in the radio was busy..."

"...I know I know...it's just nice to have that perpetual bead of sweat running down my back and into my bra dry up for a minute or two..."

"...hey guys what's up?..." Jodie strolled into the room with her paperwork book in hand.

"...not much...how you guys holding up?..." I rolled my chair up next to her.

"...it's beastly out there...we just had to do a third-floor code..."

"...ugh..." I rolled away. "...my condolences to your underwear..."

"...what's going on with your underwear?..." Fergie entered the room with her arms full of epi...lidocaine...atropine and D50 boxes.

"...nothing...Casey's being weird..." Ariel joined the fray. "...where was your code?..."

"...the region...RichTown..." Fergie sorted boxes. "...59 y/o COPDer..."

"...she looked more like eighty..."

"...that's a rough disease..."

"...good reason not to smoke..." Ariel directed her tone toward me. "...ANYTHING..." I just smiled...truly honored that she had my good health at heart.

"...did you hear the madness up at the rotary?..." Jodie changed the subject.

"...yeah what's going on?..." Ariel asked.

"…it's a combination of concert traffic clogging up the rotary and the temperature of the concert grounds reaching one hundred plus…people are dropping like flies…nobody can get apparatus through and it's getting all fucked up…"

"…so how long before we get dragged into it?…" I wondered.

"…soon I'm sure…" Fergie answered.

"…oh boy…" Ariel stood up quickly and suddenly was all business. "…let's go…"

"…okay…" There was no point arguing. "… see ya guys…"

…and we were off like a wet Band-Aid…

✫ ✫ ✫

Just as we expected when we signed back on dispatch immediately sent us to the fairgrounds to assist with the many people dropping like flies. It was a treacherous journey through traffic as most of the travelers were hot and severely aggravated. They had been there awhile and probably assumed they'd be inside enjoying the show by now. They definitely didn't see why they had to get out of our way.

We plodded along until we got to the security gate. The guard seemed really happy to see us and feverishly waved us in and toward the first-aid stand. Again we plodded along but this time it was because of the sea of pedestrians.

"…do we have our invisible lights on or what?…" I was amazed that nobody was moving for us.

"…no kidding…" **BOMP BOMP** Ariel hit the air horn and a smattering of the herd parted way.

"…hey check it out…the fire department's hosing down the crowd…" I pointed to a parked fire engine spraying its deck gun on soggy fans.

"...that's a good idea..." Ariel leaned on the a/c vent again. "...pull over there by the tent..." Ariel pointed to a Red Cross tent that had been deployed next to the small first-aid building. As we pulled up we could see rows of cots filled with supine concertgoers. The supervisor was waiting for us as soon as we got out of the truck.

"...four-ten...glad to see you..." Travis offered a wave and then jumped right into his report. "...what we got here is about fifty overheated paying customers with no intention of missing any of their show..."

"...it was an expensive ticket..." Ariel offered sympathy.

"...well we got four in the air-conditioned first-aid station that are on the edge of transport and we've already shipped out twelve with related chest pain and shortness of breath..." Travis wiped his forehead. "...you guys missed the real craziness..."

"...we had to babysit liquid man..." I pointed at the tent dwellers. "...what's up with these folks?..."

"...most of them are minor heat exhaustion...we handed out water...ice packs and a few IVs..." Travis' voice trailed off as he stared at the tent. Ariel and I waited wondering what was next. Then as quickly as he faded...Travis jumped back in. "...I got two basic trucks at the E Gate standing by for transport and a medic in the first-aid station and another medic walking the grounds looking for passed-out people...we've had a bunch go down in the bathrooms...I need you guys in the tent revitalizing people... think of it as a huge triage farm..."

"...got it...a triage farm..." Ariel's dry retort almost cracked me up but I held it in since it seemed like I was always laughing at Travis. Once inside the tent we discovered a whole new world that unfortunately came with its own Nashville soundtrack.

"...do you think I could get them to turn down the music?..." I asked Ariel as we picked up our sphygmomanometers.

"…not likely but who knows…maybe it'll grow on you…"

"…is that what happens?…your feet stop moving in the forest and it wraps itself around you and envelops you like a mossy fern?…"

"…you might want to lower your voice…you are extremely outnumbered right now…" Ariel smirked.

"…AHHHHH…I hate it when you're right…" I took my sphygmomanometer and turned. Just then the whole crowd on the fairgrounds let out a collective *yee-haw* and I nearly had a seizure.

✫ ✫ ✫

Ariel and I started on opposite ends of the tent and worked our way to the middle. It was quite the hodge-podge of patrons. Most of them were fine by now and completely overjoyed at being able to lie in comfort for the concert while we waited on them delivering free bottled waters and granola bars. A few were still pasty and pale from their brush with heat exhaustion. We made sure they kept drinking their water and even provided a few with O2 and IV fluids. I saw Ariel send an elderly woman into the air-conditioned shelter and I directed a basic crew to transport a pregnant woman for me. A few hours into our triage we met in the middle.

"…how's it going?…" Ariel was fairly pasty herself.

"…it's okay…I think we can start letting some people go…" I tried to no avail to wipe my forehead with my shirt sleeve… *polyester has zero absorbability…*

"…that's a good idea…maybe if we clear out the tent a little the air will start moving…"

"…it is pretty stuffy in here…"

"…hey four-ten…" We heard Travis calling us.

"…does he even know our names?…" Ariel wondered.

"…personally I'd rather he didn't…"

"…four-ten…what's my update?…"

"…you're Travis Jeffries and we're not…"

"…what?…" Both Ariel and Travis stared at me.

"…Chevy Chase…Weekend Update…" I offered my explanation. "…never mind…"

"…we were just getting ready to go through and reevaluate… we're thinking we can start letting people go…"

"…sounds good…and hey…" Travis paused. "…make sure you guys are drinking water too…you look a little pale…" Travis nodded at Ariel.

"…I'm hot…" Ariel quasi-barked. Travis looked stunned that she raised her voice at him and sulked off.

"…you okay?…" I reached in the trash barrel full of melted ice and bottled water. "…here…take one…"

"…yeah…I'm just hot…"

"…understandable…" I looked around and felt inclined to slip into my best John Wayne. "…so what do ya say we boot some of these freeloaders outta here?…"

"…sounds good to me…" Ariel was anxious to wrap this puppy up and with that we turned and worked our way away from each other for another hour and a half. As expected…people were less than thrilled that we were kicking them off their cots but we remained pleasantly persistent and by 16:00 we found ourselves alone with a messy tent and a whole bunch of paperwork.

One nice thing about a hot spring day is that the sun doesn't stay out as long as it would in August so things can start cooling down a lot quicker. The crowd had been successfully watered inside and out and the mass casualty incident seemed to have played itself out. We looked around the empty tent and with no other obvious tasks we decided to clean up. We had just started picking up empty water bottles and granola wrappers when Travis came back around.

"…you guys don't need to do that…the fairgrounds is sending over some employees to clean up…" Ariel and I each dropped the water bottles in our hands. "…what I need you guys to do is take these portable coolers around and hand out water to anybody looking ill…and check around the grounds for anyone down…"

"…okay…" Ariel answered while we each slung the cooler handles over our shoulders.

"…do we get the big buttons with five dollars written on it?…" This was not how I had envisioned my Fenway vendor fantasy playing out.

"…you're not selling them…" Travis looked tired so I didn't continue. "…see you guys back here…" Travis looked at his watch. "… at 18:45…" He turned without looking at us and walked away.

Ariel and I paused for a second or maybe even longer. The heat definitely had us in a fog and at first what Travis told us to do didn't make sense. The MCI was done…why did he tell us to go look for passed out people? Then it clicked for Ariel. "…I think we just got the rest of the afternoon off…"

"…I know…you think?…" It slowly came to me. "…the heat must have really taken a toll on him…"

"…who knows…his baseline is hard to follow…" I laughed and Ariel continued. "…so we'll do a walkthrough of the grounds to make it look good and then we can find somewhere to hide…"

"…good plan Lucy…I'm with you…" Ariel and I started walking and all of a sudden our day turned great. The sun's angle had dropped considerably and a cool breeze offered to separate the polyester from my skin. I felt the sweat that had saturated my scalp all day dry and my hair started moving again. I felt cool in my shades striding with Ariel through the crowd as official envoys of mercy handing out water indiscriminately just to get out of carrying it. She was much calmer and her more usual shade of pale white girl. She even offered to buy me a fried dough and I gratefully took her up on her offer.

"...wow...I think this is the first time I'm actually hearing the music..." Ariel tipped her head up as if to catch the passing notes.

"...yeah...it has pretty much been a distant din behind the crowd noise..." I handed out a bottle of water to a kid with chapped lips while I waited for powdered sugar.

"...let's find somewhere quiet to sit and eat these..." Ariel paid the lady.

"...good idea..." I scanned the grounds. "...the horse arena is in that building..."

"...horse arenas don't usually smell good on hot days..."

"...horse arenas don't smell good on cold days but we're not going to find seats anywhere else..."

"...true..." Ariel accepted facts. "...and I really just want to sit down..." So we grabbed our doughs and ducked into the large brick building. As expected...the aroma was less than desirable but after liquid man not much was going to smell worse that day.

A few sweaty stragglers were scattered around the arena and Ariel seemed anxious to join them. She climbed up the stairs and flopped down in the second row. I sat next to her and we both removed our coolers.

"...I got two left...what should we toast to?..." I unzipped my cooler and handed off the beverage.

"...how about world peace and goodwill to all?..."

"...what is this...Christmas?...how about to world peace and dry underwear?..."

Ariel laughed. "...okay...to world peace and dry underwear..." We tapped our bottles and drank long hard cold gulps.

"...oh brain freeze..." I stopped mid gulp and faked a shudder. "...feels good to be cold..."We leaned back in our seats and draped our legs over the seats in front of us. Ariel swung her leg back and forth to the rockin' country beat and we just hung out munching on our fried doughs for awhile. A few songs went by and then the music stopped.

"…must be between bands…" Ariel recapped her bottle.

"…who's on next?…"

"…I don't know…what time is it?…" Ariel looked at her watch and then answered her own question. "…17:40…HEY…" Ariel got real excited and punched me.

"…what?…" I was truly shocked at her violent gesture.

"…Clint Black's going on at 18:00…"

"…no way…" Ariel was very excited and even though I couldn't understand why it was fun to see her goofy. "…well then what the hell are we doing here?…"

"…resting…"

"…resting…this is no time for resting…let's go…" I put my empty cooler back on and dragged Ariel with me. "…let's go meet Clint…"

"…meet him?…" Ariel's skeptical but followed anyway.

"…yes…or at the very least…we'll make sure he sees us…"

"…sees us?…"

"…yes…sees us…"

"…how do we do that?…"

"..there are ways…"

"…oh god…"

✫ ✫ ✫

Ariel and I left the horse arena behind and I directed us toward the stage area. The devil was heading down somewhere and beach balls filled the air. The remaining sturdy crowd filled out the grounds nicely and the cool breeze seemed to be doing everybody some good.

"…where are we going?…" Ariel expressed concern.

"…backstage…how many waters you got left?…"

"…eight…why?…"

"…eight?…didn't you hand any out?…"

"…not really…where are we going?…"

"…I told you…backstage…"

"…I'm not doing anything to get in trouble…"

"…of course not but how about we just try to have some fun?…" I stopped walking and turned to her. "…here…give me some water…" Ariel handed over a few bottles. "…about ten years ago I got within ten feet of Bruce Springsteen just by running at him…"

"…what stopped you?…"

"…two security guards with cold hands…" I laughed in reflection. "…but today we are not going to have to run at all…" We approached the backstage area. "…because we have uniforms on…we can go anywhere…" Ariel still looked skeptical. "… just follow my lead…" Ariel shrugged her shoulders and I continued ahead. A cop was posted at the official backstage entrance.

"…afternoon ladies…can I help you?…"

"…hey what's up officer?…" I reached in the cooler. "…we got sent around to hand out water to the public safety workers… we couldn't believe it when we found out nobody took care of you guys…"

"…no kidding huh…" He licked his lips. "…I am pretty parched…"

"…well here you go…have a bottle…"

"…thanks and hey…they're cold…" He happily took one. "… the guys inside could probably use some too…"

"…no problem…" He let us by and I turned and smiled at Ariel. She smiled back and we continued on. Next thing you know all our water was handed out…cops were very happy and we were standing on the stage behind a large amplifier.

TAP TAP TAP on a microphone. "...HELLOOO COUNTRY FANS...HOW THE HELL ARE YOU?..." *the crowd went wild.* "...MY NAME IS SHAGGY FROM BIGCITY COUNTRY RADIO 92.5...**AND ARE YOU HAVING FUN?...**" The local deejay whooped up the crowd some more while Ariel and I watched from behind. "...SO HOW ABOUT WE GET IT TOGETHER AND GIVE A LOUD BIGCITY RADIO 92.5 WELCOME TO THE REASON WE'RE ALL HERE TODAY?...COUNTRY'S GREAT...**MR....CLINT...BLACK**..." AND THE CROWD WENT **REALLY** WILD...

Just then I saw Ariel's eyes get really big and when I turned around Clint Black was jogging by us on his way to center stage. I saw him nod a hello to Ariel. Amazingly she managed a hi back before turning a deep shade of red.

"...he saw us..." I pointed out.

"...he saw me..." Ariel corrected.

Then the band kicked in...the music got going and Clint was breaking into the newest song from his newest album. I may not have enjoyed the actual song but you'd have to be liquid man not to be excited about being on stage during a large venue event. Ariel was beside herself. We were completely out of view of the crowd but we were still no more than ten feet away from Clint as he performed. The sky had a beautiful reddish glow to it and the cool breeze continued to circulate. It was a very awesome moment.

I looked at Ariel and she looked back grinning from ear to ear. I leaned in and shouted above the bass **"...AREN'T YOU GLAD YOU DIDN'T BUY A TICKET?..."** She shook her head and smiled and we enjoyed the rest of the night...

...anybody seen Tabitha?...

CHAPTER 28 -
WE NOW INTERRUPT OUR REGULARLY SCHEDULED TRANSFER

...there is a time for everything and a season for every activity under heaven...a time to scatter stones and a time to gather them...a time to embrace and a time to refrain...a time to search and a time to give up...a time to keep and a time to throw away...a time to transport and a time to take a refusal...a time to work and a time to vacation...

So seasons changed...spring turned to summer and a young paramedic's thoughts turned to that of vacation time. I couldn't afford to make crazy extravagant plans to get myself away from it all but that didn't mean I didn't look forward to taking a day here or there to sleep late...lie around in my sweats and watch *Laverne & Shirley* reruns all morning. I was even talented enough to follow that up with a full afternoon packed with nothing. With the crazy amounts of overtime Ariel and I worked it was enough just to have time pass without someone asking me to carry them or tend to them or keep them breathing just a little while longer.

Ariel and I pretty much took our vacation days at the same time to help each other not get stuck with a potential craptastic partner and at some point during the time off our afternoons of nothing would collide and we'd end up hooking up for lunch or rollerblading or something. It's pretty cool when a vacation from work isn't about a vacation from the person you work with.

Since we both used vacation time in the same judicious manner we never used all of it from year to year. In the old days that wasn't an issue because Carter let you carry it over. Ariel easily had four weeks accrued and I had two in reserve. Then NAA came along and decreed a proclamation. Vacation time was no longer to be saved up and since Carter and Valley apparently had poor record-keeping techniques it was not entirely agreed that we all had time left over to be used. Once again a stir went up from the crowd…murmurs of dissension could be heard throughout the city and blah blah blah the union was on it.

Ariel got nervous that she was going to lose everything she earned and immediately signed up for whopping blocks of time off. She mumbled something about it being time she visited her brother in North Carolina and the next thing I knew she was making airline reservations.

I saw the schedule in the supervisor's office and developed immediate shortness of breath. True…not all the partners du jour were bad…some were actually pretty good but there were also a lot of empty holes left and you know how smooth I am with change. Here are some stories that came out of my trials…

✡ ✡ ✡

Ariel's Vacation…Day One…

"…Casey…you workin' today?…" Kelly shuffled toward the coffee pot.

"…yeah 7a to 7p…" I stood in the kitchen sipping from my travel mug.

"…well are you taking the chopper in?…"

"…the chopper?…" I was confused.

"…yeah…are you flying?…"

"…not likely…"

"…then maybe you should get going…" Kelly motioned to the clock.

"…oh…yeah…" I started to pout.

"…what's wrong with you?…you're usually a half an hour early for every shift…" She stirred in sugar.

"…I usually know I'm working with Ariel…"

"...oh yeah your girlfriend left you for the week..." Kelly appeared sympathetic. "...you'll be all right...it's only four shifts..."

"...this week..." I corrected her. "...and then four shifts next week..."

"...Casey...I haven't had a regular partner in six months... you'll be fine for eight shifts..." *I sensed the sympathy was over.* "...so grab your scope...zip your boots and hit the streets..." Kelly then pushed me through the kitchen toward the front door.

"...all right all right...I get it...I'm gone..."

...and I was...

✩ ✩ ✩

"...CASEY...you're late..."Travis yelled at me as I ran through the door and speed swiped my ID card through the time clock.

"...I know...I'm sorry...no excuse good enough..."

"...your partner's waiting in the rig for you...get going... CHOP CHOP..."

"...received..." I flew down the aisle of parked trucks and found 410 with its back doors open. I poked my head in as I pulled my uniform shirt on over my T-shirt.

"...you dare to keep me waiting?..." Jodie bellowed over the open software supply bag she was inventorying.

"...oh my god..." *I was relieved.* "...I'm so sorry...if I knew it was you I would've been on time..."

"...I'll let it slide...I know you're in mourning over Skippy..." Jodie clipped the bag snaps closed and stowed it in the cabinet. "...but buck up little soldier...she'll be back..."

"...thanks Jodie...I'll take all the slack and sympathy I can get...Kelly gave me nothing but crap this morning..."

"…well she's a big meanie…c'mon…let's go see if we can make Travis cry…" Jodie hopped out of the truck. "…it'll take your mind off of things and it'll be fun…"

…and so our day began…

✫ ✫ ✫

"…so what do you think Casey?…" Jodie cleaned the light console with an antimicrobial wipe. "…we gonna strike or is NAA gonna wise up?…"

"…that's a trick question…" I tipped the steering wheel forward. "…there's the very real possibility neither will happen…"

"…how so?…"

"…well…obviously NAA has the resources and willpower to remain unreasonable…but some days I worry about people being able to stomach a strike…"

"…well that ship's sailed…"She pulled out another wipe. "…two days from now it comes down to that sixteen-hour negotiating window…the strike vote's already in…"

"…yeah…but there's no saying how long it'll last…if people turn out to have a weak stomach for it…things could end badly…"

"…anybody ever tell you you think too much?…"

"…besides you?…"

"…yeah…"

"…of course…I hear it all the time…I do think too much…I think it's genetic…"

"…or insanity…"

"…which is genetic…"

"…FOUR-TEN…FOUR-ONE-ZERO…"

"…four-ten…61 area…" Jodie answered dispatch.

"...FOUR-TEN TAKE THE PRIORITY TWO TO 30 OPAL STREET FOR COMBATIVE MALE WITH ABDOMINAL PAIN..."

"...four-ten received...30 Opal Street..." Jodie flipped on her newly antimicrobed light switches. "...drive slow and easy...this call's got bullshit written all over it..."

I knew exactly what Jodie meant. 30 Opal Street was the address for the BigCity Police Department and a combative male with abdominal pain was probably a nice term for dick prisoner looking to sit in the ER instead of a holding cell. When we pulled on scene a couple of cops flagged us over to the side parking lot where the cops park their personal vehicles.

"...morning ladies...how are you this fine day?..." The day cop chitchatted as we approached.

"...well...so far so good..." Jodie was putting on her leather gloves over her latex ones. That meant she sensed dirtbag. See... some techs wore the leather gloves so their latex ones didn't get torn or punctured while in contact with the body of a dirtbag. I just did what I could to avoid touching the dirtbags at all.

"...well...let's see what we can do about that..." The cop really seemed to enjoy this "...this here is John Day..." He pointed at a disheveled 20 something y/o male sitting on the ground wearing blue jeans...a white T-shirt and a tan overcoat. He kept his head down the whole time the cop talked. "...John here was in lock up all night...got out this morning and missed it so much he decided to come back and break some cop car windows so we'd notice him and lock him back up..." So far I didn't understand why we were there. "...however...as much as we would love to accommodate his need to spend special time with us...he has one of them crap bags on his waist and it needs to be emptied..."

Ahhh...it was all becoming clear now...

"Okay...how lovely..." Jodie clearly frowned. "...all right Mr. Day...let's go..." She folded her arms waiting for Mr. Day to rise. "...one of you guys riding with him?..." Jodie asked the cop.

"...he's way low risk...nothing violent..." The cop answered. "...I'm gonna send an officer behind you in a cruiser..."

"...sounds good..." Jodie agreed. "...c'mon let's go..." She exhorted the patient again. He was less than cooperative and I could tell Jodie had very little patience for this dance. "...c'mon asshole let's go...I'm in no mood..."

"...up John...c'mon...let's not keep the ladies waiting..."

"...FUCK YOU...I'm not going anywhere..."

"...LET'S GO..." And having tired of waiting for him to get up on his own the cop reached under his arms and assisted him to his feet.

"...FUCK YOU...GET OFF ME..." This time John started waving his arms around and rolling on the ground so it was harder for the cop to pick him up. This caused the cop to stop in his attempt. I wondered why he wasn't already handcuffed.

"...just what we fuckin' need...a scene on the PD front lawn..." The cop looked around like he was clearing the perimeter for media and such. "...Central this is CP 22..." He talked into his collar mike.

"...CP 22 WHAT'S YOUR LOCATION?..."

"...out your front window Central...can I get an assist out here?..."

"...RECEIVED CP 22...CHARLIE 4...WHAT'S YOUR LOCATION?..." And Central went on to activate the calvary. Meanwhile the patient seemed to enjoy the building drama and didn't let things go. He started grabbing the cop's legs trying to pull him down and now I wondered why he was considered low risk...nothing violent. Then the cop almost hit the ground and that's when Jodie got more involved.

"…oh this is bullshit…let's go Casey…grab his legs…"

"…oh boy…" And before I knew it I did indeed get low and grab onto his legs which was no easy task since he was actively kicking them. Jodie was laying across his torso and had one arm successfully pinned and the cop was grabbing the other arm and struggling to get him handcuffed...*so much for not making a scene on the PD front lawn...*Much to my consternation one of his legs got loose and Jodie had to give up strategic position on his torso to help out and in the ensuing chain reaction his arm got free. Creative bugger that he was he went right for his colostomy bag. I don't know exactly how full it was when the call began but it was pretty damn empty when he got done ripping it off and smearing it all over the cop. I was real grateful to be at the distal end of the patient when that tidy turn of events occurred.

The show was soon over though as PD back-up arrived quickly and the two cops in the cruiser wasted no time getting the patient subdued. Jodie and I backed off and dusted ourselves off while the violated cop swore up a storm and peeled his uniform shirt off. Unfortunately the patient really needed transport now and he was a raging…stinking mess.

Strangely though I was feeling pretty charged up. I had never wrestled with a patient like that before. I mean…I got close a few times and that alone was quite the rush but this was completely different. It was really hands-on and kind of exhilarating. I honestly never felt like that before. It wasn't like I was mad because I was threatened or anything but I felt strong…tough...*like a cowboy in the city...*

We wrapped the patient up in a blanket and transported without further incident to the Mercy. Jodie got stuck with the transport and paperwork and I got stuck with deconning the truck.

"...Casey...you got that stench out of the truck yet?..." Jodie walked up to the open back doors and I was on my knees scrubbing the cabinet where he managed to smear feces into the door track.

"...working on it..." I sprayed the disinfectant. "...how did he get it in here?..."

"...he was pretty covered and intent on smearing his ass all over the place..." She flipped the paperwork over and copied the billing info. "...so is this what I should expect from an OT shift with you?..."

"...me?..."

"...yeah...I don't do this crap with Fergie...we always get the sweet old ladies with chest pain and DVT...none of this colostomy bag bullshit..."

"...well I don't think it's me...I've never had to help the cops wrestle anyone down before..."

"...really?..." Jodie was genuinely shocked.

"...no...me and Ariel usually stay clear until the action dies down..."

"...can't see where that would have worked today..."

"...yeah...guess not..." I started thinking about the call wondering how it would have gone if I was working with Ariel. I didn't get too far with my thoughts when Jodie interrupted.

"...hey dispatch called the ER...they got some patient on the third floor they need scooted over to Valley Trauma...I guess she's got a line so they want us to take her..."

"...okay...I think I've done all I can here..."

"...we'll leave the doors open for maximum airage..."

I wrapped up my cleaning supplies and Jodie and I headed to the elevators with our shiny...newly scrubbed stretcher.

"...so Jodie...let me ask you a question..."

"...what?..."

"...okay..." The elevator opened and we entered. "...so if Wonder Woman's plane is invisible...how does she find it in the parking lot?..."

"...she makes Gabrielle stay with it..." The door closed and Jodie pushed the number three button.

"...Gabrielle?...that's Xena not Wonder Woman..."

"...Wonder Woman...Xena...they're both the same..."

"...how do you figure?..."

"...they both got the wrist things...that chakra ain't much different than a lasso and they both hang out with Amazons...and you know if Gabrielle and Xena are hanging around the Amazon's they're gonna run into Wonder Woman..."

"...and Wonder Woman borrows Gabrielle to stay with her plane?..."

"...yes and Xena told her it was okay to treat her rough too..." Jodie got a look in her eye that scared me.

"...okay...this has officially gone farther than I feel comfortable with..."

"...oh come on Casey...this is not new to you...don't play coy with me..." Jodie gave the stretcher a couple of playful pushes into my ass. Even without seeing my face she knew it had turned red and that pleased her to no end. We rolled up on the nurses' station and mercifully the conversation concluded. It was my tech so I smiled at the nurse and accepted the wad of paperwork and cursory patient report.

The patient had an IV but everything else about the call was very basic and the patient was very stable so I decided to do the paperwork at the desk. That way I could just sit back on the ride and chill. Jodie acknowledged the plan and slipped off to find something to do while I wrote. I was deep in documentation mode when she apparently found a working TV in a nearby empty room. She was about two doors away from the nurses' station and heard first when an old familiar voice called to me from the darkness of the room in between us.

"…Jodie…Jodie Twist?…I know that's you…" At first I didn't hear but Jodie did.

"…Jodie…Jodie Twist?…"

"…Casey?…" Jodie called to me.

"…almost done…"

"…no…Casey…now…"

"…what?…" My attention came into focus.

"…Jodie Twist…Jodie Twist…I see you…" Suddenly I heard… **and shuddered.**

"…why does that woman know my name?…"

"…uhhh…I don't know…but I have heard you're pretty famous…"

"…I'm not pretty famous at all…"

"…uhhhh…"

"…yoo-hoo Jodie…Jodie Twist…"

"…Casey…why does that woman think you're Jodie Twist?…"

"…uhhh…I wouldn't say she does…"

"…PSSST…Jodie…" The woman was leaning out of her bed beckoning me.

"…Casey…that woman knows my name and she thinks you're me…"

"…well there's no accounting for taste…"

"…that doesn't make any sense…" Jodie was now closing in on me and the nurses' desk.

"…Jodie…Jodie Twist…can I have some punch?…"

"…Casey…" I feared for my safety.

"…okay…okay…I told her I was you one day so she'd stop asking me my name…" Jodie was now on top of me.

"…why me?…"

"…because…" She stared hard. "…because Ariel and I had just been talking about what a great pal you are…"

"…a great pal?…" Jodie was skeptical.

"…yes and how kind you are and how well you mesh into the fabric of the community…" She wasn't buying it. "…and when this lady asked my name…your name was there and it just rolled off my tongue before I knew it…" I looked humbly to the floor. "…I'm sorry…I'm so sorry…I have toyed with your identity and I could not be more ashamed…"

Jodie paused. "…you apologize well Casey…" She softened her stance. "…and it's a good thing…" She paused before she released me. "…but don't give my name out to psych patients anymore…"

"…okay…you got it…I'm sorry…"

…to think I used to be afraid of her…

Ariel's Vacation…Day Two…

When my shift with Jodie ended I immediately went back into my *dreading-my-next-partner* mode. My and Ariel's next shift was a twelve-hour overnight and not too many self-respecting medics volunteered for the overnight. They just weren't any fun. Sure the first few hours could be exciting but once the shine of the bright lights and funny-acting people wears off it gets old quick. Then around 02:30 your eyes start demanding to close and they don't make allowances for things like driving to Boston on a long-distance transfer. Working the overnights can also put you in touch in a very up close and personal way with your Circadian rhythm. My experience with the overnights taught me that my personal internal clock demands that everyday…no matter what I'm doing I have to fall asleep at exactly 04:30. I particularly experienced it in a most violent way in dispatch where many a times my head would bounce right off the counter in front of me without fail every morning at 04:30. You can try to suppress it but that's as feasible as fighting anesthesia. I...among others...have managed to prove that you can sleep standing on your feet asking a patient questions or leaning on a counter writing your paperwork or sitting in the cab of the ambulance drinking a coffee...***nobody was going to want to work this shift with me...***

"...hey Casey what's shaking?..." I looked up to see Fergie walking across the fluorescent-light-lit line of ambulances.

"...are you working tonight?..."

"...yeah..." She nodded.

"...who ya workin' with?..."

"...you ya Loser..."

"...me?..."

"...yeah..."

"...all right...let's get coffee..."

"...of course...what else?..."

☆ ☆ ☆

I hadn't even thought about Fergie working the shift. She was actually one of those rare people who can work endless hours at crazy intervals without it affecting her cognitive skills. Probably that was because she had way more cognitive skills than the average bear to begin with so she could absorb the loss a little easier.

I had never worked a shift with Fergie but I'd been around her long enough to know she was pretty cool. She was one of those people that when you were working with them you hoped something big happened because you knew they'd be amazing and bring the disaster to a suitable conclusion.

Universally it was also agreed that she had to be one of the most evolved and patient people as evidenced by her ability to be Jodie's everyday partner for five years running now. I mean... we all love Jodie and she's a very talented...skilled medic but she also has a very intense personality and day after day it can be challenging to keep up with her. Fergie pulled it off masterfully.

I wasn't the only one who noticed her "Fergie-ness." As I've pointed out many times EMS is filled with very intelligent people. However…every now and then someone comes along that everyone agrees is a much higher intelligent life form than the rest of us and Fergie was one of those people. Even Kelly…who was no slouch herself…met and got to know Fergie and started calling her "Doc." It may be the cliché nickname for a medic but it really made sense for Fergie. In fact nobody would have been surprised if one day Fergie showed up and told us she had been accepted to and managed to graduate from Harvard Med School without any of us knowing. She was that smart and that humble. The two of them displayed a strong respect for each other with neither one of them ever believing the praise the other one gave. It was all so disgustingly noble it made you want to puke.

On a shallower note Fergie also had impeccable taste in coffee. Normally we standard coffee rats are divided into two groups… either you loved Dunkin' Donuts or you loved Bess Eaton. Neither was even close for Fergie and in order to feed her finicky addiction she kept herself up on all the relevant out-of-the-way places to get freshly ground amazingly flavored beans. These places also usually came with fantastic baked goods.

"…The Human Bean…" I looked up at the neon sign. "…I like it…it's very hip…very chic…"

"…you're funny Casey…" Fergie put it in PARK and I grabbed the portable radio. "…and just to let you know…they got the best chocolate chip scones here…"

"…I'm thinking brownies…" I drooled at the mere thought of it.

"…oh…well…you know what they have?…they got this monster caramel…turtle kind of chocolate thing…" Fergie demonstrated the mass of the chocolate mound with her cupped hands and I became giddy at the thought.

"…YES…WHY ARE WE STILL IN THE TRUCK?…let's go…"

"…LET'S GO…" Fergie cheered and we hit the ground running. We both got to the door at the same time and squeezed our way in…giggling and providing amusement for the two pretty stoned teenagers manning the counter. We noticed right away that they found our every move…even the more reasonable ones…humorous so we just played along with it. In fact…Fergie even played it up a bit asking me if I had any weed.

"…on me?…" I curiously asked.

"…yeah…" She smiled wide and shook her head.

"…ah no…I left it in the truck…"

"…you guys got weed in the ambulance?…"

"…sure…" Fergie continued to pull their chain. "…we gotta get through our night too…"

"…cool man…I wanna get a job as an ambulance driver too…" The counter help smiled and poured. I laughed to myself since I knew Fergie was just as square as Ariel when it came to contraband. She just seemed to have a better sense of humor about it.

When we were done tormenting the teenagers and had sufficiently loaded up on all kinds of gooey things and super large caffeine products we headed back to work. From my estimation I figured I'd stay revved up on the goods for at least four to six hours.

For the first part of our buzz Fergie and I spent our energy on very typical no-nonsense calls like chest pains and diff breathers. I was hoping we'd get to do some really cool mysterious disease calls so I could pick Fergie's brain and watch her diabolically diagnosing mind turn. But unfortunately…there aren't too many virally infected monkeys being dumped off on the streets of BigCity so there's not a large call for super cool mysterious disease diagnosing. Come 02:00 we were doing yet another typical "bar doors open and spit out all the drunks to the streets" calls. We found this particular drunk in the breakdown lane of Rt. 291.

"…so I was out doing my patrol…"The state trooper pointed toward the breakdown lane. "…and I come around the bend and this dope is parked in the right travel lane…" Fergie and I stared at the Honda Accord now parked in front of the cruiser. "…I know he's blotto…but he told me he's a diabetic so I gotta call you guys to check him out…"

"…yeah sure…no problem…" Fergie smiled. "…are you gonna stay here while we evaluate?…" Fergie wanted to make sure the trooper didn't leave our sixes exposed.

"…yeah…you got my lights as long as you need…"

"…thanks…we'll be quick like…" Fergie and I turned and headed over to the car. Two tractor trailers blasted by us and I felt myself being sucked forward.

"…whoa…" Fergie's eyes got big so I knew she felt it too.

"…glad my boots are tied tight…" I took big steps in toward the guardrail.

"…hey…what's going on?…" Fergie approached the car and leaned into the driver's side window.

"…not much babe…how 'bout you?…" The very charming 50ish y/o dude answered.

"…she's fine buddy…but she wasn't parked in the travel lane of the interstate…" I leaned in the passenger side and nearly passed out from the fumes.

"…oh hey…a friend…" He turned his charm to me. "…hey sweetie… what's up?…"

"…not much…you been drinkin'?…"

"…nooooo…a little bit…ha hah ahahahaa…" He now shared his charm between the two of us.

Fergie pulled her head out of the window and I joined her above the car roof.

"...this guy is snockered..." Fergie expressed disgust. "...the easiest thing to do is just get him in the ambulance and take him..."

"...yeah...sure...whatever's the fastest..."

"...I have an idea..." Fergie ducked back into the car. "...hey Buddy...what's your name?..."

"...Robert...Robert Mitchum..." He closed one eye and pretended to shoot Fergie with his thumb and forefinger. "...but you can call me Bobby..." He smiled and Fergie and I met back up over the roof again.

"...his name is not Robert Mitchum..."

"...no...huh..." Fergie feigned disappointment. "...damn... and I was going to ask for an autograph..." I shook my head and we ducked back in. "...okay Bobby...here's the deal..." Fergie laid out the proposition. "...that nice officer over there wants to take you to jail..." Fergie pointed back to the lit-up cruiser. "...me and my partner..." Fergie pointed between us and he slowly turned his glassy eyes toward me. "...we wanna take you to the hospital... isn't that better?..."

"...oh yeah..." He nodded slowly.

"...but if you don't come quietly with us the officer is going to hear you and take you to jail..."

"...okay...shhhhh..." And he put his finger up to his mouth in an exaggerated pattern. "...I'll be real quiet..."

"...good..." Fergie shook her head and opened the door for him. Amazingly he kept his promise and did his best to quietly walk past the cruiser and scoot into the ambulance. Of course the trooper didn't care because he was just going to complete the arrest later at the hospital. He might even get someone to obtain a blood sample for him to make it all really official. He gave me a wave as I walked past his door and I smiled hoping maybe he'd remember my face for future reference.

Once in the ambulance Fergie wasted no time checking the guy's blood sugar. There always was the chance he was telling the truth and he was a diabetic.

"…one-eighty…" Fergie held the glucometer up to the light.

"….one-eighty…we have a winner…" My humor suffers in the early morning hours.

"…what we don't have is a diabetic issue…" Fergie reached up front and grabbed the paperwork book. "…I'll take one slow ride to the Valley Trauma please…"

I took my gloves off. "…you got it…"

Once at the Valley Trauma Fergie finished up her paperwork at the counter and I hung out by the laundry cart making up the stretcher. Our patient got put in one of the low priority beds in the hallway. There was nothing medically wrong with him. He just needed to be watched to make sure he didn't hurt himself or choke on his own vomit. That placement unfortunately put me right in his sightline.

"…hey sweetie…" I ignored. "…pssst…honey…babe…" *I swear I was gonna punch him in the head.* "…hey…hey…"

"…what?…what do you want?…" I walked slowly toward him.

"…hey…I'm sorry…" He put on the drunken apology face. "…I'm really sorry…I hope I wasn't too much of a problem for you and your friend…"

"…for us?…no…for everyone trying to safely drive on the same highway as you…well that was a bit of a problem…"

"…oh hey…you're right…" He continued. "…I'm really sorry to them…but hey…" He reached forward. "…I need a favor…"

"…a favor?…" I stopped walking. "…you want a favor from me?…keeping you out of jail tonight wasn't enough?…"

"…it was…" He belched. "…that was a lot…but…"

"…but what?…what else do you want?…"

"…well…I can't remember…uhhhh…I can't remember…can you tell me what car I was in?…"

"…what car you were in?…"

"…yeah…what car….'cause they towed it right?…"

"…yeah…they will…"

"…and I gotta get it outta impound right?…"

"…yeah you will…"

"…well I can't remember what car I left in tonight…was it the minivan or the Honda?…"

"…you can't remember what car you were driving on the interstate?…"

"…I know…it's awful…I know…I'm sorry…" He tried to give me another charming look.

"…the minivan…"

"…the minivan…oh thank you…are you sure?…"

"…am I sure?…" I mockingly laughed. "…well I do get tired this time of morning but yes…I am sure because I remember saying to my friend…what is a hot guy like that doing in a geeky minivan?…"

"…you did?…really?…"

"…oh yeah…"

"…it's my wife's…but we're not close…"

"…oh too bad…"

"…no really…"

"…oh yes really…really too bad…"

✧ ✧ ✧

"…so what do you think about negotiations?…" I broke into conversation while Fergie punched the gas card code into the keypad.

"...negotiations?..." Fergie leaned while she pumped. "...I don't know...I honestly don't put a lot of energy into it..."

"...how do you do that?..." I peeled the wrapper from my gum.

"...well...it's not so much how you do...it's more like how you don't..."

"...okay..." I waited for elaboration.

"...I just don't pay much attention to it..."

"...how do you manage that?...it's all anyone talks about..."

"...yeah..." Fergie shifted her weight and adjusted her glasses. "...I guess I just end up leaving the room on a lot of conversations...I can't get caught up in all of it...you know?...I got school going on and I'm working a lot of hours...I can't take on all that drama too..."

"...but it's more than drama...it's about our jobs..."

"...true and I'm not saying there's not some importance to it but really in the scheme of things what about it is worth getting all worked up about?...there's always been crap and there's always going to be crap...it's the nature of the business..."

"...exactly and that's why we have to at least attempt to resist the crap..."

"...how?...how are you going to resist?...it's the way it is..." Fergie chose her words carefully. "...that's like saying you're going to resist gravity or inertia...you can give it a shot and you might have some limited success but in the end you're going to get sucked back down to earth..."

"...well I think we resist by sticking together and not letting them steamroll us uncontested..."

"...absolutely...you're right but you gotta be really careful not to get too wonky with your expectations...some things are just never going to change...you know?..." I shook my head that I knew. "....try to think of it like this...there's a city...actually...there's a bunch of cities and some small towns right?..." I nodded my head in agreement. "...and in those communities are people and where you have people you have ambulance calls...we know this because it's been going on longer than there's been ambulances to do the calls...as far as we know it's been going on since the caveman days when Grog hit Bogg over the head with a club and then dragged his hairy butt over to Steve and said '...hmmm...you fix..."

"...Grog...Bogg and Steve?..." *I might have been focusing on the wrong details.*

Fergie continued. "...and as long as there're calls there's always going to be some company here to make money off those calls and they're always going to do that by exploiting young underpaid lackeys like us willing to give our vertebral discs to science..." Fergie gestured sternly with her hand. "...and it doesn't matter what uniform you're wearing...they all come with dumb rules and unrealistic expectations for the labor forces...but they can never affect what happens when you're out of their sight and on your calls...and that's where the real work happens anyway and you should always have total control of that..." *and with that the pump clicked off.*

"...and what about posting and crappy shifts and swapping off partners?..."

"...just the rules of today...and rules of today are like the weather in New England..." Fergie tapped the nozzle and put it back in its cradle. "...you weren't around back in the day when Jodie and I first started working together...at least once a month the bosses would realign the schedule and tell us they didn't want women working together...it was too dangerous..."

"...for who?...you guys or the patients?..."

"...good question...but anyway...we took care of it and they never split us up..." She removed the nozzle.

"…that sounds great but those were the old days…those were small companies with local bosses…"

"…I get that…and I'm not saying that some of the crap NAA throws at the walls isn't going to stick…but what makes you think the union is any more on our side?…"

"…they have to be…that's what we pay dues for…"

"…you're right…that's what you pay your dues for but don't be naïve…the union is as much a business as NAA is…you think it's a coincidence there's a business manager in the union?…"

I hadn't thought of it like that. "…yeah…I guess not…"

"…so NAA is out for NAA and the union's out for the union and we're at the bottom of the crap pile just trying to get by…"

"…now I'm depressed…"

"…don't be depressed…just keep it in perspective…isn't all that matters is that you get to be a paramedic and you get to use your skills to take care of people and play this little game that we play?…no one's ever going to take that away from us…the rest is just fluff…"

"…posting is just fluff?…"

"…posting is just the rule of today…and it or we could be gone tomorrow…you just don't know…"

"…interesting…and definitely a different way to look at it…" We walked toward the cashier together. "…so how is it you and Jodie make this work?…especially with the close tight spaces of posting…"

"…she is pretty fiery…" Fergie smiled and signed the gas receipt.

"…so are you…but you're also on opposite ends of opinions…"

"…we've been working together a long time…we got dirt on each other so it keeps us both in line…" She laughed again and pointed to the magazine rack by the door. "…wanna check out the porn?…"

"…sure…"

"…FOUR-TEN…FOUR-ONE-ZERO…"

"…oh well…guess the porn must wait…"

"…four-ten at the pumps…" I answered dispatch. "…go figure…story of my life…"

✡ ✡ ✡

Fergie's protest notwithstanding…it was not lost on either of us that the end of our shift also marked the beginning of the highly anticipated sixteen-hour final window of negotiations. I went home my usual tired self but I wasn't sure how much sleeping I'd get in. As I was walking in the door Kelly was heading out.

"…hey Casey…how was your shift?…" Kelly stopped to stuff the cable bill in the mailbox.

"…excellent…I worked with Fergie…" I leaned on the porch rail. "…we had massive chocolate snacks and didn't get slammed too bad…"

"…glad to hear it…" She broke down the stairs. "…today's the big day huh?…"

"…yeah…I feel like I'm on that episode of the *Bionic Woman* when she has to beat the doomsday clock…"

"…of course you do…" Kelly laughed. "…but ya might want to make sure you get yourself some good REM sleep today Casey… and be at Sully's tonight for 22:00…a bunch of us are hanging out to wait for the report from negotiations…"

"…sounds good to me…" I started walking toward the door. "…have a good shift…"

"…will do…over and out…"

✡ ✡ ✡

"…hey Casey…over here…" I walked into Sully's and a table of people called to me.

"…hey guys…what's up?…" I asked Kelly…Rickie…and Jodie…all who were sitting behind empty beer bottles and half-filled drink glasses.

"…not much yet…" Kelly answered first. "…get yourself a drink and join us…"

"…yeah…sure…anybody need anything?…"

"…I'll take a beer…" Rickie held up a near-empty Amstel bottle.

"…I'm good…" Kelly waved me off.

"…seven and seven Casey…light on the ice…" Jodie instructed.

With fear in my heart I turned to Kelly. "…is she okay?…"

"…so far…we're keeping a close eye on it…" Kelly patted Jodie on the back and smiled so I felt better. I gathered the refreshments and returned to the table.

"…so Casey we've been discussing your plight…" Rickie's words took me back.

"…my plight?…what am I a UNICEF child?…" I get unusually defensive after a night shift.

"…you'd think the way you've been carrying on…" Jodie chirped. "…you know…the whole living-without-Skippy shtick…"

"…yeah I guess I've been a little mopey…"

"…a little mopey?…" Kelly exaggerated her reply. "…you're making the dog depressed…" I smiled hopeful that they were just playing with me but tired enough to be paranoid.

"…not to worry though…me and O'Brien are going to save you next week…"

"…me too…" Jodie interjected. "…don't forget me…"

"…of course not Jode-ster…" Kelly jabbed. "…if it wasn't for you we wouldn't know Casey wasn't a load to work with…"

"…a load?…" These guys were killing me.

"…actually…we all took the extra shifts 'cause we figure we'll be on strike anyways so we won't have to work 'em…" Rickie's words cut deep.

"…you guys are awesome…" I raised my glass in a mock toast. "…no finer friends could be found…"

"…hey hey…" Jodie toasted back.

"…here's to us…" Kelly joined.

"…TO US…" they all said in unison.

"…O'BRIEN…KELLY O'BRIEN…" the bartender called across to us. "…YOU GOT A PHONE CALL…"

We all got quiet and then Rickie made Dracula movie music noise. "…DUH DAH DAH DUHHHHHH…" Kelly popped up and walked over to the bar. We all stared intently even though we couldn't hear her and she had her back turned to us. Finally… *after what seemed like forever…*Kelly handed the phone back to the bartender and came back to the table. She was not smiling.

"…that was Mahan…" Kelly pulled her chair out sharply and sat down.

"…what's up?…" Rickie was brave enough to ask.

"…the fucking union screwed us over…"

"…why?…what happened?…" Jodie got real serious.

"…as expected the negotiation window passed without an acceptable contract offer so the team informed NAA that we would officially be on strike at midnight…that's when NAA pulled out some statute pertaining to emergency services workers that says we have to give ten days written notice before we can strike…"

"…WHAT?…" Rickie exclaimed.

"…are you kidding me?…" I was shocked.

"…oh what kind of bullshit is this?…" Jodie was loud.

"...and apparently when NAA pointed this out all our union geniuses could manage was '...oh yeah...we thought something like that might apply...'"

"...are you fucking kidding me?..." Rickie was pissed.

"...what the hell?..." Jodie slammed her glass down.

"...so now what?..." I was almost afraid to ask.

"...now we head back to the negotiating table looking like clueless wonders...the union did a real good job of undercutting us..." Kelly started peeling the label off her bottle. "...and now we got a monster task ahead of us to keep everybody motivated..."

"...yeah...I've already heard rumors that some medics have gone to management to negotiate side deals if they cross the picket line..." Jodie threw out.

"...yeah...I heard that too...I guess Siano offered to cross if they promised him the next supervisor's spot..." Rickie added.

"...that fat bastard..." Kelly sneered and the rest of us got quiet. I started thinking about what Fergie had just said about the union and couldn't help but note the irony of the timing. I don't know what anyone else was thinking but looking around the table everyone was frowning with disappointment. "...well this is getting us nowhere..." Kelly stood up and pushed her chair in. "...I gotta get out of here...I'll see you guys later at the house... Jodie...as always a pleasure..."

"...see ya O'Brien...don't worry...we'll get this thing nailed..."

"...yeah Kelly...it ain't over..." I encouraged.

"...yeah I bet the worst thing that comes out of this is that we all get stuck working those shifts with Casey next week..." Rickie laughed hard.

"...oh that's right..." Kelly remembered. "...oh man that sucks..." And she smacked me on the arm. "...see ya guys..."

...and she was gone...

CHAPTER 29-
WE ARE EXPERIENCING TECHNICAL DIFFICULTY

...a time to tear and a time to mend...a time to be silent and a time to speak...a time to love and a time to hate...a time for war and a time for peace...a time to tear down and a time to build...a time to negotiate and a time to vandalize...

The three of us wrapped up our evening up at Sully's on that less than happy note. Even with putting our heads together and brainstorming it was really hard to get a handle on things. NAA's behavior was understandable and certainly to be expected but what was up with the union? Was it incompetence...laziness or were they somehow in cahoots with the enemy? Or was it like Fergie said and they were just another business looking out for their own interests? A strike by emergency workers was not anybody's idea of a good time but that was supposed to be our leverage...***not our undermining...***

Then again...did any of that even matter? The only fact that remained pertinent was that we were quickly losing ground and momentum and it was starting to feel like those were just illusions to begin with.

Back to the melodrama of Ariel's vacation. While it was true my pals were going to bail me out the following week there were still two shifts left to this week...

...anything could happen...

☆ ☆ ☆

"...oh look...a memo to the people..." I stared at the employee notice posted on the board above the time clock.

"…what now?…" Jodie swiped her ID badge. "…no talking in the trucks between calls?…company physicals will now include anal probes?…"

"…ANAL PROBES…" Fergie walked in the door and toward us. "…any shift that starts with the term 'anal probe' cannot end well…"

"…relax…Jodie got way off track…" I pointed at the memo. "…I was talking about the big ceremony coming up…"

Fergie swiped her badge. "…ceremony?…what are we commemorating?…"

"…anal probes in the company physicals…" Jodie giggled.

"…you truly frighten me…" I took a step back from her.

"…no…a special ceremony to mark the grand opening of NAA's new BigCity headquarters…" Fergie read from the memo. "…all are encouraged to attend…there will be a BBQ lunch on the front lawn…special treats for the kids include a clown and face painter…"

"…grand opening?…" I scrunched my forehead in honor of Ariel. "…haven't we been open a while?…"

"…ever since my last anal probe…" Jodie laughed.

"…let's go Twist…" Fergie grabbed her by the arm and laughed. "…you're scaring the new people again…"

✵ ✵ ✵

The last two shifts of the week were filled by nameless schmoes who did nothing to raise my spirits. One of the schmoes entertained me unmercifully with retellings of his personal ad conquests. My personal favorite being "…when I woke up and found the wig and dentures on the nightstand I got nervous… hahahhahahahaha…"

The other schmoe was less obnoxious but his people skills left a lot to be desired and I spent all day apologizing to everyone he left in his wake. At one point he fell asleep in the passenger seat and I didn't wake him up until I needed him to drive to the hospital.

"…the Valley Trauma…we're going to the Valley Trauma?…" He wiped the drool from his acidic lips. "…why?…"

"…because Mr. Lynch here believes he is having a reaction to his penicillin…" I pointed to the blotchy guy on the bench seat.

"…where'd he come from?…"

"…his living room…you were asleep…"

"…and you didn't wake me?…"

"…didn't see the point…"

…and that's all I want to say about those two shifts…

✧ ✧ ✧

"…Casey…hand me that can of White Lightning…" Rickie asked while wiping down her sprocket.

"…here ya go…" I flipped the bottle. "…you still got a big chunk of goop on your derailleur…"

"…what the hell are you guys doing?…" Kelly entered.

"…cleaning our bikes…" Rickie nonchalantly offered.

"…in the living room?…"

"…it's raining out…" I retorted.

"…what's wrong with the porch?…"

"…can't see the TV…" Rickie motioned to the screen. "…*Law and Order* with the hot chick DA is on…"

"…ADA…" I corrected.

"…ADA…" Rickie confirmed.

"…don't get grease on the rug…" Kelly looked around. "…and is this my toothbrush?…"

"…was it in the downstairs bathroom?…" Rickie casually asked.

"…yes…"

"…then yes…it's your toothbrush…" Rickie sprayed lubricant. "…I thought it was an extra one…"

"…an extra one?…" Kelly tapped the toothbrush on the coffee table. "…what are we a Holiday Inn?…we don't have extra toothbrushes lying around…"

"…oh…"

"…anyway…" Kelly flipped the toothbrush. "…we need to talk…"

"…what's up?…" I wire-brushed my chain.

"…we need to get serious about this negotiation crap…"

"…we're serious…" Rickie cranked down on her wheel tightener.

"…but we can get seriouser…" I transitioned through my gears.

"…seriouser'?…" Rickie started laughing. "…is that even a word Casey?…"

"…I don't know…" I started laughing too. "…it could be if we want…"

"…are you two stoned?…" Kelly seemed frustrated.

"…of course…" Rickie chirped.

"…who would clean their mountain bike sober?…"

"…got it…" Kelly sat down in the recliner. "…do you two goofs think you can temporarily handle a serious conversation?…"

Rickie and I looked at each other. "…I'm willing to try…"

"…me too…seriously…"

"…alright let's go…" Kelly reclined and we put our tools down and sat on the couch. "…as you know…we really got hosed by the union…"

"…seriously…" Rickie laughed.

"…stop saying seriously…"

Now I laughed and Rickie just smiled. "…sorry…"

"...the union really dropped the ball and the worst repercussion from that is we're losing momentum...we got nine days left on our ten-day notice and we could end up with a really ugly strike if we don't get people back together...everybody feels like NAA is laughing at us and nobody wants to be on the losing side..."

"...time for another union meeting..." I suggested.

"...no...I think we've maxed out on the rah-rah speeches..."

"...we need to set something on fire..." Rickie proposed yet again.

"...no but close...setting shit on fire attracts a large scale investigation...we need a more low-key form of anarchy..."

"...yeah...what are you thinking?..." Rickie was definitely getting into this.

"...I'm thinking..." Kelly paused. "...I'm thinking we need to do something to coincide with that ridiculous grand opening they have planned next week..."

"...it'd be cool if we could arrange a horde of locust or plague of frogs..." I randomly suggested.

"...easier to employ a righteous act of vandalism..." Kelly seemed to already have a plan.

"...YES...I love vandalism...what are we breaking?..."

"...I don't think we should break anything...I think we need to redecorate...you know...as in add some color to their world..."

"...color?..." Rickie caught on. "...like the color of spray paint?..."

"...why yes...that's exactly the color I'm thinking of..." Kelly smiled.

"...what are we spray painting?..." I leaned forward.

"...well I noticed there's a foundation being laid on the front lawn and some sketches on Sommer's desk seem to imply there's some sort of large signage being unveiled at the grand opening..."

"...you were shuffling around Sommer's desk again?..." I found that humorous.

"...oh yeah...at least once a week...it's the only way to know what's going on..."

"...that's true..." Rickie concurred. "...they don't tell us anything anymore..."

"...do you think people would get what this means?..." Kelly picked up a pad and pen off the coffee table and wrote something down and handed it to us...

FY NAA

"...fuck you NAA..." I read it aloud.

"...why don't we just write 'fuck you'?..." Rickie queried.

"...do you know how long it'll take to write it all out?...we're going to be on a time limit..."

"...I like it...I think it's subtle but pointed..." I approved.

"...maybe we could throw in an 'unfair to labor' or something..."

"...time limit Loser...we gotta think time limit...that's a pretty busy street so we gotta be quick..." Kelly reinstructed. "...which brings me to the next part of our mission... reconnaissance..."

"...advance scouting...." Rickie cheered. "...I'm good at that..."

"...good...because we need a lot of it...we need to know when the sign's officially being placed...what the supervisor's night schedule is like and most importantly if there's any kind of security cameras on surrounding buildings...I know there aren't any on ours..."

"...how'd you find that out?..." I asked.

"...a recently dated memo on Sommer's desk requesting a committee to study the cost verses need of a building security system..."

"...perfect...I love it..." Rickie laughed.

"...and obviously I don't have to say this but I'm going to anyways...we can't tell anybody about this..." Kelly got real serious. "...nobody...not Ariel...not Jodie...not MaryAnn...not anybody...not ever...it's a forever secret...got it..." Oddly that was the first thing that felt wrong...*keeping a secret from my friends.* "...you with me Casey?..."

"...huh?...oh yeah...I'm with you..." I refocused. "...so what's next?..."

"...you guys get your bikes out of the living room and Loser goes to the store to get me a new toothbrush...medium bristles..."

...meeting adjourned...

Ariel's Vacation...Day Five...

As expected Jodie did indeed jump in to bail me out and we ended up working my first shift of the next week together. The morning was pretty slow and we spent a bunch of time in the truck posting. Jodie was in a feisty mood and her humor was unusually cutting edge so we spent most of it laughing. A couple of times when I was headlong into an hysterical chortle I'd feel a bit of a twinge when I remembered I was holding out on a her with a secret. I knew why we couldn't tell anyone but if there was anyone who could be trusted it was Jodie. She not only was as loyal a friend as they come but she also had a huge hatred of the corporate monster we all called NAA. She would never compromise the mission and could even be a valued member of the reconnaissance team. Jodie definitely had the constitution to be a great spy. Still...I knew my loyalty in this case had to belong to Kelly and Rickie so I pushed back the twinges and just rolled with the jokes.

✪ ✪ ✪

"...so then Travis ran around the room yelling '...who said that?...who said that?...'" Jodie barely got the words out between runs of laughter.

"...did he ever figure it out?..." I laughed hard too.

"...no...the guy's got the freakin' IQ of a pair of sweat socks..." She breathed deep. "...I could pull that prank on him daily..."

"...FOUR-TEN...FOUR-ONE-ZERO..." a voice harkened.

I fought back the laughter and answered. "...four-ten...51 area..."

"...FOUR-TEN...PLEASE   HEAD   DOWNTOWN... PARKING GARAGE CORNER OF STATE AND MAIN...LEVEL 1 BY THE ELEVATORS FOR THE MALE WITH UNKNOWN PROBLEM..."

"...four-ten received..." I looked at Jodie. "...oh joy..."

"...yup...I feel a doozy coming on..." She flipped on the lights.

Spreadsheet Status Management prevailed and we navigated quickly to the parking garage where we were immediately flagged down by a tall 50'ish y/o male standing by the elevator. He didn't appear to be in much distress so we pulled up and casually approached.

"...you called for an ambulance?..." Jodie took the lead.

"...yes...I need a ride to my doctor's..." He spoke very matter-of-factly.

"...what's wrong?..." Jodie continued.

"...I have an appointment at three o'clock..." I looked at my watch and it was 14:45.

"...where's your doctor's appointment?..."

"...FOUR-TEN FOUR-ONE-ZERO..." Jodie's voice trailed off to the background as dispatch interrupted. I stepped back to answer.

"...four-ten...parking garage...corner of State and Main..."

"...FOUR-TEN WHAT'S YOUR STATUS?..."

"...four-ten on scene...assessing...possible BLS transport..."

"...FOUR-TEN PLEASE KEEP US UPDATED AS WE ARE CODE E..."

"...four-ten received..." I moved back toward Jodie and the patient. They were now in a heated debate.

"...I don't care if your car won't start...we're not a taxi service..."

"...you cannot talk to me that way...I am a taxpayer..."

"...we're private service..."

"...you're 911..."

"...and this ain't a 911 call."

"...Jodie..." I broke in and she turned to me.

"...can you believe this Casey?..."

"...I can...happens everyday..." I gave the pseudo-patient the evil eye. "...we're down to no trucks..."

"...well we're done here..."

"...no you are not...you are not done until you give me a ride..."

"...oh no...we're done..."

"...I need to get to my doctor's and that is an emergency..."

"...DISPATCH TO ALL UNITS...BE ADVISED WE ARE SITTING ON A POSSIBLE CARDIAC ARREST...ANY UNIT WHO CAN CLEAR PLEASE EXPEDITE..."

"...Casey...take that call..." Jodie directed. "...we are done here..."

"...you sure?..." Jodie flashed me a look and I knew she was sure. Our pseudo-patient continued his protest but I did indeed contact dispatch. "...dispatch be advised...four-ten is clear and will be responding..."

"...FOUR-TEN YOU'RE CLEAR?..." dispatch asked. I looked at the guy who began to follow us to the ambulance.

"…yes dispatch…four-ten is clear…" He now yelled at us through our closed doors "…patient refusal…can we get a location?…"

"…FOUR-TEN THAT LOCATION WILL BE 821 STEVENS TERRACE…68 Y/O MALE…POSSIBLE CARDIAC ARREST…"

"…four-ten received…"

"…that fucking wad…" Jodie fastened her seat belt. "…he couldn't get his car started so instead of calling AAA he called 911 for a ride…"

"…what was he going to the doctor's for?…"

"…his glaucoma check-up…"

"…WHAT?…are you kidding me?…"

"…yeah…people dropping dead around the city and he wants a ride to the eye doctor…" Jodie was pretty heated so I just let her cool off. Stevens Street wasn't anywhere near where we were but since we were the only available truck nobody could quibble with how long it took us to get there. On the way another truck called clear and started heading in the same direction.

"…what truck was that?…" I asked Jodie.

"…four-twenty-nine…I'm pretty sure Mahan was talking…"

"…who's he working with?…"

"…no idea…"

"…well it doesn't matter…whoever it is we can't let them beat us there…"

"…got that right Casey…" Jodie howled. "…stand on it…"

"…I love working with you…Ariel never lets me drive fast…"

"…she's a stick in the mud…" Jodie was feeling better again. We wound and winded our way down consecutive side streets and made our way across the city in pretty good time. We did indeed arrive on scene first…arriving second only to the cops.

We expedited gathering equipment because we knew the cops would be real grumpy if they had to do CPR. As we made our way up the driveway we did indeed see the two cops on the screen porch kneeled down doing compressions. And as expected… they were not happy. As soon as they saw us approaching they jumped up…abandoned task and met us a third of the way down the driveway "…ladies…good to see you…" I was horrified to see them just stop CPR like that but if there's anything that makes a cop grumpier than doing CPR it's being told they should get back and do more CPR.

"…yeah…whatta ya got?…" Jodie squeezed out an amiable question while I scurried to kneel down and resume compressions.

"…this is Tate Caulfield…61 y/o guy came home from the grocery store with his wife and granddaughter and collapsed while bringing in the groceries…"

"…where's the family?…" Jodie gave two quick breaths with the BVM while I rolled some oranges out of the way.

"…inside calling other family…" The cop continued backing down the driveway. "…we'll hang out down here in case you need anything…"

"…thanks guys…appreciate it…" Jodie waved while hooking up the monitor leads. I continued compressions and managed a few squeezes of the BVM along the way. "…stand back Casey…" Jodie adjusted dials and stared at the screen. "…okay…asystole… two leads…" She squinted her eyes. "…let's try pacing…" She kept working the buttons and within a minute declared that she had capture.

"…good job Jodie…" Jodie nodded her head and moved on to the next task. That's when we heard the diesel rattle of a second ambulance pulling up on scene. It would be nice to have help.

"…HEY…YOU GUYS NEED ANY EQUIPMENT?…" Mahan had gotten out of the rig first and was yelling up the driveway.

Jodie raised herself up and yelled back. "…NO…JUST HANDS WOULD BE AWESOME…"

"…YOU GOT IT…" Mahan acknowledged and put a little quick in his step. I was working on the tube and Jodie had just started searching for an IV sight. Mahan moved a brown bag stained with a smashed carton of eggs to the side and kneeled down across from Jodie "…whatta ya need?…"

"…first round of meds…"

Mahan looked at the monitor screen. "…atropine and epi coming up…"

"…tube's in…" I started taping and securing.

"…where's your partner?…" Jodie asks while taping down her line.

"…should be right behind me…hey…there she is…"

"…hey…wassup?…" I looked up and Rickie was joining us. "…sorry about the delay…dispatch was not answering me…so what do you need?…" Before we can answer Rickie ran through the checklist. "…tube's in…line's good…meds…ew…little girl watching us through the window…let me go deal with that…" The three of us paused…horrified as we looked over to see two sad little eyes peering out the door window at us. We had all gotten so engrossed in our tasks that we never realized we were being watched. This certainly was not the way a little kid should remember their grandfather…ghastly blue…prone on the screen porch with groceries littered around him. By now we had him half naked with tubes and wires and needles flying around and even worse…she probably had some expectation that all of this was being done for a good reason. We all knew that by the time a patient is asystole not much is going to change…*but that little girl probably didn't know that…*

It was an alert move on Rickie's part to catch it. Now came the hard part for her...walking in the house with the sole purpose of helping the family. Our patient was very cooperative and not much of a complainer. Her patients were a little needier but I gave her a lot of credit. She walked in that house with no fear or hesitation...*I was impressed*...When she opened the door we heard the little girl cry out "...IS MY POPPA GOING TO BE ALRIGHT?..."

"...good luck with that one Rickie..." Jodie mumbled.

"...no shit..." Mahan agreed. None of us heard what Rickie said after she closed the door but you could hear the little girl continue to cry. Deep down inside...all three of us knew we were much better off with the stiff.

With the extra hands we were able to wrap things up fairly quickly and avoid much more lingering on the emotional edge. We got off the porch...progressed to the ambulance and finally on to the hospital. Mahan drove our truck so Jodie and I could be in the back and he left Rickie on scene with the family and their truck.

We were actually at the hospital awhile before Rickie and the family arrived. By then the ER doc had stated the merely obvious and pronounced the patient dead so Rickie brought them right in to the family counseling room. You could hear the wife and granddaughter crying and it was pretty sad. I wondered how Rickie was holding up.

"...hey guys I'm back..." Rickie made a grand appearance in the tech room. "...did you miss me?..."

"...of course we did..." Jodie looked up from her paperwork.

"...hey there's my hot partner..." Mahan spun in his chair. "...come sit on Daddy's lap..." He pat his leg and Rickie perched on it.

"…how's the family doing?…" I asked while munching on Lorna Doones gainfully acquired from the nurse's break room.

"…not good…the little girl was really upset…" Rickie put her arm around Mahan's shoulders. "…she saw the whole thing happen…"

"…aw man…" Jodie stopped writing. "…that really sucks…"

"…yeah…" Rickie stared.

"…why don't you go make me a sandwich?…" Mahan interjected.

"…WHAT?…" Rickie blasted. "…I'm not making you a sandwich…"

"…well you're not doing anything else right now…"

Jodie let out a howl. "…in a minute she's going to be busy beating your ass…"

"…yeah…" Mahan conceded. "…but until then…" he continued "…get busy…" And then he started laughing. Rickie smacked him hard in the arm and then they got into some kind of wrestling match where Rickie actually got a lot of good licks in. Jodie and I stared for awhile and then she sent me to get a water extinguisher so we could hose them down…

…*I love this job…*

CHAPTER 30 -
PLEASE STAND BY

...a time to weep and a time to laugh...a time to mourn and a time to dance...a time to kill and a time to heal...a time to be born and a time to die...just sometimes not when you'd think...

Jodie and I got a late call and ended up being held over for almost an hour. That meant we ended up at the time clock with Rickie and Mahan who were scheduled to get off at 20:00.

"...hey Loser..." I walked up behind Rickie and felt the urge to give her a shove.

She regained her balance...turned around and smiled. "...wassup Casey?..."

"...hey I noticed your name isn't on the schedule to work with me this week..."

"...oh yeah?..."

"...yeah...and it's a limited time offer...you may wanna hurry before supplies run out..."

"...sure...I'll take some OT with you...what's left?..."

"...tomorrow..."

"...yeah..." She thought for a moment "...I'm off tomorrow..."

"...well actually...tomorrow night..."

"...what?...tomorrow night?..."

"...tomorrow night?..." Mahan entered the fray. "...what's tomorrow night?..."

"...an overtime shift with me...I'm trying to get her to work it..."

"...oh...work the shift ya pussy..." Mahan pinched Rickie's arm.

"...ow you fucker..." She smacked him back. "...yeah...okay... if you buy me coffees I'll work the shift..."

"...what?...buy you coffees?..." I stopped and thought of my other choices for partners and realized it was a small price to pay. "...all right...I'll buy you coffees..." I rolled my eyes.

"...and I don't mean coffees from the nurses' break rooms at the hospitals either...that coffee sucks..."

"...I'll buy you real coffees...your choice...Bravo Echo or Double D's..."

"...hmmmm..." She mulled her choices. "...I think I'll take the Bess Eaton..."

"...good choice...it's my favorite too..."

"...why don't you go make me a cup of coffee?..." Mahan tried again.

"...fuck you...get your own coffee..." Rickie hauled off and slugged him and they started wrestling again.

"...see ya guys..."

"...see ya Casey...ow...you fucker..."

...and I'm off like a diabetic's toe...

Ariel's Vacation...Day Six...

The next night Kelly had a really worried look on her face when she shuffled in to the kitchen and found Rickie and me sitting at the table...in uniform...giggling and drinking coffee out of really large mugs.

"...it's freakin' 10:00 at night...what are you two losers doing drinking huge coffees?..."

"...we're getting ready for work..." I answered.

"...you're working together?..."

"...yup..."

"…Casey's gonna buy me coffees all night so I agreed to work the overnight…"

"…for now we're just preloading…" I held up my oversize coffee mug and smiled. "…want some?…"

"…no…I'm allowed to have REM sleep tonight…" Kelly shook her head while heading to the fridge. "…but thanks…" She grabbed a yogurt and walked back to the door. "…have a safe shift and make sure you two goofs don't leave all the lights on when you leave…"

"…thanks Mother Kelly…maybe we'll see you in the morning…" Rickie waved as Kelly fled.

"…don't worry…we'll protect you while you sleep…" I giggled and Rickie laughed.

Kelly didn't bother turning around and merely offered a wave as she repeated "…DON'T LEAVE THE LIGHTS ON ALL NIGHT…"

"…why does she think we'd do that?…" I asked.

"…I don't know…" And we giggled some more.

☆ ☆ ☆

"…you know…we should be able to get a lot of recon done tonight…" Rickie proclaimed as she threw her backpack in the truck.

"…yeah…whatta ya have in mind?…" I spoke low…paranoid that everyone could hear me.

"…well…we can check out surrounding buildings for cameras and do some time test on the supervisor…see where they hang out and stuff…"

"…'kay…sounds good…"

"…what?…I can't hear you Casey…"

"…yeah…sounds good…" I lowered my voice again. "…let's wait until we're out there to talk…" I pointed toward the door.

"…riiiigggghhht…because Travis can hear us way over here…" Rickie was unimpressed by my paranoia. "…he's probably not even awake…"

"…I know…you're right…" I felt ashamed. "…I just get nervous…but I'll be all right…I'll be ready…you'll see…you and Kelly might be worried but I'll be there…"

"…okay Dianna Ross but for now you're babbling…"

"…it's the coffee…"

"…okay but pull yourself together…" I feared Rickie would slap me so I stopped and just smiled. "…that's better…let's get out of here before your head explodes…I'll drive…"

"…fine…" I hopped in the unfamiliar passenger seat. "…let's go get some coffee…my treat…"

✳ ✳ ✳

"…that could be a camera…" Rickie pointed to the roofline of the building across the street from World Headquarters.

"…doesn't matter though…there's no way it can pick up the angle at the front of the NAA building…"

"…yeah true…good…" Rickie leaned forward and scanned outward. "…I don't really see where any buildings would have the right angle…"

"…you sure?…what about that one?…" I pointed across the street. "…remember…they caught the Oklahoma City Bombers by piecing together security video from ATMs and convenience stores and they traced every one of their steps…"

"…Casey…again with the paranoia…do you really think the FBI lab is going to conduct the investigation?…" I thought for a moment. "…NAA is going to ask the BigCity cops to investigate and how hard do you think they're going to work on it?…everyone fuckin' hates NAA…we're going to be heroes…"

"…heroes?…" I laughed. "…now who's deluded?…" I peered through the ambulance binoculars.

"…I'm not deluded…this is a good idea and it's gonna get people fired up enough to stick with the strike…I don't even care if I get caught and fired…"

"…really?…"

"…yeah…what do I care?…I can get another job…I don't even really want to stick around this area anyway…"

"…really?…where do you wanna go?…" I was disappointed to think Rickie might leave.

"…I've been looking into being a park ranger…I've always wanted to go out west…"

"…to the Berkshires?…"

"…no…" She laughed. "…to the Rockies…you know… Colorado or Yosemite…maybe even Joshua Tree…"

"…wow…that's cool…I never knew you wanted to do that…"

"…oh yeah…it's one of the reasons I got my medic…"

"…so why are you still here?…"

"…I wanted to get some experience first…you know…get good at doing a bunch of different things before I go somewhere where I only do three calls a week…I have sent some applications out though…"

"…that's awesome…" I stopped again and thought about how much I'd miss her. "…have you heard anything yet?…"

"…no…but I just sent them out like last week…" She took the binoculars from me and scanned another roofline. "…I figure with things getting kind of crazy it was a good time to start exploring my options…and I gotta do something because I cannot take posting much longer…"

"…yeah…" I immediately agreed. "…it really does suck…"

"…oh my god yes…it is so freaking boring…sitting in a box in a parking lot…how do they expect us not to go insane?…"

"…you gotta wonder…"

"...so yeah see Casey...I don't care if I get caught because I don't think I'll be able to take this much longer anyway..."

"...yeah but that's even more reason for you not to want to get caught...vandalism to private property is not looked on kindly by the Park Services..."

"...don't worry about it Casey...we're not going to get caught..."

...she seemed so sure...

☆ ☆ ☆

"...anybody in that car going Casey?..." Rickie met me half way between the two cars in the collision.

"...no...they're all fine...and I got the signatures to prove it..."

"...cool...we're out of here..." Rickie keyed the portable radio and talked. "...four-ten...we're clear...four refusals...no PI..."

"...excuse me..." A tall skinny woman who had been hanging out on the fringes of the scene approached and tugged on Rickie's sleeve.

"...one second..." Rickie deflected her.

"...FOUR-TEN RECEIVED YOU'RE CLEAR AT 23:30... STAND BY FOR POSTING ASSIGNMENT..."

"...excuse me miss..." The woman tugged again and Rickie answered her just as I approached.

"...yes?...what can I do for you?..."

"...I need a ride..."

"...a ride...are you kidding?..." Rickie laughed. "...we're not a taxi service..."

"...I know...I know but my car just broke down and my foot hurts...can you give me a ride?..." The woman was persistent.

"...you want a ride to the hospital?..."

"…Casey…" Rickie muttered. "…no giving hints…"

"…no I don't want to go to the hospital…I want to go home…"

"…see…I didn't give a hint…"

"…Casey…may I have a word with you?…" Rickie grabbed me by the arm and pulled me to the side. "…why are you engaging this person in conversation?…"

"…I don't know…it's late…we're in a bad section of the city… should we just leave her here if her car's broken down?…"

"…she doesn't have a car…she's a crack whore…she just wants a ride…"

"…okay…so she wants a ride…what's the big deal?…maybe it's on the way…"

"…I don't believe you…"

"…c'mon…even crack whores need love…and it'll be good karma for us just before we knowingly perpetrate an evil deed… we're going to need the cosmic favor…"

Rickie turned away disgusted but she approached the woman. "…where do you live?…"

"…up that way…" The woman pointed up the street.

"…how far?…"

"…not far…"

"…not far?…just a mile or two?…"

"…yeah…a mile or two…"

"…get in…" Rickie opened up the passenger door and the woman happily got in. "…you get in the back…I can't even believe you got me doing this…"

"…it's good for your soul…" And I climbed in the back like a third rider. I didn't bother trying to squeeze my way up front so I could barely make out the conversation going on between Rickie and our fare. I did notice though that we were making a lot of lefts and rights and not really getting anywhere. That's when Rickie pushed the issue and demanded she tell her what street we were looking for.

"…Alaska Street…" The woman innocently answered.

"…ALASKA STREET?…" Rickie shrieked. "…ALASKA STREET?…THERE'S NO ALASKA STREET IN BIGCITY…"

"…yes there is…that's where I live…"

"…there's no Alaska Street…now either give me the name of a real street or get out…" Rickie was pretty pissed off which of course cracked me up to no end.

"…I live on Alaska Street…"

"…no you don't…"

"…yes I do…"

"…that's it…" Rickie pulled over and slammed the truck in PARK. The next thing I knew she was opening the passenger door and booting out our disappointed traveler.

"…well someday you will learn there is an Alaska Street and that is where I live…"

"…okay…bye-bye…" I saw the crack whore walk by the side window of the ambulance muttering to herself. Then Rickie opened the side door. "…and you can just stay back there…" And she slammed it closed again. I laughed really hard because it was really funny.

"…you know…" I poked my head up front. "…you were so right…you really could see that coming…"

"…shut up…you have lost your right to be up front with the grown-ups…" And with her free hand Rickie closed the door between the cab and the back of the ambulance.

…so much for good Karma…

☆ ☆ ☆

Rickie stayed mad and made me stay in the back until we got dispatched to our next call. Normally I would have just taken a nap but a gallon of coffee had made that impossible so I took the opportunity to number all the software supplies in the entire ambulance for the ease of future inventories.

By the time the paperwork was completed on our dif breather all was forgiven and I was allowed to ride up front again. We got ourselves another coffee and headed downtown to watch the hookers and male prostitutes line up to work their magic. I always get a kick out of how TV and movies portray the pros. In real life the ones we see on the streets are the ugliest human beings going. Drugs...lifestyle...diseases and other humans beat on them in every possible way you could think of and then probably a few ways you wouldn't. Scabs from diseases cover their flesh...abuse and neglect cost them their teeth...their hair is always straggly and greasy... sometimes they lose clumps of it. Yet for some reason the line of cars passing through is never ending. I guess that means either there are some pretty scanky looking housewives in the burbs to which the pros are seen as a step up or it really is true what Rickie says...*a blow job is a blow job...*

☆ ☆ ☆

The rest of the shift was pretty generic and 08:00 found us bleary-eyed...punched out and making our way home. It was a beautiful warm summer morning so before we escaped into the house to seek out sleep we sat on the front porch stairs and smoked a joint. I was hopeful it would help me ease down some so I could sleep since my hands were still shaking from the caffeine overdose. Kelly opened the front door and stepped out to join us.

"...hey guys...how was your night?..." We parted on the stairs and she walked past us.

"...good except for the part where Casey opened a travel agency specializing in trips to Alaska..."

Kelly looked understandably puzzled and I interrupted. "…you know…I never knew you were so insensitive…it was a chance to do a good deed…"

"…it was ridiculous…"

"…it was compassionate…"

"…Casey…"

"…Connors…"

"…Casey…"

"…Connors…"

"…THE TWO OF YOU…enough…" Kelly snapped. "…I should clunk your heads together…" Rickie and I stopped…sneered at each other and then started giggling. Kelly stared blankly and waited for us to return to normal conversation. Sensing that she may soon make good on her promise to clunk our heads together we focused on regaining calm.

"…so we got a lot of recon work done last night…" Rickie adjusted herself on the top stair.

"…really?…good…"

"…yeah…there aren't any cameras we need to worry about…" I muffled a giggle and stretched my lips tight to keep from smiling too wide.

"…and the supervisor is always where he says he is…we hid behind the plumbing supply company from midnight until about 02:00 and World Headquarters was empty…"

"…that's when we figure Travis was making the rounds… restocking at the hospital…getting dispatch coffee and doing whatever else it is Travis does…" I quivered at the thought.

"…it's also the only time when there aren't any crew changes…so it's probably the best time to engage…"

Kelly shook her head and thought for a moment. "…good job Losers…I've been thinking about it and I think we need to plan on doing this Friday night…"

"…Friday night or early Saturday morning?…" I queried.

"…I guess technically early Saturday morning…" Kelly corrected. "… and it sounds like between 24:00 and 02:00…"

"…cool…we're ready…" Rickie stood up to stretch.

"…yeah…this is pretty exciting…" I found myself yawning.

"…are we keeping you up Casey?…" Kelly leaned forward on the porch rail.

"…yeah…I think the caffeine finally wore off…" I yawned again.

"…not me…I feel like doing something…" Rickie stretched some more. "…I'm gonna head up to the Rail Trail…wanna go for a ride Casey?…"

"…no…" I slowly rose from the stairs. "…I'm going to bed…"

"…I'm going to work…I'll see you Losers later…" And like a flash Kelly was down the walk to her car. In a blurry haze I headed up the porch stairs toward the house. Fifteen minutes later I was nestled in my bed with thoughts of vandalism dancing in my head as I drifted off to sleep.

...tomorrow we rule the world...

✠ ✠ ✠

One of the worst things about working overnight shifts was having to sleep during the day. Even in a quiet neighborhood like ours it was impossible to sleep really deep. The room was bright…cars drove by at an increased rate…neighbors yelled out windows and doors for kids and spouses***…Rickie knocked over the coatrack bringing in her bike…***

By 14:00 I found myself numbly sitting on the couch staring at *Beverly Hills 90210* wondering why my friends aren't that cool. Oh wait a minute***…they are…***

I lingered in that painful state between being completely awake and being tired enough to sleep. You just kinda hang out on the outskirts of uncomfortable edginess. You can't get cozy in your skin and all your joints feel like they need to be popped. It makes me wonder if being tired is painful for your body and we only change levels of consciousness so we don't have to feel it. Here I was lingering without enough anesthesia to put me down.

Rickie got up around 15:00 and joined me on the couch. Together we sat in silence staring at *Seinfeld* wondering if our friends would make a funny TV show...*they would...*

The coma ward aura was broken when Kelly blasted through the door around 20:00 and proclaimed **"...WHAT A FUCKING MISERABLE DAY..."** Rickie stared intently at the TV and my eyes followed Kelly as she whipped off her boots...tossed her cooler on the kitchen counter and whipped plastic containers into the sink. She disappeared upstairs for a bit and I drifted back to the TV. By the time Jackie and Roseanne had won the lottery she had rejoined us in the living room and flopped down in the recliner.

"...bad day?..." I smiled meekly and offered the bong.

"...yes...thanks..." Kelly accepted. "...calls were off the wall...all stupid stuff and Travis had some bug up his ass..." She paused to take a hit. "...it was just annoying..." I shook my head in acknowledgment. "...what's up with her?..." Kelly pointed to Rickie.

"...*Third Rock's* on..."

"...oh..." Kelly watched Rickie. "...hello...Loser..." Kelly picked up a ball of socks off a pile of laundry and whipped them over my head and at Rickie. It bonked off her head.

"...hey...what the fuck?..." Rickie's trance was broken and she looked around. "...oh hey...O'Brien's home..."

"...yes...hello...how are you?..."

"…good…how was your day?…"

"…fucking awful…weren't you listening?…"

"…huh…oh…I love this show…it cracks me up…" Rickie smiled and unaffectedly returned to prime time.

"…she only got a couple of hours of sleep…" I offered.

Kelly shook her head and took another hit. "…I'm just in a miserable mood…"

I shook my head and we all watched TV in silence for awhile. Then at the commercial break Kelly broke in with an announcement. "…oh hey Casey…before I forget…I took OT with you tomorrow…"

That perked me up. "…really?…awesome…"

"…yes and I think we should try to go shopping if we can…"

I was tired and very slow. "…shopping?…"

"…yeah…we gotta get supplies for the mission…"

"…oh yeah…the mission…" *how could I forget the mission?*

"…and I think it will go a long way to making me feel better if we're actually getting paid by NAA to go on our shopping spree…"

"…even better…you'll be on an overtime rate…"

"…exactly…you know…I *am* starting to feel better…" Kelly smiled and relaxed a bit.

"…it truly is the little things in life…"

"…it is…let's watch a movie…"

Ariel's Vacation…Day Seven…

The next morning the alarm went off and got smashed in the usual fashion. Then I remembered I was working with Kelly and suddenly I was motivated to spring out of bed and dash through my morning routine…*we were going to have some fun…*

"…Casey…you mind driving?…" Kelly waited at the toaster for her Pop-Tarts. "…I gotta make my gas last until we get paid…"

"…no…not at all…" I poured coffee. "…if you don't mind going topless…"

"…exuuucuse me?…" Kelly exaggerated her response.

"…my Jeep…I took the top off last night…" I smiled and suggested "…but if the other one interests you…"

"…no…not at all…"

"…ouch…"

"…sorry…" POP "…when did you say you took the top off?…"

"…last night…after the movie…I couldn't sleep…"

"…oh…I see…" Kelly wrapped her Pop-Tarts in a paper towel and grabbed her cooler. "…shall we?…"

"…sure…let's boogie…"

…let the games begin…

☆ ☆ ☆

"…we should try to get ourselves posted at 81…" Kelly stashed her cooler behind her seat and hooked her stethoscope on the PA mike. "…there's a hardware store that sells those paint cans made for graffiti…"

"…the ones with nozzles on them?…"

"…yes…" She climbed in. "…anything will do in a pinch but I'd like to try to get those…"

"…yes…I hear that they're all the rage with the gangstas…"

"…they are…so if we get busted we'll at least get some street cred out of the deal…" Kelly laughed and I thought I may have unconsciously turned a shade of green. "…what's a matter Casey?…you nervous?…"

"…uh…a little bit…" I lowered my voice. "…I've never done anything like this before…"

"…yeah…" Kelly leaned in. "…but you've wanted to… right?…"

"…yeah…" I smiled. "…I guess…" I started to feel a little better.

"…relax Casey…it's an adventure and adventures aren't meant to have predictable outcomes…and if we get caught we'll all keep each other company while we look for new jobs…"

"…yeah and Rickie's probably got a year's stash of protein bars we can live off of…"

"…there ya go… worst case scenario….protein bars and beer…" Kelly picked up the mike and prepared to speak. "…best case scenario…we become legends…"

"…Rickie says we'll be heroes…"

"…heroes or legends…it's all the same…"

☆ ☆ ☆

We pulled out of the garage and into the bright morning light. Kelly signed us on and showing no respect dispatch immediately put the legends to work.

"…FOUR-TEN…YOU'RE MY ONLY TRUCK SO I NEED TO SEND YOU TO 42 BRADFORD STREET…APARTMENT 3A FOR THE FEMALE STABBED…"

"…four-ten received…" Kelly answered calmly and then turned to me. "…what could make someone so angry so early in the morning?…"

Kelly went on in her relaxed glib manner and all I could muster was a dumbass grin. I was afraid that if I opened my mouth the screaming in my head would leak out and she'd hear **"…YES…I GET TO DO A STABBING WITH KELLY O'BRIEN…"** Instead I focused intently on navigating through traffic.

"…you know where you're going Casey?…"

"...I think so...Bradford's off the rotary...right?..."

"...yes and 42 is the huge apartment building halfway down on the left...everything else on the street is a three-family..."

"...'kay...that makes it easy..." I continued to zig and zag and with a little guidance from Kelly's internal atlas we smoothly made our way across the city. When we pulled up in front of 42 three cruisers were pointed nose in to the apartment building but there weren't any cops hanging around outside.

"...something must be going on..." Kelly scanned the area. "...we should keep ourselves light on our feet...let's just take the first-in bag and O2..." Kelly laughed. "...you know...in case we gotta run..." She pretended to throw the O2 bottle over her shoulder. "...and don't be afraid to throw things if you need to..."

"...oh I have..."

We split up the bags and made our way up the stoop. Our forward progress was stopped at the front door because nobody thought to leave it unlocked for us. Kelly started pushing all the doorbells and finally a crackly voice buzzed back "...what?..."

"...ambulance...let us in..."

"...I don't need an ambulance..."

"...no but your neighbor does...let us in..." A few seconds went by without activity and then we saw a shade open on the second floor. An elderly woman peered down at us and we waved back. Finally the door buzzed and we were able to gain entry.

Sometimes in larger buildings it can be difficult to locate the right apartment. I went in expecting to find doors missing numbers and letters and poorly lit hallways branching off of each other like bronchioles. This time however a trail had been left behind for us.

"...oh look...a clue..." Kelly pointed at a gelatinous glob of blood on the stairs.

"…and another and another…" I pointed as a bloody string of dots connected all the way up the stairs. "…if that goes on for three flights we got troubles…"

"…we'll see…" Kelly pulled out her penlight and flashed a mini beam up the stairs. "…stay to the side…technically that's a crime scene and we don't want our footprints photographed in it…"

"…got it…" I did my best to take Kelly's advice and straddled the edge of the creaky stairs. The trail did in fact go on for three flights and actually the puddles got bigger the closer we got to the actual apartment. It also got a lot noisier the closer we got. A baby was screaming at the top of its lungs and everybody else was talking loud to be heard over it. Kelly and I danced around a significant puddle of blood outside the apartment door and made our way inside to the madness.

It was a large apartment but the front rooms were completely empty of people. We didn't find anyone until we got to the back and found everyone in the kitchen. Four cops were shuffling around asking questions…taking photos and writing everything down. A young woman holding a screaming 2 y/o was standing at the center of it all. They were both crying and she was bleeding significantly from her face. She had a huge laceration that extended from her left cheek…just under her eye…down to the corner of her mouth and the skin flapped open revealing anatomical layers of tissue and tendons. I don't know if she knew how bad it was because she kept talking and walking with the baby and that made the flap bounce around. My initial reaction was to go "…ewwww…" and take a step back so it was a good thing Kelly moved right in and took charge.

"…is there someone here who can take the baby?…"

The woman looked around. "…my sister's in the next room but I don't think he wants to leave me…"The baby eyeballed Kelly and drew closer to his mother. Kelly peeled him away anyway.

"…I understand…but we need to take care of you and he doesn't need to see this…"The kid couldn't cry any louder but he sure did try. Kelly was persistent though and the woman called for her sister. When he was finally cleared out me and Kelly got down to the business of patient care. We got the woman to finally sit down and we controlled the bleeding and flapping of skin with various software supplies.

"…here Casey…hold this here while I wrap…"

"…got it…"

"…so Maria…what happened this morning?…"

Maria was still kind of crying so she spoke very softly to begin. "…last night my husband told me he'd been sleeping with some woman he works with…he said she was crazy and he didn't know what she might do…I guess she got real angry with him at work yesterday and threatened to cut his balls off…"

"…sounds like a good idea to me…" Kelly mumbled and I agreed.

"…well this morning I was doing the dishes and my baby was eating his breakfast and she shows up at the window over there…" She motioned to the window over the kitchen sink. "…and she's got this long knife and she's banging on the window…" She started to cry hard again. "…I grabbed my baby and ran and she busted in the back door and chased us all the way downstairs… she was screaming '…where's Luis?…I'll cut his balls off…' but then she swung the knife at me and cut my face…she almost cut my baby…" Kelly and I looked at each other and she spoke what I felt. "…holy shit Maria…you've had a horrible morning…" Maria looked at her with sad eyes and you could tell Kelly was moved by her expression. When we were done wrapping and taping she put her hands on Maria's shoulders "…well…let's get your son back out here and we'll get you two to the hospital…" Kelly leaned in and spoke reassuringly. "…don't worry…we're going to take care of you both…"

Kelly asked the cops if they were all set with the patient and they confirmed they were. She let them know we were going to get the kid and leave for the hospital.

The patient's injury may have been gruesome but it was not life threatening. It still was pretty much the talk of the ER though as the nurses couldn't get over the balls of the girlfriend to break in the wife's house and cut her face up like that in front of her kid. It was pretty much agreed that she had to be some kind of freak show. Then the story got even better when Fergie and Jodie brought in the husband. Turned out after the psycho bitch hit the wife she blazed her way down the road to the factory where she and the husband worked and she delivered him a couple of slices to the gut. It would appear…Jodie confirmed…that she was going for the Bobbitt.

"…unbelievable…" Kelly shook her head in amazement as they wheeled the husband by us. "…just couldn't keep it in your pants…" He groaned a little bit and the orderly just kept pushing him toward X-ray. "…well now you can keep it in a jar…"

Kelly and I cleared up and she let dispatch know that if it was at all possible we'd like to get sent to 81. Dispatch was glad to hear her request but things were still fairly busy so they had no choice but to keeping ping-ponging us in between 51 and 61. At this point we were going to have to be satisfied with just not having to do any of the stupid calls going down. In between 51 and 61 was one of my favorite pizza shops and the third time we drove by it I asked Kelly to pull in so I could get something to eat.

"…sounds good…I need to get a soda or something…"

The small shop only had on-street parking so we pulled up out front and parked the ambulance about three car lengths away from the door. Walking in we each focused on our own needs as I went right for the counter and put in my order for a tuna… cheese…tomato…mayo… eight-inch grinder…heated please and Kelly beelined for the cooler in the back of the restaurant and started perusing beverage choices.

It was just early enough in the afternoon that the shop wasn't too busy so I was hopeful it wouldn't take long to get my food. In the excitement of our first call I had burned a lot of calories and I was really hungry. I almost considered not getting my grinder heated so it would take less time to make but…well…I just love melted cheese so I decided to risk it. I tucked my hands in my pockets and meandered around the counter a bit. I checked out the covers of *Wheeler Dealer* and *The Valley Advocate* and then I stumbled upon a gumball machine full of M&M's. I was contemplating whether or not to part with the quarter and buy a handful to hold me over…

…when suddenly…

sssqueeeall…**crrasshh**…Sscraaapppe
…and the pizza shop shook…

I moved toward the door and when I looked to see where Kelly was she was already on the move too.

We had gotten to the door and taken one step onto the sidewalk when all of a sudden a car came flying by. Only it wasn't your typical car flying by. This car was on its roof and as it passed us the metal roof and pavement rubbed together to make a god-awful grinding sound. The tires that had just been accelerating on the pavement were flying feverishly on their axles and made a sci-fi whooshing noise.

"…whoa…watch out Casey…" Kelly grabbed me by the arm and pulled me back as the car continued down the road. "…those wheels'll rip your head off …"

"…yeah…I've never seen them quite so close up…"

The car came to rest about twenty feet past the pizza shop and Kelly and I jogged up to meet it. There were huge gouges in the pavement and a strong smell of incomplete combustion filled the air. Kelly kneeled on the ground and made contact with the driver while I called dispatch and let them know what was going on.

"…how ya doin' in there?…" I was behind the vehicle and couldn't hear the patient's reply but Kelly kept talking and even laughed a couple of times so I got the impression nothing was too serious. Dispatch said they'd send fire and police to assist and I stepped back to direct the traffic that had already started to plug up the scene. Kelly walked over to me and requested an update.

"…fire and police are on their way…nobody seems to believe it when I say slow down and two cars almost ran over my foot because they were staring at the rollover and not me…"

"…okay…that's a little more detail then I needed but good job…"

"…how are things in the vehicle?…"

"…so far so good…60'ish y/o female…she seems fine…just kinda hanging around…the roof's pretty crunched which makes opening the doors impossible…as soon as you're cleared from traffic duties bring over the c-spine stuff…"

"…'kay…"

It actually didn't take long at all for a cop to show up and take over for me and while I was gathering c-spine equipment fire rolled up. Kelly let them know the patient was stable so they could take their time doing what they do. Still they wasted no time getting chock blocks tucked…air bags deployed and the crunched-shut doors pried open with the jaws.

Kelly and I used the now-peeled-open front doors and crawled into the car. We got the collar on the patient and eased her out of her seatbelt and onto the longboard. I have to say she was really calm about the whole thing. Most people who get tipped upside down and uncontrollably skid fifty feet down a fairly busy city street usually get a little flustered. Not our patient though…you'd think it was just another day of test pilot school for her.

Kelly and I got the patient out of the car and when we crawled from the vehicle wreckage and stood to lift her…the crowd that had gathered on the sidewalk broke into spontaneous applause…

Well…actually…we dug our knees and elbows into the shattered glass shards and sharp metal edges covering the ground and when we stood to lift her the pizza guy yelled across the street **"…HEY…YOU PAYIN' FOR THIS GRINDER OR WHAT?…"**

…oh the life of a 911 medic…

✷ ✷ ✷

After we cleared up from the rollover Kelly and I again got sent to 61. This time though the whole city seemed to get eerily quiet and nobody was doing anything. Eventually as trucks cleared up dispatch maneuvered things around and sent us to 81. We immediately got giddy.

"…let's go shopping Casey…"

"…excellent idea…" We proceeded directly to the hardware store and Kelly pulled the ambulance around the back of the building. We were making our way around to the front of the store when we saw another ambulance blast into the small parking lot.

"…Jesus…who that hell is that?…" Kelly strained to see past the sun reflecting off the windshield. Then the lights on the ambulance went on and the air horn got honked a couple of times. "…oh boy…it's the Loser…"

The ambulance pulled up next to the sidewalk and sure enough Rickie was in the cab "…wassup you guys?…"

"…what are you doing?…" Kelly walked over to the driver's side door and I started around to the passenger side. "…who are you with?…"

"…nobody…"

"…nobody?…" I heard Kelly question.

"…yeah…I'm supposed to be bringing this truck to a show-and-tell at the Kid's Health Fair at the mall…" Rickie pointed to the side of the ambulance where a bunch of jungle animals wearing BAND-AIDS were painted.

"…oh yea…" I cheered as I climbed in and sat down in the passenger seat.

"…sounds like you're having fun…"

"….yeah…" Rickie sighed. "…and every time I have to stop at a stoplight assholes make barnyard animal noises at me…"

"…well it's hard to make zebra noises…" I pointed out.

"…whatever…Mary Ann went home sick so I guess it's better than cleaning trucks…what are you guys doing?…"

"…we're on a mission…" Kelly answered. "…they sell the cool spray paint here…"

"…oh…alright…I'm coming in…" Rickie reached down and unsnapped her seatbelt.

"…yeah sure…just leave your ambulance on the sidewalk…" Kelly stepped back and waved.

"…oh yeah…I should probably move it huh?…"

"…we're parked around back…put it next to ours.…" I suggested.

"…yeah that sounds good…oh wait a minute…what time is it?…" Rickie looked at her watch. "…13:30…hmmmm…do I have time?…" I waited for her answer. "…yeah…fuck it…what do I care if I'm late?…"

"…well there you go…" And then for some crazy zany reason I thought it would be fun to open the passenger door and hang out of the truck while Rickie pulled around to the back parking lot. She thought it would be fun to goose the accelerator and try to whip me out of the truck. And she almost accomplished it. That of course led to a sustained giggling episode that lasted as long as it took for us to park and walk around to where Kelly was waiting for us.

"…oh for fuck's sake…" was all Kelly could say as she turned her back on us and proceeded into the store. We did our best to contain ourselves and raced to the door to catch up with her. It appeared Kelly was now trying to ditch us and despite having shorter legs than the two of us she glided effortlessly away.

"…I think we're embarrassing her…" I smiled at Rickie.

"…I know…" Rickie smiled back. "…WHAT A SNOB…" Kelly heard her and waved her off without turning around.

We arrived at the paint section and Kelly had already found the spray cans we were looking for. "…excellent…many choices…" She mulled over the selection. "…we gotta figure out what color will stand out the best on the sign…"

"…what color's the background?…" I scanned the blacks and grays.

"…the schematic said white with blue and black lettering…" Kelly informed and just when I was reaching for what I thought was an appropriate complement to the design Kelly blurted "…perfect…I got it…" and she held up a can for us to see.

"…yes…that's awesome…" Rickie exclaimed. "…that's the one…"

"…florescent pink…" I saw it next. "…that's pretty wild…"

"…exactly…" Kelly smiled. "…this will make a statement…"

I laughed. "…maybe we should write TOWANDA instead…"

"…Towanda…" Rickie laughed. "…I love that movie…"

"…me too Casey but that might actually give us away…"

"…and pink spray paint won't?…" I contended.

"…true…"Kelly conceded. "…but there's another reason…" She turned to Rickie. "…spell 'Towanda'…"

"…uh…T…E…H…"

"…wrong…"

"…uh…T…A…"

"…wrong…" Kelly turned to me. "…see why Casey?…"

"… yeah I see…"

"…so I'm not a good speller…that's why I became a paramedic…"

"…oh yeah…'spell paramedic'…"

"…that's easy…G…O…D…"

…and we giggled…

☆ ☆ ☆

We each grabbed a can of paint and left the paint section. We seemed to be taking the scenic route back to the register as Kelly and Rickie stopped to play with everything. They turned all the lights off and on in the electrical department…rang all the door bells and then I saw Rickie screwing PVC pipes together and ranting something about storming the beachhead. I think the excitement was really getting to Kelly too because as we passed a big bin of playground balls she grabbed one off the top and bounced it off Rickie's head. "…watch out Loser…coming through…"

"…oof…ow…" Rickie absorbed the beaning. "…why does everyone always wanna beat me up?…"

"…not sure…" Kelly free throwed the ball back into the bin.

"…I think you just bring it out in us…" And I responded by shoving Rickie into the bin of balls.

"...ooof..." Rickie tumbled in and a bunch of balls came bouncing out into the aisle.

"...oh my god Casey..." Kelly laughed while she tried to gather them. "...you're gonna get us tossed out of here..."

"...me?...I did one little thing...you guys are the menaces..."

"...somebody help me up..." Rickie struggled to balance on the rolling rubber. Despite my continued giggling I reached in and helped her out. Several old people walked by our mess and scowled. "...oh sure..." Rickie muttered "...look down on us now..."

"...but later when you can't breathe..." Kelly evilly giggled while she soccer kicked some balls back into the bin. "...you'll be calling our number..."

"...that's right people...because we're 9-1-1..." And with my grandiose boast we all burst into hysterics.

"...that was so queer Casey..." Rickie laughed. I shrugged my shoulders***...well aware of my queerness...***

We paid for our product and the clerks seemed grateful to see us split for the parking lot. Kelly tucked the bag of cans into her backpack stowed behind the driver's seat and we said our good-byes to Rickie. She looked at her watch and shrieked **"...14:15... OH CRAP I'M LATE..."**

"...ohhhh...you're in trouble..." I taunted.

"...yeah...you and your Zoo Mobile should get out of here..." Kelly shooed her. "...tell 'em you got lost..."

"..yeah...I'll think of something.."

"...you always do..." Kelly waved and Rickie and all her jungle friends zipped away.

✡ ✡ ✡

With our day's mission successfully completed there was a renewed excitement that had our truck all abuzz. True to my normal schizzy self I didn't know whether to be excited or scared.

It's a good thing there really isn't much of a difference between the two so I didn't end up too confused.

There was no mistaking how Kelly felt. She was grinning from ear to ear and her normal upbeat tempo was cranked up a notch. I could tell just the thought alone of perpetrating an obnoxious deed on NAA was making her giddy and where my conflict came from the questions of legally right or wrong…Kelly was steadfast in her convictions.

See…Kelly isn't much of a complainer. In fact…quite the opposite…*she's a doer…*It's part of what makes her an outstanding medic. While most people are impressed that they're able to notice a problem Kelly skips that step and gets right to fixing it. And she does it across the board without consideration to who has the problem or what kind of clothes the problem's wearing or how the problem smells. If you need her help Kelly will give it to you and she'll give it to you in a way that maintains your dignity and humanity.

Then along came NAA and all their attacks on the things that mattered most to her. Her job…the profession and all her friends that were forced out the door. In her mind she had exhausted all legal forms of protest to no avail and the major contributing factor to the legal protest failing was the underhanded tactics NAA so blatantly employed. Therefore…if NAA was going to walk on a morally vague edge she was well within her rights to do the same. If for no other reason than to hold a mirror up to the emperor so that all others knew he could no longer legitimately claim ignorance of his nakedness.

The souped-up energy emanating from us made it impossible to stay cooped up in the truck so Kelly drove us down to the duck pond located near 81. At least there we'd be able to get out of the truck and walk around. She parked the ambulance in the shade and we took our portable radio with us to the benches that lined the north end of the pond. We each sat on the backrest of the bench and Kelly propped the portable radio up between us.

The radio was quiet and Kelly and I each took a moment to soak up the scenery. It was a fairly small pond but it was pretty in the **surrounded by leafy green trees and clean brown sand** kind of way. It also served as home for about fifty ducks and at least two large snapping turtles that I had counted. Across the way there was an older guy fishing but I'm not sure you'd want to eat anything you caught here. A small kid who appeared to be with him occupied himself with whipping chunks of bread at the ducks.

"...listen to the ducks Casey..." Kelly pointed across the water. "...hear the one duck telling a joke?..." I listened and sure enough one duck was quacking. "...and now all the other ducks will laugh..." And sure enough on cue all the other ducks started quacking. "...isn't that funny?..."

"...yeah..." I laughed. "...I guess we know which duck is you..."

"...I'm the funny one..."

"...yes you are..."

"...of course I am..." And she laughed.

...as do all the other ducks...

Kelly and I hung out with the ducks for awhile. In fact we hung out with the ducks a lot longer than we expected. Things had really ground to a halt in the city. Not that that was overly unusual. A lot of times calls ebb and flow and since everybody was running ragged all morning it made sense the afternoon would slow down. The mystery was always found in how long the calm would last because as sure as paralysis causes bedsores the calm would end.

Meanwhile...*in all the calmness*...I got bored and climbed in the back of the ambulance to take a nap. Kelly had walked over with me and stopped to take a book out of her backpack. To reach it she had to move the bag of spray paint...*which caused her to laugh maniacally for a moment*...and then she said she was going to sit in the sun reading.

"...don't sit out there too long...you don't want to catch on fire..."

"...am I turning red?..."

"...a little..." That caused her to reach in her backpack again and pull out sunscreen "...you carry sunscreen at work?..."

"...I'm full-blooded Irish...I got no melanin..." She dabbed the lotion on her cheeks. "...I gotta put sunscreen on to go spelunking..." That made me laugh as I settled on the stretcher and she went off properly protected.

About a half hour later I woke up shocked to find we still hadn't moved. I meandered out of the back of the ambulance... rubbing my eyes when the sun hit them.

"...what the hell's going on?..." I asked Kelly.

"...what'd ya mean?..." Kelly looked up from her book.

"...we haven't moved..."

"...we haven't had to..."

"...well that's weird...what's going on?..."

"...I don't know...the region went out... LittleCity's got a call or two happening but not much else..."

"...hmmph..." I sat next to Kelly.

"...you're not disappointed are you?..." Kelly dog-eared her book.

"...no...of course not..." I lied. Of course I was disappointed. We went from having a thrill-packed morning to now hitting an absolute standstill. Normally I wouldn't have minded. In fact normally I'd be thrilled at the thought of getting paid to watch ducks…take naps and drink coffee. Oh…coffee…that sounded like a good idea. "…hey…do you mind if we head up to Double D's?…I could use some caffeine…"

"..sure…let's go…" Kelly stood up quickly and we trekked back to the truck.

Back to what I was saying…normally I'd be thrilled at the lull but who knew when I'd get to work with Kelly again and I wanted to make the most out of it…

…we could sit around telling jokes with the ducks anytime…

✼ ✼ ✼

An hour later and Kelly and I were still without a call. We got bored at the duck pond so Kelly just started driving around and after about fifteen minutes of that she pulled into a parking lot.

"…this is fucking ridiculous…" She leaned forward and tipped up the steering wheel. "…I can't stand this posting shit…"

"…you're just not keeping an open mind…" I muttered. Kelly gave me a blank stare. "…Travis said that to me the other day when he caught me complaining…"

"…Travis that wad…what the fuck does he even know about posting?…"

"…only what NAA made him digest from the brochure they force-fed him…"

"…that's true…I do feel bad for some of the supervisors… they're really stuck in the middle…"

"…I know…guys like Dan Stone or Stu…they were good medics and they deserved to be promoted…"

"…now for their troubles they get to be hammered on by corporate and treated like narcs from the ranks…"

"…I wonder how people will react when they see them cross the picket line…"

"...that'll be tough..." Kelly stared ahead through the windshield. "...but maybe we'll be so busy beating Siano's ass we won't see them..."

"...yeah that motherfucker..." I felt an angry tide rise inside. "...how do you live our life and then sell out your comrades for a piece of shit supervisor's job?..."

"...some people are just selfish fucks Casey and nothing's ever going to change that..."

"...I get that...but if you're going to sell out get something worth it...."

"...I agree..."

The next hour passed just as uneventfully and Kelly and I were now not only bored but kinda getting sick of sitting on top of each other. She drove us back down to the duck pond and this time we just got out of the truck and hung on our respective doors.

"...we should have brought gloves and a ball..." Kelly folded her arms on the open window.

"...I thought I saw a Frisbee in the c-spine compartment when we were on that rollover..."

"...a Frisbee?..." Kelly had a little spark in her speech. "...well what are you waiting for?...find it..."

"...well okay..." I turned from the window and opened the side compartment door. I had just started taking out bags to make my search easier when I heard dispatch call out our number.

"...FOUR-TEN...FOUR-ONE-ZERO..." Kelly opened the door...reached in and answered.

"...four-ten...general area of 81..."

"...YES MA'AM...COULD YOU TAKE THE PRIORITY TWO TO THE CORNER OF ABBOTT AND ABBY ROAD FOR THE ELEVEN-YEAR-OLD FELL?..."

"…four-ten received…Abbott and Abby for the eleven-year-old fell…" Kelly hung up the mike. "…Casey…"

"…coming…" I reversed thrust and stowed the bags back in the compartment…tucking all the handles in neatly so I could close the door on the first try. I came back around to the passenger side door. "…wasn't a Frisbee…just a paper plate…so what are we going for?…"

"…some kid took a digger…I say unless he's got a limb hanging off he gets a BAND-AID…ice pack and a kick in the ass…" Kelly laughed. "…get out of here ya whiner…" She mimed a dropkick just before climbing in the driver's seat. "…turn the scanner up… let's see if the cops are there yet…"

I reached over and turned the volume up. We listened a minute and it didn't sound like anyone was anywhere near the scene.

"…wow…for as slow as it's been for us it sounds like the cops are pretty busy…"

"…yeah…they also don't have a lot of sector cars out here…" Kelly was right. We were heading toward the quieter residential area on the outskirts of BigCity. Most of the cops spent their time closer to downtown and as we got closer to the call the more it looked like we'd be getting there first. "…okay…here's Abbott…" Kelly casually wheeled around the corner and Abby came into view.

"…wow…that's a fairly large crowd for a kid who fell…" I noticed the group gathered on the corner.

"…slow day for everyone…" Kelly skillfully maneuvered the ambulance close to the sidewalk…careful to avoid biffing any curb stragglers. I picked up the mike and radioed off to dispatch and then Kelly and I got out of the rig and waded through the crowd.

"…excuse us…hello…let us through…" Kelly and I each exhorted the people with their backs to us. Then some lady from deeper in the crowd cried out to us "…OH THANK GOD YOU'RE HERE…HE'S NOT BREATHING…"

"…what?…" I looked at Kelly and we pushed our way through the last few civilians in the way. When we finally got to the kid we were both very taken aback by what we saw.

"…okay…didn't expect this…" Kelly looked back at me. "…Casey…go get everything…"

I knew right away what she meant "…got it…" And I turned and jogged back through the crowd. "…OKAY EVERYBODY… YOU'RE IN THE WAY…BACK UP PLEASE… EVERYBODY PLEASE BACK UP…" I waved my arms dramatically hoping the motion would help back people off. It did seem to work some and a workable space was made for me to get all our code equipment back to the scene. I loaded the stretcher up with a longboard…the monitor… airway bag and first-in bag and boogied back toward Kelly and the kid.

*About the kid…*It was easy to see why someone thought he fell. He was lying on the ground up against the bottom stretch of porch lattice*…oddly twisted and blue…*When I got back with the equipment Kelly had just finished transitioning him to the supine position.

"…he got hung up on the porch rail with this jump rope…" Kelly worked on getting the long braided cloth off his neck. It wasn't going easy because he had been hanging on it long enough for his neck to swell around the rope and it was very much buried in his flesh. While she worked to cut it off I cut off his shirt and put the defib pads on his chest. The quick look showed a very fine v-fib and I let Kelly know I was going to shock.

"…hold on…" She struggled with the trauma shears. "…I got it…" And with a snip she cleared the jump robe from his neck and scooted back a foot or so on her knees. "…go ahead…"

I set the joules and delivered the shocks. Kelly continued working on the airway and I watched as the fine v-fib dissolved into a discouraging asystole. "…fuck…we lost it…" I mumbled under my breath.

"…easy Casey…" Kelly whispered. "…there's a lot of kids watching…" I looked up and around and she was right. At least five pairs of large scared young eyes stared back. I looked back down at the young half-opened baby blue eyes of the patient on the ground. They were already bloodshot and sunken in his blue swollen skull but they still looked just as young as the other eyes watching.

"…bang out some compressions Casey…then we'll work on pacing…" Kelly's words redirected my attention and I searched for my landmark. She had the tube secured and was already dumping epi and atropine down it.

A cruiser pulled up behind our ambulance and Kelly asked the cops to move some people back. They got right on it and Kelly picked up our portable. "…four-ten to dispatch…." I looked up from my compressions and couldn't believe how cool her voice was.

"…FOUR-TEN GO AHEAD…"

"…yeah dispatch we got a pedicode here…could you send us some extra hands?…"

"…FOUR-TEN YOU HAVE A PEDICODE?…"

"…oh for Christ's sake…" Kelly looked up at the sky and then keyed the radio. "…yes dispatch…we have a pedicode and we need some extra hands…"

"…RECEIVED FOUR-TEN…WE'LL GET SOMEONE OUT YOUR WAY…"

Kelly kneeled back down at the kid's side and gave the BVM a couple of puffs. "...go ahead and try pacing...I'll work on the line..." She continued searching through the first-in bag and came up with an IV start kit. I stopped compressions and started fiddling with the monitor buttons. I adjusted the volume and worked with the rate but I couldn't get any kind of capture. I stopped and resumed compressions and then dove in again... *volume...rate...rate...volume ...nothing...*

"...how's that going Casey?..." Kelly taped down her line.

"...it's not..."

"...guys...whatta ya need?..." Because of the noise generated by the larger-than-usual crowd gathering on the sidewalk I hadn't heard the second ambulance pull up but now Rickie was approaching.

"...help Casey pace..." Kelly directed.

"...I got it..." I looked at the monitor wondering why this wasn't working.

"...no you don't..." Kelly pointedly stated. "...let Rickie have it...take the airway..."

I was frustrated but Kelly was right. I slid up to the head and Rickie took over. I continued bagging and Kelly pushed a round of meds through the IV. When she finished she banged out some compressions and asked Rickie for an update.

"...I got electrical capture...check for mechanical..." Kelly dug her fingers deep into the kid's femoral artery and waited a few seconds.

"...you got it...nice job...let's start moving toward the truck..." Kelly dragged the longboard next to the kid and we got ready to roll him. I was leaned over listening for her count when all of a sudden somebody hit me in the back of the head. At first I just ignored it figuring someone in the crowd bumped into me. "...okay...on my count Losers...one..." And I got biffed again.

"…two…three…" and as we coordinated the rolling of the kid on the longboard I got hit yet another time. That was the final straw as now I was thinking it was one of the cops losing his mind. Sometimes they get a little nutty around dead kids but really… hitting me in the head was unacceptable. "…WHAT…WHO'S HITTING ME?…" I spun around and an un-uniformed person was staring at me.

"…that's my son…what's going on?…"

"…oh…I'm sorry…" I stammered suddenly super over thinking everything I said.

"…Casey…" Kelly called. "…lifting on three…"

I turned to acknowledge her. "…this is Dad…" I nodded my head toward him and she understood.

"…Rickie…take the airway…Casey…stay with Dad…"

Rickie slid up to the head and I peeled off handing over the tube and BVM. Then I took a deep breath and stood up to talk to Dad.

"…hi…sir…step over here please…" I tried to direct Dad away from the stragglers still gathering on the sidewalk.

"…no…" His tone was very firm. "…I wanna know what's going on with my son…now…"

"…I understand…" *crap are you supposed to say that?* "… well when we found your son he had a jump rope around his neck that had somehow got caught on the porch rail and it cut off his breathing and stopped his heart…"

"…is he dead?…" *of course not…state law says no one dies in an ambulance.*

"…no…we have a tube down his throat to breathe for him and we're using the cardiac monitor to provide paced cardiac stimulation to his heart…and we're giving him oxygen and all the drugs the ER would give…"

"…what should I do?…"

"…you should go to the emergency room to be with your son…do you want to ride with me?…"

"…no…I'll take my car…where are you bringing him?…"

"…are you sure you want to drive sir?….I can give you a ride…"

"…I'm fine…and I don't want a ride…" His tone escalated so I backed off the offer. "…now where are you taking him?…"

"…we were going to take him to the Valley Trauma…unless you want us to go to Mercy…"

"…no….Valley Trauma's fine…" And he quickly turned on his heels and left. I was glad the interaction was over because he was truly scaring me. Maybe it was his military tone or the fact he hit me three times in the head but this guy was intimidating.

I caught up to Kelly and Rickie and they had everything strapped down and ready to roll. "…Casey…get back here…" Kelly instructed when I opened the back doors of the ambulance. "…Loser you drive…we're going to beach the Island Hopper here…" Rickie tagged me in and we switched places. I scampered up to the captain's seat to resume airway duties and she slammed the back doors of the ambulance shut.

"…how's the father?…" Kelly asked while she administered another round of meds.

"…very angry and on his way to the Valley Trauma…"

"…he's angry already?…"

"…he hit me in the head three times and I thought he was going to hit me again when I asked to drive him to the hospital…"

"…oh boy…well we certainly got nothing here to make him less angry…" I looked down at the young boy's small face. Our oxygenation had turned him a lighter shade of blue but it was clear the damage had been done. His half-opened eyes exposed fully dilated pupils and despite Rickie skillfully gaining capture his heart had long ago stopped being motivated to do anything on its own. He was dead...*and we were merely the twenty-minute ride to the hospital that delayed the inevitable...*

"...Casey...you with me?..." Kelly didn't thump me on the forehead like Jodie but I felt the same popping back feeling.

"...yeah...what's up?..."

"...change the c-med channel for me..."

"...oh sorry..." I reached to my right and turned the switch. Kelly hailed a dispatcher and began her patch to Valley Trauma. Rickie continued to navigate through city traffic but we were still a ways out. Kelly wrapped up her hospital report and I hung up the mike for her. I continued bagging and she pulled the jump rope out of the O2 bag.

"...check this out Casey..." She held up the cut loop she had dug out of the kid's neck "...there's a knot here..." She moved her finger down the rope to a very tightly pulled half knot.

I looked at it closely and thought I understood. Kelly clarified it for me. "...he tied this...he didn't accidently choke on it..."

I looked down at his little face. "...he killed himself?..." Kelly leaned back on the bench seat and shook her head...*she was genuinely sad...*

"...yeah...can only imagine why..." She looked at him. "...couldn't have been a good reason..."

I squeezed the bag again and stared. I didn't say anything as a hot wave of sadness washed over me. I didn't think I'd cry or anything but I was truly overwhelmed.

Rickie pulled into the Valley Trauma parking lot and soon enough we were transferring him from our ambulance to the ER's capable hands. The nurses were a lot more businesslike with a kid than they were with an old person. You could tell they were also sad and they didn't even know about the knot yet. Once he was off our stretcher Kelly quietly exited and went directly to the tech room. I grabbed the stretcher...threw all our gear on it and wheeled it out to the ambulance. Rickie quietly followed me out. I had hopped up in the back and started putting equipment away. Rickie stood by the stretcher and ran a code summary off the monitor.

"...well that call sucked..." She watched as the tape rolled out. I didn't say anything and just shook my head. She ripped off the strip. "...I'm gonna bring this in to Kelly...I'll be right back..."

She walked away toward the ER doors and I continued cleaning and putting away stuff. From the dark inside of the ambulance I saw the Dad walk in the public entrance to the ER. I was glad he didn't see me. Once inside someone would hook him up with Social Services and they were way better trained to handle angry grieving parents.

Rickie walked back out the ambulance entrance doors with a bed sheet in her hand and she started making up the stretcher. I hopped out of the bus with the dirty laryngoscope wrapped in a glove. "...I'm gonna clean this inside...the orderly's closet has good disinfectant..."

She looked at the pile of empty med boxes strewn about the ambulance floor and bench seat. "...okay...I'll finish this up..."

I headed through the ambulance entrance...past the tech room where Kelly had her head down and was dutifully writing her report...through the main ER where I saw they had already stopped working on the kid and the curtains were closed around him...all the way to the back hallway where all the good supplies were kept. I ducked in the orderly's closet and proceeded to sterilize my blade. Chris...the cool nurse...saw me and came over to ask me about the call. I told her what happened and she made a sad face and then she moved on to assist one of her patients with an updraft.

When I felt my blade was sufficiently de-spooged I wrapped it in a clean paper towel and exited the back doors of the ER. That took me around past X-ray…through the Fast Track and dumped me out by the main triage area. Taking this route I hoped to completely avoid seeing the dad since he should have been brought to the family counseling room by now. Unfortunately though… because we all know how well avoidance usually works out… when I walked through the triage doors there he was…smack dab in the middle of triage. I thought about quickly reversing direction and bolting back through the door I just came through but before my legs actually responded to the command he turned around and saw me. Backing up now would just be wrong.

"…hey you…" he barked "…what's going on with my son?… no one will give me a straight answer…"

"…no one's come out to talk to you?…"

"…no…"

"…let me go get someone…they can answer your questions…"

"…NO…" He grabbed my arm. "…you've ducked me long enough…now what's going on?…"

I looked down at his hand squeezing my arm and then I looked over at the security guard who would come rescue me if I called out and then I looked back at the guy. He was just a dad who wanted to know what was going on with his kid. It wasn't his fault I didn't want to be the one to tell him.

"…sir I'm sorry…" I pulled my arm away as he loosened his grip. "…we did everything we could but…" I looked at his hard face and wished to the gods I could say anything else and still be right. "… your son's dead…"

"…my son's dead?…" His forehead tightened and he drew his hand back. I stiffened…preparing to be decked.

"…yes…I'm so sorry…" *please don't hit me.*

"…my son's dead…" His voice faded and his arm dropped back to his side. Instantly he went from menacing to heartbreaking and I felt the need to put my hand on him. Only tenderly on his shoulder…not threateningly or defensively.

"…come with me sir…" I directed him to turn. "…I can get someone to take you to your son if you want…" He didn't say anything and turned to walk with me. I brought him inside to the Social Services office and handed him off. Then I turned and left the ER walking briskly past Kelly and Rickie's confused expressions in the tech room…

…I didn't want to talk to anyone else right then…

The thing about a tough call is not to dwell on it too long. It may be sad…it may raise questions you can't answer directly but there's nothing you can do about it so just try to deal and move on.

That was made a little more difficult this time since the other two people who were on the call and shared the sadness came home with me and would be sitting across from me at the dinner table. I wasn't going to have the option I so many other times exercised. Just pretend nothing happened at work that day. To give myself a breather I came home and stashed myself away in my room. I smoked a bowl…cracked a wine cooler and cranked Garbage…*I only listened to the sad songs…*I took a shower and let hot water pour on my head and then I lied naked on my futon letting the cool evening breeze blow through my window and across my body. After about an hour or so I felt better enough to get dressed and head downstairs to see what was going on with Kelly and Rickie.

When I got to the kitchen Rickie was sitting at the table in front of a makeshift lab set-up and Kelly was rummaging through a cupboard.

"…what's up guys?…" I eyeballed the assortment of pots on the table.

"…O'Brien's making fruit fondue…" Rickie chopped a banana.

"…fruit fondue…" I laughed. "…where the hell did you get three fondue pots?…"

"…a tag sale in '82…" Kelly appeared with a jar of hot fudge. "…right after I got out of college…"

"…you mean I've been living in a house of fondue pots and had no idea?…"

"…I got an 8-track player too…" Kelly stirred the caramel pot. "…make those slices bigger Loser…you need enough to kabob them…"

"…so what do we have cooking here?…" I lifted the lid off the third pot.

"…oh…that's your classic cheese…" Kelly dove into the drawer to find skewers.

"…it's awesome on Granny Smith apples…"

"…hmmm…this could be good…"

"…of course it will…it's the traditional feast following the crappy-ass call because fondue…as it turns out…is very good for the soul…" Kelly popped a chocolate-covered strawberry in her mouth and I was convinced. Then Kelly laughed through the strawberry. "…and then we'll play *Clue*…"

That caused Rickie to look up from her cutting board and howl "…no fuckin' way…I am not playing *Clue*…"

"…oh come on…you're the best Mr. Mustard ever…" Kelly taunted.

…no sadness on their faces…

✵ ✵ ✵

We sat around the kitchen eating delicious snack treats for awhile...*I don't even know how long...*but it was true...fondue is good for the soul. Something about jabbing a helpless little piece of fruit with a metal prong and stirring it in a pot of boiling sugary substance reaffirms your power and place in the universe.

We barely talked about the call other than Kelly saying that kid must have had one horrible reason for killing himself and hopefully we'd never find out what it was. Rickie and I agreed and then we changed the subject and talked about the more pleasant topic of our upcoming mission. We even reenacted the hardware store playground ball scene when Kelly hip checked Rickie into the laundry basket sitting on a kitchen chair.

Being in the rare mood that I was I decided that I was going to concentrate on getting drunk. Kelly and Rickie were drinking too and by midnight the fondue was broken down and Kelly was crawling her way up to bed. Rickie and I were pretty buzzed though and as it turned out...we were just getting going. We started off in my room looking at the stars.

"...when you're out west you'll see beautiful skies like this all the time..."

"...real ones even...."

"...smartass..." We got quiet and stared for a while. Then the fluorescent glow started to fade and Rickie declared that she needed another beer. We left the serenity of my ceiling behind and slid down the banister to the downstairs. Then before she opened her beer Rickie had another thought.

"...you know...I don't really feel like drinking here...let's go find a bar..."

"...you mean in town?..."

"...yeah...but let's not drive...let's just start walking and see what we come up on..."

"...sounds good...it'll be an adventure..."

So Rickie grabbed a beer for the walk and we hit the streets. The beauty of living in a college town is that you don't have to walk far before you strike bar.

"...let's hit this one Casey..."

"...it's a VFW..."

"...yeah...cheap drinks..."

"...cheap drinks that they spit in...they don't really like our kind in there..."

"...what kind?...I don't even know what kind I am..."

"...all the more reason to hate you...c'mon..." I pointed across the street. "...let's go in there..."

"...the Cigar Bar...that's cool..."

Rickie and I entered under the blue neon-lighted sign and proceeded directly to the bar. We pondered purchasing a Punch but passed simply because we knew it would slow us down. We both were in agreement that we needed to hit-and-run any bar we stopped at. That way we could consume alcohol products but work in outdoor walks to counteract the claustrophobia we were both continuing to suffer from.

After breaking my personal best by making last call in three different bars we stumbled our way back out to the streets. Neither one of us felt like going home though and all our drunken ramblings led us to the cemetery up the street from our house.

As far as cemeteries go it was really cool. It was so big that when you were in the middle of it you couldn't see the street on any side and even in the bright light of day you felt surrounded by somberness. From a historical perspective it held record of the town's founding fathers in the oldest section where they were all buried. They obviously had money and they spent it on their deaths as well as they had on their lives. There were a few mausoleums holding entire families and you could follow maiden names and trace how the daughters were passed around and married off to other founding families. Some of the tombstones were humungous and had the actual story of the person's death engraved like a short story on them. I don't know who John Stuart was but I know he died in 1875 in a tragic whitewater incident in New Hampshire and at great expense his father had his drowned remains brought home to be laid to rest with his family who waited for him with open arms at the gate of our Lord. Not quite sure how they knew about the last part but there it was in stone so it must have been true.

I thought about the tombstone that should be written for our patient today. **"...here lies Jeffrey Burgess...he was only eleven years old but things were already so bad he had to tie a knot in his jump rope so it would be tight enough to kill him as he swung off the porch rail... at great expense his father raised his hand many times driving young Jeffrey into the open arms of the other dead relatives in the family...God wasn't around so much for Jeffrey as a boy...no telling if anyone will show up at the gate for him either...it would appear Jeffrey just didn't matter and now that's all he is...*matter...*"**

...god I feel so angry...

✧ ✧ ✧

Tonight however there would be no reading of the tombstones as it was way too dark to see detail. This was going to be all about bravery as walking through a cemetery at night is about as scary as it gets in suburbia.

"...you ready Casey?..." Rickie and I stood at the wrought iron gate entrance and even drunk I could tell she was taunting me.

"...yes I'm ready...let's go..."

"...let's go..." And in we went and yes it was scary but no...I was not going to let her know. From my daytime walks I felt confident that I knew the important paths and it was a good thing because there was zero light. Rickie had a small flashlight on her key chain but it was made for lighting keyholes not guiding drunken fools down cemetery paths.

"...you ever watch that ghost show on the *History Channel*?..." I decided to take a shot at freaking Rickie out.

"...yeah...they go to historic places and look for ghosts..."

"...in a nutshell...yeah..." I paused almost forgetting what I was going to say. "...well they got this really freaky way they check for ghosts..."

"...proton packs?..."

"...no...they leave tape recorders on all night recording all over the cemetery and then the next day they play the tapes back...and sometimes they hear voices on the tape..." *a shiver went down my spine and my voice quivered.*

"...it's probably the drunk people walking through the cemetery..."

"...oh yeah..." *so much for freaking her out.* "...I never thought of them..."

"...face it Casey...cemeteries may be scary but they're the last place you'll find a ghost..."

"...yeah?..."

"...yeah...with the whole world and netherworld at your disposal why would you stick around here?...there's nothing but dirt and stone..."

Rickie's words made sense and gave me cause for reflection. That gave me time to reach into my pocket and pull out some treats. "...hey...look at what I got..." I held up little bottles for Rickie to see.

"...Casey...it's pitch black...I can't even see your hand..."

"…well here…put yours out…" Rickie extended her hand and I placed the nip in it.

"…sweet Casey…what flavor is it?…" I heard her twist the cap and sniff. "…orange…huh… yes…Grand Marnier…I love it…"

"…yeah…I got them from Kelly's St. Patrick's Day stash…I'll have to replace it tomorrow…I hope I remember…"

"…I'll remind you…" and with that silly comment we both giggled for a while. When we were through I remembered I had another treat stashed. FLICK went my lighter and in the glow of the flame I could see Rickie smile. "…awesome Casey…weed and Marnier…" She took a hit. "…this is perfect…" We leaned against one of the larger stones and relaxed…taking our time smoking most of the joint. I was feeling really buzzed now and with my inhibitions severely lowered I ventured where I had previously not dared.

"…so where do you think our patient from today is?…"

"…lying on a cold slab in the ME's office…" Rickie answered without hesitating.

"…not his body…" I slurred. "…him…the part that made him a person and not a walking hunk of carbon…"

"…oh…" Rickie thought for a moment. "…I don't know… somewhere happy I hope…" Rickie handed me the joint. "…you gotta hope a kid sad enough to kill himself at least gets to go somewhere happy when he dies…"

"…yeah…true…" I reflected. "…you know…I know we don't know why he killed himself but his father was really scary…"

"…how so?…"

"…well I know he was upset and all but he did hit me three times on scene…"

"…what?…"

"..yeah...when we were leaned over rolling him on the longboard...I guess I wasn't noticing him fast enough so he swatted me in the head..."

"...three times?..."

"...yeah and then at the hospital he grabbed my arm and I thought he was going to deck me when I told him his son was dead..."

"...well there you have it...probably the reason the kid killed himself..."

"...yeah but why today?...what was different about today?..."

"...today was probably just the day he couldn't take it anymore..."

"...yeah..." I stared at the stars for a good long time. "...god that sucks..."

...you'd think he'd know that...

✡ ✡ ✡

Rickie and I drank...smoked and roamed the cemetery for about another hour. Then around 04:00 I remembered something important***...I had to be at work in about three hours...*** Obviously that was not going to happen so I told Rickie I needed to get home so I could bang out.

When we got in the house Rickie sang something about having to wicked pee and she ran across the downstairs to the bathroom off the kitchen. I called dispatch and I'm sure it was obvious to them why I was calling out but I didn't care. Tomorrow...or should I say today...was the last day of Ariel's vacation and it had been two hellacious weeks. I missed her...got screwed by the union...plotted anarchy and now had the face of a strangled 11 y/o etched in my brain***...I needed a break...***

I started rummaging around in the refrigerator and Rickie joined me when she got out of the bathroom. "…what looks good Casey?…"

"…I got half a burrito from Veracruzana and some pizza from Paradisio…"

"…ooh…Paradisio…I'll take that…" I handed Rickie the to-go container and we both headed toward the microwave. After our food was sufficiently zapped we sat at the table to eat. "…you know where I'd rather eat this?…" Rickie spoke between chews.

"…Rome?…"

"…yes…Rome would be awesome but I think it would be easier for us to go out on the roof…"

"…oh yeah…the roof…let's go…" We grabbed our containers and in a drunken clumsy manner aimed for the upstairs. Somehow I don't think we were very quiet and I wondered how long it would be before Kelly came out and shushed us.

"…would you like me to hold your pizza while you climb out?…" I giggled while watching Rickie execute ballet moves out the window.

"…no I got it…oof…" Rickie ducked her head quickly. "…watch out for the screen Casey…it slides down…"

Good advice in hand I held the screen and began my ascension. "…here…hold my burrito…" Rickie helped me out and soon we were sitting on the porch roof once again staring at the stars.

"…do you believe in god?…" I leaned on the house and quizzed Rickie.

"…nope…" Her answer was swift and definitive.

"…wow…there was no hesitation there…"

"…no reason to hesitate…I know how I feel…what about you?…"

"…ahhhh…well…not a single god…you know like a Christian god or Jewish god…I guess I want to believe more in the structure like the Greeks or Romans where there was a god to represent all the powers of the universe...like a wind god or thunder god..." I paused for a moment. "...or maybe I just believe in the wind and thunder and I think there needs to be a god in charge..."

"...if there was a god he'd be in charge but since no one's in charge I'd say there's no god..."

"...maybe he's an absentee landlord god...he just collects the rent and lets the property go to hell..."

"...again...that's not a god..." Rickie stared at the stars. "...I just have a hard time believing someone all powerful would let a fraction of the shit that goes on happen if they could do something about it..."

"...people say that just means God's letting things play out to see how we'll handle it..."

"...right...but if you let someone bleed to death in front of you you'd get sued for neglect...try telling the courts you were just letting it play out to see how it would be handled...but now if you're God you let little kids get fucked up the ass so you can see how it plays out...what the fuck?..."

"...no...you're right..." I leaned back and chewed my burrito. The early morning air had a slight chill through it and it made me shudder. "...damn...should have grabbed a sweatshirt..."

"...you know what really pisses me off..." Rickie remains serious.

"...no...what?..."

"...in a few days a bunch of people are going to show up to bury this kid and they're all going to call for the glory of God when it was God who let that kid suffer..."

"...but you don't believe in God..."

"...I don't...so let's just keep him out of it...let's be real... take his death as a chance to tell parents not to hit their kids...not to talk about some mumbo jumbo that means nothing..."

"…it's how people find comfort…"

"…what's with you Casey?…you almost sound like you're defending it…"

"…no…" Rickie's words pushed me back a bit. "…no… god no…I guess those words just come out after years of indoctrination…but I'm not defending anything or anybody…I'm not sure where I stand on the God thing but I know how I feel about religion…"

"…oh…don't even get me started on religion…that's just a way to make money off the illusion of God…"

"…absolutely…and there's nothing more frightening to me than a leadership group who's entire platform is based on faith… you know what the definition of faith is?…"

"…not really…"

"…it's the assured expectation of things hoped for though the evident reality of such is not yet expressed…"

"…the who what?…"

"…translation…just shut up and do what we tell you…"

"…that sounds about right…" Rickie folded her arms around her drawn-up knees. "…at least that's what I got out of Sunday school…as soon as I asked any questions I got told to work on being humble…"

"…HA…" I laughed. "…how's that going for you?…"

"…not so good as it turns out…"We both laughed for a bit.

"…you know what really gets me?…"

"…what?…"Rickie pulled out a beer she had stashed in the windowsill.

"…the Pope Mobile…"

"…the what?…" **PSSSSSHH.**

"…the Pope Mobile…that little bulletproof golf cart they built for him after his assassination attempt…here we are…we're supposed to trust implicitly in the will of God and the Pope himself doesn't trust him as the supreme body guard..."

"...this is what I'm saying..." Rickie seemed content that she'd made her point.

"...but if there is no god...what happens to us when we die?..."

"...I don't know...." Rickie looked pensive. "...I've had patients code and come back...even if it's just for a little while... and I've asked them if they saw anything..."

"...and?..."

"...nothing yet...who knows...maybe we do just die..."

"...no...there's no way...I can't accept that...the universe is endless...time is infinite and the only living intelligent creatures we know of only get seventy...eighty maybe ninety years of all that time and space...what's the point?..."

"...it is weird when you think about it...people die and then they come back...where do they go?..."

"...and why do some come back and some don't?...does it all just boil down to acid base relationships?..."

"...I don't know..." Ricky sipped. "...but I know what it doesn't have anything to do with..."

"...what's that?..."

"...us...it like we really are just there for the ride..."

"...so we are like God...people call us in a time of need...we come if we're not busy doing something else and we pretty much have nothing to do with the outcome except we bill for it..."

"...there ya go..." Rickie looked up. "...wow...what a beautiful sky..."

✵ ✵ ✵

We finished eating and the combination of food and lateness of the hour diminished my buzz. For the first time since yesterday morning I actually felt tired and ready to sleep. My overnight drunk had served its purpose and by chemically wailing on my body I had gotten it back under my control. I would have already been in bed but by now I had to work up the energy to go back inside. Instead I leaned back resting against the house with my eyes closed. I may have even drifted off but then I heard Rickie's voice.

"...you know...I've never gone home and cried after a call..." Rickie was also leaning against the house.

"...no?..." I'm actually surprised...*I don't know why...but I am...*

"...no...but I hear other people have..."

"...do you think less of me?...I have..."

"...no...God no..." She paused. "...I'm just worried why I haven't...am I a fucked up person?..."

...no Rickie...there's more to sadness than tears...

CHAPTER 31-
DELIVERANCE TO MY SIN

...and most important...a time to sleep it off...

By 05:00 the sun was coming up and I was going down. With a bottle of water by the futon and the ceiling fan keeping the room cool I drifted off to restless repose and in the process ***I had a strange dream..***

I dreamt I was sitting in a dark movie theater anxiously staring at the screen waiting for the flick to roll. I was by myself but I could hear a couple of people whispering in the background.

"...this movie's a classic...the director does fine work...no one can touch his vision..."

Then the movie started. Much to my annoyance somebody opened the theater door and a bright light cut through the room. Then the door closed and the room returned to its normal viewing darkness. My eyes were squinting to adjust and I felt the seat next to me fold down. Somebody sat next to me. As my eyes came around I noticed she was a chick...and a cute one at that...

"...I know how this movie ends..."she looked at me and smiled.

"...yeah?...well I don't...so...don't tell me..."

"...why not?...they're all the same..."she kept smiling. "...somebody wins...somebody loses...somebody gets hurt..."

"...you're gonna get hurt in a minute if you don't shut up...go sit over there..."

So she got up...her chair folded up and she walked across the theater and sat down. I turned to the screen and intended to get back to my movie.

"...just because I'm over here doesn't mean I can't talk to you..."I looked over and she was talking to me. "...hi..."and she waved.

"...do you mind?...I'm trying to watch the movie...could you leave me alone?...please..."

"...leave you alone?...huh...from where I sit you are alone...you were alone when I got here...you're alone with me over here and you'll be alone when I leave...which is now...so there...I'm leaving and you're alone... proud of yourself?...good-bye..."

And she left...and I was alone...and...**I woke up thrashing on my futon...in the dark...alone...**

...and very thirsty...

✧ ✧ ✧

Ariel's Vacation...Day Eight...

Weird dreams aside I still managed to sleep in pretty late. I didn't even start to stir until 13:00 and I didn't actually get out of bed until 15:00 or so. Rickie...*amazing specimen that she is...* apparently had already gotten up...showered and taken off to go hiking with Mary Ann... Mahan and some of her other buddies. This was confirmed to me by Kelly when I finally oozed my way to the living room couch.

"...you guys were up pretty late last night...huh?..."

"...yeah...I think I finally passed out around 5:30..."

"...yeah feel any better?..."

"...yes simply by virtue of the fact that I have managed to make myself more nauseous than I was yesterday at the Valley Trauma...so yesterday doesn't feel so bad in comparison now..."

"...it was a crappy call...if you wanna talk just let me know..."

"...thanks..." I was touched by Kelly's offer. "...but I'll be all right...I think I just needed a good drunk to get it out of my system..."

"...okay..." Kelly nodded and left it at that. "...what's on now that's good?..." She picked up the remote.

"...college softball...ESPN..."

"...very good...channel 49 it is..."

✵ ✵ ✵

I was still at one with the couch drinking lemonade from a gallon jug when Rickie pounced through the front door in her customary manner. "...hellloooo...I'm home..."

"...hey I'm in here..."

"...hey wassup?..." Rickie poked her head into the living room. "...where's O'Brien?..."

"...food shopping...she left about an hour ago..."

"...cool...what's on the tube?..."

"...*A League of Their Own*..."

"...ahhh good flick..." Rickie flopped down and jeered. "...girls can't play ball..."

I laughed and was impressed at the same time. "...how was your hike?..."

"...awesome...we hiked for about an hour and then we went four-wheeling in Mahan's Bronco..."

"...really?..."

"...yeah...it was a blast..."

"...I don't know how you do it...I'd a been pukin' my guts out..."

"...yeah...I almost did at first...but then it went away..."

"...amazing..."

"...helllooooo...I'm home..." Now it was Kelly popping through the front door. "...can somebody give me a hand?..." Rickie and I both got up and joined her on the porch. She was surrounded by a sea of grocery bags and we waded in to help her out.

"...what's all this O'Brien?..." Rickie quizzed. "...I've never seen you buy so much at once..."

"...I bought dinner for us tonight..." Kelly grabbed some bags. "...I thought before our mission we should eat good...you know…in case we get arrested and don't get anything but bread and water for a while…"

"…ugh…" I groaned.

"…oh god…easy…" Rickie cautioned. "…don't get Casey started…"

"…she'll be fine after she eats…" Kelly held up a package. "…'cause look what I bought…I got steaks and corn on the cob and potatoes…"

"…and strawberry shortcake stuff…" Rickie looked through her bag and cheered. "…all right…what's in your bag Casey?…"

"…shampoo…"

"…huh?…"

"…well it wasn't all about our dinner…" Kelly headed for the kitchen. "…and don't bother looking in the CVS bag either…"

"…oh well now I'm curious…"

"…stay out of it…" Kelly yelled from the kitchen.

"…let me see it…" I opened the bag and Rickie peeked in. "…oh…" And she started laughing.

Kelly came back and snatched the bag. "…thank you…"

"…what was it?…" I whispered to Rickie.

"…I'll tell you later…"

"…aw c'mon…"

…she's not gonna remember…

Rickie and I were assigned grill duty and Kelly stayed in the kitchen cutting potatoes …onions and strawberries…***hopefully not on the same cutting board…***

"…you gotta turn the knob…click the button once and then three times real fast…" I directed Rickie on official grill procedures.

"...I got it Casey...I've lit this thing before..." **click click**

"...but it's not lit now and the well is filling up with...

click wooooooooooooofffffffffffff

...gas..."

"...oh my god Casey...did you see how high that just flashed?..."

"...yes...I felt the breeze and I think my hat made it to the neighbor's yard..."

✵ ✵ ✵

"...this was a great idea O'Brien..." Rickie gnawed her way through a corn on the cob.

"...yeah...nice cut of meat too..." I scooped up the last of the onion and potatoes on my fork. "...I'd have to say this would probably be my choice for a last meal..."

"...that was the theme..." Kelly took a drink off her beer. "...so you feeling better Casey?..."

"...yeah...a gallon of lemonade later and I was finally able to produce urine..." I pushed my plate up and put my elbows on the picnic table. "...I think the worst may have passed..."

"...good...because we're all going to need to be bright eyed and bushy tailed for tonight's mission..."

"...so what time are we leaving?..." Rickie looked over another ear.

"...12:45..." Kelly answered sharply. "...that'll give us time to get there and drive around a little bit to work up our courage without wasting all our time..." Kelly laughed and for the first time I wondered if I wasn't the only one who was nervous.

"...oh we are not backing out..." Rickie showed no sign of flinching. "...I've been looking forward to this all week and we are doing it..."

"...relax little soldier...it's going down..." and just like that Kelly's swagger was back.

...Zero Hour minus 5:45...

☆ ☆ ☆

"...oooh...I love Raymond..." Rickie flopped down on her end of the couch.

"...me too Loser but this episode is just about over..." I flopped down on my end of the couch.

"...hand me the paper Casey..." Kelly reclined. "...there's gotta be a movie on..."

I handed Kelly the entertainment section. "...let's try to find something in keeping with the theme of the night..."

"...yeah...something about fighting back against the forces that live to fuck you up the ass..." Rickie suggested.

"...perfect...9:00...channel 14...." Kelly pointed the remote and the movie came on the screen...***cue the banjo music...***

"...*Deliverance*...yes...I love this movie..." Rickie stretched her arms out in celebration.

"...oh boy..." I rolled my eyes and lied back on the couch. "...this is going downhill fast..."

"...no it's perfect..." Kelly smiled. "...by the end of the flick we'll be all fired up and righteously indignant..."

"...I'm already righteously indignant..."

"...yes but can you spell it?..." I teased.

"...r...i...g..."

"...quiet...movie's on..." Kelly scolded.

Rickie began to whisper. "...g...h...t...o..."

"...wrong..."

"...oh..." Rickie groaned...I laughed and Kelly glared.

...Zero Hour minus 3:45...

✵ ✵ ✵

Deliverance had its desired effect as by the time the credits were rolling I had already counted ten "for fuck's sakes" from Kelly and Rickie had groaned herself all the way down to the floor where she sat with her arms wrapped around a pillow. I barely watched the movie as my head was spinning from nerves. I was able to look like I was paying attention but my mind was everywhere else.

The second half of our double feature turned out to be *Pulp Fiction* which led to Rickie proclaiming that the powers that be must have known the special kind of encouragement we'd need.

"…yeah…nothing like anal sex to keep you focused…" Kelly stated as she got up to get another beer.

…Zero Hour minus 1:45…

✵ ✵ ✵

We weren't going to be able to watch all of *Pulp Fiction* as our time was running down. Kelly got the bag of spray paint from the hall closet and handed out product.

"…Casey…Loser…your weapons…make sure you shake them a lot before we get to ground zero…we don't want to be waiting around for the little metal ball to clank for a minute…"

My hand shook as I took the spray can but Rickie broke out into poetry. "…this is my can of spray paint…although there are many like it…this one is mine…"

At 12:30 we smoked from the ceremonial bong of anarchy and Rickie asked Kelly if she had any face paint. She didn't but that led to all three of us deciding to change our clothes to more camouflaged apparel. Once we were appropriately decked out in black jeans…T-shirts and toques we agreed we had wasted all the time we could and now it was time to hit the road. We loaded into the Saturn in the customary manner with Kelly driving…Rickie riding shotgun and me perched quietly in the backseat. On the way to World Headquarters we debated who we'd call with our one phone call and then we decided who'd fake what to get out of lockup so we could sit in the ER like so many other perps had done to us.

"…I can fake a pretty good seizure…" Rickie declared. "…I know I can even get a good foaming going on…"

"…cool…very cool…" Kelly affirmed. "…I know I've smoked enough weed to squeak out an asthmatic wheeze or two…how about you Casey?…"

"…hmmm…you guys took the good ones…I don't want to do anything vanilla like abdominal pain…" I thought for a moment. "…I know…I can have a panic attack and I probably wouldn't even have to do a lot of symptom faking…"

Kelly looked at me from the rearview mirror. "…yup…that'll work good…"

"…just make sure you go apneic a couple of times to really get your heart rate up…" Rickie suggested. Then a good song came on the radio and Rickie cranked it up and started passenger seat dancing.

…Zero Hour minus :15…

✯ ✯ ✯

"…okay…there it is…" Kelly pulled the Saturn up to the front of the World Headquarters. Where there previously had been just a laid foundation there was now a large object covered by a huge tarp. "…Loser…go check the tarp and make sure we can get under it…me and Casey are going to ride through the parking lot and make sure the supervisor's gone…"

"…got it…" Rickie reached for the door handle.

"…but keep your eyes open and don't do anything until we get back…just in case the building isn't empty…"

"…got it…" Rickie reached for the door handle again and this time actually got out. I dove over the seat to the front. Kelly turned off her headlights and drove around to the back of the building. Once we were convinced the building was clear we drove back around. Kelly parked on the long driveway near the sign with her nose pointed out for quick escape. We couldn't see Rickie until we got closer and then we realized she was already tucked under the tarp.

"…update Loser…"

"…oh hey…" Rickie was deep in logistical thought and looked surprised to see us. "…well…we can get under it but we'll never get it off…it's huge…"

"…that's fine…it'll actually give us cover…" Kelly started shaking her spray can and mostly out of nerves I copied her. "…all right…everybody knows what they're doing right?…LOCK AND LOAD PEOPLE…"

And just like that we all jumped in to our assigned lettering. My job was easy. I had to clearly paint "FY" to be followed by Rickie's "NAA" while Kelly tagged several objects around the sign. She got a manhole cover…a telephone pole…the stop sign at the end of the driveway and then she took the lookout position. When I was done I joined her in the lookout spot while Rickie finished up. Out of sheer terror and nervousness I started laughing and couldn't stop. Kelly was giggling too but it seemed to be more out of glee than anything else.

"…this fucking rocks Casey…" She laughed.

I was just about to agree with her when I saw headlights over her shoulder. "…CAR…"

Kelly spun around "…yes it is…" And then she yelled loudly so Rickie could hear her "…ABORT LOSER…ABORT…" Kelly and I then turned and bolted for the Saturn. She reached it first and opened the back door for me. In my nervous escape I leaped headfirst into the backseat and when I came down I landed on the spray can and painted a beautiful pink streak across the back of the front seat. I also managed to fill the car with a very lovely fine pink mist. Kelly kept yelling for Rickie who seemed oblivious to her cries to abort. I looked out from the backseat to see Rickie's legs not moving under the tarp. Kelly even seemed to be getting nervous. "…c'mon Loser let's go…"

Finally Rickie broke away and ran back to the car. She wasn't even completely in the door as Kelly threw it into DRIVE and took off. We were all pretty high now and the car was loud with cheering and hootin' and hollerin'.

"…YES…we fuckin' did it…WAHOO…"

"…unbelievable…I'm a cowboy…who'd a thought I could be a cowboy?…"

"…fuck you NAA…FUCK YOU AND YOUR BULLSHIT…"

BEEP BEEP

CHAPTER 32-
SIGNS OF THE TIMES

...as Jesus was sitting at 61 the disciples came to him privately "...tell us..." they said "...when will this happen and what will be the sign of your coming and of the end of the shift?..." Jesus answered "...watch out that no one deceives you...for many will come in my name claiming '...I am a paramedic...' and will deceive many...you will hear of gang wars and rumors of gang wars but see to it that you are not alarmed...such things must happen if there are to be good calls...Bloods will rise against Crips and Latin Kings against Jamaican Posse...there will be famines and earthquakes in various places...all these are the beginning of birth pains...and if you deliver the baby...do two sets of paperwork so we can bill two patients..."

Despite the lateness of our returning hour all three of us had every intention of getting up the next morning to be at the unveiling of our sign. Kelly was the earliest riser and took off before I got up. Rickie was already in the kitchen drinking coffee when I stumbled downstairs.

"...hey...what's up Loser?..."

"...not much...coffee's still hot..."

"...is it fresh?..."

"...no but it's hot..."

"...ah...just like I like my women..."

"...oh no...I like them fresh too..." *we giggled.* "...so you wanna ride in together?..."

"...to the shindig?..."

"...yes...the shindig at Shangri-La...I wanna go in your Jeep..."

"...sure...we can take the Jeep...where's O'Brien?..."

"...she had some errands to run...she said she'd see us up there..."

"...cool...I'll go shower..."

✵ ✵ ✵

When we got to the Grand Opening celebration there was another surprise waiting for me. A very tan and smiling Ariel was already there. Oh was she a sight for sore eyes. While she stood there grinning I reached down and picked her up over my head. "...SKIPPY...I'm so glad to see you..."

"...put me down...I'm glad to see you too..." I put her down and we got into the business of catching up.

"...so how was your trip?...what's new in North Carolina?... nice shirt..." I pointed to her North Carolina State Trooper T-shirt.

"...thanks...my brother gave it to me..."

"...your brother the highway Nazi?..."

"...yes...my brother the highway Nazi..."

"...so how is the family?..."

"...good..." She smiled and nodded. "...oh my god the kids are so big...I didn't even recognize my niece..."

"...they glad to see their Aunt Ariel?..."

"...I think so...how about you?...did I miss anything?..."

"...you mean since we were last hanging out with Clint Black?..." Ariel laughed in reflection and I thought for a second. "...yeah...a few things happened...we'll have a lot to talk about Monday..."

"...Ariel the flirtin' Guertin..." Kelly laughed as she approached. "...I'm so glad to see you're back in town...you wouldn't believe what a downer Casey was without you..." She gave Ariel a hug and Ariel smiled.

"...I'm sure you took good care of her while I was gone..."

"...yeah we found a few things to keep us busy..." Kelly smiled and looked at me. "...can I see you by the dunk tank Casey?..."

"...sure...hey...is that a tear drop on your cheek?..."

"...yes...I had the face painter put it on..." She got very serious. "...now it's known that I've killed people..."

"...you're killing me right now..." *we walked a ways.* "...so what's up?..."

"...nothing...I just think we should be together when the tarp's removed and our work is there for all to hail...and remember...we gotta look surprised too..."

"...oh my god..."

"...what?..."

"...you have pink paint on the edge of your glasses..." I'm horrified to see the evidence so outwardly displayed.

"...I what?..." Kelly took her glasses off and examined them. "...I'm blind without my glasses Casey...I can't see anything..." Kelly started laughing really hard. "...I'm serious...I can't see it..."

"...well it's there..."

"...oh my god that's too funny...good thing I took them off while they painted my tear...I think I was talking to Sommers..."

"...you think?..."

"...I couldn't really see him...oh my god Casey...that's so funny..." Kelly was really cracking herself up.

"...there's an ambulance parked over there...I'll go get some alcohol preps..." Kelly just kept laughing and as I walked away Rickie walked over to see what was going on.

"...wassup O'Brien?...I could hear you cracking up way over there..." Rickie pointed to the grill area where Mahan was holding a spatula and looking over with a confused look on his face. Kelly showed Rickie her glasses and as I walked away I heard Rickie burst out laughing too.

I got back with some alcohol preps and we quickly got rid of the evidence. It was just in time too as when I got back to the group a Borg representative had just commenced with the Grand Opening auditory tripe. By now we had all grown so accustom to the predictable hollow ball-washing that was synonymous with any company meeting that there was very little emotion coming from the audience. Looking around...all I really saw was a bunch of whipped peasants hanging out for the free food. Pretty much the only thing missing for the flavor of a Renaissance fair was someone collecting unfair taxes and stocks filled with the delinquent poor.

Then the Borg spoke of marking this momentous occasion with the unveiling of the vital sign heralding change...*dumbass play on words...*Change that may be scary but change that will be good...*because I said so I guess...*Join with me now as we herald the new sign of the times...**DUH DUH DUHHHHHH...**

And with a tug and a swoosh the signs of the times were unveiled and behold...*yes...*the signs were all pointing in the right direction. The right direction of a fluorescent pink...highly visible

FYNAA

Apparently after I had laid the framework Rickie tirelessly went back over every letter until it was highly defined and quite visible from a distance. So that was why she was under the tarp so long...*I just thought she was huffing...*It was all so perfect. The crowd gasped and collectively giggled and then Mahan instigated a "strike" chant which got everyone waving their fists in defiance. Now the fair just needed a tree and a short rope. The Borg felt it too as the Grand Opening ceremony was abruptly cut short and everyone was sent home...*including the clown...*

What else was cool though was that as everyone was leaving... the previously faint and almost indistinguishable FYNAAs on the manhole cover...telephone pole and stop sign now seemed to stand out even clearer in support of the huge FYNAA. As everyone peeled out of the driveway they honked their horns and pointed at the tags.   Someone shouted "...let's head to Sully's..." and a caravan was formed...*I think I saw the clown in Mahan's Bronco...*Suddenly it was like a cloud had been lifted off of everyone and for the first time in a while...*nine days to be exact...*everyone was back on track and on the same page again. Kelly and Rickie were right. It was the perfect gesture of anarchy to get everyone refocused...

...momentum had been shifted...

As expected the caravan landed at Sully's and the bartender's eyes got really big when he saw the twenty or so of us piled in the door. Seemed his life was already complicated enough with the bar's softball team hanging out...*oh well...*

Our crowd got set up with the first round and we piled a bunch of tables together successfully taking over half the bar. Everyone was stirring and obviously intent on trying to figure out who had perpetrated the deed. I heard Rickie tell Mary Ann that she thought it was a supervisor. Maybe Travis had some balls after all. Then they burst out laughing. Kelly threw her hat in the ring and said it had Mahan written all over it. He laughed and said it had O'Brien written all over it and she commented that she would have loved to but she wasn't tall enough. Then Mahan said maybe Rickie did it since she was tall enough and that just made me and Kelly laugh. "...are you kidding?...Rickie can't spell..." *and the mystery lived on...*

At first I was offended that no one even suggested that I could be involved. Then I realized that was just me being ridiculously ironic. After all...a mere twelve hours earlier I was petrified everyone would know...

...time to pick a side girl...

✫ ✫ ✫

The revelry continued through the afternoon and we all gathered around the bar TV and watched the Red Sox engage the Rangers in an offensive slugfest in which Nomar went two for three. No finer day could there have been. Around the fifth inning Mahan got a call from the negotiating team to say that NAA was requesting a last-minute negotiating meeting. At midnight we would officially be legal to strike. It was now 16:30 and everyone was fired up and ready to go. NAA...*it would appear...*was finely starting to feel the heat. Mahan downed the last of his beer and headed off to shower and put on his suit. We had all long stopped being susceptible to false hope but this did ring true of promise.

...we'd see...

✫ ✫ ✫

The baseball game ended disappointingly when the Red Sox failed to hold on to a ninth inning lead and so with heavy heart and stomach full of pizza I headed home. It had been an exciting eventful last few days and I really wanted to get some productive REM sleep. That wasn't to be though as sometime around midnight Kelly and Rickie busted in my room and woke me up.

"...Casey...they signed...Casey...wake up...they settled with us...we got almost everything we wanted..."

"...they what?..." I had been deep asleep.

"...they signed..." I focused on Kelly's face. "...and we got everything we wanted except they get to keep posting..."

"...for real?..."

"...yes..." Rickie cheered. "...so c'mon get up...everybody's downstairs..."

"...downstairs?..."

"...yeah...everybody's here...let's go..."

"...cool..."

...I guess I'd sleep tomorrow...

CHAPTER 33 - BRING ON PARADISE

...and he said "...these are they who have come out of the great tribulation...they have washed their robes and made them white in the bleach of the disinfectant...therefore... they are before the throne of the God of EMS and serve him day and night in his ambulance...never again will they hunger...never again will they thirst...for they will get lunch breaks...the sun will not beat upon them nor any scorching heat during posting...for the God of EMS will be their shepherd...he will keep the a/c charged in their trucks... and the God of EMS will wipe away every tear from their eyes..."

Monday morning I bounded out of bed with a renewed energy in my step. The contract was signed...Ariel was back in town and we were going to get to keep our shifts and partners. It was unbelievable. And on top of it all I had played a silent but integral role in making it all happen. Turns out I was a cowboy...I was a revolutionary even...I was a revolutionary cowboy...

...oh boy...

✡ ✡ ✡

When I went in to work there was a new posting near the time clock. This one also decreed that there was to be a celebration but this one was to be a true celebration. A celebration of the people as this one was to be hosted by labor***...Mahan was throwing a pig roast...***

"...did you see this?..." I pointed as Ariel approached from my flank.

"...see what?..."

"...Mahan's having a pig roast...two weeks from yesterday..."

"...Sunday the eighteenth?..."

"...yeah..."

"...aren't you working that day..."

"...oh no...is that the day I told Fergie I'd work for her?..."

"...yes and it's her brother's wedding so you better work it..."

"...ugh..."

✳ ✳ ✳

What to do...what to do...A little voice inside of me told me this party had all the makings of a real humdinger. Anytime you get a substantial group of frustrated people together and add alcohol...high jinks and hilarity are sure to ensue. Ariel didn't understand. She just didn't get into parties...large or small...so she couldn't see how enticing this was to me. Still...I did promise Fergie I'd work her 8a-8p and there just never was a good reason to back out of a swap. Oh well...for now I placated myself with the thought that there was still enough time between now and Mahan's pig roast to find a replacement for myself. In fact...there were plenty of medics who would pass up a party to take overtime and I'd just have to work fast to make sure I secured someone before everyone else who wanted the day off got to them.

Then we ran into Fergie and Jodie at the Valley Trauma. Ariel told Fergie I was trying to back out of my shift which led to Fergie pleading with me not to. I reassured her that if push came to shove I would work the shift and that her brother's wedding was not in peril. Then Jodie handed me a slip of paper.

"...what's this?..."

Jodie put her hands on her hips. "...a list of suitable partners for me..."

"...what for?..."

"...listen Casey...I only consented to Fergie getting the day off because I was willing to work with you..."

Fergie was shaking her head in agreement with Jodie. "...it's true...she did..."

"...over half of these people are going to want to be at the pig roast..."

"...hey...I want to be at the pig roast but we can't all get what we want but at the very least Casey I'm not getting stuck with a jerk off..."

"...okay...okay...no jerk offs..." I took a deep breath. "...I better get crackin'..."

✡ ✡ ✡

It wasn't until Ariel and I got sent to our first call that I realized I hadn't done a call since the kid last week. It was a rare occasion that Ariel drove but I think she was feeling a little bit adventurous fresh off of vacation and she was driving us to a well-being check. I was supposed to be looking up Beckett Street but for some reason my mind drifted to that call. I couldn't stop thinking about how crazy it was that we thought we were just going to a kid who fell and he ended up not only dead but having killed himself too ***...weird...***

"...am I taking a left up here?...HELLLLOOO..." Ariel rapped me on the head. "...anybody in there?...helllloooo..."

"...oh yeah...sorry...yes...left...then left again...."

"...thank you..." Ariel flashed a look. "...where were you?..."

"...nowhere...sorry..." I concentrated really hard. "...Fifty-three...fifty-seven...sixty-three's right there..."

✡ ✡ ✡

"...so Jodie really tied your hands...huh?..." Ariel peeled the lid back on her coffee.

"...yeah...it's quite the restricted list..."

"…you know…I'm probably not going to go to the pig roast… if you want I'll come in at noon and work the second half of the shift with Jodie…"

"…thank you and I'd love to ask you to but you're not on the list…"

"…what?…"Ariel shrieked louder than I ever heard her shriek before. "…that's gotta be a typo…"

"…a typo?…" I smiled. "…this isn't the *New York Times*…this is more like the ramblings of a mad woman…she wrote it on a paper towel with a dry-erase marker…"

"…yeah…but who keeps me off their list?…" Ariel was sincerely offended and it was pretty funny.

"…don't feel bad…Mindy Grant's not on the list either…"

"…Mindy Grant…of course she's not…she's got B.O.…"

"…I don't know what to tell you…"

"…I do…it's a typo…"

"…well if it is great…we'll confirm that with Jodie and then you can work the half shift for me…"

"…no way…I wouldn't work with Jodie now if you paid me double time…"

"…great…thanks for your help…" I breathed deep yet again.

☆ ☆ ☆

"…you're really pretty…anybody ever tell you that?…" The drunk grinned at Ariel and I counted at least four missing teeth.

"…no…she's really pretty but you're the first one to notice…"

"…I wasn't talking to you…"The drunk repositioned himself on the stretcher in an attempt to turn away from me.

"…why don't you just stop talking…"

"…why don't we all just stop talking…" Ariel smiled at me and attempted again to get the triage nurse's attention.

"…is she your girlfriend?…is that why you won't look at me?…yoo-hoo…look at me…"

"…yeah…we found you sleeping in a Dumpster but that's why she won't look at you…"

"…again…I wasn't talking to you…"

Finally the triage nurse made eye contact and gestured toward a bed in the hallway. Ariel and I moved the stretcher over to the wall and dropped the railing to begin patient transfer. That's when the drunk got fresh. As Ariel reached over he reached up and grabbed her. I took exception to that and reached my fist straight down and square into his chest. It's not that I hit him but more like I pushed him and knocked him back down on the stretcher. He looked up at me and sputtered. "…what the fuck?…"

"…just lie there and shut the fuck up and keep your hands to yourself…" My voice was tight and resolute.

"…okay…all right…"

"…what was that?…" I looked up and Ariel had a puzzled look on her face.

I realized what I had done and I'll admit I was a little puzzled myself but not wanting to lose face I stuck with the plan. "…crowd control…you're welcome…" And I turned and walked away leaving her with the patient.

…no idea where that came from…

✡ ✡ ✡

"…are you all right?…" Ariel stood at the open back doors of the ambulance.

"…yeah…why?…" I stared at the floor not wanting to make eye contact.

"…because I've never seen you respond to a patient like that before…I figure something must be wrong…"

"...no...I just didn't think he should be grabbing you like that..."

"...and I appreciate that but you can't be putting your hands on patients...it's a dangerous habit to get into..."

"...okay...." I continued to stare at the floor.

"...so we're good?..."

"...yeah...we're good..."

"...look at me..." I looked up and she smiled at me. "...we're good?..."

I refused to smile. "...we're good..."

"...okay...I'm gonna go do paperwork..." Ariel still looked concerned.

"...yeah...I'll work on getting the dirtbag smell out of the truck..."

"...okay..." And she walked away.

✮ ✮ ✮

"...oh my God I can't believe it...is it really you?..." I walked across the Valley Trauma ER parking lot and smiled at an old friend.

"...heeeyyyy...it is me...how the hell are you?...." Blossom stood at the back doors of his ambulance and smiled back.

"...I'm great...what are you doing here?..."

"...long-distance transfer...we brought a trauma down from Ben Medical..."

"...cool...anything good?..."

"...yeah actually...he fell asleep early this morning and drove into a barn...broke himself into little pieces...check him out... he's in the trauma room along with some really cool X-rays..." Blossom giggled in his customary manner.

"...I will...so how you liking Country?..."

"…it's good…we don't do a lot but what we do is usually pretty good…we get to call the chopper out a lot…I'm getting good at setting up LZs…"

"…that's cool…get to ride in yet?…"

"…yeah once…" Blossom rested his boot on the bumper. "…they ask us every time but it all depends on who's left for coverage in town…it's tough to fly to Hartford in the middle of the night if I'm the only medic covering three towns…" I nodded my head in understanding. "…so what's new with you?…how's NAA life?…"

"…as sucky as you predicted…"

"…yeah?…huh…"

"…oh my God…tons of rules and unique punishments outlined for each infraction…but at least we got our new contract…"

"…yeah I heard…so that's a good thing…"

"…good enough…posting's here to stay but we get to keep our shifts and partners…"

"…you still working with Ariel?…"

"…yeah…"

"…well that was worth keeping…" Blossom giggled again.

"…seriously…and guess who I'm living with?…"

"…I heard…"

"…you heard?…"

"…yeah…Kelly O'Brien and Rickie…that's awesome…"

"…yeah…we have a lot of fun…"

"…and cause some trouble too I'm sure…" I just smiled and Blossom laughed. "…yup…I knew it…" We both laughed some more. "…you gotta love it…right?…this is a special life we're living…"

"…it sure is…"

"…we just gotta remember to keep it simple and take it as it comes…" Blossom smiled and was wise beyond his years…

…just gotta take it as it comes…

CHAPTER 34 -
THE LOWEST OF THE LOW

...then the God of EMS will say to those on his right "...come...you who are blessed...take your paycheck prepared for you for your week's work...for I was hungry and you gave me a Happy Meal...I was thirsty and you gave me a Gatorade...I overdosed and you gave me Narcan...I was sick and you started a line...I was in prison and you came to visit me...I needed a transfer and you transported me..."

...then the righteous will answer him "...God of EMS when did we see you hungry and hit the drive-through or thirsty and stop at AllStar Variety?...when did we see you posting and invite you in?...when did we see you sick...overdosed or in prison and go to visit you with IVs and Narcan?...when did we take you priority three to the Valley Trauma?..."

...the God of EMS will reply "...I tell you the truth...whatever you did for one of the least of these brothers of mine...you did for me..."

Sometimes it is so hard to tell what wakes you up in the morning. Is it the bright light of the sun reflecting off the store window onto your unprotected face?...Is it the smell of early morning bus exhaust dumping on you after it drives away from the curb or is it the sound of the store manager barking "...HEY YOU...TIME TO GET UP AND MOVE ALONG...?"

James sat on the bench in Court Square contemplating such mysteries of life. Bottom line...it didn't really matter much...but contemplating gave him something to do...

...something to do...

...something to do...

Oh how he wished he had something to do...

People don't realize it but they're slaves to their schedules...
Oh sure...people think they're slaves to the tasks on their
schedules...They gotta get the kids to soccer...they gotta hit the
dry cleaners and post office...But they're not...they're slaves to
the schedule themselves...It doesn't matter what the tasks are...
you just gotta have something to do...

...something to do...

...something to do...

God how he wished he had something to do...

He could go for a walk...nothing new there...he walked a
lot...but he didn't have anywhere to walk to...It would just be
walking to move...not walking to get anywhere...and really...he
didn't walk so well anymore...

Oh there go those ambulance drivers again...

They always got somewhere to go...they're always movin'...
they're always doing something...Weird though...lately they've
been around more...parked...parked and not going anywhere...
Not sure why...they used to only be around when someone called
for them or when you saw them driving by going somewhere
where someone called them...Now they just parked...parked and
got out and stretched...hmmm...funny...they look bored too...

God do they look bored...

They look bored in a different way though...it's not that they
don't have anything to do...they just can't do it here...So they
wait and they wait until there's something they can do...and then
they do it...I admire that...I'm drawn to that...I want to walk by
and be near it...

Oh thank God...I have something to do...

"...hey James...what's up?..." The blond one was pretty and
she knew my name...I think I recognized her...maybe not...

The other one stared at me and commanded "…that's right… keep walking…" But I just walked to get here…I didn't want to walk to get there yet…She stared at me some more…The blond one smiled and told her to relax…She didn't relax…now she was staring at the blond one…the blond one smiled some more and offered her a cookie…She said "…you can always bribe me with chocolate…" and she smiled…I wanted to spend time with them…I could make that happen…I had something to do…

> …something to do…
>> …something to do…

"…911 WHAT'S YOUR EMERGENCY?…"

"…um yes…I'm feeling suicidal…"

"…YOUR'RE FEELING SUICIDAL?…"

"…yes…I believe I could hurt myself…"

"…ARE YOU WITH ANYONE RIGHT NOW?…"

"…no…I'm alone…"

"…DO YOU HAVE A WEAPON OR A MEANS TO HURT YOURSELF?…"

"…no…but I could look until I find one…"

"…NO SIR…PLEASE DON'T DO THAT…WE'RE GOING TO SEND SOMEONE RIGHT OVER…I SHOW THAT YOU'RE ON A PAYPHONE IN COURT SQUARE…"

"…yes…I'm next to the Courthouse Coffee Shop…serving courtside for twenty-five years…"

"…YES SIR…WE'LL SEND SOMEONE RIGHT OVER… PLEASE STAY ON THE LINE UNTIL YOU SEE THEM… "

"…oh I see them right now…they're walking toward me…"

"…OKAY SIR…WHY DON'T YOU HANG UP AND WALK OVER TO THEM…"

"…okay…"

OH YES…I had something to do…

> …something to do…
>> …something to do…

"…what the fuck James?…you see us sitting over there and you just couldn't resist calling 911?…" She scared me…so I looked to the blond one…

"…I'm feeling suicidal…I'm pretty down…"

The blond one didn't smile but she nicely said "…for real James or are you just looking for something to do?…" How did she know?…I had no answer I felt comfortable with…I stayed quiet…she opened the door to the ambulance and I stepped in.

"…not on my clean sheets…" The scary one pointed to the right. "…sit your ass down on the bench seat…" I went to the right…then she thought she was whispering but I heard her. "…that's right…you're lucky I don't make you sit on the floor…"

"…go ahead and drive…I'll take this…" Oh yes…the blond one was going to sit next to me. "…put your seatbelt on James… we don't need any more problems for you…" She was so nice. "…and I'll tell you what I'm going to do…if you sit tight and don't make my day any harder than it has to be I'll give you this…" Oh a cookie…a huge chocolate chip cookie covered with M&M's.

"…okay…" I would have liked it now…but she pulled it back…

"…no…when we get to the Valley Trauma…" She smiled and I was willing to wait…she asked me questions…I answered them…the driver yelled at someone in a wheelchair sitting in the crosswalk…hey…that was Miriam…

The scenery out the back window swirled and I thought we must have been at the hospital…this part made me dizzy… the driver put the ambulance in PARK and talked on the microphone…I knew she would open the back doors soon…

"…okay James…you know the drill…" The blond one still talked nice. "…undo your belt and hop down…"

"…do I get a cookie?…"

"…do you get a cookie?…" The driver got loud. "…this isn't fucking IHOP…get out of the ambulance…"

"…yes James…you get a cookie…" The blond one was still nice. "…I'll bring it in to you when you're settled with the nurse…"

"…what?…are we serving in flight meals now?…"

"…be nice…"

"…this is nice…we gave him his useless ride to clog up the emergency system some more and now we're done…get out James…"

"…I'm coming…I'm coming…" I got out of the ambulance and the blond one walked me over to the door…she punched numbers on a keypad and the door opened…we walked inside…everybody said hi to the blond one…everyone called her Fergie…

…Fergie…

…Fergie…

…oh yeah…her name is Fergie…

Fergie told me to sit on a bed…I did…she walked away and started talking to a nurse…the nurse looked at me…she smiled but she was not happy…sometimes people smile when they're not happy…they walked over to me…

"…hello James…my name is Chris…" She still smiled. "…not feeling well today?…"

"…no…"

"…okay…let's see what we can do about that…" She smiled again. "…I'm going to check your blood pressure…" she took my arm.

"…all set with me?…" Fergie smiled at the nurse…again… not really happy.

"…yeah…me and James should be good…" The nurse smiled at me. "…so how's school going?…"

"…good…one more semester…"

"…where you going to work?…" The nurse really smiled at Fergie. "…hint hint…here maybe…"

"…oh I don't know…I gotta pass my boards first…"

"…oh come on…you'll be fine and I'm sure you've thought about what kind of nursing you'd like to do…"

"…yeah a little bit…"

"…so keep us in mind…we can use smart talent like you around here…"

"…thank you Chris…I will…" Fergie smiled and turned red… she started to walk away.

"…and tell them I sent you…" The nurse said…she didn't answer her.

"…I'll be back with your cookie James…" She answered me.

The nurse asked me the same questions the blonde did…I tried to answer them the same…

"…okay James…the doctor will be over to talk to you soon…why don't you just lay back and relax…" The nurse put up the railing on the bed. "…are you hungry?…did you eat breakfast?…"

"…I'm gonna get a cookie…"

"…you are?…okay…well how about some real food first?…" Real food?…a cookie is real food…Sucking the cheese off a tossed-out hamburger wrapper isn't but a cookie is…

"…okay…" I laid back…maybe she knew I wasn't getting a cookie…

"…here ya go James…" The blonde was standing next to me. "…here's your cookie and a milk…" I reached up and took them.

"…milk and cookies…a nice little treat for abusing 911…" The angry driver was back. "…nice…what's next?…a back rub for opening hydrants on hot summer days?…"

"…easy Twist…" They walked away…they kept talking…I didn't hear what they said…

"...Mr. Zoya..." A man in a white coat put down my railing. "...I'm Dr. Rice...I understand you want to hurt yourself today..."

"...yes..."

"...any thoughts as to how you would hurt yourself?..."

"...no...I just feel like I want to..."

"...okay...have you ever tried to hurt yourself before?..."

"...oh sure..."

"...you have?..."

"...yes..."

"...and how did you try to hurt yourself in the past?..."

"...mostly drinking and fucking up..."

"...I see..." he wrote on a piece of paper. "...I'm going to say three words Mr. Zoya and I'd like you to remember them...I'm going to ask you to repeat them later...okay ...understand?...."

"...yes..."

"...okay...the three words are zebra...twenty and red..."

"...okay..."

"...have you had any drugs or alcohol today?..." He put the paper in his coat pocket....he started poking me...

"...no..." I tried though...turned out the beer bottle I found was just full of piss...

"...do you hear voices in your head?..."

"...no..."

"...do you feel as though you're being watched or chased?..."

"...only when a cop drives by..."

"...but not any other time?..."

"...no..."

"...what were the three words I asked you to remember?..."

"...zebra...twenty...red..."

"...okay Mr. Zoya...I understand the nurse is getting you some breakfast...why don't you go ahead and relax..." He put the rail back up...I ate my cookie and drank my milk...That cookie was really good...

The nurse brought me a tuna fish sandwich...a small scoop of coleslaw and a bag of chips...I couldn't eat just one...I finished everything and when I was done I pushed the container off my mattress and I heard it hit the floor...I rolled over and fell asleep and I had a strange dream...

...I was climbing a tree on a warm summer day...I leaned back from the tree and for a moment let myself relax...It was a beautiful morning and it was going to be a beautiful day...one last deep breath with my head back and the sun on my face...I leaned out and extended my arms to reach the tree...My left heel kicked out and while I waited I realized something...

...oh my god...I was falling...

......

......

...and I woke up with a start...

...I was lying on the stretcher...

...I heard talking...

"...so are you going to Mahan's pig roast on the eighteenth?..."

"...the eighteenth of this month?...no..."

"...are you working?..."

"...no..."

"...can you work for me?..."

"...no..."

"...no?...why?...it's a good shift with Jodie Twist..."

"...I'm sure it is...I like working with Jodie but I'm going to Boston for my sister's birthday..."

"...oh...okay...well thanks anyway..."

"...sure...hey try J.D. Crocker...I hear he's looking for OT that day..."

"...oh thanks...he's not on the list..."

"...the list?..."

"...yeah...long story...thanks anyway Shirley B...I'll catch ya later..."

I watched the two ambulance drivers walk down the hallway to go back outside...I thought I knew them...Oh well...they were gone...A lot of people walked quickly past me...they all looked very busy...I wondered if they really were...The clock said it's 2:45...Wow...I must have slept for a long time...Should be getting to be lunchtime soon...Maybe I could get a ham and cheese...oh well...whatever would be fine...I wondered how long they'd let me stay here...

"...I'm just saying...maybe you could have expanded your list just a little bit more..." Hey...the blond was back...I sat up and smiled and hoped she saw me as she went by. "...hi James...still here?..." I shook my head yes...

"...big surprise there..." The angry one was with her...they were pushing someone on a stretcher. "...look Fergie...a standard is only a standard if you stick to it...I can't go abandoning things that have gotten me this far..."

"...I get that...and I respect that...but you're tying Casey's hands and she's doing me a favor so maybe you could do..." And now they were too far away for me to hear...

"...Mr. Zoya...how are you feeling?..."

"...good...okay I guess..."

"...very good...okay...what we've done Mr. Zoya is call ahead to detox to reserve a bed for you..."

"...ah no that's okay...I don't want to go to detox..."

"...okay...I understand Mr. Zoya but there are no psych beds available and it would seem detox is your greatest need right now..."

"…no…I don't need detox…"

"…Mr. Zoya…we checked your blood alcohol when you came in and it was .28…that's particularly high considering it was 10:00 a.m. when we checked…"

"…you checked my blood alcohol?…" When had they done that?…I looked at my left arm and sure enough there was a BAND-AID in the elbow fold…When had they done that?… What else had they done?…What were they doing now?…They were trying to send me to detox that's what they were trying to do…I couldn't go to detox…In fact…I had to get a drink soon. "…I can't go to detox…"

"…very good Mr. Zoya…I'll have some paperwork for you to sign and then you're free to go…"

"…okay…"

"…good luck to you Mr. Zoya…" He left.

"…okay James…I got you a lunch…" The nurse was back. "… go ahead and eat while the doctor does his paperwork…"

I opened the container…peanut butter and jelly…disappointing but what could you do?…I needed a drink…Kahlua…Kahlua goes good with peanut butter and jelly…not that I would drink that sweet stuff…although a shot of vodka toughens up anything…even milk…well maybe two shots of vodka for milk…Anyway…this sandwich wasn't bad and it came with a bunch of wafer cookies… three of each kind…yellow…brown and red…aren't those the colors wings come in?…God I needed a drink…I had to get out of there…what the hell did I care about paperwork anyway…What the hell?…I had to get out of there…

…I had to get out of there…

…I had to get out of there…

…I was so out of there…

"…James…where are you going?…" The nurse saw me crawl off the end of the bed…I grabbed my clothes and walked out the door...I couldn't hear her anymore...I had to get a drink...And well I wasn't going to find one around there...I put my pants on...crap...I didn't grab my shirt...crap...I'd just keep that Johnnie on...where could I get a drink?...I'd walk...I'd walk away from there and find something...and so I walked...and walked...and walked...and kept on walking...I didn't find anything...I was tired...I sat on the first flat surface I could find...and that's when I found it...In the bushes...in the front of some big business big building on Main Street...a bottle...a bottle in the bushes...Lord Calvert...about one-third full...can you believe it?...one-third full and it wasn't piss...Some other guy must have been drinking there...He probably...*GULP GULP GULP*...where was I...oh yeah...*GULP GULP GULP*...some other guy must have passed out or forgotten it...or stashed it for later and now I got it...I should ...*GULP GULP GULP*...I shouldn't stay there 'cause he could come back and if I was sitting there drinking his Lord Calvert...well...I should...I would...and I was...I was walking again...*GULP GULP GULP*...I had nowhere to go but I was walking again...and I was happy...I was happy because I had Lord Calvert and he didn't...*GULP GULP GULP*...Hey there went an ambulance again...Hello...I waved to my good friends...*GULP GULP GULP*...my good friends who gave me cookies and rides...They gave me rides and there they went again...*GULP GULP GULP*...There they went again...Oh yeah that sun was bright...felt good too...I was gonna sit down...I was gonna...*GULP GULP GULP*...sit down...I was gonna...God that felt...

"...HEY ASSHOLE...GET OFF THE MOTHERFUCKIN' SIDEWALK..." OOF...it felt like I got kicked in the stomach...or something...I woke up to yelling and I couldn't breathe. "...GET...GO...GET YOUR RANK ASS OUT OF HERE..." I looked up into the sun and an angry man was yelling at me...he looked like he wanted to kick me again...soon...so I rolled

around and got away from him...I held Lord Calvert and slid...
rolled and slid and got out of there...*GULP GULP GULP...*That
was bad...Back to walking...

                    ...back to walking...
                            ...back to walking...

...and I walked...*GULP GULP GULP...*and...

                                    ...the...
                                        ...sun..
                                            ...went...
                                                ...down...

    ...I didn't want to walk anymore...I wasn't...*GULP GULP
GULP...*getting anywhere...so I decided that this was where I
was...McDonald's...McDonald's had a table outside...I sat at the
table...cars came in and out of the parking lot...I...*GULP GULP
GULP...*stared...

    Hey...that was an ambulance...it pulled in the parking lot...
another ambulance was behind it...it kept going down the street...
everybody waved...the other ambulance flashed their lights and
hit the loud horn...*GULP GULP GULP...*wonder where they
were going...

    "...you're getting out of the truck in a McDonald's?..." Oh
no...it was the angry one...

    "...I need the bathroom..." Hey it's the pretty blond one...

    "...better bring some 4x4s...this McDonald's isn't known for
its maintenance and upkeep..."

    "...I got napkins..." They went inside...I watched them
from the window...the angry one got in line...the blond one
disappeared...I was going to go inside...I could...I could
go inside...I got in line...I stood behind the angry one...she
ordered...

    "...yeah...give me a number four with a Coke and barbecue
sauce...thanks..."

"...hi..." She saw me.

"...oh what the fuck James?...nice Johnnie..."

"...I want a cheeseburger..."

"...that's great...should I supersize it for you too?..."

"...I just want a cheeseburger..."

"...wonderful...but I don't work here and I don't give out handouts to drunks...beat it..."

"...I want a cheeseburger..."

"...and I want you to get out of here...you're a walking health code violation...scram before I catch something off you..."

"...I want a cheeseburger..."

"....GET OUT..." She took her flashlight and pushed me toward the door with it...I was not getting a cheeseburger...I walked out the door...I was outside...*GULP GULP GULP*...I was next to the ambulance...it was running...I wondered if the door was open...it was...I was inside the ambulance...I was sitting in the driver's seat...the ambulance was running...

...GULP GULP GULP...

"...fuck it..." I was driving...

...I was driving...

...I was driving the ambulance...

...and I drove...and I drove...wig wag...flasher...strobe...I turned them all on...cars moved...well some did...*GULP GULP GULP*...cars moved...and I drove...and I drove and cars moved...and cars moved and just one big gulp...a police car was behind me...

...I wasn't driving anymore...

CHAPTER 35-
MAYBE I DON'T WANNA BE BLESSED

...then little children were brought to Jesus for him to place his hands on them and pray for them...but the disciples rebuked those who brought them "...keep the little children away from Jesus...don't you know they're germ factories?..."But Jesus said "...let the little children come to me and do not hinder them for the Kingdom of Heaven belongs to such as these...and besides...I've been taking my zinc..."When he had placed his hands on them he went on from there...two days later...he had pink eye...

"...hey...are you guys going to the pig roast at Mahan's Sunday?..." I walked into the living room and Kelly and Rickie were in their usual positions.

"...uhhh...let's see Casey....wild crazy people from work crammed into Mahan's back yard...drinkin'... playing volleyball...eatin'...and heebin' the jeeb...I don't know...do ya think we should?..." Kelly answered...*her words dripping with sarcasm...*

"...you know...it was possible to treat that as a simple yes or no question..."

"...true...so what's your point?..." Kelly continued sarcastically.

"...I don't think I'll be there..."

"...what...are you insane?..." Rickie queried. "...of course you'll be there..."

"...I know...I want to be there...but I told Fergie I'd work for her months ago and now..."

"...now everyone's going to the pig roast so you can't get coverage..." Kelly became more sympathetic. "...I heard Crocker was looking for OT that day..."

"…he's not on the list…"

"…what list?…" Rickie asked.

"…the shift is with Jodie and she has carefully outlined her selective criteria for who she'll work with in the form of a list…"

"…oh fuck that…" Kelly snapped. "…get whoever you can… we all gotta work with everyone…"

"…I know that and you know that but believe me…it's easier just to follow Jodie's list…" I paused for a second. "…I mean…she is my friend and she is asking for a favor…"

"…I don't know Casey…" Rickie stood up and started walking toward the kitchen. "…I'd grab Crocker while I could…" She continued walking unaware of her faux pas.

"…you'd what?…" I started smirking.

"…no way Loser…it's hard to grab a guy who always has himself close at hand…" Kelly started laughing. "…know what I mean?…"

"…oh my god…" Rickie howled…now aware of her misspoken words. "…I can't believe I fucking just said that…"

"…well you did…" Kelly laughed some more and took a drink of her beer. "…I don't know Casey…I think you and I both know you need to be at that pig roast…" She nodded at me.

"…I know…I know…"

…what the hell was I going to do?…

☆ ☆ ☆

"…our activated charcoal is out of date…" Ariel scrunched up her forehead while she read the small imprinted stamp on the end of the tube.

"…I'll get some…we need ice packs too…" I slid the cabinet door shut and stood to exit the ambulance.

"…grab some more electrodes …we've been using a ton of them…" Ariel threw an empty box at me. "…fill that up with them…"

BONK "…HEY…" The box hit off the side of my head. "…control your cardboard…" I picked the pillow up off the stretcher and whipped it off her.

"…hhhheeeeyyyyyy…" Ariel whined as her glasses got knocked askew. "…watch it…."

"…ladies…ladies…do I need to break this up?…" We both looked out the back of the ambulance to see Travis drooling and being creepy.

"…NO…" we answered in unison and immediately stopped having fun.

"…ah…too bad…" He slurped and turned to walk away. "…and hey…let's wrap up that inventory…we're down a truck today…"

I watched him disappear around the side of another ambulance. I looked at Ariel as I stepped off the gator plate. "…what's new about that?…"

She just shrugged her shoulders and then smiled evilly. "…think fast…" *a tube of glucose whipped by my head.*

"…hey…" I ducked quickly. "…no heavy stuff…"

✫ ✫ ✫

I took my time in the supply room as I was not the least bit sympathetic to the lack of personnel on the street. NAA would never get it that their Spreadsheet Status Management bullshit was ridiculous if we always double-timed to cover the flaws in their system. Besides…if anything significant occurred dispatch knew where to find Ariel and she knew where to find me.

When I got back to the truck I could tell Ariel wasn't in a big hurry either because she was now out of the truck and leaning on the back doors talking to Fergie.

"…hey Fergie what's up?…" I approached from behind and when Fergie turned around I could see she was upset.

"…hey you…" She still smiled.

"…what's up?…" I looked at Ariel and she didn't look too pleased either.

"…our ambulance got stolen last night…"

"…out of the garage?…" I looked around.

"…no…out of the South End McDonald's parking lot…"

"…what?…"

"…James…" Ariel offered.

"…James stole your ambulance?…"

Fergie shook her head. "…yup…he was sitting in the parking lot when we pulled in and he followed us in…I was in the bathroom and I guess he got really aggressive with Jodie… demanding she buy him a cheeseburger…so she booted him back outside…we had the truck running for the a/c and I guess he just hopped in and took off…"

"…what the fuck?…" I was stunned.

"…of course he was trashed…" Fergie continued. "…so he's driving hammered through the South End when he biffs a parked car and the cops nail him…"

"…holy shit…where's Jodie?…" I looked around anticipating the more animated retelling of the tale that I was sure she'd supply.

"…she's not here…" Ariel answered.

"…they fired her…"

"…they what?…"

"…they fired her…James told the cops she was driving when we got to McDonald's so NAA blamed her for leaving the keys in the ignition…they tried bagging me too but Jodie wouldn't have any part of it…when she found out she was fired anyway she took the whole blame saying I had insisted on shutting off the truck but she insisted on keeping it running…"

"…really?…" I was truly impressed and deeply touched by Jodie's loyalty. "…so they listened to that douche bag?…"

"…well…she was driving…"

"…yeah but we all leave our trucks running…" Ariel reasoned. "…we can't have our meds sitting in a hundred degree oven while we live amongst the homeless in the city…" Her ire rose and now all three of us were agitated. Of course that's when Travis strolled by.

"…four-ten…let's go…I told you we're down a truck…"

"…and that's our fault?…" I spun around. "…you fire a good medic for some bullshit reason and now it's our fault you're down a truck?…"

"…watch it Casey…" Travis stiffened his back.

"…why?…" I also stiffened. "…you gonna fire me too?…"

"…easy…" I barely heard Ariel.

"…just get your ass in your truck and go…"

"…yeah go…" I started walking toward the driver's side door. "…hurry up and go babysit a parking lot…" I opened the door and got in. "…let's go Ariel…it's very important that we go fucking sit our asses in the parking lots of BigCity…" I slammed the door and started the engine. "…this job sucks…" Travis stood his ground as I backed up by him. **"…AND YOU FUCKIN' SUCK TOO…"**
…insert squealing tires…

✵ ✵ ✵

Ariel and I drove in silence to our all-important posting location. It's amazing how loud silence can be when all you hear is angry screaming in your head. Angry screaming that I was providing. I was so freakin' pissed and sitting confined in the cab of a truck was the last thing I needed. I drove to the most remote area I could find and when I parked the truck I bailed out and slammed the door about six times and yelled *fuck* as loud as I could. Ariel got out of the truck too but she stayed to herself on the other side.

Finally I felt like I got the rage cleared out and I sat down on the curb to seethe more stoically. Ariel slowly walked over and sat next to me. "…you're pretty mad…huh?…" she meekly offered.

I looked over and she had a very sheepish…nonthreatening grin on her face. Something about it perfectly complemented her dry humor and the combination cracked me up. I started laughing and couldn't stop and probably out of relief she started laughing too. Finally I felt sane enough to speak.

"…I can't believe they fired Jodie…"

"…I know…" She picked up a stick and started jabbing at ants scurrying along the edge of the curb. "…but she's a good medic and she'll get another job…"

"…oh is that all that matters?…as long as we can get another sucky job we'll be all right…that's what we're supposed to be grateful for?…"

"…our job's not sucky…it just has sucky moments…" Ariel kept jabbing. "…right now you're having some sucky moments strung together but that'll end…"

"…yeah…maybe I'll get fired…"

"…yeah…maybe with the way you almost ran over Travis you will…" Ariel giggled. "…that was not your brightest moment…" I knew she was right but I really didn't think there was anything that could be done about it now. She continued "…you gotta relax though…you've been really high-strung lately and that's not a good approach to be taking…"

"…I know…you're right…" I felt expected to put how I felt into words. "…I don't know what's been going on lately…I feel like I'm in a good mood and then something happens and I'm not..."

"...we all get a little frazzled...you probably just need some time off..." Ariel continued to jab with the stick. "...you got some time you can take...take it..."

"...I want the pig roast off..." I started getting irritated again. "...I want to be able to go to that party..."

"...well...then here's some good news..." Ariel's tone lightened. "...Jodie's fired so now her list doesn't apply...I'll come in and work the second half of the shift for you..."

"...yeah?..." My mood suddenly lightened. "...that would be awesome...thank you..."

"...and c'mon...we'll go find a payphone and call Jodie...I bet she's already got another job..." Ariel put her arm around me. "...c'mon...it'll be fun..."

I didn't think it would be fun but I wanted to talk to Jodie... although a big part of me would have also liked to just stay on the curb with Ariel killing ants and hugging me. Oh well...she stood up and chucked her stick so I got up too and we headed back to the ambulance...

...and all the ants breathed a sigh of relief...

✲ ✲ ✲

Ariel and I found a payphone in the Bess Eaton parking lot but when we called Jodie we got her machine. We figured she was either out job-hunting or hiding from the press so we left a message and went back to work.

Later that day we ran into Mahan at the Valley Trauma ER. He was busy modifying his pig roast flyers and didn't notice me walking up behind him.

"...oh man...please tell me you're changing the date to a day I'm not working any part of..." I peered over his shoulder.

"…no…why?…" He turned and looked at me. "…what do you mean you're working?…you don't work Sundays…"

"…previous swap…I gotta work the morning…"

"…just the morning?…it doesn't start until one…"

"…I know…I just like being off the whole day…that way you can truly relax and ease into the party mode…so you'll change it?…"

Mahan laughed. "…I can't change the date…the pig's already ordered…besides I planned it on a day I knew everyone was pretty much off…including you…"

"…I know…I know and I am off for the afternoon so it's not a big deal now…so what are you doing?…" I stared at the flyer.

"…well in light of recent circumstances I've taken the liberty of changing the name of the event from the "…'I GOT PORKED BY NAA AND LIVED TO PARTY Pig Roast' to the 'Jodie Twist Memorial Bash'…"

"..oh nice…does she know yet?…"

"…yeah…as a matter of fact I got her changing flyers at the other end of the ER…"

"…she's here?…" I looked around.

"…yeah…she popped in about a minute ago…"

"…ah…cool…"

…and I was off like a bathing suit on spring break…

✡ ✡ ✡

I wandered the alleys of the ER until I found Jodie holding court in the usual manner by the nurses' station. In fact…the only thing that didn't look like just another day in the ER was the fact that Jodie was in civvies instead of her blue uniform.

"…Jodester…" I hollered. "…how the hell are you?…"

"…Casey…I'm angry…how the hell are you?…" And she hugged me.

"…I'm angry too…what are you doing here?…"

"…visiting my friends without the spying eyes of NAA…what are you guys doing?…"

"…bee sting with full anaphylaxis…we gave an epi drip…"

"…cool…where's Skippy?…"

"…explaining to med con why we gave an epi drip…"

"…oh no…" She laughed. "…you wanna come to unemployment with me now?…"

"…no…" I smiled. "…actually med con gave us the order…it was pretty cool…"

"…oh…okay…"

"…so what are you going to do?…"

Jodie kept smiling. "…I don't know…sell a kidney maybe… make my husband support me…whichever turns out to be more fun…"

"…yeah they both sound like a hoot…" I was relieved she still had her sense of humor. "…but seriously…are you okay?…"

"…yeah…I'm fucking bullshit but we're fine…"

"…I can't believe they fucking fired you…"

"…really?…you're surprised NAA acted like a bunch of pussies?…"

"…I guess not really…" I looked around kind of surprised Jodie was taking it so well. "…so are you really good?…"

"…yeah…I'm fine…it's summer so I'm going to take my vacation early and mostly unpaid and then I'll scope out my options…Country already called me or who knows…maybe I'll go shake up LittleCity EMS…and there's always Connecticut…I do have reciprocity…don't worry Casey…I'm good…"

I stared at her to make sure she wasn't just bullshitting me. She smiled back and I realized I still had no idea how to read her.

…but I was honestly not afraid of her anymore…

✫ ✫ ✫

"…so you got to see Jodie?…" Ariel clicked in her seat belt. "…do you feel better?…"

"…yeah…at least she seems like she's all right…" I put the truck in DRIVE and pulled out of the ER parking space. "…I don't know how she's doing it…I'd be a wreck if I got fired for bullshit…"

"…you mean if you got fired from your sucky job?…" Ariel almost sneered.

"…yeah…my sucky job…"

"…FOUR-TEN…FOUR-ONE-ZERO…"

"…four-ten…leaving Valley Trauma now…" Ariel answered.

"…FOUR-TEN…I KNOW IT'S A WAYS BUT COULD YOU PLEASE RESPOND PRIORITY TWO TO THE BIGCITY MALL?…PARKING LOT IN FRONT OF SPENCER'S GIFTS FOR THE PSYCH WITH PD…"

"…four-ten received…BigCity Mall…with PD…" Ariel answered again as I flipped the lights on.

"…priority two for a psych?…that's odd…"

"…probably a violent psych…" Ariel figured.

"…so why not just cuff and transport themselves?…" I still wondered.

"…I don't know…" Ariel had no other answer.

"…a psych at the mall…that's kind of funny when you think about it…have you ever people-watched at the mall?…"

"…yup…" Ariel giggled.

"…who isn't the psych?…right?…"

"…yup…" She giggled some more. "…car…"

"…got it…" I dodged all further obstacles and despite the delayed response we arrived at the mall in a fairly decent amount of time. The cruiser was parked right out front and I pulled up to it. I leaned over to pull some gloves out of the box in the console and when I sat up I saw the cop walking toward me. He was an older day cop...he'd been around forever...but this was the first time I actually saw him with someone in custody. Something else wasn't right either. He wasn't the sharpest dresser on the force but as he approached I noticed his collar was wonky and his hair was mussed and his pen was hanging precariously out of its pocket.

"...what's up officer?..." I asked mostly out of concern for him as I soon noticed a scratch and a welt under his right eye.

"...I got a live one for you...he's a real Tasmanian devil this one..." He walked toward the back door of the cruiser.

"...can we walk him?..." I slowed him down a bit.

"...more like can you contain him?...he's a handful...even cuffed..."

"...okay hold on..." I looked over to Ariel who had hung on the perimeter for an update. "...hey Aire...stretcher time...and leg restraints too..." I smiled and shook my head.

"...okay..." Ariel didn't smile so much and turned to get everything. That's when I turned back toward the cruiser and peered in the backseat to see who the ball of energy we'd be transporting was. That's when I realized.

"...oh my god..." I looked back at the cop.

"...oh my god what?..." Ariel sounded concerned as she approached.

"...he did this to you?..." I looked back in the window.

"...yeah...I'm telling ya...he beat up his social worker too... that's what I got called for...and then when I tried talking to him he got crazy on me...I had to tackle him and he put on one hell of a fight before I could get the cuffs on him..."

"...he's a kid..."

"…yes he is…officially his birth certificate says he's nine…his name's Scotty and he's a terror…you are looking at one pissed-off kid…"

I kept staring in the back window of the cruiser at the little guy with his hands cuffed behind his back. As soon as he saw me he rushed right up to the window and bashed his forehead off it. I swear he had foamy sputum around his lips.

"…hey…don't bang your head…" I put my hands up like I could stop him through the glass.

"…fuck you…let me out…" And he bashed his head again.

"…fuck you…are you kidding me?…" I looked at the cop. "…this kid's tough…"

"…this kid's been beaten on his whole life…Daddy's in jail for killing his baby sister and Mom's just a strung-out crack whore… he can't be placed in foster care…he's literally being raised by the state and even they don't know what to do with him…can't wait till he's eighteen…"

"…fuck you…" And he bashed his head yet again.

"…okay…can we get him away from the window so he'll stop doing that?…" Ariel suggested as she attached the leg restraints to the stretcher.

"…you got it…here we go…" I could tell the cop was in no hurry to re-engage with the kid but I give him credit. He was putting a maximum effort forward. He opened the passenger door and talked to Scotty through the cage. "…hey Scotty…buddy…I need you to go for a little ride with these nice ladies…"

"…NO…FUCK YOU…THEY'RE CUNTS…FUCK YOU…" Scotty screamed the whole time the cop tried to smooth talk him. The cop didn't stop though…he just kept trying to explain everything like you would with any other kid. Amazingly…even when the kid tried spitting at him through the cage…he just kept giving him the benefit of the doubt and kept talking to him like any loving dad would.

I looked at Ariel and we were both thinking the same thing *...CRAP...we gotta restrain a kid...*There is nothing good about having to forcibly restrain a child. There is no good feeling that comes from wrapping your adult-size hands around the small structures of a 9 y/o's body. There is no power in bringing down a weaker being. There we were though...soon grappling with flailing limbs...walking the fine line between squeezing too hard and hurting him or letting go and getting scratched and mauled to the point of injury. He screamed...he spit...he put up one hell of a fight and even though we knew it was for his safety that we were tying him down to the stretcher...there was no satisfaction in becoming just another adult who put their hands on him in a forceful manner.

When we had him safely secured Ariel quietly took off her gloves and went up front to drive. I sat on the bench seat next to him. He looked lost in the largeness of the stretcher. He was crying now...sobbing almost in defeat. His little face was soaked with tears and spit and pain. His demeanor softened and the voice of the little boy buried deep inside him spoke. He began to beg me to let him up.

"...please lady...I'll be good...please lady...untie my hands..."

"...no..." was all I could say. "...I can't let you up..."

"...please...please lady..." He cried harder and couldn't even turn or curl up to comfort himself like little kids do because of how he was restrained. He pulled from side to side trying to get his hands loose. The restraints started to dig into his wrist. Presented with the scared little boy side of him I started to really feel like an evil child-hating ogre. I even briefly considered unstrapping him.

"...lady...please..."

But something inside me just wouldn't let me do it. "...I don't want you to hurt yourself...I can't let you up..." Very quickly his tone changed again.

"...LET ME UP BITCH...I WILL KILL YOU...I WILL KILL YOU BITCH..."

Grateful as I was that he was still restrained the regression back to angry-human-in-child's-body was painful to watch. I considered moving and sitting behind him so I wouldn't have to see his face. I looked up front and Ariel was intently staring out the windshield. I knew she was glad not to be back there with him. Still I stayed...and I stared...I stared at the face of a young child and wondered...what's wrong with us?...why do we do the things we do?...and fuck yeah how can there be god?...because how could a god let us do the things we do?...

...and what's with all the sad little kids?...

✵ ✵ ✵

"...that was one sucky call..." I spoke as Ariel and I headed down the 291 off-ramp leading back to World Headquarters.

"...that's for sure..." Ariel stared ahead. "...but not as bad as it will be when he gets bigger and figures out how to really hurt someone..."

"...hope we get to do that call too..." I mocked as we cross the railroad tracks...*we drove quietly another half mile...*

"...you doing anything for dinner?..." Ariel broke in.

"...not sure...you?..." As we drove down the long street we came upon the sign still labeled FYNAA and I silently chuckled to myself.

"...I really wanna check out that new Indian restaurant downtown..."

"...Indian?...hmmm..." I pondered. "...I've never had Indian food...is it hot?..."

"…some…not all…" We pulled into the long driveway and Ariel keyed the mike. "…four-ten off Cabin Street…" We held our breath waiting for the verdict.

"…FOUR-TEN RECEIVED YOU'RE OFF CABIN STREET…HAVE A GOOD EVENING LADIES…"

"…four-ten received…thank you…you too…" Angie politely answered.

"…oh thank god…I am so done with today…" I pulled the ambulance up to the building and stopped as a chairvan was still occupying the wash bay. I rubbed my face to see if I could jump-start my circulation.

"…so what about it?…" Ariel squawked.

"…huh?…" I stopped mid rub. "…what about what?…"

"…dinner…downtown…Indian restaurant…"

"…oh…yeah…right…" I sheepishly smiled. "…you asked like ten minutes ago…" Ariel stared silently…not the least bit amused. "…yeah sure…I'm feeling brave…let's do Indian food…" The chairvan cleared out and we pulled in the wash bay. I was feeling really tired and had no desire to wash the barely dusty truck but Ariel's a rule-follower and the rules say you gotta wash your truck after every shift…no matter what…*so here we go…*

I pulled two brushes off the rack on the wall and Ariel started to fill up the five-gallon bucket with soap and water.

"…four-ten…you're home…" Travis appeared around the masonry wall separating the wash bay from the parking area. "…I need to talk to you…" Travis pointed at Ariel and that made me really wonder if he knew her name. It's unusual for Ariel to get singled out by the supervisor so immediately she looked confused. When she looked at me I'm sure I looked confused too. Still… she remained composed enough to finish filling up the bucket and then she walked toward Travis.

"…make sure you ask if you need union representation…" I spouted Weingarten as she walked away and Travis shot a dirty look back at me.

"…I'll be fine…" Ariel muttered as she walked off with him and I knew she would be as Ariel could more than handle herself with any supervisor…including Travis. It was just so odd for her to get called away. Oh well…I dutifully continued washing away wondering what might be up. Then I wondered why I was still doing a super primo job when Ariel wasn't around to enforce it. New philosophy in hand I ignored several caked-on bug corpses and wrapped it up. In fact…by the time she came back not only was the truck washed but our paperwork was organized in its envelope and I was getting ready to drive around and drop off our medic gear. Ariel came around the wall with a dazed look on her face. Then when she saw everything was done her look turned incredulous.

"…you finished everything?…"

"…yeah…"

"…you finished everything the right way?…"

"…what?…"

"…you checked everything?…you didn't cut corners?…"

"…I know how to finish a shift…now get in before I leave your skinny ass over here…" She shook her head and mumbled something about it not really being a long walk. Still…she opened the door and hopped in. When she did I noticed she had a down expression on her face.

"…what's up?…"

"…nothing…"

"…you lie…what's up?…"

"…nothing…you got everything done so let's just park and get out of here…" Since it was a short drive to the supervisor's door I didn't push it. I was confident there'd be plenty of time for that later. We parked in our spot and got out of the truck for the last time that day. My ass was still sweaty from the confinement of the bucket seat but I took pleasure in knowing it would soon dry off and I would...*at least for the moment*...own my ass again.

I stayed to gather my belongings from the day and Ariel dragged what she could of our gear over to the supervisor's door to turn it in. I followed behind her with the monitor and set it on Travis' desk. He didn't say anything to me and I didn't even bother trying to look at him. It was clear we were both hanging on to the anger from the morning. Times like these it was great to have Ariel on my side because she could translate asshole. I know she didn't like it any more than me but she could always manage enough congeniality to get us through a day.

With the day's chores all wrapped up...Ariel and I punched out and started walking toward the door. That's when I decided to push it. "...so what's up?...because something clearly is..."

Ariel waited until we were outside to answer. "...Travis just told me they're putting on extra trucks for the pig roast..."

"...yeah?..."

"...well they know there's probably going to be a bunch of bang-outs so they're doing mandatory call-ins for the day and evening..."

"...meaning?..."

"...meaning they're telling people now that they have to work certain shifts that day...I just got assigned to a 8a-8p truck..."

"...what?...did you tell him that you were already working for me?..."

"...yeah...and he didn't care...he said since the paperwork wasn't in yet it wasn't official so their move supersedes that one..."

"...what the fuck?..."

"...I know...I'm sorry..."

"…it's not your fault…" Another wave hit me. "…but what the fuck?…"

"…I know…I even asked him if we could work together…I'd just take Jodie's slot but he was being a prick and said no…the schedule was made up and they weren't complicating things by agreeing to swapping around…they're stressed enough about the day already…"

"…WHAT?…" Oh now I was livid. "…they're motherfucking stressed?…THEY'RE THE MOTHERFUCKERS MAKING ALL THE STRESS…"

"…I know…"

"…where is that slimy ass prick?…" I started for the door.

"…no don't do that…" Ariel waved her arms to stop me. "…he's being a major prick because he's still pissed at you for this morning…don't make things worse…"

I stopped and looked at Ariel. "…how can he make it worse?…"

"…you still have to work the shift with him on as supervisor…" she explained. "…believe me…he can make it a lot worse…" At first I was not convinced and I still considered going inside to find him…but Ariel held her ground and kept repeating "…really…he could…he could make it a lot worse…"

Finally I had no choice but to hear her and concede defeat. "…all right…let's get out of here…" I turned and headed for my Jeep. I was so pissed off that I couldn't get the thought of beating Travis' head with a bat out of my mind.

"…you going to meet me at the restaurant?…"

"…no…" I turned back. "…I'm sorry…I gotta get out of the public view so I can act immature without consequence…"

"…what?…"

"…I'm going home to punch a wall…you don't really want to see that…do you?…"

"...no..." I could tell Ariel was majorly disappointed in me.

I tried to soften my stance and offered a weak explanation. "...look...I'm sorry but I'm really tired and I just wanna go home...I'll see you tomorrow..."

"...yup..." *oh yeah...she was not happy.* "...I'll see you tomorrow..."

✧ ✧ ✧

I barely remembered the ride home. My head was spinning and I couldn't seem to get two uneventful occurrences strung together so I could have time to regroup. I felt like I was hanging on a yo-yo string...slave to the rhythmic up and down...pulling and tugging with each snap of the wrist and not at all the fun kind... *yeah...you know what I mean...*

I pulled off the highway and descended upon Main Street College Town. Of course the pedestrians were even way more out of control than usual and it felt like forever before I pulled safely into the driveway. I remember sitting in my Jeep...maniacally drumming on the steering wheel believing I really wanted to get up and get into the house*...but my body only made it to the porch stairs.* Man...was I tired. I flopped down and leaned against the railing and wondered to myself if I'd ever be able to make it back in the house*...maybe Kelly and Rickie would bring me food on their way by to work...*

"...oh hey...I thought I heard your Jeep..." Kelly came from around the back of the house and joined me. "...what's up Casey?...you look beat..."

"...long fucking day..."

"...yeah...I heard about Jodie...that sucks..."

I laughed to myself knowing that by now that was only the half of it. In fact by now it seemed like such a long drawn-out story I could only muster up a cryptic metaphor. "...you know what Hawkeye Pierce said once?..."

"...Hawkeye Pierce of *M*A*S*H* fame?..."

"...yes...that Hawkeye Pierce..." I continued and Kelly listened. "...he said war wasn't hell...it was worse than hell because as far as he knew only evil people went to hell and had to put up with shit...everybody including old ladies...kids and small pets have to tolerate war..."

She stared. "...okay..."

"...well...I think working for NAA is in that category of war... we're not evil people and we have to put up with their shit...and little old ladies and small pets...they all get dragged into it too.."

"...and little kids?..."

"...yeah...and little kids...they seem to get dragged the hardest..."

"...you okay Casey?..."

"...yeah..." I paused. "...I can't get the pig roast off and it's pissing me off...I jerked around with that stupid list trying to get Jodie a suitable partner and now everyone's got other commitments and Jodie's not even working the shift..."

"...and you really feel like you need to be at that pig roast?..."

"...yeah...I just really feel like I need something for me...just to have fun and I know this is going to be a kickass party..."

"...it'll still be going on after you get out..."

"...yeah...great...so after I serve the almighty master all day I can take a moment or two for myself...that's not what I want...I want the whole day...just one...but the whole day to myself without NAA fucking with it somehow...I just want to know that I still have some control over the fun in my life and that my only purpose is not to serve that money-grubbing corporate demigod..."

Kelly put her arm around me. "...I hear you..."

"...thanks...I know you do..."

"...no...you don't understand...I hear you...I hear you wheezing and I hear you coughing late into the night...you're ill..."

"...ah...I get it..." I smiled. "...yeah maybe..." But in my head I knew I wouldn't do that to Fergie. I had made a promise and I wasn't going to break it. Hell...Jodie remained loyal even under the threat of losing her job and this wasn't even close to being that kind of noble.

Still I smiled and Kelly got up to go back into the house. "....c'mon inside...Loser rented some scary flicks...we're gonna see if we can freak each other out till one of us pukes..."

"...oh my god..." I rose from the stairs.

...how could I say no to that?...

CHAPTER 36 -
HITTING THE WALL AND OTHER SOLID OBJECTS

...at dawn Jesus appeared again in the temple courts... where all the people gathered around him and he sat down to teach them...the teachers of the law and the Pharisees brought in a woman caught in adultery....they made her stand before the group and said to Jesus "...Teacher... this woman was caught in the act of adultery...in the Law Moses commanded us to stone such women...now what do you say?..."They were using this question as a trap... in order to have a basis for accusing him...but Jesus bent down and started to write on the ground with his finger.... Matthew go long and Peter Button Hook...when they kept on questioning him he straightened up and said to them "... listen if any one of you assholes is without sin...let him be the first to throw a stone at her..." Again he stooped down and wrote on the ground...maybe Matthew should Button Hook and we'll send Andrew long...

So that day's events pretty much sealed my fate and the seventeenth came and went without me finding someone to work my shift. Sunday morning I had no choice but to rise...dress and drive in for the shift I never wanted to work. It sucked seeing Ariel at the time clock and knowing that we'd be separated the rest of the day. It sucked thinking she might have been happy at that thought since I had stopped being pleasant company at least a week ago. It sucked when Alyssa walked in and we each realized we'd be working together. I thought she was an overbearing... loud-mouth...inappropriately out lesbian kid and she thought I was a prudish... uncool...too-conforming old person...*in retrospect we both were right...*

It sucked when we got dispatched right off the bat to the scene of a carjacking for a perp attacked by neighbors. It sucked when we arrived and found a scared 17 y/o dumb enough to attempt a carjacking in broad daylight and then it sucked when he got caught and some neighbors held him down while other neighbors called the cops and then it sucked that he squirmed free as the cop arrived and he grabbed a brick and it sucked when he whipped it off the cop's head and then it sucked more when the cop got done beating the snot out of him and that's why we had to be there at all but nothing sucked quite as much as what I did next...

...*because that my friends was the really big suck...*

He lay handcuffed...face down on my stretcher...he could not have been much more vulnerable...He had already proven himself the day's punching bag...Everyone took a shot at him... Everyone leveled their anger at his body...He already had the swelling to prove it...But he kept running his mouth...He kept shouting threats and continued to assert that he was in charge... And I don't know why but for too long a moment I believed he was...He threatened me and I didn't see that he was just a stupid kid...I didn't see that he was already defeated and that words didn't really matter much anymore...I just saw him attacking and I heard his menacing words and I felt an anger like I had never felt rise in me before and I exploded...I exploded in rage and anger and I beat him until my hand hurt so badly that I had to stop...And I still felt rage and anger...Even when he was unconscious and no longer threatening...I didn't know where it came from...but I still felt rage and anger...and it pounded inside my body...it pounded in my head and it pounded my gut in waves...waves of anger and rage...

✵ ✵ ✵

…and then I got scared…

…because while it's true I should have never even been at work…I was and that meant I had to keep control…I was suppose to lead by example…but they bullied me and they made me feel inferior for being human…and I turned right around and took it out someone weaker…I searched and searched until I found the family dog and then I kicked it hard with everything I had*…I sold my soul with nothing to show for it…*

Then to top it off while I sat brooding in the ER all of my friends…the mob of formerly frustrated and angry people…were gathered in Mahan's backyard…where I needed to be to heal in a spiritual celebration of fleeting moments devoted to liberation from the horde called Borg*…I craved to be there…*Instead I sat in X-ray across the hall from where my patient laid unconscious and handcuffed to his bedrail…I stared at him waiting for him to make another move…He didn't…He didn't move at all…He just lay there and I just sat there*…and nothing happened…*

Needing a ride and wanting to avoid the supervisor I called Kelly. I offered her just enough of an explanation to let her know that I really needed a ride. She wasted no time and picked me up but we didn't say much on the ride about what happened. I think she knew enough of the details that she wanted to call me a stupid ass but deep down inside she knew there would be plenty of time for that afterward. Right now she appreciated what I really needed…a judgment-free ride home and time to change into more appropriate casual wear…

✵ ✵ ✵

When I got in my room I took my uniform off as fast as I could and I crumbled it up in a ball and threw it on the floor as far away from me as possible…

...today I didn't like my job at all...

✫ ✫ ✫

To me the pig roast will always remain a drunken haze blurred by Percocet...confusion and pain. Everyone was impressed by the swelling in my hand but I still don't know how I felt about being patted on the back for "...decking the fucker..."

With every good person's accolades I slammed another shot and rested my hand in the keg ice***...nothing was touching the racing thoughts in my head...***

I initiated a free-for-all mud wrestling event and later pushed five people into a Sani-Can just so we could all palpate Alyssa's belly ring***...she loved it...***The activities at least occupied my time long enough to get me through the *gee I'd really like to hurl myself into route 202 traffic* phase.

I went home early the next morning and collapsed into bed like the cliché broken hero. There is a deafening sound that echoes from the crash of your world and you can get quite the headache from it. For the next two days I didn't get out of bed. I believe I may have suffered from some form of paralysis often associated with hand fractures. The phone would ring and I would ignore it. Rickie knocked on my door around noon. Kelly yelled up when free food was served. The sun went down...the sun came up and I ignored it all. Rice Krispie treats and Fresca sustained me when and if the urge for food came along. The TV was on with the sound muted and I got just as much out of staring at my candle.

I hated myself. I hated everything that I began to feel I stood for. I was the bad guy in every movie I ever booed. I lost my mind and snapped and because of my lack of self-control another human ended up unconscious***...then I became liar...***Sure all my friends knew I decked him but management was told he slammed my hand on the ground during a struggle to restrain him. That's assault on EMS personnel and the company pressed charges. Now I would be a perjurer or I would be convicted of assault myself. All because I snapped…

…weak fuck that I am…

✻ ✻ ✻

I had a wild dream last night..

I was lying in a cheap hotel room bed and I heard a loud BOOM. It was the same hotel we stayed at when I was ten…*it was the one I liked…*It stands out as such because as a youth my vacations were foggy memories of rundown cheap hotels. The adventures didn't come from water parks and amusement rides. They came from bugs in the bathroom…fire hazards in the Dumpster and angry maids who would steal your loose change. But once we vacationed on the runway of an airport and where previously I had cringed at the horror the rooms presented…the airport hotel was cool…The room had a big window and when you opened the curtains at night that window was a wormhole that could magically transport you to anywhere around the world. I stared out and hung on the neon taillights of silver jets taxiing in and out…*for once in my life I ignored TV…*

Tonight was different though and when I jumped out of bed and opened the curtain I saw two silver jets screaming at each other. Collision was inevitable…*so was overtime…*At first my stomach turned for the passengers. Then I realized there would be fallout. Steel shrapnel would rain from the sky and that would make for tons of casualties…bodies laid out on the grass…broken from the twisted wreckage. I was supposed to be excited. Instead I was petrified…I couldn't think…my head was spinning like the burning fuselage streaming from the sky.

I took off from the room…blindly running down the runway. I refused to look up and I grabbed my ears to block out the sound of screaming engines torpedoing to the ground. I was confident I could make it all go away but it was so loud and not going down easy. I felt my knees buckle from the echoing booms slamming through the earth as huge monuments of steel burrowed in from above...I heard people shouting...squelching and shrieking in horror...fear dripping from their tones...*and I looked for a safe place to hide...*

Body parts began pelting me...forcing me to look up...That's when I saw the parade of ambulances...*red lights blaring and sirens lacerating the event coming toward me...*All my peers were in uniform and ready to perform their duties. I didn't stop running and I didn't change my direction. I never wanted to be a paramedic again...I couldn't do it... I couldn't handle it...*I shouldn't have been let in the door in the first place...*

     I woke up on my futon...hot and dry mouthed...*Xena stared disapprovingly from the TV screen...*

I didn't care how sunny it got today...I refused to be anything but depressed...

"...so did I tell you the nice thing Jodie said to me the other day..." I had dragged myself from my cave and sought company with Fergie.

"...no..." But she looked quite interested over the ridge of her bagel.

" ...it was at Mahan's Pig Roast...the one I got to late because I was in the Emergency Room...remember?...getting my hand X-rayed because I beat the crap outta that Puerto Rican kid... only I don't think I hit him because he was Puerto Rican...I just know that's how I remember him...young and Puerto Rican...

but he was stupid too….and actually I hit him because he was stupid and he resisted and fought and he hit the cop in the head with a brick…so Jodie said '…if they hit the cops you can't be nice…you don't want the cops to be nice to them if they hit you'…so Alyssa grabbed his pants and we dragged him across the sidewalk…you know…facedown no shirt on…he got some scrapes…but the cop's hands were shaking…he chased us down as we approached the scene and he had my door pulled open before Alyssa even stopped…he dragged me out screaming…and he was spitting in my face yelling at me so hard and the back of his head was bleeding '**…THAT SON OF A BITCH TRIED TO KILL ME…**' he screamed in my face when I opened the door…next thing you know I had my foot in the back of his head…I jammed his head against the wall with my dirty black boot…and the fucker wouldn't shut up…he couldda made it easy and shut the fuck up but he just kept screamin' '**…I CAN'T BREATHE…I CAN'T BREATHE…**' and you know he could 'cause he's screamin' so I fuckin' slammed him…I came up full swing…BOOM…I pasted him wherever my fist landed…and it fuckin' hurt both of us…I broke my hand…he went unconscious…I can't believe I hit 'em…I never knew I could lose it like that…"

Fergie popped the last of the bagel in her mouth. "…so what did Jodie say?…"

"…oh I digressed…sorry…she told me what I should have done instead was looked at Alyssa and said '…you didn't see nothin'…' and Maglited him…"

"…yup…that's Jodie…"

"…yeah…but I don't know if that's what I should have done…"

"…I'm going to go with no…"

                    …Fergie appeared so calm…

✯ ✯ ✯

I spent days lying in bed staring at the ceiling. My hand hurt less as time passed but my head stayed fucked up. I couldn't believe I hit him...*I was supposed to be the good guy...*

Speaking of which...I still hadn't talked to Ariel since the whole thing happened. Well...she was in the ER when I came in that day but I think she was actually pretty pissed at me. See...I was scared. I never lost control like that before. I really thought I could've killed that guy. If I didn't break my hand I couldn't think of anything else that would have stopped me from hitting him more...*it just seemed so justified at the time...*Now I couldn't wrap my head around what the fuck I did. They train us to take a time-out when we're frazzled. They just can't seem to teach us how to know when we need the time-out. And who the hell wants to take a time-out anyway?...*time-outs are for pussies...*We're supposed to be tough...we're supposed to stay separated...we're just supposed to know better...*why didn't I?...*This job had taught me so much about myself. Sadly the latest tidbit I learned was just how stupid and pathetic I could be...*I could have killed him...*

When I saw Ariel in the ER I played up the bravado. As soon as I saw the look in her eyes I knew that she knew what I did was wrong but I hung with it anyway. I pretended I was proud of what I had done. Yeah I was a street medic now...I was tough...no motherfucker punk ass was going to read my name tag... threaten me with gang violence and get away with it.

I would have been better off crying and letting Ariel hug me. She would have too...maybe...*if I hadn't been such an ass...*

✯ ✯ ✯

"...so how's your hand doin' Casey?..." Kelly and I sat alone in the backyard keeping watch over a barrel fire.

"…okay…I think it actually looks worse than it feels now…" I looked over my varying shades of healing bruises.

"…that's good…" Kelly poked at a smoldering log. "…so how are you feeling?…"

"…I'm good…it doesn't hurt really…"

"…I'm not talking about your hand…" Kelly kept jabbing at the log. "…I'm talking about your head…"

"…my head?…" I wished I didn't know what she was getting at. "…my head's fine…I'm good…"

"…really?…you're good?…"

"…yeah…I'm fine…"

"…so you lose your shit on a call and pound some kid unconscious but your head is fine?…"

At first I didn't answer or look at Kelly. In fact…I was kind of hoping some excuse of any kind would appear to call me away so I could avoid the whole conversation I saw forming like precipitous plumes.

"…no…I guess that's not so great right now…"

"…that's good…I'm glad to hear it…" Kelly stopped jabbing and looked at me. "…I didn't want to think my good friend was turning into a heartless bastard…" This time Kelly's words stung me and my face got hot. I fought hard not to give in to the emotions rising inside and since I knew my voice would most likely betray me I chose to stay silent. Normally I ached for the chance to be taught by Kelly but right now I just really wanted all of this to go away.

"…maybe your friend is just a heartless bastard…"

Surprisingly Kelly laughed. "…you are not a heartless bastard…I was asking a trick question…I already knew the answer…" Kelly smiled at me. "…you just made a mistake…"

"…just a mistake?…I beat some kid unconscious because I was pissed off at something that he didn't even have anything to do with…what the fuck was that?…"

"…okay…it was a big mistake…but you're human…" Kelly shrugged her shoulders as if to say "…right?…"

"…yeah…sure…I'm human…"

"…you are and this time you got lucky and you got away with it and now you gotta learn from it and move on…it kills me to see you beating yourself up so badly…"

I stared at the flames. "…this just feels pretty unforgivable…"

"…I'm sure it does right now but it certainly is forgivable and that's what you need to focus on or you're never going to get past this…" Kelly seemed to pause for effect. "…you're not special Casey…this stuff happens to all of us…and eventually we all do something that leaves us struggling to make peace with ourselves but how can it not…we don't live in a black and white world and we certainly don't work in one…that means it's not always easy to know what the right thing to do is…never mind actually do it all the time…so we're gonna screw up…we're not freakin' machines…but unless you want it all to be over right here…right now…you gotta let it go…"

"…that's it?…just let it go?…"

"…yeah…learn from your frickin' mistake and move on… like we've all had to…"

"…really?…" For some reason I didn't believe her. "…you've had to?…"

"…yeah…I have…" Her tone was convincing. "…what?…do you think I'm perfect?…"

"…you know how I feel…"

"…well I'm not…and I wasn't always this calm…cool and kickass street medic you seem to think I am…"

"…you think so too…"

"…I know…" Kelly smirked. "…and I really kind of am…" She laughed and the mood lightened just a bit. "…but seriously…I'm not who I am because I never fuck up…I'm who I am because I do the best that I can and if I screw up I admit it…deal with it and move on…"

I still had a hard time believing Kelly ever could have done something that bad. "…you ever lose your shit and pound on some patient?…"

"…no…but that's not the only sin we can commit…" Kelly sat back in her beach chair. "…I let some asshole push my buttons once so bad that I booted her out of my ambulance before we got to the hospital and I considered myself under control because I waited for my partner to sort of slow down before I opened the door and pushed…then I told dispatch she bailed out on us… totally lied about it to cover my ass and then I sweated it out for weeks waiting for her to call and complain…even in the old days that would have gotten my ass fired…and I would have deserved it…." I shook my head in agreement. "…my long brilliant career very well could have been over then but it wasn't and the fact that I dodged a bullet wasn't lost on me…that's when I knew that my only option was to decide if I really wanted to do this for a living and if so was I capable enough to not do stupid things again that could cost me my job…" Kelly continued. "…or even more importantly…my soul…because we both know that the books…the training…the classes…they don't mean much…it's what we learn on the street that makes us who we are…for better or worse…because what's the worst thing that can happen to you reading a book?…you get a paper cut?…but learning on the streets has a whole other world of challenge to throw at you and it's not always pretty…we get paid to show up to everyone's worst day…and if we're not careful we can let it turn into our worst day too…not to mention that as long as you're a street medic you're gonna come in contact with a lot of dirtbags who live for nothing more than to push our buttons…it's like a dirtbag pay-per-view event…" I smiled and she continued. "… so you're just going to have to make up your mind that you're not going to let them get to you like that…and you do that by changing your priorities… remember…it's not about us and sometimes we are only in the way…do what you can to keep yourself out of the formula…"

"…you actually make it sound kind of simple…" I stared incredulously.

"…well…it is…" Kelly poked at the fire again. "…you just need to relax…" She left it at that for the moment and I took the chance to regroup. I took a couple of deep breaths and considered the option of relaxing. Then Kelly broke in again. "…and hey… while we're solving the mysteries of the world…Rickie and I came up with a solution for your Wonder Woman question…"

"…oh yeah?…" I smiled at the thought of what might be coming next. "…what'd ya come up with?…"

"…well it's quite simple really when you think about it…she just chirps her car alarm and the lights flash…"

I laughed. "…that's awesome…and it completely makes sense…"

"…well credit Loser for coming up with it…as it turns out…that's usually how she finds her car …and it's not even invisible…so you see Casey…everything is easier when you just keep it simple…"

…okay…so I was just going to have to work hard to relax…

☆ ☆ ☆

Then Ariel called*…and just when I had just started feeling better…*When I recognized her number on the caller ID I cringed at the possible lecture I was most likely about to endure.

We really hadn't talked yet like Kelly and I did and I was afraid of what she might say. However...*to my surprise*...her tone was very casual and exceptionally nonjudgmental.

But what she did say that sent a wave a fear through my heart was that she was coming over. When I told her I didn't want company she told me to get over it. Realizing that this was not an argument I would win I hung up and went up to my room and prepared for the impending doom.

About an hour later I heard the doorbell ring and Kelly letting her in. Next thing I knew she was in my room...plopping down on my futon.

"...how are you?..." she deadpanned.

"...good...how are you?..." I answered while relocating the magazines she threw herself on.

"...I'm good..." She paused. "...I miss you..."

"...you do?..." I was skeptical.

"...yeah ya butthead...I miss you...and I miss working with you..."

"...oh now you're just being nice..."

"...no...just being nice would be telling you I don't care what you did..." *ouch.* "...I'm not going to say that..."

I shook my head. "...sure...I wouldn't expect you to...or believe you if you did..."

"...but I do miss you..."

"...thanks...I miss you too..." I lied back on my pillow. "...and I'm sorry...I'm sorry I let you down...you especially tried to warn me and I totally blew you off..."

"...yeah...why were you so stubborn?..."

"...I don't know...I still got some figuring out to do..."

"...but you're coming back to your sucky job?..."

"...yeah...I'm coming back to my sucky job...in fact my return is Monday when I have to start light duty..."

"…oh yeah…light duty…"

"…yes…light duty…that cavalcade of office tasks…answering phones…filing stuff and making photo copies…a street medic's true wet dream…"

"…easy…it's only temporary…"

"…I know…and I probably really should look at it as due penitence…"

"…yeah…well at the very least you probably shouldn't be heard complaining too much about it…all things considered you've pretty much lucked out…"

"…yeah…Kelly and I just had a long conversation about that…"

"…yeah…and did you learn anything?…"

"…oh yeah…I've learned a lot…a lot about myself…this job…this world…I gotta stop having so many expectations and just go with the flow a little more often…"

"…sounds like a good start…" Ariel paused for a second. "…there's something else you need to do too…"

"…there is?…" I cringed at the thought.

"…yes…you need to take me out to dinner…"

"…what?…take you out to dinner?…"

"…yes…because you still owe me dinner at the Indian restaurant…"

"…I owe you?…"

"…oh yeah…and you owe me a lot more but I'll start with the dinner…" She smiled that goofy way she does and I knew I couldn't argue. Not only was she cute…she was right…I did owe her a lot…and I owed a lot to others too…

…I guess I should get busy on that…

✵ ✵ ✵

So that's my story…I hope you enjoyed it even a fraction as much as I enjoyed living it. These truly were the best of my times and the friendships and the memories I made were exciting and enduring. It took me awhile but I even managed to learn some good stuff along the way too. While it's true we're surrounded by pain we have to ask ourselves...*are we really?...*If the child lies dead in the street...dead or killed by some accident or stupidity...*is it our pain?...*or is it the pain of the mothers and fathers... brothers and sisters...friends and neighbors? If problems lay out in front of us...is it our problem if we go home and find shelter and food and love in many forms? Is it really our sadness or is it just our job...is it just what we do?...

...are we what we do?...

☆ ☆ ☆

Eventually I pulled myself together and found my way back to work and World Headquarters. Thank God I had great friends who were willing to cut me some slack and forgive. I thought long and hard about the lessons life just schooled me in and the ache of shame stayed with me for awhile. I found myself overly nice to everyone...I guess to compensate for the evil I had just added to the world's bounty but like everything else so far...eventually that faded too and I meandered back to the mean.

Ariel and I kept working together for another year or so but the wholesale changes at NAA never let up and soon nothing looked the same anymore. Ariel completed the true meaning of the merger when she married a former Valley medic and their offspring were born as hybrids. Jodie was gone and soon ended up working for the LittleCity medics. True to her style she really shook things up over there and soon feisty little basics like me and Blossom were the least of their problems. Fergie soon followed when she got her nursing degree and took a real...good paying job. Then she fell in love with the very strong athletic male at the time clock. See...he was around all the time...*but he really prefers* *stealth mode...*and the children they made were very strong athletic bookworm types*...a truly wonderful combination...* Mahan announced shortly after the pig roast that he was taking a job on a local fire department and he and his shit-stirring ways were soon serving the PFFM. Kelly never did get a regular partner and eventually just slid into a supervisor's slot vacated when Travis lost his mind...screamed **"...CHECK THIS MILEAGE ASSHOLE..."** and tried to drive a chair van into Sommers' office. I was happy for her since she clearly deserved the promotion but I did feel a twinge of sadness for all the up-and-coming EMTs and medics who would no longer have the privilege of working on the streets with her. I think everyone should have had that chance because without her guidance most of us would only have been a fraction of what we became.

Rickie never headed out west like we expected. Instead she started seriously dating a MiddleCity firefighter and soon she didn't have to look that far away to find what really made her happy. When they moved in together it broke up the household and marked the end of our college town living. I remember standing on the porch looking into the foyer of the house I had called home for most of those great years. A can of pink spray paint rolled out of the closet when I opened it to grab my jacket for the last time. I just couldn't believe it was over*...yet again...* another chapter in my life abruptly closing. I guess that's what it's about though. Maybe it's because I'm getting older but change has become a little less imposing to me. It's just the way it is. Embrace it...grow with it*...evolve...*In fact...in the end...change ain't what's so bad...not changing is...

...so just take it as it comes...

I had a fairly pleasant dream last night...

I was in a bar and I was surrounded by a group of women... Only I didn't feel surrounded...I felt encompassed and secure...I was happy and I was having a good time...A psych patient was doing push-ups in the corner and I heard several people counting them off...A group of women played pool and music was playing gently in the background...*I was gettin' through my night...*The crowd parted and one woman separated from the rest...*what a beautiful smile...*She walked over to me and to my surprise she kept smiling...*and that was all right...*and she sat on my lap and told a funny joke and I held on...because I just knew I shouldn't ever let this one go...

I woke up on my futon...smiling and holding my pillow tight...feeling all right...

Before the beginning...

...and oh yeah...definitely at the end too...

It was late…and it was getting later…My life was careening down narrow windy roads completely in the dark and constructed with blind corners…Careening is a subjective motion…You can feel it standing still if you're dizzy…But when you feign control careening is fun…Sitting next to the Almighty Kelly O'Brien it was intense…

*This is the story of a 24 y/o GWF who grew up wanting to be Johnnie or Roy who then grew up and met Kelly O'Brien***…who was way cooler than Johnnie or Roy could have ever hoped to be…***and suddenly it all made sense…There is no feeling more liberating than the realization that one has stumbled upon their destiny…Now I'm scared to think where else I could have turned up…There are so many fine lines in life…friend-lover…lord-devil…***blah blah blah***…And you can end up in the strangest places for a sixteenth of a degree's difference in fate's line…***I was a sixteenth of a degree away from a life as doomed whiskey tango***…Now I don't believe there is anywhere else to be***…anywhere else would not be as true…***I thought I was applying for a job…What I got was a new perspective…I began to see life for what it isn't…I saw it from the bottom up***…And I liked the view…***In fact I have grown afraid that they might try to take it away from me and if they did I don't know what I'd do…*

…ours is not a profession…it is a religion…

✶ ✶ ✶

…and I think all religions are basically the same…They all teach that the world sucks and it's because evil kicks good's ass…The only chance good has is the gods…The gods who have the right to say anything they want because whatever they want is right…

…they are gods and that's what gods do…

✶ ✶ ✶

*I believe in the God of EMS…He is a he right now***…but Kelly O'Brien is giving him a good run for his money…***I'm able to* *believe in the God of EMS because I have seen him in action...This is a god who can be fair...**sometimes he just chooses to be a bastard...** However...fair is fair and at least he doesn't care if you call him a bastard when he deserves it...*

> ***...I don't know how Kelly will feel about being called a bitch...***

☆ ☆ ☆

*The God of EMS operates on certain rules...I share them as I figure them out or as they are shared with me...**only a few are allowed to the inner sanctum...**Ariel taught me my first rule...**be careful what you wish for...**Because you will get it...Like if you wish for a code because you're bored you'll get a pedicode...And for some strange reason looking at a dead kid and knowing you wished for it kinda sucks...*

Ariel also explains that there's a special angel for drunks...kids and EMTs...Sometimes I think Ariel is my angel...I mean with her by my side I have carried a lot of drunks...cried with a lot of kids and drank with a lot of EMTs...

☆ ☆ ☆

*Ours is a religion passed through stories told well...You are taught respect...Respect for yourself...Respect for your patients...Most importantly respect for learning...One reason we share the rules as we figure them out is because nobody knows all the rules yet...**maybe collectively we can come up with a complete set...***

Dark nights are the best time to learn...Sit next to the almighty Kelly O'Brien in florescent truck stops...under the neon glow of the light bar...and listen to her as the stories pour out...They tell our history...a history loaded with heroes...leaders...goats and devils...

All religions have a book that explains the rules...The book also outlines punishment for failure to comply...Some people might think regional protocols are our bible...but they're not...We have no such book...because no one can tell you how to feel holding a dead baby...

Sometimes it just gets to you and no one holds it against you if you go home and stay there...So like any good religion...guilt is all the punishment we ever need...But I was lucky...I had the privilege to learn from an angel how to be like a goddess...

...bless me Hoppy for I have sinned...

COWBOY JARGON
...know what all the cool kids are saying...

y/o: medical shorthand for year old. As in a 60 y/o male.

whiskey tango: a term using the military phonetic alphabet to identify white trash.

EMS: Emergency Medical Services.

code: cardiac arrest.

EMT: Emergency Medical Technician. Some people think it's funny to call us ambulance drivers.

newbie: a term of endearment used to identify new people. You can be new to the job or new to a provider level (eg: a newbie paramedic).

intercepts: in order to provide a higher level of patient care en route to the emergency room, an ambulance staffed by higher trained EMT's fights through traffic, meets up with an ambulance staffed by lesser trained EMT's and takes over patient care for the rest of the transport.

ALS: Advanced Life Support. In Massachusetts, an ALS provider is either an intermediate or a paramedic.

ALS truck: an ambulance staffed with at least one paramedic or one intermediate.

MVA: motor vehicle accident or car crash.

CMED: a special radio channel for communication between an ambulance & the hospital.

c-spine: cervical spine or your neck and back.

c-spine precautions: using a longboard and collar to protect your neck and back from further injury.

O2: oxygen.

nonrebreather: a type of O2 mask that delivers 100% O2. That's a lot.

trauma shears: those cool scissors that really can cut pennies in half .

radial pulses: the pulse you can feel in your wrist. Patients going into shock will lose their radial pulses before their carotid pulse (the pulse you feel in your neck).

GSW's: Gun Shot Wounds.

chairvan: a vehicle used to transport patients who can't ride in a car but don't need medical treatment from an ambulance provider.

bravo sierra: a term using the military phonetic alphabet to identify bull s@#*t.

a forty: A forty ounce beer.

whoop: someone who goes a bit over the top with their love for all things EMS related.

PI: personal injury or people are hurt.

COPD: disease of the lungs & airway.

BVM: bag valve mask. Used to oxygenate patients who are SOB or not breathing at all.

SOB: medical shorthand for shortness of breath. Still not a nice thing to call your patient.

cardiac pacing: using electricity to stimulate the heart to beat in a steady rhythm.

EKG: the strip of paper that comes out of the heart monitor.

Epi drip: an IV solution of Normal Saline and Epinephrine.

Made in the USA
Charleston, SC
02 June 2011